PASSENGER

13

Compiled & Edited by
Ben Thomas & D Kershaw

**Also available and coming soon
from Black Hare Press**

DARK DRABBLES SERIES
WORLDS
ANGELS
MONSTERS
BEYOND
UNRAVEL
APOCALYPSE
LOVE
HATE
OCEANS
ANCIENTS

SPECIAL EDITIONS
STORMING AREA 51
EERIE CHRISTMAS
BAD ROMANCE
TWENTY TWENTY

OTHERS
DEEP SPACE
WHAT IF?
KEY TO THE KINGDOM
DEEP SEA
BEYOND THE REALM

Twitter: @BlackHarePress
Facebook: BlackHarePress
Website: www.BlackHarePress.com

Passenger 13 title is
Copyright © 2020 Black Hare Press
First published in Australia in May 2020 by Black Hare Press

The authors of the individual stories retain the copyright of the works
featured in this anthology

*All characters and events in this publication, other than those clearly in the
public domain, are fictitious and any resemblance to real persons, living or
dead, is purely coincidental.*

All rights reserved. No part of this production may be reproduced, stored in a
retrieval system, or transmitted, in any form or by any means, electronic,
mechanical, photocopying, recording or otherwise, without the prior
permission of the publisher and copyright owner.

HARDCOVER : ISBN 978-1-925809-66-4
PAPERBACK : ISBN 978-1-925809-65-7

Cover design by Dawn Burdett
Formatting by Ben Thomas

Adieu, farewell, earth's bliss;
This world uncertain is;
Fond are life's lustful joys;
Death proves them all but toys;
None from his darts can fly;
I am sick, I must die.
Lord, have mercy on us!

> Rich men, trust not in wealth,
> Gold cannot buy you health;
> Physic himself must fade.
> All things to end are made,
> The plague full swift goes by;
> I am sick, I must die.
> Lord, have mercy on us!

Beauty is but a flower
Which wrinkles will devour;
Brightness falls from the air;
Queens have died young and fair;
Dust hath closed Helen's eye.
I am sick, I must die.
Lord, have mercy on us!

> Strength stoops unto the grave,
> Worms feed on Hector brave;
> Swords may not fight with fate,
> Earth still holds open her gate.
> "Come, come!" the bells do cry.
> I am sick, I must die.
> Lord, have mercy on us!

A Litany in Time of Plague, Thomas Mashe, 1593

Table of Contents

FOREWORD

So, here we are…

Bob Dylan said it best, *the times they are a changin'*, and boy are we in for one hell of a bumpy landing.

I'm not sure this is what Bob had in mind back in 64' but this is where we are heading, and we better get used to it because we ain't coming back to just shoes off and body scans at airports anytime soon. It's all handwash, greed, and house arrest for the foreseeable future and I don't have a clue how we actually got here. I mean, it's not like we were warned about globalisation and the problems open borders would create.

No wait, what…we were?

When I saw the prices of cruise ships offering holidays around the world coming down, enticing a new generation of travellers to sail the seas, with all you can drink vouchers and relaxed dress codes, I wondered how long it would be until we had what was the equivalent of a floating drunken stag party

cruising from port to port, historical monuments being visited by what can only be described as roaming Griswold, drunken wolf packs, causing mayhem each time their cruise docked in some exotic location.

When videos emerged of bar fights breaking out on these ships and people being locked down for spreading diseases running rampage throughout the guests, I knew it was only a matter of time before we had a containment problem.

Ships would be quarantined.

When the *Diamond Princess* became the first to report the COVID virus, I pitied those quieter travellers; stuck in their inside berth cabins, isolated and quarantined for not just days, but weeks—cabin fever must have been terrible—and I got to thinking about a worst-case scenario for those trapped. Would they be taken away from the infected ship? Where would they go if they were refused entry?

What if they were just cast away and forgotten, escorted from each country's boundary until the ship disappeared over the horizon?

How would folks survive? Would it be like Mad Max of the high seas?

I sent my idea off to Black Hare Press and

quickly received a reply asking me if I would like to expand on this idea, perhaps get together some other writers to contribute to a similar kind of tale, something different.

How could I refuse?

A collaboration with my very own handpicked 'Dirty Dozen' crew—folks who I could count on to tell a fine tale of horror and humour.

"Three weeks?" I repeated. "You want me to do this in three weeks?"

Dean gave me a virtual *shrug*.

It wasn't impossible, we had done it before…or rather BHP had done it before. All I had done was submit a couple of ideas to their anthology and check the edits when they came back to me. Easy really.

What they were asking me to do now was admin a group, find a crew, sell my idea to said crew, give them a deadline, and then set up an order of events!

"Easy!" they said.

I mean, it's not like I had my own little black book of names I could call on. All I had was a bookshelf full of anthologies and drabbles to recruit from. I was going to have to go through them all, find an assortment of varying voices to make sure I didn't recruit 13 writers who followed the school of Jason

Bourne or Lizzie Bennett.

Man, did I have myself a list by the end of the weekend, though!

Needless to say, my list was long. I had about twenty candidates I really wanted to write for this anthology, but only room for 13. It was a tough choice, so I picked names from the list at random, sending out Willy Wonka tickets in order, with an "RSVP as quick as you can".

Spaces filled fast.

Four beers later, my wish list was done, and my first load of Messenger requests were put out into the cloud, telling my candidates about my idea for what could be an awesome tale. The few at the end who didn't get to the email in time…well I apologised to them, explaining that the positions filled up faster than toilet rolls were being ripped from supermarket shelves.

Those who were quick off the mark, well I told them my idea was writing a tale about a passenger onboard a plane from somewhere, en route to somewhere else. This passenger would be infected. This passenger would infect another 12 travellers. They in turn would infect others as they moved around the globe.

Infection would spread and stories would grow. It would be their tale to take wherever they wanted. Slow, fast, romantic, apocalyptic. Their choice completely. Give it a Cormac McCarthy feel, make it slapstick. Go full Dustin Hoffman, chasing monkeys. Hell, add some Captain Trips if you want.

All I had to do was crack open another stubbie and wait for the madness to flow.

One hour and two stubbies later, my recruitment drive was done, my pen, along with my vast wish list, was placed aside, and I slowly realised I had my assembled team of travellers, just like Lee Marvin.

Why I put Brian MacGowan in the first batch of Messenger request still baffles me. I suppose I needed to adhere to international laws and add at least one Canadian to the anthology.

Inside these covers are 13 infectious tales told by 13 cracking story tellers. Story tellers whose work I have read and admired immensely over the short time I have been in the writing game. What we ended up with inside these pages is 13 stories of love, panic, distress, payback, apocalyptic emptiness, debauchery and even espionage.

So, here we are…

The Eve of Destruction.

Buckle up thrill seekers, it's gonna be a bumpy landing. The captain has lit the seatbelt sign and it's time I checked on one of the passengers on board. That's him over there, looking all smug as he stifles another coughing fit…Passenger **13**!

"Ain't we a pair, raggedy man."
-Auntie, Mad Max Beyond Thunderdome, 1985

"If a Hot Toddy makes you feel better, go for it."
-Dr Alan Weiss, Cleveland Clinic Ohio.

Gregg Cunningham

X-DAY -5

POTUS interview with "Squawk Box" co-host Joe Kernen:

We have it totally under control. It's one person coming in from China. We have it under control. It's going to be just fine.

Isobel and Shen

BLAKE JESSOP

WUHAN HOSPITAL, CHINA

"It isn't that they might be watching you," Shen said. The British journalist looked as if she'd been about to say something else, but his words stopped her dead. "They are watching you. Every shadow is watching you."

They sat together on plastic chairs outside a noodle stand on Hubu Street. The journalist had introduced herself as Isobel Pang, and she looked depressingly fresh and eager. Doctor Wei Shen had been just starting breakfast when she'd sat down with him, uninvited, with a plate of the same reganmian he was eating. He hadn't slept at all and was eating his hot dry noodles mechanically. Med school had taught him that food was often a convenient counterfeit for sleep.

"Thank you for the warning, but I still want to do this," Isobel said seriously. Her age was hard to pin down, and Shen's first reaction was to write her off as a disaster tourist or Weibo blogger. Not a serious journalist; she was too young. The more she spoke, though, the more he doubted.

"Tell me honestly," he said, "are you willing to risk your life for this? Maybe you should be a fashion commentator. Are you willing to die here?"

The girl's face went blank, and for a moment Shen didn't feel so much older than she was. The look that came over her started as anger but finished in emptiness. As if she'd meant to be scornful, but remembrance of what had made her that way had taken her back to some place she'd tried to forget. It was not just the look of a woman used to being misjudged; those blank eyes had seen death up close, had sensed mortal danger, had stared over the edge to a long drop. It was like looking in a mirror.

"Am I willing to die here?" she said after a moment.

"I'm sorry I asked," Shen replied.

"I don't look like a journalist to you?" Shen ate another mouthful to give himself time to think, and the journalist waited like a cat.

"You're right." Shen sighed. "It's what's on the inside that counts."

This was a terrible idea; they would certainly be

caught. Shen reached up to run a hand over his face and made a very large decision before he stopped the very small gesture. "How would I sneak you into a hospital?"

Isobel smiled, and her eyes came back to life.

"Wearing a mask, I imagine."

***

"This is Xia, a transfer nurse from Jingzhou Central Hospital," Shen told his team. They were gathered in a break room that all had the tables stacked against one wall to make room for cots. Isobel was already in full scrubs, and only her pale brown eyes were visible above a surgical mask. "She will be recording video to send to the ministry of health in Beijing, so don't ask her for help unless you really need to. She knows how to stay out of the way."

Dr Wei introduced Isobel, and the hardest part of their charade was over before it started. No one asked any questions, and they accepted Isobel easily. There was enough to do that any help at all was better than nothing. Shen was surprised by the fluency of his lies, and how little he felt about deceiving his

23

13

teammates. *Perhaps I am not deceiving them at all; someone has to show the world what is happening.*

***

Time blurred, and for a week, Isobel followed Dr Wei on his rounds. Those never really ended; they slept only rarely, and Isobel discovered how rare a treat leaving the hospital to eat had been for the doctor. His staff worked every day, and as the virus took over Wuhan, they started working every night, too. Every hour. Every minute.

Not for the first time, Isobel filmed death. Patients were lined up in the corridors, on every surface that could accommodate them. Some of the slightly less sick sat in waiting room chairs where it was a little easier to breathe. People coughed, and begged, and woke up wheezing with pain or didn't wake up at all. She learned the layout of the hospital and snuck out the back to take a break. Found an orderly there, smoking a cigarette.

"Do you want one?" he asked. He pulled his mask down every time he took a drag. "It cuts down the smell."

"No," Isobel said, and raised the camera. The

orderly leant against a wall by the sliding doors to one of the hospital's loading bays. In the opening behind him, pure white body bags were stacked like cordwood. They looked like slick, bulbous cocoons that had fallen from a tree.

***

"Doctor?" Isobel—*Xia,* Shen corrected himself—had a tone in her voice he'd never heard before: panic.

The patient Shen was attending was an old man who gasped in every breath as if the air had no oxygen. He led Isobel to one of the examination rooms to calm her down.

"What is it, Nurse Xia?" he said once they were alone. Isobel's eyes were wild.

"Why do they gasp like that?" She was shaking.

"What happened? Why are you so worked up?"

"Like fish out of water. It doesn't look like there's anything wrong, but he couldn't breathe."

Shen tried to think of a way to break through to her. *She's a reporter; give her answers.*

"Take this and pin it up to the light board." Shen handed Isobel a set of x-rays. Not the patient he had

just been looking at, but it hardly mattered. "The switch is over there. No, film this, too. It will be useful."

Isobel's chest stopped heaving, and she levelled the camera robotically.

"It's true that patients don't look all that bad when the virus starts, but it's what's inside that counts. Look." Dr Wei indicated the x-rays against the backlit panel. "Do you see how the lungs look like solid masses of white? That's called ground glass opacification, we should be able to see black between the ribs, but it's hazy."

"Ground glass? Like a shower stall?"

"Exactly. The virus causes something like a cytokine storm. The resulting fibrosis strips your ability to take in oxygen. Is that clear?"

"Yes," Isobel said.

"Now," Shen said, and saw himself reflected in Isobel's camera lens, "what's wrong?"

"I saw the body bags. Where are they going? How many people have actually died?"

"Showing you this is going to be another risk, and will be very hard. No one is supposed to see. Are you ready?"

Isobel nodded.

***

Wei Shen didn't see Isobel for more than a day after showing her the morgue. It wasn't actually a morgue, of course; it had once been a university gymnasium. Plastic tarps covered the floor, and every window had been left open to let in cold winter air. Trucks came and went endlessly, some dropping off fresh cargo, others taking it away. Men in grey suits spoke into cellular phones in the parking lot, and the military patrolled in full hazmat combat gear. The rows of dead lay side by side like cigarettes in a carton, each body bag scrawled with hectic characters. Hundreds to a row. Dozens of rows with just enough room to walk between them.

Shen did not react to the sight; he felt everything there was to feel through Isobel. He watched her as he greeted the staff and made excuses for their presence. Listened to the catch in her breath the first time she saw the entire lifeless panorama. Felt the stupor of her muscles as she raised her camera. Smelt the scents of decay he had long since stopped noticing in the shiver that passed through her as she panned. He wondered if the little shake would

13

transmit to film.

She came back a day later and cornered Shen the first chance she got.

"I have to get out, now. I have to stop being Xia." Shen raised a hand. "No, don't ask questions, I'm out of time. I'm leaving you the GoPro and my sat phone. If I upload anything straight to the internet they'll know. Record everything you can, and I'll call that phone when I get back to London."

"What about the footage you already have?"

"I'll smuggle it out on my portable hard drive. Assuming I get on the plane without getting strip searched, it'll be no problem."

Time stretched between them. They couldn't hug, couldn't shake hands. Dr Wei gave her a very slight, old fashioned bow. Isobel nodded, and her eyes glistened behind the face shield.

"Good luck," she said, and he felt her desperate tension and grief only until she vanished from sight.

***

"What do you need us to do?" Shen asked the captain. The soldier looked like something out of a nightmare; full hazmat gear, a gas mask, and a QBZ assault rifle that looked like a weapon from a science fiction film. Isobel had been gone for three days, and Shen was making his first house call since the outbreak began.

A squad of PLA soldiers had driven Shen and two nurses to the apartment complex as dawn broke, and the streets were eerily empty.

"We'll check to see if the building is safe, then you'll help us scan the residents." The man's voice was muffled under his gear. Shen had a portable thermal scanner that looked a lot like the kind cashiers used at supermarkets. It used an infrared thermometer to scan body temperature, and anyone with a temperature over 38.5 degrees would cause a loud beep.

"No problem, anyone who doesn't want to see you will just run out the back, though." Shen had recently started making jokes to alleviate the sense of dread the empty city gave him.

"We welded all the doors shut except for the front," the soldier said, taking him completely seriously. Shen checked his scanner as the soldiers gathered around the door.

As soon as there was any play in the hinges, the door crashed open and a screaming man charged out

13

at them.

"You bastards! How dare you lock us in there?" he croaked. There was a stunned moment of silence, and the distraught civilian started running, his flip-flops slapping noisily against the street. The captain didn't yell or issue commands. He raised his QBZ in a motion as smooth and mechanical as a piston firing in a cylinder. The crack of the rifle echoed and re-echoed between the buildings as though between mountains, and Shen saw curtains draw back all along the street. Hundreds of faces stared from windows and balconies at the bloodstain spreading beneath the sprawled figure. The city wasn't empty; it was a powder keg with the lid screwed on tight.

"Check him," the Captain said, and Shen did, walking down the road like an actor walking onto a giant stage to deliver an obsequy. He knelt. The man was around sixty and his last few breaths came in tight gasps. Shen pretended that the mask was a shield between him and what he was doing, and scanned the man's temple. There was a loud beep.

"How could you?" the man gurgled very softly.

"Don't worry," Shen replied, "tomorrow it will be me."

X-DAY -1

POTUS Tweet:
CDC and my Administration are doing a GREAT job of handling Coronavirus

ISOBEL AND SHEN

BLAKE JESSOP

```
WUHAN TIANHE AIRPORT, CHINA
        FLIGHT: WUH-AMS
```

Isobel Pang tried not to think about the video footage on the portable hard drive in her bag and thought about it anyway. For a while, there had been a temptation to hook it up to her phone and watch it, but it turned out she didn't need to; images from the quarantine zone invaded her mind all by themselves. They changed her dreams, made food slide tastelessly down her throat, and turned her stomach into a cauldron of bile and anxiety. She was navigating from the intercity rail station into the Wuhan Tianhe International Airport through a throng of nervous travellers, so it wasn't a good time to start having flashbacks.

A deep breath meant to steady her nerves instead smelled like smog and cigarette smoke, and Isobel thought about a cop she'd seen smoking outside a line of police tape at the Wuhan Wet Market. Wei

Shen had already snuck her onto his medical team by then, and her features were concealed by a full plastic hazmat mask. As the cop had lifted the tape for them, he'd handed Isobel a cigarette, the action pure reflex. She'd wondered what she needed it for, until she'd seen the cages. Stall after stall plastered with menu cards advertising a dizzying array of animals for sale. Tables with cutting boards still sticky with offal, cleavers and knives discarded in pools of old blood. Behind each were stacks of cages, and in the cages were the animals that had spawned the epidemic. One of them, she didn't know which. No one had fed them since the security forces cleared the market, and the bats and civets and pangolins and peacocks had died behind their bars. They'd scratched at each other trying to escape, and those on top had defecated and bled on those beneath, dying en masse stacked one atop the other. It was more death than Isobel had ever seen in one place, and she'd watched loyalist tanks shell civilians in Homs.

They're just animals, she'd told herself, and believed it until Dr Shen had managed to get her and her Go-Pro into some of the temporary hospitals to see just how similar her species looked when it died. The same writhing, the same heaving breaths, the same blood.

Isobel shook her head, almost violently, and tried to read departure signs through eyes suddenly blurred with tears. She took another deep breath, and this one did settle her nerves. She finally felt the old combat coldness coming back and focused on where she was; in the middle of a disaster no one knew was happening yet, trying to get out. Trying to get the proof of it out, anyway. She looked over one shoulder and strode into Terminal 1. Looked again.

The first thing Dr Wei Shen told Isobel when she entered the Wuhan quarantine zone wasn't a warning about the virus. Not *wear this mask,* or *wash your hands.* She had told him who she was, that she wanted footage, that the BBC would air it, that she wanted his help. She'd told him they'd have to be secretive, that the Ministry of State Security would start sniffing around if she wasn't careful. The doctor had laughed.

"It isn't that they might be watching you," he'd replied. "They are watching you. Every shadow is watching you. Now, wash your hands and wear this mask."

She hadn't believed in the shadows then, but she did now. They were as pervasive as the virus, as

13

subtle and impossible to avoid as malignant microbes, unless you knew what to look for. Isobel did, and when she walked past the check-in counters, she finally saw them.

The last two weeks had been so full of sickness, of danger and paranoia, that Isobel had started seeing ghosts, and now the ghosts were looking back. She knew she was being followed with animal clarity, and felt the way she thought suicide bombers must feel; sick with fear, carrying something that could kill her, and absolutely certain of her cause. Certain down to the core of her being that what she had would blow up very, very big. Headlines, in her case, but the videos were just as likely to make her disappear in a burst of chaos as any conventional explosive. A few news stories had already run about the novel Coronavirus, mostly comparing it to SARS. She had proof that was about as accurate as comparing a hand grenade to a bunker buster.

Isobel walked the main concourse like a businesswoman with places to be, took a blue medical mask from a bin proffered by a harried looking airport worker, and covered her face. Her father was British and her mother Taiwanese, so her skin was a little too light to blend in perfectly. She let her hair down, a curtain of black that might partially shield her from notice.

This was not the first time Isobel had fled a war zone. Not the first time she'd been tailed. Two casual looking men in sport coats loitered behind her. They followed her at oblique angles, constantly keeping her in sight. Nausea tugged at her guts, clammy and cold, and she veered into a bathroom.

Isobel rushed into a stall, locked it behind her, and despaired at the tiny metal catch that was her only defence against the outside world. She sat on the toilet and set her laptop bag across her thighs. Tried to run down what was about to happen to her. *I am going to be caught and searched. When they find my footage, I will never leave China again.*

Isobel breathed as evenly as she could, heart racing, and the mask pulled against her lips with each inhalation. She worked on the simplest difficulty first; visibility. She texted a friend at the British Consulate and let him know what was about to happen. Maybe he could apply some pressure—renditioning a BBC journalist had to be a bad look, even for the MSS.

After that she made a list of her remaining problems and found them singular; the outbreak

footage. She couldn't upload it using her unsecured cellular phone and expect to make it out undiscovered. One of literally millions of worker bees who monitored internet traffic in China would stop her or report her. A satellite phone would solve the problem, but she'd given hers to Dr Wei along with the camera. She'd already wiped all traces of the footage from her laptop; the only place it still existed was her portable hard drive, and there was no way Chinese security would let her leave with that. She dug it out and held it in her hands. The drive was the size of a paperback novel, a terabyte of flash memory encased in burnished steel. It felt like holding something radioactive. For an instant, Isobel considered dumping it in the toilet tank and washing her hands of the whole thing.

"I am not doing that. No fucking way."

She drummed her fingers against the case and wondered how long she had before a female shadow came to roust her from her hiding place. Five minutes? Four?

Isobel had a desperate idea. It's what's on the inside that counts.

With trembling fingers Isobel used her nail file to unscrew the two halves of the case. A thin line of glue resisted as she pulled it apart, but in a moment, she was looking at the guts of the drive. It was mostly empty space, a green plastic chip board, and some wires that lead to the USB port. She tore the connectors from the flash memory and teased it out of the case with the file. It was about the size of a credit card. Excitement surged through her. She dug out her wallet, wobbling for a second and trying not to let her the entire ersatz workshop fall off her knees.

Someone entered the bathroom and Isobel froze. Sweat formed under her arms and trickled down her ribs. There was the click of high heels and the snap of a makeup case. A young woman's voice talking to a static little buzz on the other end of a cell phone.

Isobel felt a moment of relief and then jumped as her own mobile vibrated. A text from the consulate. *We can get you on the plane, but you're going through security. That's as good as it gets. Ditch everything. GET OUT.*

Isobel cuffed sweat from her forehead and dug a credit card out of her wallet. She used leftover glue from the case to stick the flash memory to it, then slid the card back into its slot. It bulged a little, so she got rid of her frequent flyer's card to make space. That

13

done, Isobel carefully screwed the portable hard drive back together and slipped it deep beneath the cardboard stiffener at the bottom of her bag.

Someone hammered on the door, and Isobel saw booted feet surrounding her stall. Felt the same feeling she got the first time she heard an incoming artillery shell.

Here we go.

***

Isobel shivered in a bare room. The obvious thing to do was be terrified, but she was locked into a restraint so surreal that it was hard to think of it as reality at all. They'd sat her in a chair with a little desk not unlike the ones she'd crammed into at university, except that this one had a cage that locked around it like an iron maiden. It looked enough like being shoved into a shopping trolley that she wanted to laugh hysterically.

Chinese state security laid her stuff on a table and searched it with methodical precision. Isobel tried to keep her expression as neutral as possible. She wondered why the bloody hell there needed to be a little desk in her Orwellian torture chair.

The men in grey removed the sim card from Isobel's phone and the SD memory from her e-reader. They took the old-fashioned paper-and-pencil notebooks she used when there was no way to recharge electronics and put them in individual plastic evidence bags. They whisked her laptop and out of the room before she could even begin to protest.

"Ms. Pang, is this everything?"

"Yes," Isobel replied, trying to keep the fear out of her voice. "Am I free to board my flight?"

"We have the right to confiscate anything deemed a threat to national security, as well as a right to detain you. Do you understand?"

"Yes," Isobel repeated. "Am I free to board my flight?"

They turned her carry-on bag inside out. They rummaged through her toiletries and underwear. They cut open the hems of her raincoat. Isobel felt like someone had broken into her flat and was tearing the place apart while she sat tied up with duct tape on the couch.

"Agent Cai, look!"

From underneath the board that stiffened the base of her laptop bag, one of the agents pulled out

the flat steel rectangle, the USB cable still dangling from it. Agent Cai took it.

"One terabyte hard drive," Agent Cai said, "we'll be taking this, too."

Isobel looked up at him with all the loathing she could muster.

"I understand, am I free to get on my flight?"

Agent Cai started to laugh, but the buzz of his phone interrupted him. He frowned.

"Are you prepared to sign a confession?" he said after a moment. "It will make your case much easier."

Isobel smiled. The petty part of her liked knowing what the desk was for, and the rest knew what the question really meant.

"Got a complaint from the British Consulate, did you?"

Cai paused again. His eyes were unreadable. He said nothing.

"Can I have my passport? Am I free to board my flight?"

"Yes," Agent Cai said.

***

Isobel took her seat, and the tension in her didn't relax until she felt the sharp exhilaration of the Emirates 757 accelerating down the runway. When it did, she felt giddy, like she'd gotten away with the crime of the century. The only things the MSS had returned to her were her passport, wallet, and shoes. They'd taken everything else and assured her she would be mailed a receipt. One of them had thumbed through her cards, actually put his fingers on the flash memory, and then hurried to take all of her cash. Just thinking about it made her grin for ten seconds solid, and then exhaustion settled over her like a wave crashing over a beach.

So much fear, so much tension, and her work had only just begun. She hadn't even written any copy yet. There was no script. No treatment. Nothing but hours of the most terrifying footage she'd ever seen. She would need to find an editor, someone good. Someone who could work fast. She'd been in China long enough to get out of touch with just how bad things were in the rest of the world. She had to get up to speed.

Isobel took a deep breath and rang for a stewardess.

"The first thing I need is a drink."

She ordered a gin and tonic and watched the harried flight attendant keep her balance amidst a bit of turbulence as she brought it over. She closed her eyes, and when she opened them the drink sat on the tray in front of her, ice slowly melting in the clear liquor. She must have nodded off for a moment. Isobel yawned, and pulled the mask down to her neck for a moment. She raised the plastic glass and sniffed. The bitter, beautiful pine scent of Tanqueray. Bubbles tickled her nose, and she took a long, luxurious sip.

TONY GRANT

STEPHEN HERCZEG

ON BOARD FLIGHT: WUH–AMS

Tony splashed cold water on his face and looked into the mirror. Through his red-rimmed eyes, he watched the droplets run down his haggard face and catch in the three-day growth on his cheeks and chin.

Christ, I'm knackered.

He dragged several paper towels free. Dabbing the water from his face, he popped his glasses back on and let his eyes settle back onto his tired features, their focus adjusting until he could clearly make out the devastation.

If only Claire could see me now. No way she could refuse a stunning example of manhood like me.

He hadn't thought of Claire for a while, hiding her memory behind a wall inside his mind. A wave of sadness washed over him before he succumbed to another mixed feeling of rage and depression.

Why the hell am I here?

13

His mind raced and wandered back to a week before when life had been going along nicely.

Tony was well placed in NextGen Consulting. He specialised in ICT architecture, advising clients on the correct mix of technologies to satisfy their business needs. To the layman, his job would be as boring as watching grass grow, but he was damn good at it and he was proud, and they paid him handsomely for both his skills and his ability to connect with clients; how he understood their needs and respected their wants.

He was currently with the Home Office, assisting with securing the borders in preparation for withdrawal from the European Union. Visa and Passport processing had always been slow but would degrade now that non-nationals would be treated individually rather than like UK residents.

They were bringing in a system of cameras that would capture and pre-process passenger details as they walked through the terminal. Not easy, as it required linkages to the EU passport database, real-time processing and integration with the intelligence network. There were security implications aplenty, as well as the difficult part of sticking within budget.

Tony, in his role with NextGen, had designed the overall system and was in negotiations with a local company to purchase the camera and facial matching systems. The talks with the EU regarding access to their database had progressed amicably, and they were ready to begin final negotiations before signing contracts.

Then in walked Milan.

The client at the Home Office had introduced Milan Curlis as a specialist in procurement, helping to ensure that large-scale contract negotiations went smoothly and represented the best value for money to the government.

Alarm bells had fired off immediately in Tony's mind. Milan presented as a well-dressed businessman, much like Tony himself, but with a thick head of blonde hair. He held himself with an air of smarm that irked Tony straight away. Then there was his asthma puffer that came out whenever he talked. To Tony, it seemed a way to garner sympathy, rather than a need. Tony even hated the thick gold ring he wore. Milan told anyone who'd listen, he earned it at Harvard. Tony smelt bullcrap. Within the hours the alarms in Tony's head were signalling.

Milan's first interaction with the project was to

13

listen quietly as progress was laid out and the choice of vendor explained. At the end, he simply asked why they hadn't considered Hubai Optoelectronics; a China-based company that had recently installed a facial recognition network across all of China's major airports. The system linked back to the main database of the Ministry of State Security in Beijing.

Tony had simply stated that Chinese systems of this type were considered too questionable for consideration.

Milan responded with a flippant, "But, they are half the price of the one you are considering."

The ears of the main client from the Home Office had pricked up at that remark. Tony immediately sensed doom wafting across his project at that point. That tide swelled over the coming weeks, washing away any hope of signing the contracts he had negotiated. Eventually, the client had ordered a personal inspection of the Chinese systems to ensure they were fit for purpose.

Expecting Milan to be sent to China, Tony's shoulders slumped when the finger was pointed at him.

The trip would involve an entire week of travel, with visits to Beijing and Shanghai, and a side trip to

Wuhan province to see the factory where they were built. Tony ended up flying for almost three full days out of the seven, a day to and from China, with each leg inside the country taking about two hours.

Apart from the continuous question of why he was there, the trip was uneventful. The Chinese hosts were accommodating. They relished the opportunity to show off their systems and took him through every aspect, including a visit to the MSS offices in Beijing, something that very few outsiders ever managed. His appreciation for the technology grew, but a nugget of doubt still sat in the back of his mind. The system was virtually the same as the one they'd already chosen. The only difference was price.

As he stared as his haggard appearance once more, one final moment with Milan began to bring all his fears to realisation. As Tony was about to race to the airport, Milan had eyed him with that supercilious look and said, "Don't worry, I'll look after the project while you're away."

An off-the-cuff remark at the time, but Tony believed it was tantamount to a declaration of war. If he didn't trust his NextGen compatriots, he thought he'd probably be tossed out of the Home Office

project the moment he landed in London.

Anger grew inside. He almost swore out loud when a knock on the door snapped him back to the present.

A voice filtered through the doorway, "Are you awake in there?" The tone of the voice told him someone was in desperate need of the toilet.

Tony checked his watch.

Still twelve hours to Amsterdam. Good god, I'm tired.

***

Tony's dreams were filled with vivid fantasies of Milan dying in horrible ways. A smile crossed his face beneath his shuttered eyes. In his fantasy, Milan was bound to the trunk of a tree. The bane of his life pleaded for forgiveness, his eyes wide in terror, the asthma puffer jammed up his nose.

Just as Tony raised a chainsaw, gunned the motor and stepped forward to deliver the killing blow, the machine turned into a lollipop. Tony popped the candy into his mouth and his senses were overloaded with the sickly, sweet taste.

His supine form smacked and licked its lips as

the sweet sensation filled his mind. His dreams blew away and his eyelids flickered open. A large pair of almond-shaped eyes stared deep into his own. The face was framed with a mop of jet-black hair. A wide, bright smile broke across the little girl's visage and she let out a delighted squeal of laughter.

She held the same lollipop from Tony's dream and he quickly realised where the sweet taste came from. She pulled her wet sticky hand away from his face, popped the lollipop back into her mouth and ran off up the aisle, a string of high-pitched giggles following her.

He'd seen the little girl earlier in the flight, running up and down the aisle several times, chased by her mother. At one point, she had suddenly stopped making noise. An event that was strange, although a blessing. Tony had peered towards the cockpit and spied the little girl. A hand reached out, the owner hidden from his view, and presented the little girl with a lollipop identical to the one she had placed in his open slumbering mouth. Part of him thanked the passenger for trying to placate and calm the little girl, another part damned him for the resultant taste in his mouth.

Tony sat up straight and smacked his lips again.

13

His roused mind now grimacing at the sickly taste. He downed the remainder of his complimentary water. The aftertaste of the lollipop persisted. He pressed the call button to order another bottle—and something a little stronger—then dragged a handkerchief from his pocket and dabbed at the sticky residue left by the toddler's hands, regretting that he'd finished off his water and resigned to wait for the attendant so he could finish cleaning his face.

His eyes strayed towards the windows and fixated on the crack of bright light shining beneath the shutter. His body said it was late at night, but reality said it was the middle of the day and would stay that way until they landed in Amsterdam.

His musings on the time of day were interrupted by the arrival of a shapely young Asian flight attendant. His eyes flicked across the polite smile on her face. He smiled and ordered another water and a scotch. As she disappeared into the kitchen, the little girl with the lollipop ran down the aisle, squealing at the top of her voice, followed by her flustered mother, whose face darted from side to side in an attempt to project a blanket expression of apology to all and sundry. The mother returned a moment later with the struggling child in her grasp.

Tony lay his head back, a slight smile on his face at the thought that running after a small child was in his distant past; his boy was fully grown and gone from the house. Tony's eyes snapped open as he realised his son was old enough to produce his own offspring that, in all likelihood, would be thrust upon him with a moment's notice. Part of him was horrified, but part of him knew Claire would have loved it.

Finally, the attendant returned with his drinks. He sat the scotch to one side while he moistened a napkin and dabbed at the remaining stickiness on his face. The little girl must have had some fun while he was asleep. With a lack of a controlling force, she'd planted her tacky paws all over his face and lips. He presumed she'd stuck the lollipop into his mouth, which was probably open as was his body's habit when he slept. He considered himself lucky that he hadn't sucked it into his lungs as he dozed.

He tipped half of the scotch into his mouth and let the fiery liquid spread warmth through his stomach as he swallowed it. He followed with more water to rinse his mouth clean and keep the cloying taste at bay.

Checking his watch once more, he realised he

still had another two hours before they touched down in Amsterdam. His choices were to chase sleep, pull his laptop down and write up some notes, or watch a movie. The movie won out. Cycling through the choices, he narrowed it down to a clear choice.

Guns, bullets and lots of gratuitous violence. He ordered another scotch with some snacks, and nestled back, focusing his attention to ensure that Milan Curlis's face appeared on as many bad guys as possible.

The time screamed by as fast as the body count in the movie was racked up by the black-suited hitman. Just as the hero was approaching the domain of the big bad boss, the movie stopped, and the pilot broke in informing the passengers that they were about to land.

Tony grimaced.

Damn. Every time I fly, we land with five minutes to go in the movie.

Tony prepared for landing, giving his empty glasses and bottles to the attendant as she hustled past. He kept the movie going, hoping that it would conclude before the plane reached the terminal.

No luck. The hero had entered the big boss's home and offed a few of his bodyguards just as the screen went black and the pilot welcomed them to Amsterdam. Tony grumbled under his breath and simply hoped that the movie was showing on the London flight so he could at least finish it off.

****

The hour and a half stopover in Amsterdam was an exercise in tedium following the eighteen hours since they'd left Shanghai. Not enough time to leave the airport precinct, or even the transit lounge. Tony managed to find a small café and ordered coffee and a pastry to tide him over until London.

His first instinct was to call his son, James, but his mobile was off. It was Friday night; James could be anywhere. Tony sent a quick text to say he'd arrived in Amsterdam and would call when he was home.

While waiting for a hopeful reply, he scanned through his social media feed, and seeing nothing, he dulled the screen and put the phone away.

Sitting back and sipping coffee, he scanned the passengers milling around the transit lounge. The little girl—and her overly sweet lollipop—was performing a small whirling dervish dance in the

middle of the causeway, causing people to divert around her amidst a myriad of grumbles and curses aimed at the exhausted mother sitting nearby. Tony felt a pang of pity for the poor woman, but his tongue touched a lone remnant of sweetness on his lips and his sympathy vanished. He grabbed a napkin and wiped frantically, then downed coffee to rid himself of the taste. He half wondered if any hint of sugar would trigger off memories of the little girl for the foreseeable future.

X-DAY

POTUS statement at press conference in James S. Brady Press Briefing Room:

And again, when you have 15 people, and the 15 within a couple of days is going to be down to close to zero, that's a pretty good job we've done.

SAM THE CODER

JACOB BAUGHER

Sun Tzu said: There are five ways of attacking with fire. The First is to burn soldiers in their camp; the second is to burn stores; the third is to burn baggage-trains; the fourth is to burn arsenals and magazines; the fifth is to hurl dropping fire amongst the enemy."

—Sun Tzu, The Art of War.

"Passenger-13 is in place. Compromised. Audio/visual stream live."

I didn't know who the statesman was, just that he looked like the biggest tool this side of Mars. He was a big, balding man in an ill-fitting, dusky, slim-fit navy suit that poorly concealed the pistol shoved down his pants like he was some sort of West Baltimore gangster. He swaggered about the room like a tiny god with a potbelly that hung over his gun

belt. I hated him. I hated the whole goddamn situation. That's why I had the tape recorder shoved in my pocket. The second I got out of here, I'd leak this to the press, flee to Australia, and live in the Kimberleys with my wife and daughter. I already have the ticket bought. They're waiting for me at the airport, and the reporter is sitting in Maan Cafe on Wuche Road. Just a few more hours and I could have spent the rest of my life sitting on a beach with Lily in a bikini and teaching my daughter how to build sandcastles and hit baseballs.

The statesman's entourage stood on either side of the door in the dimly lit room. They were who I was most worried about. If they'd discovered the tape recorder, I'd be shot immediately. I would know. I wasn't the first person to try to leak this. Their rifles glinted in the flickering blue fluorescents that hung from the ceiling. Rows and rows of empty seats at vacant computer terminals bathed the would-be blackness in the light of the blue screen of death. The place reminded me of a lecture hall from university or those CIA buildings from American thrillers.

My computer was the only one running a program. On the far wall, a giant television screen was mounted and showed the inside of a plane—KLM flight 667, inbound to London, Heathrow from Wuhan, via Amsterdam. I wasn't sure how the government installed cameras on the KL-997 and broadcasted the feed without disrupting the aircraft's navigational instruments (for all I knew it was quantum mechanics).

"Bring up Passenger-13 on the screen, please," the statesman says.

"Yes, sir. Coming online."

I input a few lines of code into the terminal and the cameras cut to a young American man who was staring at the stewardess with a glazed-over expression.

"That's him?"

"Yes, sir."

"He doesn't even look sick."

My supervisor, who has been sitting next to me, clears his throat. "We pumped him full of meds before we cut him loose. Trust me, he's asymptomatic but highly contagious."

"And we have full control over him?"

"Yes, sir." He gave me a gesture that I think he meant to mean 'show him,' but I didn't move. This man had a gun and I wasn't about to get shot. I'd

heard rumours about the statesman. I was too close to that beach in Australia to mess this up.

"Coder?" The supervisor knows my name but he's to refer to me as "coder" in case this ever leaks to the public. I find this ironic, as I'm literally the leak. I refer to him as "supervisor" and we both refer to the statesman as "statesman."

"Yes, sir." I input a line of code. Passenger-13 orders a beer from the stewardess, perfectly polite, takes a sip, unlatches the tray on the back of the seat in front of him, and sets it down.

"Coincidence," the statesman says. "Do something else."

I input another line of code. Passenger-13 licks his palm. Then, when the person next to him isn't looking, he rubs it on their arm rest.

The statesman lets out a chuckle. "And we can make him do *anything*?"

"Well," my supervisor says, "Anything that a person might do that's not too far out of what's normal for them. Basic tasks, sure, but we couldn't get him to, I don't know, take his clothes off or compromise himself without breaking the illusion. His brain is already rejecting the *Yoshimo Chen* persona, but as long as we can keep him from concentrating on it, he should remain ours."

"Excellent. How many are infected so far?"

"Right now?"—the supervisor checks a monitor—"Just him and the guy next to him. All we have to do is sit back and wait."

"No," the statesman said. "The chairman must be sure.'

"Sir—"

I'm not sure what signal the statesman gave his men, but three short bursts of gunfire, ungodly loud, interrupt my supervisor. Hot blood sprays across my face as he drops to the floor. I keep my face carefully blank.

"Coder," the statesman says, "plug these commands into the terminal. We want to optimise infection."

He hands me a piece of paper. Lines and lines of code are written out in what seems to be 5-point font. Fuck me, I should never have taken this job.

"Yes sir," I say.

I start the entry...

We're going very substantially down, not up (when asked if *"U.S. schools should be preparing for a coronavirus spreading."*)

GUS DYSON

JACOB BAUGHER

ONBOARD FLIGHT: WUH-AMS

<INITIALIZING COVID-20. SUBJECT CONSCIOUS. PASSENGER-13 ARMED,

LIVE. RUNNING DIAGNOSTIC:

<STIMULI?>

<STIMULI?>

<CONFIRMED INFECTION. RUNNING FULL SYSTEM SCAN>

<RESPIRATORY: STATUS - INFECTED>

<DIGESTIVE: STATUS - INFECTED>

<NERVOUS: STATUS - COMPROMISED - WITHIN FULL CONTROL OF THE STATE>

<IMMUNE: STATUS - ACTIVE>

<IMMUNE: SUDO: RUN [SUPPRESSION.EXE]

<STATUS: CONFIRMED SUPERSPREADER.>

<SUDO: PASSENGER-13; COVID-20 ENGAGED>

Gus Dyson thinks his name is Yoshimo Chen. He has flight anxiety, and the bumpy ride from Amsterdam to London isn't helping. I engage his nervous system and give him a shot of dopamine. He

relaxes, slumps back in his seat and stares at the stewardess' buttocks that he finds so attractive. His own shot of dopamine, triggered by his arousal, mixes with mine and sufficiently distracts him.

He knows something is wrong. He thinks his name is Yoshimo Chen, like it says on his passport, but knows, somewhere deep in his mind, that it's really Gus, and that he's really worried about his fiancée, and that he just can't seem to work out how he's gotten here.

His brain reacts against my suggestion and tries to show him an image of a young woman with red hair trying on a wedding dress in a small shop on Cuyahoga street in Akron, where he's from. I block it and, instead, direct his attention back to the stewardess. He relaxes, scratches his chin, takes a sip of beer.

Yoshimo-not-Gus has three small glowing phials under the skin of his left wrist that he keeps picking at. I send him a command to stop. It's not time yet. Those are the kill switches. One command from me, and his wrist will spasm, breaking the vials and releasing a mega-load of our nanite-infused COVID-20 supervirus into the air. There aren't nearly enough infected for the statesman's liking.

Just Gus, who thinks he's Yoshimo, and Nigel, who we made Yoshimo cough on as he passed by when he boarded the plane. Nigel has had too many beers in preparation for a stag party and is beginning to think his name is Zhang-Wei (though he won't admit it to himself yet). The statesman wants me to blow the fuse at Chicago O'Hare. I'm trying not to think about that.

Maybe I deserve to die.

Tommy, a man sitting three rows ahead of Yoshimo, is also infected. I've made Gus lick his palm every fifteen minutes since getting on the plane and made him touch pretty much everything he sees. Tommy, though, is stewing in his own oxytocin and dopamine as Stacey, the sexually frustrated mother of three with an absent husband, who is sitting next to him, begins to infiltrate his gym shorts under the fleece blanket she's brought with her for just such an occasion. She's not ours yet, but she soon would be, so I let the situation play out.

As for the rest of them…

```
<Engage:  sudo  "Bladder.exe";  "Cough.exe";  "Mutation -
'contact' .exe">
```

POTUS statement at press conference:
We're ordering a lot of supplies. We're ordering a lot of, uh, elements that frankly we wouldn't be ordering unless it was something like this. But we're ordering a lot of different elements of medical.

ALEX LOGAN

PAMELA JEFFS

ONBOARD FLIGHT: AMS-LHR

I thought I was ready. But I'm not. Not really. Flying passenger class in a plane under clear skies is one thing, but strapped in riding the back of a storm is quite another. Lightning. Turbulence. The crying of a baby and the smell of fear from the woman sitting next to me. They are triggering my responses. I suck in a stabilising breath. I'd be a lot better up in the cockpit. In control. But I'm not permitted to fly. Not until I prove to Her Majesty's Armed Forces that I've recovered. I clench my teeth and grip my seat tighter. My fingernails press into the worn leather. British RAF pilot, Alex Logan—that's me—Mr Fucked Up In The Head ever since the last covert ops I undertook with Special Forces in Syria, went wrong.

I lean back. I focus on the small details around me, the smell of the recirculated air, the flickering

images of the TV show—re-runs of *The Fresh Prince of Belair*—playing on my neighbour's iPad screen. But it doesn't help. All I keep thinking about is how I lost my wings that day over Syria—how I fell from the sky, losing both my plane and best friend, Connor Johns, in a hail of ISIS militant fire.

"Oh, c'mon, Alex," says Connor. "Don't be so melodramatic. You need to let this go. You didn't kill me. *They* did."

I glance to my left. Connor is standing in the aisle. His pilot's uniform clings slick to his skin, soaked in blood. The left half of his face is missing. The man sitting across the aisle and just behind me— a bald, bearded man with glasses—is visible through my friend's transparent body.

I turn back. Connor isn't really here, I remind myself. He's dead. He is just my imagination. The plane suddenly drops as the crosswinds outside shift. My seatbelt constricts around my waist.

He's dead. He's dead. He's dead.

The view of the cabin suddenly shifts, changing from a dimly-lit, people-filled space into a day from my past—a blistering day in a far away desert filled with fire, smoke, blood and sand. I blink, pushing the flashback away. Connor died there in the shadow of the plane's ruptured wing with a punctured chest and his face torn away. I tried to revive him. I still taste his blood on my lips.

This is a different plane. Syria is far away.

"Hey, Alex. Look at the sky," says Connor, his voice rasping.

I know I should ignore him, but don't. I turn my head. The porthole window offers a small glimpse of broken clouds, lightning skittering along their skirts—silver against dread grey. Once I would have thought it beautiful. But I don't find anything beautiful anymore.

Not even the black-haired airhostess who stops with her drinks cart next to me.

"Can I get you anything, sir?" she asks. I'm stuck by how her blood-red fingernails are an exact shade to match her painted lips. And those lips—the way they smile—just a little too friendly. I'm pretty sure she would give me her number if I asked for it.

"Sir, are you okay?" she asks again. Her blue eyes remind me of the skies over Syria.

"Ah, yes," I manage to say. Connor grins. "Just water, thanks."

"No problem." The woman reaches through Connor's transparent chest and into her drinks cart.

13

The clear water bottle she places on my tray table drips with condensation.

"You should definitely get her number," says Connor, his gaze following the airhostess as she moves further along the aisle.

My ex-girlfriend, Alice's voice muscles into my head. "You are seriously screwed up, Alex. I'm leaving. And do womankind a favour and don't go inflicting your fucked-up-self on any other poor unsuspecting girl."

I frown and unscrew the lid of the water bottle. The liquid is cold as it slides down my throat.

"Don't listen to what she said. Alice was a bitch," says Connor. He leans his elbow on the backrest of my seat. Phantom blood dribbles from his sleeve onto the floor.

"Shut up," I mutter. Alice was well within her rights to leave me.

"Excuse me?" says the woman sitting next to me. "Were you talking to me?"

I shake my head and wink. I tip my chin and pretend I was talking about the people in the seat behind us.

The two men. The woman nods knowingly and turns back to her iPad. The men's voices have been an annoying litany for the entire flight. I listen as their current topic of conversation leaks in through the crack between the seats.

"Have you heard about the COVID breakout? Chinese government is apparently in full lock down. Crazy shit like shooting people in the street."

"Yeah. But you never can tell the truth of those stories. Sure, the government is pretty brutal, but they wouldn't just kill people for no reason."

"No reason? You are so fucking naïve. This virus is spreading. People are dying over there. I saw it on the news, they didn't show bodies but whole complexes were being barricaded to keep the sick out—or in maybe, I don't know. But it looked bad. You can't tell me they aren't afraid."

"Well, hopefully they'll find a cure. It's just cold symptoms, right? Yeah, the old and young are at risk, but you know, more people die of cancer every day."

"True, but I got a friend who works in virus research. He reckons things like this tend to mutate— you know, get real bad, real quick…"

I've heard enough. I've got more important things to worry about than a virus infecting people half way across the world. I unclip my belt and stand. The airhostess has the aisle blocked down the back,

but the path to the toilets at the front of the cabin is clear. I step out, gripping the headrest. The man sitting on the aisle opposite me stands up suddenly.

His tray table is covered in beer cans, another one is held in his fist. Sweat slicks his brow. He frowns as he leans into the aisle—a clear challenge. But while he towers over me, he is slimmer in build. I know I could take him if he wants to start something. I don't move back, but instead slowly lift my chin to lock gazes with him. A challenge of my own. But Connor growls low at my back. A warning. I take note. He was always smarter at picking fights than me. I smooth out my features and place my hand out, palm up.

"After you," I say. The man glares at me for a moment longer, and then steps out. As he does, he stumbles and the beer in his hand slops over me. He clutches his chest and coughs, beer-tainted spittle sprays across my face. He coughs again. This time the wet sound is followed by a slew of vomit that shoots across his chin and over my boots.

"For fuck's sake, dude," I snarl stepping back from him. I wipe the back of my palm across my face in disgust. My boots are beyond salvaging.

The man grins weakly. "Hostess won't think

you're so pretty now."

"Hit the fucker!" whispers Connor in my ear.

But I'm not fighting anyone while covered in puke. "Get out of my way," I say.

The man wipes his mouth. "Look, sorry. Air sickness and a few too many brews. I didn't mean anything by it."

The hostess minus her trolley arrives, her hands full of napkins. "Please gentlemen. Move aside. Let's get this mess cleaned up."

She's smiling, but the tightness of her lips betrays her disgust. The sick man nods, but then doubles over and coughs again. Before the hostess can move, her shirt is sprayed in more vomit.

I'll give her credit. She looks like she is about to gag, but doesn't. A consummate professional.

"Oh shit, I'm sorry, love," murmurs the sick man, trying to pat away the rivulets of vomit from her blouse.

"Please," says the hostess, pushing his hands away. She reaches past him and pulls an airsick bag from the seatback. "Take this and sit down."

The passenger complies. I feel sorry for the woman as she kneels down and starts to clean. She glances at me as I squeeze past her, heading for the

13

toilets. No smile on her face this time.

There is someone already in the cubicle when I get there. I curse. I have a desperate need to clean up. Behind the closed door, a cough barks out. A deep, wet sound. Then a rushing swoosh as the bowl is evacuated and the gentle gurgle of water in the sink. The door clicks open. A young woman steps out. Her hand rests for a moment on the door handle. "All yours," she mutters, blowing her nose on a tissue as she passes. I notice a small smear of blood on the tissue as she folds it away. Jesus. Is everyone on this flight goddamn sick?

Fuck.

I step in and pull the door shut. The handle is still moist from the woman's grip. I turn the tap on and scrub my face. I feel marginally better. I kick off my boots and tip the toe of the first under the tap. Chunks of vomit slide away from the black patent leather, falling to clog up the drain. I poke at the mess with a paper towel. It jerks thickly past the drain and down into the pipe. Fucking disgusting.

I drop my shoes, rinse my hands again and rest both palms on the bench. I take a deep breath. My reflection glares back at me from the mirror—my sandy-blond hair in its military cut, grey eyes and a week's facial growth. Even I can tell I look tired. Just a little while longer and we'll land. Then I can rest and finally get back to work.

All will be good.

"We both know you aren't good." Connor appears behind me, his reflection staring at me from the mirror.

"Leave me the fuck alone." I mutter.

"You know I'm not really here so I can't technically leave you alone."

"Jesus. I just want to go to the toilet in peace."

"Fine. I'll wait outside. But we need to have this discussion. You can't go back to work while still having hallucinations like this. You'll end up killing yourself or someone else."

I swallow. Connor is right, or maybe it's my conscience talking. But the problem is, I can't stay off work like this anymore, either. It's a slippery slope to Hell if I have to spend much more time twiddling my thumbs on forced medical leave. I need my next meeting with the base psychologist to go well. She needs to clear me this time round.

I just want to get back. I'll be okay once I'm in the pilot seat again.

"That's if they ever let you back in a plane," says

Connor. "Trust me. They'll work out what's going on with you."

"No, they WON'T!" My anger peaks. I punch the mirror. The glass splinters, erasing the ghostly image of Connor's face.

"Doing that just proves my point," says Connor's voice, now disembodied. "Your fucked if you go ahead with this review."

"Don't worry. I'm ready." I slowly reach down to turn the tap on. The blood welling on my knuckles slides away in the cool current of water. Outside, the intercom address system activates.

"Please fasten your seat belts and lift your trays into the upright position. Crew, prepare the cabin for landing."

I pull a clean paper towel out and wrap it over the cuts. I push open the door and head back to my seat.

Connor is already there, waiting, when I get back.

ERIN

LANNAH MARSHALL

ON BOARD FLIGHT: AMS-LHR

New life never started easy.

Turbulent.

Uncertain.

Time stretched and condensed into abstraction, cradled and smothered until one emerges into the breathlessly wide world anew. A laborious, unrelenting journey on the newborns; young and old alike.

Swaddled in her plane seat, Erin promised herself the world and changes. Her eyes watched the light of the sun chase the passenger jet, an old life refusing to leave her behind.

A hiccup.

More turbulence.

Erin's eyes darted to the infant beside her.

He can't find you here. A lump in her throat. Uncertain, but necessary, she promised herself. A

deep breath ached in her wavering heart, but she held it there and slid the window blind shut. A false night now, huddled with doubts and smatterings of coughs and grunts.

Nothing but the low rumbling engines to remind her that they were suspended in the air by science and optimism.

An air of optimism, a chant in her mind as a brief smile twitched her lips.

A cough behind her breaks her thoughts, and she returns to watching the sleeping babe in the cot. A beautiful, delicate thing she'd made and brought into a world so cold and empty. She wasn't strong enough. Never strong enough.

No. She adjusted the cloth wrapped around her son. *I was strong enough to carry him aboard. I will be strong enough to carry him off it. One step at a time.*

Erin pressed her temples. The low chatter of the plane was an unwelcome static in her ears as she tried to imagine her mother's expression when she opened the front door.

She would pale, Erin suspected, so white her freckles would blossom on her cheeks. The whites of her eyes, so clear in the mind, were haunting. It knotted her stomach and stabbed at wounds previously lost to time.

That expression was once etched in the back of Erin's mind and with a blink of her eyes, it vanished again.

Like the infant beside her, Erin coddled herself in her complimentary blanket and self-soothed to an improvised lullaby. One day she'd have words for it, maybe she'd sing it to her son.

Those eyes flashed bright again. Her mother's nasal-high pitch surfaced. Distraught. Grieving. The child she raised, the woman Erin could have been, was dead. All those dreams were scattering and fading, like fireflies and long nights through Hubei Province.

"You stupid girl," her mother would say. Her nose would wrinkle in that way it did whenever the PM's Question Time was on, and her R's would roll with venom. A toxin she usually reserved for her father. Those eyes. Pale and unloving.

Erin sunk lower into her seat.

Her father was not much better. No. It would be a cold day in Hell before she'd bring Jian to him.

On the topic of Hell, maybe now was a time to visit the church. Skip the sour reunion all together and seek refuge in a confession box. It was too late for the nunnery, but maybe God would offer some peace, even if only for a little while.

That was too far ahead. This was a long flight and Erin was tired from teetering on the edge of maybes and could've beens. In this moment, on this flight, she straightened herself up and feigned the greatest smile as the stewardesses walked down the aisle.

Glimpses to the left and right offered little confidence. There was nothing comparable to travelling with a child, an infant no less, knowing everyone onboard internally groaned at the sight of him.

"Drinks?" A stewardess asked, her red-polished nails appearing before Erin registered the question.

"Um, no," was her soft reply. "No, thank you."

The stewardess cooed at the sight of Jian and pretended to paw at his blanket but made sure not to disturb him. A small mercy. For everyone.

***

Jian's peace didn't keep.

He awoke as though startled by a phantom and

screamed as one would imagine the wind sounded outside, ripping against the plane's metal.

Before the groaning could start, or the judgement, Erin pulled Jian from his cot and brought him into the toilet cubicle. The acoustics. The claustrophobia. The ringing of screaming dragged knives through her brain. Jian was an unearthly shade of red. His gummy mouth open, barely a moment to take in air before unleashing a louder, more violent scream.

"Shush, shush," whispered Erin as she quickly, gently, tried to remove his onesie. Her fumbling fingers were numb and shaking as her eyes blurred to stinging tears. "Please, please, shush, shush."

Jian kicked out, curled his legs towards his stomach and wailed louder and louder, until Erin was sure her ears would recognise no other sound for the rest of her life. Skull-cracking, pain-fuelled cries split through her ears and across her vision as she tried to remember how a nappy worked.

No poop.

She took his tiny feet in hand and wiggled, motioning them as though riding a bike. She picked him up and soothed, swooned and danced in the tiny box with his screaming face pressed against her shoulder. He wriggled and kicked and used his newly grown nails to grip and grab at her cheeks. So much strength and noise for such a tiny, delicate thing.

She sang and tried to drown out his worries with a lullaby she knew, but she couldn't hear any other sound than her son. She rubbed at his back, patted and pawed. Rocking back and forth on the toilet, she pictured the faces of the midwives at the hospital, the ones that had tutted and took over soothing him during his first cry.

The ones that thought she couldn't speak Mandarin.

"She's heavy handed," one had said.

"She's knows it's a baby, right?"

Then, to her face, in broken English, "Don't worry, try again."

"Thank you for your support," had been her curt, fluent Mandarin, response.

They paled. Some left.

She prayed for Chen to be on the other side of the doorway, the midwife that had visited her in her apartment and promised her, "it gets easier."

"Does it" Erin whispered into Jian's cheek. Her tears soaked his black, fluffy crown of hair. "I can't breathe." She held tighter and rocked and watched the door. She pictured the frustrated and angry passengers waiting for her. Cursing her son. Maybe even wishing she'd kept her legs shut.

"Kill it," Hongqi had said when he found out. Those once loving eyes had darkened and, in a moment, in a word, he became an entirely different man.

Just as those once doting flight attendants and cooing elderly women were now sat in their seats, rolling their eyes and blaspheming.

"W-What? Why?"

"You think I haven't been blackmailed before?" He rose, older now, experienced not as a principle in a school, but as a liar, a negotiator and a fraud.

"You're not divorced, are you?" she remembered whispering.

"You *stupid* girl," she pictured her mother spitting.

"Kill it."

No, no, no. She pressed her face into Jian's and kissed and cried. "Please, tell me, what do you need me to do?"

A knock.

So soft, but Erin heard it. She slid open the cubicle door to face a sheepish-looking flight

attendant.

"Is everything okay? You've been in there a long time," she said.

Jian screamed against her chest, and Erin's eyes wandered beyond the pleasantries of the stewardess and to the ever-watching, ever-grumbling, ever-coughing passengers.

"I am," said Erin, raising her shaking head.

People were waiting to use the restroom. Erin could see them grimacing at Jian's banshee wails. One was visibly ready to carve their ears from their head. She apologised and stepped aside.

He can't find you here.

Scurrying back to her seat and desperately trying to soothe her son, Erin found herself in the epicentre of stares.

It was relentless.

His cries made sitting unbearable, but walking up and down the aisle irked her neighbours and then some.

"Must you bring that brat down here?" their eyes would ask.

Her clammy hands felt swollen and boiling, and with her heart beating faster than she'd ever known, her arms were growing weary. Jian had never been so heavy. Heavy on her chest. Heavy on her shoulders. Heavy on her heart.

Burning with embarrassment, she could no longer make eye-contact with the other passengers. She had tried feigning dignity, but the tears won. They sealed her eyes shut like salty blisters, but on she marched her screaming son with a stiff upper lip.

"Darling," said a quiet voice beside her, spooking her from her monotony.

"Y-Yes?" Her voice broke.

"Would you like a break?"

Before Erin could reply, Jian was gently pulled from her shaking arms, and Erin wiped her face free of snot and tears. An old woman held her son, smiling at her with big steel-blue eyes and warm leathery cheeks.

The anchor gone from her chest and Erin felt light-headed, breathless, and stammered a thank you with the same fickle strength that kept her from her knees.

"You go have something to eat, some water," said the old lady. "We'll be right here."

Erin nodded, hesitating as she backed away towards her seat. It was easier holding him than to walk away from his screams. Something in her gut

13

resisted her freedom, but she needed it.

Her seat didn't register as she passed it. Instead, she carried on walking towards the tail end of the plane, to the farthest toilet she could reach, and locked herself inside. Her son's cries were there, half-real and half-tinnitus.

She sat there for some time, her head awkwardly placed on the tiny sink, and she cried out what little energy she had. After a few intermittent tears, she wiped her face, washed her hands and prepared herself for the last ten hours of the flight.

****

Moira and Paula were nothing if not patient.

Blessed with hundreds of grandchildren between them and faulty hearing aids, they passed Jian back and forth until the boy settled. Then, with Erin between them, they showed off their flock using their 'fancy gadgets' such as phones and tablets.

"He's going off to university next year," said Moira about her eldest son's youngest.

"Studying engineering," finished Paula with a tap on Erin's wrist.

Moira sighed and swiped through her family

tree, and Erin watched with a peaceful numbness she hadn't felt since before she'd fallen pregnant.

At some point, dazed, she moved back to her seat, slipped Jian back into his bassinet and fell asleep. All eyes could have been on her, but hers were too heavy to care.

The flight could have lasted days. Erin's frame of reference, the sun, was lying to her. The tension among the passengers was palpable, and no level of fatigue allowed her genuine rest.

As the plane glided down to land, the reality refused to sink in.

Stepping off the plane gave rise to sea legs, and Erin hobbled through the terminals with Jian strapped to her chest.

Strong enough, Erin reminded herself, one step at a time.

Moira and Paula found her at the carousel, huddling together and giggling. They poked and prodded at Jian's squishy cheeks as he pouted at them and collected their luggage as it made its way around the bend.

"They've done it again, Paula," said Moira as she groaned at a dent in her suitcase. "Heavy-handed bastards."

13

"*Oof.*" Paula rolled her tongue, and in her eyes, Erin saw a thousand curses. "They'll get a dent in their head if they do it again."

Erin's lips broke into a light smile, and Paula wrapped her arm around her and squeezed.

"Where're your bags, lovey?" Moira asked.

Erin took a deep breath and pointed to a small purple case that had circled twice. The disgruntled passengers, the ones Jian had tormented, stood between them. A dizzying amount of people to upset. Yet, even as the crowd lessened, she struggled to find her bearings and courage to cross them. Jian was small. Loud, but fragile.

"There you go, lovey," said Moira as she plucked the case from the conveyor belt. "Ah." Her lips flattened. "Looks like they've dented yours too."

"Bastards." Paula winked at Erin. "You look awfully tired."

"Sorry?" Erin frowned and rubbed her temples. "I didn't sleep very well."

"Do you have far to go?"

"Canterbury."

"Ah, that just won't do," said Moira. "Come stay with us, we have a spare. Have a nap. Rest yourself up a bit before travelling again."

"The bairn will need it too," said Paula.

Erin nodded her cheek against Jian's head and followed the women through the relentless waves of people. From the dim plane's cabin to the eternally day-bright Heathrow, Erin's eyes stung from the overexposure of colours and noise. She recognised the English and the Mandarin, with layers of French and Arabic in between. It was a lifetime ago when she sprang through Heathrow's doors, two suitcases and a carry-on bag. She'd gripped the tickets so tight with excitement that her nails dug into her palms. Everything was shiny and new. She was almost skipping through the airport, high on graduation and feverish to explore the world. Next stop was China. A new life.

Erin stared at where she'd once stood, where she'd once gazed up at the flight information with wide eyes and a wider heart. Fatigue had yet to plague her the way it did now. It was all in the mind, she told herself. All she needed to do was look out to London and imagine a future as bright and wonderful as the one she'd longed for in China.

A new start, she chanted. *Another step.*

POTUS press conference at Centers for Disease Control and Prevention:
I like this stuff. I really get it. People are surprised that I understand it. Every one of these doctors said, 'How do you know so much about this? Maybe I have a natural ability. Maybe I should have done that instead of running for president.

GUS DYSON

JACOB BAUGHER

ON BOARD FLIGHT: AMS—LHR

For the slightest moment, despite his better judgement, Yoshimo Chen could have sworn his name was Gus Dyson, that he was very afraid, didn't know where Megan, his fiancée, was, and that a man in a white lab coat was about to inject him with a Big Needle.

The feeling of dysmorphia passed and, all at once, the overpowering urge to urinate came over him at the exact same time that he took a swig of the overpriced beer that the stewardess (whose ass he'd been eyeing for the past half hour) had handed him.

He choked on the beer, spewing it all over the stewardess's blue KLM uniform, the sleeping man with black hair next to him, and the buff ex-military-looking guy in the row across the aisle who, in his opinion, had taken entirely too long ordering his drink while the stewardess ogled his white t-shirt and

blue jeans that were so tight that they showed off a significant trouser snake.

He got up, still coughing, and profusely apologising to all involved, and made his way to the small lavatory at the back of the plane. He ignored the stares that followed him.

Not-Gus-Yoshimo unzipped his trousers, tried to aim through his hacks, and let fly. He picked absently at the itchy spot on his wrist as he finished up. For some inexplicable reason, he thought there were three glowing bars underneath his skin, like the cell phone symbol on his phone, but on closer inspection, there was only an angry patch of eczema that he'd always had…hadn't he?

He turned on the water to wash his hands, thought better of it (he really hadn't touched anything), took a deep breath, cleared his throat, opened the lavatory door, and puked stale beer directly onto the stewardess's shoes who was standing at the coffeemaker.

A young Asian woman who was sitting in the last row of the plane, wearing a BBC news polo, gave him a disgusted look, said, "What the fuck is your problem, asshole?" and then returned to watching footage of Hong Kong protesters on her laptop.

The stewardess, who he had thought was hot when the flight took off, was approaching him. She handed him an airsick bag and said, "Sir, return to your seat," and gave him a pitiful smile that one usually reserves for sick puppies.

Yoshimo did, flushed red, and apologised profusely to her, but not before he dipped his finger into the journalist's gin and tonic. He didn't know why he did it, but it felt good. He sat back down in his chair, the barf bag clutched in his hand, and closed his eyes. He was almost to London. The journey was almost over.

The journey to what? some alien voice in his head asked. *The journey to where?*

Suddenly very tired, Yoshimo closed his eyes and went to sleep.

POTUS White House meeting with African American leaders:
It's going to disappear. One day — it's like a miracle — it will disappear.

ERIN

HEATHROW AIRPORT, UK

Vomit. Everywhere. A stranger bent double beside the suitcase, spewing bile and undigested food onto the floor.

Erin's blood drained and stomach rose as she side-stepped the man. Her hand rested on Jian's head as she turned away.

"Are you okay?" she asked over her shoulder.

The stranger grumbled and staggered out the exit.

"That's disgusting," said Paula as she brought out wet wipes from her purse.

"Drunks," muttered Moira, taking a handful for herself.

Already patting down Erin's case, Paula cursed in whispers. "All over your wheel."

"You don't have to do that," said Erin.

"You look after the bairn," said Moira. "You don't want him near this mess."

"Of course," said Erin as she stepped back.

The stares had already begun, and the cleaning crew emerged from the crowd. The rest became a blur as Jian began to squirm. As she stepped out of Heathrow Airport, Erin took one last look back and recalled how she'd been so spritely. How she'd been so excited, her heart swelled in her chest and she couldn't seem to talk fast enough. She was jet-fuelled, powered by the pride her mother and teachers held for her.

Just one step at a time.

***

Moira and Paula lived in a small, cat-friendly estate. The neighbours, while vibrant, were hardy people. Their brows furrowed at the sight of Erin stepping out of Moira's car, and a few of the children playing hopscotch stopped and ran to greet them.

"Moi!" they cried out. "What did you get from China land?"

"Just China," said Paula, "and we said we wouldn't be there long."

Erin helped Moira with the suitcases in the boot. Her gaze drifted to the teenagers that watched them from their place in the carpark, but she shrugged off their curious glares. The children picked up their pitches as Paula began handing out sweets bought in Beijing, and then crashed into groans of disgust at the sight of caramelised insects.

"They're good for you, you know?" Paula told them. "Protein."

"Not in all that sugar, deary," said Moira as she pulled up her case handle and cleared her throat. "We went to Oz."

"Oz?"

"Been to see them 'roos," said Paula with a gummy grin. "Now, where's your mams?"

"Inside."

"At work."

"The pub."

Erin assisted Moira with the cases. For a moment, she felt normal. It seemed like a natural moment, and when she looked over her shoulder, it wasn't for Hongqi or his friends. He can't find her here.

The pair lived in a much-loved home with an air of tranquillity about it. It housed many of the antiquity associated with the elderly, such as porcelain plates and china dolls, but also rollerblades and football boots with freshly chewed up dirt in their spikes. The dining room table had six places set already, and the walls were decorated from skirting boards to ceilings with their children, their children's children and all the friends in between.

Erin recognised many of the faces and respected the space set around the two urns placed on the mantlepiece.

Frank and George. Erin gave a polite nod. *Pleased to meet you.*

They were clean. Recently dusted—by Misty if Paula had remembered correctly.

"This is Erin," said Moira to Frank's urn. "She'll be staying with us until she's ready to go home."

Erin's smile faltered, but she feigned it when Moira clasped her elbow and offered a nod of support.

"You know, I was a single mother," she said as she headed back to her suitcase.

Erin perked. "Oh?"

"Frank's parents were loathed to let him marry me."

"Thirty-five years," called Paula from the kitchen. "Do you take sugar?"

"Um, no, thank you," said Erin as she joined Moira on the sofa. Her eyes flicked to Jian. He still slept in his seat.

"It was a different time," said Moira. She turned her attention to the build-up of letters on the coffee table. "I was all kinds of things. My son, more so."

"What do you mean?"

"My priest at the time, Father Jacobs, refused to let me christen him." Moira's lips flattened. "A bastard, they called him. Do you know what happens to children that are not christened?"

Erin nodded, recalling the horror of reading the titular Tess in Tess of the D'Urbervilles bury her infant son. Erin's eyes betrayed her, staring at Jian as he slept. She was only a child herself when she read how Tess had pleaded to save her son's soul. The chapter where she'd buried his corpse as close as she could to the church wall's left her empty, drained and staring into the ceiling for hours on end. In her mind, Tess was Erin, and Jian's cold body hung limp in her arms.

"It's not the baby's fault," she'd told Hongqi. Her hands sat on her stomach. It rolled with unease. She'd thought it'd be easy, but it wasn't. "I want to keep it. You don't have to have anything to do with it."

Hongqi had lowered himself over her. His

presence knocked her backwards as his eyes locked on hers. I, his lowest, cruellest tone, his voice rumbled, "I said, '*kill* it'."

"Don't you worry," said Moira, "as I said, a very different time."

Erin blinked the memory away and smiled as she took Paula's freshly brewed tea. A finely missed British delicacy, and the surest sign she could tell herself that this wasn't a dream. This was real. "Thank you."

"You said you taught in the schools," said Paula as she sat opposite them in an armchair surrounded by family photos. Not long was she sat did a cat join her. "What was it like?"

"Oh!" Blood drained and rose across Erin's face.

"We don't need to know," said Paula. A passing glance to Jian.

"No, it's okay, I'm just jet-lagged." Erin forced a laugh that grew into a cough. She cleared her throat and tried to imagine a time before Hongqi. There never was in China. She blurred him out of memories, like burning faces from photographs. A distorted, unpleasant view of the world formed, and it sat uncomfortably on her shoulders. "I was originally sent to the city of Guangzhou, in the

Guangdong Province. I was teaching age groups from, say, four to seven? They were beautiful children. They'd had a lot of English teachers. A lot of turnover." Erin stared into the jittery surface of her tea. "It was the most fun I've ever had in my life." She took a deep breath and focused on the smiles of those children, and how they'd tried so hard to please her with their broken English and how receptive they were to her support. These were the children of businessmen and women. The middle-class Chinese. The lessons were long and arduous, but some parents invited her over for dinners and others weren't there for birthdays. Then she stepped in. She expanded their world with English, but not as much as they expanded hers. It was a lifelong debt that could never be repaid. "But then I went to Hubei."

Paula and Moira watched her but said nothing. They had experienced eyes, and Erin knew she needed to say nothing more for them to fill in the gaps—Paula's eyes kept flitting to Jian, and Moira gave Erin a gentle nod.

SAM THE CODER

JACOB BAUGHER

SECRET GOVERNMENT FACILITY, CHINA

<Sudo: COVID-20, Diagnostic-1>

<Results: 78% Sentients infected within margin of viability. Acceptable margin for error>

<Sudo: Run VirusMultiplier.exe>

<Sudo: Run YoshimoSleepCylce.exe[Duration: 40min] | WakeCommand "Welcome+to+Heathrow">

<Sudo: Run stage2.exe>

<Sudo: Run immunosuppression.exe>

I sit back in my chair. It squeaks. On the monitor, the flight attendant cleans up Passenger 13's vomit and takes the soiled rags to the wastebasket in the rear of the plane. Yoshimo-not-Gus is asleep. The statesman and I wait as the minutes tick by until the plane starts its descent into London. The small green bar on the side of the monitor continues to climb, representing infections, until it reaches 100%.

13

The statesman sits back in his chair as well. "Well done," he says softly. He digs into his jacket and pulls out another slip of paper.

"His final instructions. Then you may go."

I take the paper, glance at the screen. The plane has just touched down and Passenger-13 was stirring, so I assumed that the "Welcome to Heathrow" message was playing out of the speaker. The paper contains commands like "Visit Bathroom," "Visit Coffeeshop," "Visit Giftshop," "Walk to food court," "Order food," and "Board plane for O'Hare." The very last command on the paper reads simply `<kill>`.

"Is this wise?" I ask, before I can stop myself. *Think of the beach, man, think of Lily in the bikini and your daughter and baseball.* "Surely, it'd make more sense to let him roam?" I didn't want to kill this man. I shift ever so slightly so the tape recorder in the front pocket of my flannel is aimed toward the statesman.

"The chairman believes it's best if he's terminated. Outside psychological counsel have advised that he may have memories of our suggestions and will be able to trace them back to us after the quantum entanglement is broken, which would link China to the weaponisation of COVID-19 to COVID-20."

I glance over my shoulder at the two men standing by the door. Their guns are pointed at me now.

"But of course," I say. I take the paper and start coding. I had what I needed. I squash down the guilt that I was essentially killing Gus and think about my wife and kid. Gus was weak. He broke in the Wuhan lab, so many floors below us. It's like that scientist said: the weak exist to serve the strong. I was one of the strong. I was playing the long game, so I kept coding. I convinced myself it was for my family. For the world. For the journalist waiting for the tape recorder. But I knew that was an empty lie.

POTUS interview with FOX News:
If we have thousands or hundreds of thousands of people that get better just by, you know, sitting around and even going to work—some of them go to work, but they get better.

GUS DYSON

JACOB BAUGHER

ON BOARD FLIGHT: AMS-LHR

Thunder cracked outside, drowning out the loudspeaker's "Welcome to London-Heathrow" announcement, and Yoshimo-Chen-not-Gus-Dyson startled awake and into a coughing fit. The man sitting in the window seat next to him glared.

"You better not puke on me, buddy."

"No, no," he struggled to say through his coughs. He was getting sick, he could feel it. All he wanted was to take a hot shower when he got back home to Chicago. His mouth tasted like vomit, his hair was sweaty and matted to his forehead. He needed a stiff drink, 2,000 mg of acetaminophen, and a sleeping pill, FDA regulations be damned.

The man looked away in disgust, and out of the plane's window, lightning flashed across the sky. Turbulence buffeted the plane as it came in for the landing. He always hated this part, this last gasping

breath of controlled free-fall when the ground seemed entirely too close for comfort.

Gus clutched the seat's armrests and tried to keep his coughs in as the ground rushed closer in sporadic flashes, illuminated by the raging lightning outside the rain-slicked window. He closed his eyes again, laid his head back on the seat, and decided he'd up his self-prescription to two stiff drinks, a large coffee, and the big bottle of paracetamol from Boots the Chemist. He started the mental list in his head as the plane touched down and deployed its drag flaps, rushing to a stop. Boots, coffeeshop, food court, bar…in that order. His stomach gurgled and he shifted uncomfortably in his seat. Gus added "bathroom" to his list and gave it top priority.

One hour, four extra-strength Tylenols, a chicken nugget combo, and three gin and tonics later, Gus was sure he was sick, and the Tylenol wasn't helping. He'd staggered through the airport, made all his stops, and was now in a window seat in the Boeing 767. A pretty woman sat next to him, but he barely noticed her.

A voice came over the loudspeaker and said something in Icelandic. Then, *"Ladies and gentlemen, welcome to flight BA 925, service to*

Chicago via Reykjavik..."

Gus closed his eyes. His head was pounding. A vague, disjointed thought floated up through the darkness, mingling with the jarring intercom voice.

Is this death?

POTUS Tweet:
I NEVER said people that are feeling sick should go to work.

X-DAY +1

POTUS press conference at Centers for Disease Control and Prevention:
I think we're doing a really good job in this country at keeping it down.

LILY AND JOSEPH

D.M. BURDETT

LHR ARRIVALS HALL, UK

I spied the enemy through my night vision goggles as he infiltrated the main headquarters. Slow and focused, like a cat stalking a butterfly, I tiptoed around the edge of the vast room, my crosshairs trained on his every move as I watched his yellow hard hat bob down the corridor.

"Joseph, can't you sit down and behave," Mum said, but seeing an open expanse between me and the foe, I bolted across it to the safety of a stone pillar, my breath coming in short gasps as I leaned my back up against it, my gun tight to my chest. After pausing for a moment, I peeked my head out over my shoulder and peered around my hiding place.

"Ugh, why do I have to have such a moron for a brother," Lily complained, but I put my finger to my lips to silence her and tipped my head in the direction of the enemy. She acknowledged the signal with a

roll of her eyes.

The enemy was still distracted by his mission, treading carefully through the moving throng, but then he looked my way, and I dropped to the floor like a ninja. I don't think he saw me, but I kept my head down for a count of five, just in case.

When enough time had elapsed, and I was satisfied the enemy wasn't about to pounce on me, I crawled on my stomach, pushing myself along on my elbows in the strange terrain, until I reached a row of chairs. Then I slid beneath them, weaving between chair legs, the machine gun following the slow progress of the insurgent's heavy boots on tiles.

Suddenly, the slow careful footfalls stopped, and my breath caught in my throat as the black boots turned in my direction. Was it possible he'd seen me?

As fast as I could, I wriggled forwards, still on my belly, knocking into legs and bags on the way. Listening to the tuts and groans of the dirty sympathisers above me, I followed my gun to the end of the row. At the end, I jumped out, and seeing the infidel across the room in the hi-viz jacket raise his trigger hand, did the most awesome forward roll across the waiting area that I'd ever managed before.

Unfortunately, my night vision goggles failed

me for a moment, and I crashed into a man pushing a trolley who went sprawling across the floor in front of me, and a bottle of smelly brown liquid smashed open and splashed my new camo trousers.

"Jesus Christ, kid," he yelled. "What the hell are you playing at?"

I lifted my night vision goggles to peer down at him. "Ninja assassins," I told him. *Well, durr!*

"Ninja what?" he muttered before grabbing me by the wrist. "Where's your mum, numbnuts?"

I turned, but Mum was already running over. "Oh my god, I'm so sorry," she said, fussing around the downed man.

"I'm okay," the man said as he climbed up from the floor and flashed a hot look in my direction. I smiled back, leaning my imaginary machine gun against my shoulder. "But my weekend's entertainment is gone."

Mum put an arm across my shoulders. "I'm so sorry," she said softly. "He gets so excited. Can I pay for your…gifts?"

A cleaner and a man in a black uniformed turned up then. "You OK, mate?" the uniformed man asked as the cleaner started to mop up the stinky brown mess. I watched all this through my night vision goggles, the blue light trained on the ill-disguised terrorist I'd just neutralised.

"Na, I'm good, nobody died," the man said, and then he bent down and ruffled my hair. "But you make for a lousy assassin." He leaned in and whispered quietly, "You gotta be silent but deadly, wee man! Attack them when they least expect it!"

It made a lot of sense. A silent but deadly ninja would be like a superhero.

"Got it?" he asked, and I nodded as he turned and made his way to the automatic sliding exit doors.

"You're so lame."

I turned my head and the goggles lit up my sister's face; her top lip was curled up, her eyes narrowed at me.

"I just vaporised the enemy." I pulled my gun from my shoulder and lay it across my arms. "One down, trintyseven million to go."

Lily rolled her eyes. "I wish someone would adopt me, so I didn't have such a freak for a brother. You're embarrassing."

I lifted my gun to my shoulder again and pinpointed the end of Lily's pimply nose in the crosshairs.

"Now, I'll neutralise you, infidel," I whispered menacingly.

"Neutralise this," Lily said, giving me the finger.

"Moooom," I whined at the top of my voice, trying to squeeze out some dramatic tears for extra effect. "Lily called me a freak and gave me the finger."

Mom, still wiping her hands on her jeans to clean off the man's sweat, was returning to her chair.

"Lily! That was your fault," she said. "I asked you to take care of him while I wait for Dad. Can't you do anything I ask?"

Lily huffed and unfurled her folded arms. "Me? But Mom, he's totally feral!"

With a victorious smile, I turned back to the crowded arrivals area, and seeing a new rebel soldier pulling a bomb on wheels—cleverly disguised as a suitcase—I dropped to the floor once more, army-crawling under the next row of chairs.

***

I saw him before he saw me.

"Daaaad!" I shouted, and he waved across heads as he made his way down the short walkway from the

glass doors. I raced down the length of the hall and jumped up at him as he turned the corner.

"Hey, buddy. How're you?" he said, picking me up.

"Dad, look at my new goggles," I said, patting them. "And my new camo trousers. And my new gu—"

"Woah," Dad said, plopping me back on my feet. "Slow down, tiger."

"Hi, Daddy." Lily hurried towards us and put her arms around Dad's waist.

He kissed the top of her head. "Hi, Princess." I put two fingers in my mouth and gave Dad the sicky face thing with my fingers down my throat, and he winked at me.

"Where's Mum," he asked.

"Here," she said from behind him, and he turned and kissed her right on the lips. Right. On. The. Lips. With everyone looking. *Ugh!* Me and Lily looked at each other and did the sicky face and Dad laughed at us both.

"C'mon, you two. Let's go home."

Nigel

GREGG CUNNINGHAM

ON BOARD FLIGHT: AMS-LHR

Somebody shut that fuckin' kid up before I pop a vein!

Nigel cursed under his breath sat in row 7B of the cramped aisle seating, sensing the tension building inside the shitty air-conditioned flight cabin as the coughing started up again behind his reclining chair.

This was his second flight of the day; Amsterdam to Heathrow being the last leg of his long journey home.

He shook his head slowly, clutching the whisky glass propped on the tray as the kid behind him kicked his seat for the hundredth time and wrapped his small sweaty hands around Nigel's headrest and pulled hard. If he was back on the terraces watching his beloved Spurs, he would turn around and let the parents have an earful, maybe even lash out at how

shitty they were for letting their kid act like an arsehole. However, two weeks in the sun had calmed Nigel, and he wasn't about to give up on that holiday feeling just yet. The longer he could control his aggression, the longer his holiday would last.

He would soon be back on the streets of London, with the traffic and the roadworks and the fines and the shitty passengers to deal with, so the longer he held onto the thoughts of the sunny beaches and the scantily clad beauties and the fights on the terraces while watching his team romp through Europe, the longer he could keep his cool.

So instead of turning around and throttling the kid, he simply smiled and finished his whisky, then pressed the button above his head to call the hostess for another beverage to kill his brain. The drinks trolley battering ram had barely passed his aisle, so hopefully the hostess would turn and serve him once more before they landed. After all, he had been no trouble during this flight for a change, some would say even pleasant. Which was not what they'd be saying about the little shit using his chair as a set of monkey bars behind him, or the dude with the hacking cough spluttering over most of the plane as he wandered the aisle muttering to himself.

"Ladies and gentleman, please return your seats to the upright position and fold away your trays as we prepare for our descent into London Heathrow."

Nigel cursed as he tipped the dregs of the miniature into his mouth but was relieved this part of the journey was over. Now all he had to do was join the melee of bleary-eyed ignorant passengers who would be jostling impatiently to leave the plane before it had even rolled into the gateway, collect his bag from the scrum of sweaty foreigners at the carousel, queue through the long, stationary lines as stony faced migrant customs crew searched luggage, hoping they wouldn't find his extra stash of cigarette cartons and Johnny Walker duty free. He could already envisage the conversation at the declaration desk. Why did he have to explain himself to those fucking bob-a-jobs at customs anyway. This was his country not theirs.

Nigel was already starting to return to his dubious factory settings before the plane had even touched down.

The biggest issue playing on his mind though, was the fight for his space on the courtesy bus with the unclean, being harangued by the rent-a-wanker security guards trying to maintain some sort of order at the ranks, then remember which fucking car park he had left his taxi in for the last two weeks and hope to Christ that the car battery still held a charge. If he had to call Vinnie out to jump start his motor, it would cost him a hefty packet, not to mention a right good ribbing from the lads down the Hope and Anchor.

As he watched the nervous passengers around him fidget in their seats, he could almost feel the holiday shine wash away, like the roar of the stadium crowd's rowdy cheering echoing from the terraces quickly turning to muted groans after VAR ruled a perfectly good goal offside. He convinced himself things would return to their normal shitty status as soon as he sat in that driver's switched and switched on the 'For Hire' sign on the taxi roof.

The rush through the airport to get to the luggage carousel was no surprise. Nigel found, to his dismay, long lines of jostling unclean at customs, and he hoped his smuggled extra whisky bottles swinging freely in the duty-free carrier bag hanging from his trolley looked inconspicuous enough. He passed through the Nothing to Declare gate without incident, happy in the knowledge he had enough Johnny walker to entertain himself for a day or two.

He was swerving his trolley through the anxious travellers staring at the departure board, checking the exits for the nearest transfer bus sign, when he felt the shoulder charge from a young kid in combats playing between the aisle of seats.

"Jesus Christ, kid!" Nigel yelled as both he and his whisky crashed to the floor with a clatter. "What the hell are you playing at?" he said, grabbing the boy by the wrist.

"Ninja assassins!" the boy mumbled, lifting his imitation night vison goggles and staring down at the liquor puddling by his feet.

"Ninja what?" Nigel cursed stumbling back to his feet awkwardly as passengers began to stare at the ruckus.

"Where's your mum, numbnuts?" The boy turned and pointed, just as the shocked parent ran forward to help Nigel to his feet.

"Oh my god, I'm so sorry!" she gasped, grabbing Nigel's sweaty palm.

"I'm okay," he sighed, "but my weekend entertainments gone!" He pointed to the wet bag by their feet.

"Oh, I'm so sorry!" She grabbed her son's hand and pulled him close. Nigel wiped down his damp

Spurs top, counting to ten silently.

"He gets so excited. Can I pay for your…gifts?" she asked as the gate security guard, accompanied swiftly by a cleaner, approached the mess.

"Na, I'm good, nobody died." He looked at the young boy and bent down, ruffling his hair with a clammy hand. "He makes for a lousy assassin!"

"You gotta be silent but deadly, wee man! Attack them when they least expect it!" he whispered in the kid's ear. "Got it?"

The kid nodded.

With that, Nigel pinched the boy's cheeks before carrying on through the exit.

His luck changed for the better outside. The black cab started first time, and he picked up a fare that wanted a ride straight into Islington. And this late at night, it was a great fare to pick up because the roads would be clear.

Happy days!

"Where to, Guv'ner?" Nigel asked, adjusting his rear-view mirror as the fare sat down and pulled out his phone.

"Britannia Hotel, Canary Wharf, please," he replied.

"Nasty business this Corona shit, eh?" Nigel

said, turning the radio up as he pulled away from the pick-up point and turned onto the empty carriageway. The overhead street lighting twinkled through the raindrops on his windshield as he increased the wiper speed to match the drizzle outside.

"I heard the Chinese are covering up all sorts of shit over there. Got the army out, locking folks in their houses and shooting anyone who breaks curfew!" he said, talking over the news reporter on the radio.

The fare said nothing as he scrolled through the images on his phone, the screen illuminating his sweaty face in the back of the dark cab.

Nigel raised an eyebrow and tried again.

"Just been over to Germany to watch Spurs lose to Leipzig. Lousy fuckin' game, but great result." He glanced in the rear-view mirror. "That Sabitzer is a bit of an animal, mind you!"

The fare said nothing, much to Nigel's disgust, so he turned up the radio and gave up, returning his attention to the road and thoughts of his bed.

"*...sources confirm the virus has now reached epidemic figures, with Japan and surrounding countries closing their borders to China. WHO*

13

Experts believe it's only a matter of time before the situation is under control and an antidote is found to quell the spread of the infection and reiterate that the public need not be alarmed."

***

"Britannia Hotel. This the right place, mate?" Nigel said. He turned in his seat, glanced around, and then rolled his window up to avoid the smell of the fish market. The fare nodded as he checked the meter before handing three warm fifty pound notes with sweaty hands, pushing them through the window slot that separated Nigel from his customers.

"Keep the change!"

Nigel rubbed the notes to check their authenticity.

"Thanks mate, you have a good night now, take care of yourself!" Nigel called as the passenger exited the cab with his luggage and wandered over to the pub.

"You too!"

"Cheers, easy!" He chuckled under his breath then spun his cab around and headed home for the night. Easiest money I've made since betting Vinnie he couldn't down a pint of Guinness quicker than me, the soppy twat.

The roads were clear all the way back to his flat, apart from the military vehicles he passed, travelling in convoy towards London. Nigel was surprised to find a couple of free parking spaces outside Shamy's, the local corner convenience store, instead of the usual parking he had to use down the road. He would have to call Vinnie next week and find out all the gossip, perhaps suggest they meet up for a drink down the Hope and Anchor at the weekend. For now though, he was knackered, and all he wanted to do was grab a cold one from the fridge and sleep. The next week was going to be full on to catch up on all the shifts he'd missed, he'd just have to keep his head down.

"Nigel, how the devil are you!" Raj, the store manager, smiled as he unpacked his rusty Nissan of stock boxes.

"Great, Raj. How you keeping?" Nigel replied, shaking Raj's hand.

"Oh, business is booming. People are going crazy for these!" He patted the boxes of Andrex toilet paper and smiled.

"It's a mad world, Raj, right enough." he grunted, eying the whisky in the back seat of Raj's car. "Say, can I grab one of those for a nightcap? I'll sort you out in the morning, mate?"

Raj nodded. "Sure, but drinking that kills your brain cells, Nigel!"

"Yeh, tell me something I don't know, mate!" Nigel grabbed the bottle of Johnny Walker and said his goodbyes.

"Catch up tomorrow, Raj!"

Foster March

SHAWN M. KLIMEK

LHR ARRIVALS HALL, UK

Turbulence. A crying baby. Some passenger coughing up both lungs.

Foster March would have found the flight from Amsterdam to London insufferable if not for the free headphones and inflight movie. Excited about the imminent reunion with Victoria, his hot British girlfriend, Foster had also splurged on an overpriced shot of rum in his Coca-Cola. Thinking about the huge grin he showed the flight attendant as he exchanged a $10 bill for a cocktail in a plastic cup, he wondered if she figured him for an alcoholic, but that wasn't the case at all. The source of his glee was the ticklish realisation that this purchase confirmed deeper feelings for his girlfriend than he had yet admitted even to himself. See, a rum and Coke wasn't even his drink of choice—it was hers. Apparently, he had come to miss Victoria so

much that he had absentmindedly ordered her a drink.

Smiling as he sipped, Foster reminisced about the night they met. He'd come to London on a 6-month work visa to serve as the chief consulting engineer for a cash-machine upgrade project. Being both a foreigner and a boss of sorts had limited his opportunities for making new friends. One particularly lonesome Friday after work, he had boorishly imposed himself on the company of some coworkers he had overheard agreeing to join up at a nearby pub. It was awkward at first, which was to be expected, but he had been deceived by their politeness and jocularity to presume himself ultimately welcomed. And then the hazing started: inside jokes and pointed laughs at his expense. He laughed it off at first, even gamely paying for the first few drinks owed for unfair bets, determined to prove what a good sport he was. But as his borrowed comrades became more drunk, they also became increasingly transparent in their contempt. Defeated at last, he paid for his drinks had been about to leave when an attractive and bosomy young woman in a short skirt emerged from the kitchen to collect dirty glasses from the tables. Victoria was the pub-owner's daughter and well known to these regulars.

"Vicki darling," one of her customers called out to her, "give us a kiss! It's me birthday!"

"Nothing like that on tap, Bill," she answered. Others teased her and flirted in similar ways, as Foster stared in admiration at her effortless aplomb. When, as fate would have it, an empty seat opened conveniently beside him, instead of continuing out the door, Foster impulsively dropped into it. When Victoria came to remove the glasses from the table, probably emboldened by alcohol, he complimented her on the way she managed such obnoxious attention. She thanked him and then replied with a wink that she found it easy to keep her cool around men without beards.

Thus began his rapid transition from misery to joy. They began to date and found that they liked each other's company.

Months later, as the end of his visa stay approached, she said to him, "Meeting you has been so lovely, Foster, but now I'm sad. Do you promise to remember me?"

"Even better, darling," he had answered, "I've earned some vacation time, and I plan to return as soon as possible on a visitor's visa. I hope we can

spend it together. It will give us a little more time to figure out where we want this relationship to go."

This suggestion appeared to surprise her, as he recalled. Had he come on too strong, or conversely, declared his feelings too late?

During their time apart, Foster did his best to stay in touch via email and the occasional phone call, but her enthusiasm seemed to have faded, and it bothered him that he seemed to be carrying most of the communication load. On the other hand, he allowed, she frequently worked late nights, and unlike himself, had no access to a computer at work. He was probably judging her unfairly. Comfortingly, once he informed her that he had finally concluded the arrangements for this return visit, her response had seemed very positive. Indeed, she had declared herself eager for the reunion, adding that what she wanted to tell him ought to be said in person.

During the long flight, Foster had had plenty of time to wonder, what could she have meant by that?

Once the plane touched down at Heathrow, he greeted her with a text: `Here in one piece. Excited to see you!`

Victoria had responded with two emojis: a "thumbs up" and a "heart". Disappointingly terse, but perhaps she was busy. After all, she had set aside her evening for their big night and was probably preoccupied with last minute preparations: cramming to get all her chores done early, managing traffic, perhaps even gift shopping. He was about to respond with three heart emojis, until the passenger in the window-seat beside him stood up and cleared his throat, impatient to join the disembarkation queue.

"Excuse me," the man said.

"Go ahead," said Foster, pulling the phone to his chest and tucking his knees to one side. The man forced his way past, openly annoyed. The manoeuvre was a tight squeeze, and Foster's phone was inadvertently knocked out of his hand into the aisle where, to his horror, it was promptly stepped on and then kicked away.

"Hey!" he protested.

He unbuckled his seatbelt and shouldered his way into the queue, already stooped to reach the phone.

"Hey, everybody wants to get off the plane, not just you, jerk," someone shouted in a thick, Dutch accent.

As he picked up the phone, he was dismayed to

13

see that the screen was crushed. Someone bumped him forward, but angry shouts from the rear of the plane made him realise the person directly to his rear was not to blame. Nevertheless, he was about to turn and apologise when the person splattered the back of his neck with a disgusting cough like a sea lion with a three-pack a day smoking habit.

Lowering his head, Foster focused instead on a speedy escape. He disembarked, collected his baggage and went through customs like a man trying to catch a connecting flight. Feeling his phone vibrate, he saw that a new text from Victoria had arrived. The text read: `Can't reach airport in time. CU@ Bullhorn Pub.` ♥

That was her father's pub. The place they had met. Foster was both disappointed and relieved. He was glad he could stop at his hotel first and have a shower. He tried thumbing an acknowledgment but discovered that the touch screen on his phone no longer responded.

During the taxi ride to his hotel, his thoughts returned to the riddle of what sort of thing wanted to tell him in person. It might be either very good, or very bad. Suddenly, a staggering possibility occurred to him. Could she be pregnant? That might explain her reticence to communicate. Keeping such a secret would have been torturously difficult had they been chatting daily, he realised.

In a daze, he paid the cab driver, a black man with a neck tattoo, tipping generously.

"Keep the change," he croaked.

"Thanks, Guv'ner", said the driver, looking at him with concern. "Watch your health," he added, before zooming away.

Foster checked in at the hotel and wheeled his luggage up to the room. His mind continued to race while he showered and changed, pondering the implications of this question. Was he ready to be a father? Obviously, if she had let it get this far, she had chosen to keep the baby. A miscarriage or abortion isn't the sort of news you reveal to your boyfriend on the same night you greet him after a long absence. And if she was pregnant, was she hoping he would propose? Her father's pub was a smelly, noisy place, but it was also the place where they had first met. It was arguably a romantic choice.

Foster went down to the lobby and asked the desk clerk to call him a cab.

"Right away, sir."

During the cab ride to the Bullhorn Pub, Foster

realised that, since he had no engagement ring handy, proposing on the spot was out of the question. This realisation lifted a load off his shoulders, and his anxiety gave way to ordinary excitement. On the other hand, proposing to her within a next week or so might not be such a bad idea. Her beauty seemed obvious to everyone; she was a prize that many had jealously asserted was out of his league. He would certainly be a fool to let her go. He resolved to tackle the challenge of discovering her ring size as soon as possible.

Soon, the cab pulled up outside the pub, a two-story, red brick building covered with ivy. Lively jukebox music was playing, and yellow lights shone through every window, including the ones upstairs. Foster craned his neck to see if he could glimpse any of the customers inside. Jutting out over the pub door was the familiar painted sign in the shape of a bull's horn, and dangling beneath the sign, reflecting the season, a pot of blooming, purple petunias. Another seasonal change was that sidewalk in front of the building was crowded with wrought-iron tables and chairs, occupied by customers smoking cigarettes.

Unable to evade the haze of cigarette smoke, Foster strode through it as quickly as possible, stifling a slight cough as he pulled open the pub's front door. Instantly, he became one with the chaos. Unlike that first awkward, but ultimately lucky night, he had long since made himself at home at the Bullhorn.

"Hey, Foster!" shouted a balding man in a business suit, lifting a beer. "Long time, no see!"

"Cheers, Danny!" said Foster. "Have you seen Vicki?"

Because the place was packed to the rafters, before Danny could respond, Foster's brief glimpse of him was eclipsed by new customers crowding the bar. Determined to get an answer, he gently pushed his way through the crowd, muttering, "Excuse me. Excuse me, please." At the same time, of course, he was surveying the crowd for other faces. Suddenly, everything went dark as two cold hands were pressed over his eyes from behind.

"Guess who?"

Recognising the voice, he turned around and beheld the twinkling eyes and smiling face of his beloved. Overcome, he took her face in his hands and pressed his lips to hers in a passionate embrace. She met the kiss willingly, or so it seemed initially. To his surprise, she pushed him away mid-kiss.

13

"Wow," she said. "That's a bit much."

"God, I've missed you, Vicki," he rasped.

"Okay, but it's been a while, right?"

"A long while, and I've been starving for those lips. You're even more beautiful than I remembered you," he enthused, looking her up and down. She was wearing short boots, the usual tight-fitting jeans, a red button-down blouse, open at the top to display her ample cleave, and a denim jacket.

"You look good too," she countered, reaching for the top of his head. "Though you've lost a bit more hair," she teased, tousling it playfully. "But what happened to your voice?"

Foster waved his hand dismissively while clearing his throat. "Oh, it's nothing. You know what it's like on aeroplanes. They suck all the humidity out of the air. Plus, I just walked through that wall of smoke outside," he said, punctuating his statement with an unexpected cough.

"Alright, well listen. We have a lot to discuss. Have you eaten, yet?"

"Hours ago. I could definitely eat. Shall we go to your place and order in,"—he wagged his eyebrows suggestively—"eat here, or head to one of the restaurants on the wharf?"

"None of the above. C'mon. Let's go outside to talk."

Foster coughed as they ducked through the smoky haze again, and then reached for Victoria's hand to hold it as they strolled.

"My apartment is out, because I have a new roommate," she said.

"Oh really? What's she like?"

"And this being a Friday night, all the decent restaurants are jammed, and likewise, the waiting lists."

"I don't mind waiting, if we're together."

"The truth is, I'm too excited to sit anyway." She pointed towards the heart of the wharf district. "What do you say to a long walk towards the food court? I know you like burgers."

"Sounds good."

"That will give us time to chat."

"I'd like that."

The rosy sunset at their backs painted every facing window a rosy hue, and the water beside them and the fountain in the square contributed to what Foster judged to be a successfully romantic atmosphere. He squeezed Victoria's hand and playfully began to swing it as if he were about to start skipping.

"Foster!" she said, giving his fingers a sobering squeeze. "I may as well tell you now what I needed to tell you in person."

He turned to face her, his eyes soft and adoring. "I'm listening," he said.

"I have a new boyfriend," she blurted, reclaiming her hand.

"A what?"

"A new boyfriend...and we've moved in together."

"A new… Seriously?"

"I'm sorry."

Shadows exaggerated the look of pained confusion on his face. "You're breaking up with me?"

"Technically, we were never more than a fling."

He threw up his hands. "If that's how you felt, don't you think you should have told me this before I flew for ten hours to get here?"

She swivelled left and right, as if appealing to strangers for support, fingers splayed in despair. "Do you see how you are? This is why it was so hard to tell you. You were always so...so serious. I just thought it would have seemed heartless not to tell you in person."

Approaching footsteps suddenly became impossible to ignore. An unfamiliar man stopped less than a meter away.

"Are you alright, Vicki?" he asked.

Annoyed at the intrusion, Foster whipped around hotly and looked the stranger up and down. Handsome, broad shouldered, athletic; probably spent evenings at the gym and played rugby on weekends; casually but smartly dressed for a night out: a clear upgrade, although Foster didn't catch on immediately. The beard should have been a giveaway.

"Butt out please, sir!" Foster snapped.

"Foster, this is Clyde, my new boyfriend," said Victoria. "I'm alright, Clyde. And this is Foster. The man I dated before you."

"Did you tell him yet?" Clyde asked.

"I just did." Separating herself from Foster, Victoria walked over and clutched a muscular bicep.

Clyde stretched out an open hand. "Nice to meet you, Foster. Tough luck, I suppose."

Foster looked at the hand witheringly until it was withdrawn. For a stretched second, he looked back and forth between the couple, fuming uncomfortably. Becoming aware of a headache, he rubbed his temples. "Well, this is just dandy," he said, at last.

"Let's go home," decided Clyde, wrapping his arm around Victoria's waist, and pulling her away.

"Goodbye, Foster," she said, looking back. "I'm sorry."

"Goodnight, Vicki. And goodnight, asshole," he added, bitterly.

Clyde turned around, pushing Victoria behind him. "Did you just call me *"asshole"*?"

Foster flinched. He'd have no chance in a fight against this brute. "*As well!*" he said, thinking quickly. "I said, 'Goodnight Vicki, and goodnight to you *as well!*'"

"Goodnight, then," said Clyde warily, and turned his back. Foster watched as their figures receded towards the Bullhorn. Once he'd recovered from his momentary fight-or-flight panic, a much more powerful sadness swooped in. His throat was beginning to feel scratchy and his headache was becoming worse, but it was hard to care about such things when his broken heart felt like someone had just put a pickaxe through his chest.

Foster reached into his pocket for his phone,

intending to summon a taxi ride back to his hotel. Only when he was staring at the fractured screen again did he remember that it had been smashed. A few hours ago, at least the pixels had all seemed intact. Now, the images were flickering and faded, as if the whole gadget was about to die. To his surprise, he discovered several urgent message notifications had been received, hitherto unnoticed. The alert banners were arrayed in a diagonal cascade beneath the spider-webbed display screen. Only the identical subject lines were visible: `Emergency Health Alert!` He prodded and swiped the broken screen, but in vain. Unfortunately, he had no way to open and read the messages, yet. Maybe there would be something on the TV about it once he got back to his room.

Calling a cab on this phone was obviously out of the question. Returning to the Bullhorn to ask someone there to request a cab on his behalf was also out—too humiliating. There seemed no better alternative than to continue walking east. Fortunately, this path would lead him almost directly to a tube station, which in turn, could take him anywhere but here. With his head beginning to throb, he quickened his step.

Brazilian President Jair Bolsonaro:
Q: *There have been 474 deaths today, bringing the total to 5017*
A: *So what? I'm sorry. What do you want me to do?*

Change of Luck

SHAWN M. KLIMEK

Bored of quarantine, Belinda snuck out of her cabin, roaming until she found the casino. Instead of a hostess, the entrance was blocked by a janitorial cart. Inside, a janitor was disinfecting the slot machines.

"Excuse me," Belinda interrupted.

"Hey! Are you sick?" queried the janitor.

"Only cabin fever. Mind if I play a few slots?"

"The money cage is closed."

"I have quarters," said Belinda, jingling her purse.

The janitor shrugged. "I'm finished sanitising. I suppose you can play until you're broke."

"Thanks!"

As luck would have it, Belinda soon struck the jackpot, her purse filling with contaminated quarters.

13

POTUS press conference at Centers for Disease Control and Prevention:
Anybody right now, and yesterday, anybody that needs a test gets a test. They're there. And the tests are beautiful...the tests are all perfect like the letter was perfect. The transcription was perfect. Right? This was not as perfect as that but pretty good.

MILTON FINE

P.A. O'NEIL

AWAITING FLIGHT: LHR-SEA

"Nope, my flight is on time, so tell Becky, I'll make it home for her concert." Milton Fine assured the person on the other end of his cell phone of his planned arrival from London's Heathrow Airport to his home in Seattle. "No, you don't have to pick me up, I'll take one of those van services home."

He had arrived early for his 9:30pm non-stop flight to Sea-Tac Airport and was standing in line before one of the many Starbuck's counters when his wife called. Most places, answering your phone and maintaining a conversation while standing among strangers might be considered rude, but Milton was more hungry than thirsty. He knew, if he got out of place the chance of getting a fresh bagel would be slim to none.

"Yeah, bye-bye, Honey. I'll text you when we take off." Milton pocketed his phone then reached for

his wallet, his other hand held his briefcase. He was turned slightly away from the direction of the line when he felt a nudge on his elbow.

"Can I help you?"

A small Asian man carrying a backpack as if it were a child lifted his chin. "The line, it's moving." His English was only slightly accented, but by the look of his new Nike's and the cut of his leather jacket, Milton figured he might've been a traveller from Hong Kong or Singapore.

"Oh, beg pardon, thanks." Milton's face flushed as he stepped forward, pacing himself behind the woman in front. For some reason, he felt the need to explain his behaviour to the man behind him. "I was chatting with my wife, Emma, she's in Seattle. I'm just waiting to catch my flight." His head bobbed as he finished talking, hoping he would get a response. When none came, he sighed, taking another step forward.

"Ah-choo!"

Milton turned back at the sound of the sneeze, only to find the small man trying to wipe his face with the sleeve of his leather jacket.

"Ah, bless you. Oh, here…"—Milton stepped out of line to reach the counter for the paper napkin dispenser. He pulled out a couple of sheets and passed them to the seemingly befuddled little man— "…these should help." He handed them over and turned just in time to find his place as the next customer to be served at the counter.

Milton turned to find seating, with his whole wheat bagel, including a cream cheese *schmeer*, and a large hazelnut latte, he nodded to the next man who was wiping his sleeve. He placed the bag holding the warm bagel in his coat pocket and carried his coffee in front of him while he walked towards his boarding gate. His mouth watered at the thought of the opportunity of licking the excess cream cheese from out the middle. At last, he made his way to the boarding gate, and setting his coffee and briefcase on the floor, he removed his coat, folded it in half and draped it over the back of the chair. Carefully, he removed the prized bagel from his pocket. He picked up the coffee, straddling the briefcase between his feet, and sat down to enjoy his snack.

The bagel with the oozing cream cheese did not disappoint, and when done, he pulled a handkerchief from his back pocket to wipe his face and fingers. From his briefcase, he took out a magazine, scratched his face and settled in for the wait.

***

The long flight home was uneventful and made good time with the airport mostly empty when they disembarked. Passing through Customs was easy, and waiting outside the overseas terminal were a couple of taxis and transport van picking up passengers bound for hotels and homes. Milton had prearranged for the van to carry him home, and after dropping off a few other passengers and twelve-hours after his plane left London, he was able to put his key in the front door.

Even though the house was dark, the familiar smells greeted him as he walked from room to room, welcomed him home. He set his luggage down in the family room before discarding his coat over the back of a chair and tiptoeing down the hall, checking each room as he passed. The first door he opened was of his son, BJ. The acrid odour of the fourteen-year-old's domain escaped as he looked in, his son sprawled across his soon too-small bed. Closing the door, he made a mental note to have a talk with the boy about cleaning his room. The next door belonged to his daughter; Becky's bedroom. A Hello Kitty nightlight shined in the darkness, illuminating her nightstand, the shadow falling on the head of her bed. Assured his seven-year-old darling was safely in the land of slumber, he moved on to his own bedroom.

He entered the room and gently closed the door. Kicking off his shoes while unbuttoning his shirt, he passed to his side of the bed to pull back the covers. Emma lay on her side, her back to him. Through what little light made its way over the top of the curtains, he could see her hair cascade across the pillows, her shoulders mostly bare from the thin straps of the nightgown clinging to her body as it rolled down her waist and over her hips. Stripped to his underwear, Milton climbed into bed and placed an arm around her waist, his hand raising up to cup a breast as he tenderly kissed her shoulder towards her neck until he was lost in her tresses.

"I wouldn't do that if I were you. My husband is due home any minute." Emma never moved as she spoke, her voice flat and reasonable.

"Hmmn, what should we do until he gets here?" He purred in her ear.

She rolled back, opening her arms to pull him into an embrace. "I'm sure we can think of something."

***

13

"Daddy, you're home!"

Milton set down his coffee, avoiding a spill, as Becky jumped into his arms. He was seated at the kitchen table, glancing over copies of the local paper which had been saved while he had been gone. "There's my princess! Give me some sugar." He pursed his lips in anticipation of a moist kiss from the little girl.

"I dreamed you came home last night, Daddy!" Her lips tapped his before throwing her arms around his neck.

"Becky, let go of daddy and sit down to breakfast."

Pushing the little girl away, he joked, "Yes, Becky, your squeezing the stuffing out of me."

"All right, Mommy. Daddy, my concert at Papa Arlo's is today," she noted between mouthfuls of cereal. "Are you coming to hear me sing?"

"Yes, Princess, I made sure to fly home just in time." Milton picked up his cup. "But I'll probably have to take a nap or else I won't be able to keep my eyes open."

"Why, Daddy?"

"It's called 'jet lag', Sweetie. It means my internal clock is off. Speaking of internal clocks, where's BJ? He's sleeping a little late, isn't he?"

Emma sat down with her own cup of coffee and pulled a piece of toast off the stack in the centre of the table. "Yes, but he went to the school dance last night, didn't get home until 11:45."

"11:45?"

"I told him he had to be home before midnight."

"Yes, but he's only fourteen, don't you think it's a little late?"

"He's growing up, Milt. We have to allow for him to use his own judgement now and then."

As if on cue, a tall youth with dishevelled hair, in sweatpants and a t-shirt, walked in carrying an open gym bag. "Mom, I brought my clothes home from my locker. Do you think you could wash them so I can take them back on Monday?"

"Oh my, is that what I smelled last night when I checked in on you?"

"BJ, the laundry room now! You know how to use the washer." Emma rose and followed the lad out of the kitchen.

"Daddy, why do boys stink?"

"You think boys stink, Princess?"

Becky lowered the cereal bowl away from her mouth as she finished the remaining milk, wiping her

13

mouth with the sleeve of her flannel nightgown. "Uh-huh, they all do."

"What about me, I used to be a boy, do you think I stink?"

Becky giggled. "Of course not! You're not a boy, you're my daddy."

Milton hid his smile behind the newspaper. "Good, you keep thinking that way, Princess. Now go get dressed, and Princess…"

"Yes, Daddy?"

"… next time, use your napkin to wipe your face."

***

"BJ, put away your cell phone, I don't want to see it once while we're at Papa Arlo's—in fact, leave it in the car."

"But, Mom…"

"You heard your mother, in fact, I'm going to shut mine off."

In the backseat, Becky giggled, until her brother's look of disappointment and disdain silenced her.

They pulled into a visitor parking space before

the Loving Hands care facility. "Hey look, it's Kari." Becky bounded from the car before the set parking brake could be set.

"Becky, come back here," called Emma. Closing her door, she instructed her son to catch up with his sister.

BJ shrugged and rolled his eyes. "Hey, Becks, slow down!"

Emma and Milton followed, she with sheet music tucked under her arm, while he rubbed his forehead. "Your nap didn't help with the jet lag?"

"No, I guess I should've slept longer. Now I have this nagging headache over my sinus area."

"We'd better not stay long after the concert, visiting with Papa Arlo, then."

"Gee, I feel so guilty, like I should see him more than just every couple of months." He held open the facility door.

"I know, but you have your own life and family, Milt. It probably was the last thing your father had in mind when he moved away."

"Let's not discuss it here, especially not in front of the kids, okay?"

"Mrs Fine, Mr Fine." A portly man in dress slacks and cardigan greeted them with outstretched

hand. "I want to thank you again for arranging this."

They returned the greeting. "Mr Porn, it's my pleasure. I hope the children who have arrived haven't disrupted anything?"

"No, no, ma'am, we just ushered them and their parents into the activity room. We'll be collecting the residents to join you in a few minutes if that's all right?"

"Yes, of course, I'll check out the piano while the choir leader sets up the children."

They turned towards a large room set with several tables, each with four chairs, bookcases with books of every shape and colour, shelves filled with game boxes, and in the corner, an upright piano. Half a dozen children were sitting at the tables near the piano, some with their parents, others alone. "Carol, Ann, I see you ladies found your way here."

"There she is," declared a woman as she rose. "I hope six voices are enough for a concert?"

"Of course,"—Emma leaned in—"I'm actually surprised we had this many show up."

As if on cue, childish giggles entered the room, upping the number of voices. "I do hope we're not late." said the nervous looking woman accompanying the new arrivals.

"No, no, of course not, I'm just glad you're here." Emma smiled and winked at her husband. "Why don't you go get Papa Arlo? That way you can visit a little bit before the show starts."

"Good idea." BJ started to rise. "No, son, you stay here and help your mother. You can come and get us when the show is ready."

Milton left to the sound of excited children as he made his way to his grandfather's room. Tinny notes from the piano followed, out of sync with his steps. He stopped at a door festooned with a white and cork board, the name Arlo Fine hanging from a small placard at the bottom. "Knock Before Entering," took up most of the available space on the white half.

Knocking, he turned the door handle, opening it before there could be a response. "Papa, it's me, Milton. May I come in?"

The raspy accented voice sounded gleeful. "Milton, my Milton, come to see your old grandpapa? Come in, don't stand out in the hall and give a show."

Milton heart melted at the sight of the old man in the wheelchair, grizzled short cropped grey hair, rimless glasses perched on the bridge of his nose, bushy moustache hanging over his lip. His wrinkled

13

face had a couple days' growth.

Bending down, he embraced the old man. "Papa, how I've missed you." He kissed him on the cheek before stepping back, blinking back tears.

"Now, now, none of that, you're here now. Here, sit down, you'll get a crick in your neck looking down, or worse, bad knees if you crouch."

Milton pulled up a chair. "How they treating you, Papa? Are you getting everything you need?"

The old man patted him on the hand. "Yes, of course, it's as good as any other place. Look around, my room is clean, my medication comes on time, and the food is Kosher most of the time."

"Do you want to move to an exclusively Jewish facility? The closest is a couple of hours away and…"

"No, no, this is the place where your parents placed me before they left to fulfil their mid-life crisis. I've been here so long, in a way it's become home."

"Now, Papa, you know my folks always dreamed of moving to Israel. When the chance to live in a kibbutz presented itself, they felt it was divine intervention. Have you heard from them?"

He tossed up his hands. "Yeah, I got a letter from

them the other day, but you can only read so many times about milking cows and picking olives."

The conversation was one Milton and his grandfather had many times before, but each time, he found himself siding more with the old man instead of his parents. "Well, they're not here, but I am. You know if you need anything, any time, either Emma or I will be here as fast as we can."

"Emma, where is that lovely *schikse* you married?"

"Now, Papa, be polite. She and the kids are preparing for the concert in the activity room."

"You mean today's concert? I wasn't planning on going, but if you say my family is singing then what are we waiting for?"

Their laughter was interrupted by a knock, but before they could answer, BJ poked his head through. "Mom, says they're about to begin, so you better come now."

"Oh, my goodness, who is this young man before my tired old eyes?"

Milton waived his son in. "It's BJ, Papa, hasn't he grown?"

"Grown? My goodness, look at all the peach fuzz on his face—he's almost a man! Come here,

Barry, and hug your old Papa Arlo."

BJ blushed at the sound of his given name but approached the old man and hugged him with a tenderness which surprised his father.

"I have a son named, Barry, did you know that?"

"Sure, I did, he's my grandfather, so I guess I have to thank you for half my name."

Papa Arlo was caught off guard, but then he laughed so hard he started to cough.

Milton was at his side in an instant. "Papa, are you all right? You want for me to get a nurse?"

Papa waived him off as the cough subsided. "I just caught the air in my throat, it's nothing to worry about. C'mon, let's go see this concert."

They approached the community room, BJ pushing the wheelchair. Papa Arlo asked, "Who's giving this concert?"

"It's the kids from Becky's Sunday School class. When Emma heard they wanted to do a community service project, she suggested they sing at nursing homes. Now, here we are. BJ, why don't you park, Papa Arlo up close so he can see Becky."

"You know, Barry, if you ever need an after-school job, I'm sure I can put in a good word with that Mr Porn fellow. You push a mighty good wheelchair."

The boy laughed as he set the brakes. "Maybe after wrestling season is over, Papa Arlo."

Emma was conferring one last time with the teacher before she sat down to the piano. She glanced at her daughter in time to see her sniff back her runny nose. Reaching into her pocket, she took out a folded piece of facial tissue and placed it over her daughter's face. "Blow!" Her one-word instruction was enough for Becky to take a deep breath and exhale through her nose, filling the tissue with the moist contents. Emma folded over the tissue to wipe her daughter's face once more before crumbling it up and putting it back into her pocket.

Becky used the back of her hand to finish drying her face. The little girl next to her began to laugh, but Becky quickly raised both hands to cup the girl's face, stifling the laughter and making her cheeks puff as she gently squeezed. The other girl's eyes widened, but when Becky dropped her hands and began to laugh, the other girl did too and threw her arm around her neck, pulling her in for a hug. The sound of their names being snapped from the director, and the opening notes of a song, brought them to full attention and they lent their voices to the choir.

When the show was done the room, filled with wheelchairs and walkers of all designs, erupted in applause from the nursing home residents and staff who had come to hear the children. Mr Porn was still clapping as he approached the choir leader to shake her hands. He thanked the children for their performance and announced cake had been provided for all to share, insisting the children help distribute the pieces. This caused another round of applause, not only from the attendees and the performers.

"Shall I get you a piece of cake, Papa Arlo?"

"No, thank you, Barry, I think I'd like to go back to my room. I'm a bit tired." The boy reached down to release the brake. "That's okay, my boy, you stay here and have my piece of cake."

BJ looked up at his father who nodded and took the handles of the wheelchair. "You stay and help if they need to reset the room. I'll take Papa Arlo back to his room." The boy nodded and trotted off towards the table with the cake.

"Milt, oh Milt!"

"Don't worry, Emma, I'm just taking, Papa, back to his room. You and the kids follow when you're all through."

She waived and returned her attention to placing plastic forks on paper plates alongside small slices of cake.

"Papa Arlo, if you feel ill, I can get a nurse." They rolled through mostly empty halls, only passing people headed in the opposite direction as the news of cake got around.

"I'm not sick, Milton, I just wanted to talk to you in private," he rasped.

"Sure, Papa, anything."

"It's about your parents, just because they dumped me here in this depot, waiting for the *Death Express* to come and get me, don't think that you have to take over what should be their duties."

"Now, Papa, they didn't 'dump' you. We all researched places for you to stay, remember? We even visited a few together."

"But they ran away, Milton! It should be them, or at least your father, coming by to see me on a regular basis. I tell you, my parents risked everything to come to this country to make a better life. Why your parents felt they had to leave it to find happiness, I'll never understand."

They turned into the old man's room. "Is this is your way of saying I don't come around enough to

13

see you?”

“No, no, Milton, you have your own life and a young family to attend to…”

“Do you want to stay in the wheelchair or move to the chair by the window?”

“No, no, I’m fine here, thank you. What I’m saying is you don’t have to feel it your responsibility to come see me at all if you don’t want.”

Milton pulled the chair from the window alongside his grandfather’s. “Papa, besides Emma and the kids, you’re the only family I have. Coming to see you is never a burden, so please don’t think that way.” He placed his hand on the old mans and gently squeezed.

“Thank you, Milton, I assure you, your visits brighten my spirits for days.”

The solemnity of the moment was interrupted by the sound of Becky bursting through the doorway. “Did you hear me sing, Papa Arlo? I sang loud just for you.”

“Rebekah, you were the star of the show. Come here and give your old Papa some sugar.”

He held out his arms to embrace the child as she flowed towards his chest. Becky pursed her lips to give her great-grandfather a kiss sweetened from cake frosting. Pulling away, she giggled, "Your moustache tickles!"

"Here now, Becky, I told you to keep your voice down. You don't want to disturb the other residents." Emma followed her son into the room, sheet music still tucked under one arm. "Hello, Papa Arlo, BJ said you weren't feeling well. I hope the children didn't wear you out." She bent down and placed a kiss on his cheek in one fluid motion while speaking. "Oh look, I left a little *shmutz* on your cheek." With practiced agility, she reached into her pocket for her ever ready tissue and wiped off the remnant trace of lipstick.

"Listen to her, Milton, we'll make a Jewess of her yet."

Becky turned from jovial face to face, but she soon joined in with her childish giggle. The laughter subsided when the old man began to cough.

"C'mon, kids, we'd better go, Papa needs his rest."

"Aww, do we have to?" whined Becky.

"Yes, yes, Becky," admonished Emma, as she gently pushed her by the shoulders towards the door already held open by BJ. "You get some rest now, Papa Arlo. We'll be back another day for a longer visit."

"One more thing…" pleaded the old man. "Barry, would you come here?"

BJ hesitated, but with a nod and a smile from his father, he let go of the door and returned to kneel before his great-grandfather.

The old man gently took the boy's head in his hands and pulled it towards his own face. Silently, he mouthed a blessing and kissed the top of his head. "There, you'll never be too old for a kiss on the *keppe*. Now, Milton, let me give you yours."

BJ rose, backed away. Becky's face peeked through between Emma's hip and the propped open door. Milton took his son's place and knelt close enough for Papa not to have to reach out. After his blessing and kiss, he hugged his grandfather, and turned to leave with a promise to come back next week. As the family walked out and the door closed, Arlo Fine removed his glasses to wipe his moist eyes.

*****

"Mommy, where's daddy?"

"He went to work early, says he's still on travel time." Emma placed the bowl of warm cereal at her daughter's place. "Who knows, since he went in early, he might come home early as well, won't that be nice?"

Becky nodded and picked up a piece of toast, but before she could take a bite, her brother swept into the room and plucked it from her hands. "Hey, that's mine!"

"Sorry, Becks, but I've got to run. Mom, did my gym clothes get done?" He placed the toast between his teeth and with gym bag in hand, strode into the laundry room.

"And good morning to you, too, young man. They should be in the dryer. If you want them warmed a bit, turn it on for a few minutes and sit down to breakfast."

He returned with the toast held precariously between finger and thumb, with one handle of the bag around his wrist, the other trying to zip the bag closed. "Can't, we have a team meeting this morning. Gotta go…"—he placed the toast back between his teeth—"see ya after practice."

Emma watched as he passed through the kitchen and out on his way to the front door. The slamming sound made her jump. Becky continued eating, her attention never leaving her meal. Emma shook her

 head and poured herself a fresh cup of coffee. Placing it on the table next to the bowl she served for her son, she pulled out the chair and sat down to the deserted breakfast.

***

"Mmnn, coffee smells good," claimed the petite brunette as she walked into the foyer of the office complex, "Who's here? I thought making coffee was my job." Laughing, she dropped her purse in a drawer at her desk and walked into the kitchenette to place her lunch in the fridge.

Coming out of his office, empty mug in hand, Milton joined in her frivolity. "I did, Barb. I got in early, so I thought I'd start a pot. I'm sure it's not as good as yours."

Picking up her favourite cup, she looked at the remnants of previous contents and frowned. "It's not too difficult, all you do is put a packet in the upper chamber and push a button to start the hot water." She rinsed her cup until satisfied with its purity, then held it out for him to fill it before he placed the carafe back on the warmer after filling his cup.

"Yeah, but you seem to do it with a natural

finesse." This made both laugh again as they walked back towards their desks.

"No, really, Milt, what are you doing in so early?"

"I don't know, guess my internal clock hasn't reset itself yet." He shrugged. "Anyway, it gave me a chance to go over my notes in peace before I have to check-in with the boss. By the way, what time is my appointment with him?"

Barb set her cup down on a coaster with a Seahawks logo, stained brown. Turning on her computer, she called back to him, "What's the matter, Milt, couldn't get any work done at home?"

"Naw, Saturday was a washout between napping and visiting my grandfather. Sunday, there was church and dinner at the in-laws. I'm sure what I need to tell him, just wanted some quiet time to organize my thoughts." *Achoo!*

Barb popped her head through his open office threshold. "Bless you. You're meeting him at 10:00 am and the rest of the team after lunch. I have the boardroom booked for 1:15 pm."

Milton was wiping his face with the handkerchief he always kept in his back pocket. "Hmmn, uh, yes thanks."

"Is everything all right?"

"Yeah, just a little fatigued, that's all. I tell you; it was sure nice to sleep in my own bed." He leaned forward, returning the soiled linen to his back pocket. "London was nice though; I think I'll take Emma and the kids there before BJ gets too old to enjoy family vacations."

"Yeah, my folks have talked about touring Britain." Barb leaned on the moulding of his office door.

"I hear others coming in, do you want me to close the door?"

"Sure, that'd be great, and if I don't come out, give me a heads up before 10:00, please."

Barb had been his secretary long enough to understand Milt would have to walk through a gauntlet to get to his supervisor's office. She knocked and then cracked open his door without waiting for a reply to give him his fifteen-minute head start.

Milton placed his notes in a binder as his nose started to run, he once again pulled out his handkerchief to clean his face. Returning the cloth, he picked up his binder and two bright coloured pens from his desk and left. All along the way, he nodded at secretary's and shook hands with fellow staffers promising he would see them after lunch.

He was met at his destination with a smile and a nod from Barb's counterpart as he turned the doorknob to let himself into his boss's office. "Morning, Carl, I hope I haven't kept you waiting?"

"Not at all, Milt, good to see you back in one piece." The grey-haired man behind the desk rose, hand extended. "Sit down and tell me about London, do you think we have the contract?"

"Well, it looks pretty good to me. When I left, they seemed open to further negotiations. Oh, by the way, while I there, I picked up some of their pens for your collection." Milton reached into his breast pocket and withdrew the two pens. "Didn't know which colour you preferred, so I picked up one of each."

"Thank you, Milt, that's mighty thoughtful of you."

***

Milton opened the bedroom door and softly walked into Becky's room. "Hey there, Princess, Mom says you have a fever."

13

Becky moaned as she turned towards the hallway light. "Mommy had to come and get me from the Nurse's Room. It was 'barassin. Mrs Bree said I just have a cold and not to worry about anything."

He stroked the stray hair from her too warm brow. "Well, I'm sure your friends would rather you be home where you can rest and get better. You'll probably be back at school soon." He picked up a damp washcloth, warm from her fever, off the pillow next to her head. "Now, I'm going to get you another cool rag, you just keep quiet now and try to get some rest."

Becky gave a feeble nod and turned away.

***

"Morning, everyone, gee the coffee smells good."

"Sit down, Milt, I've got your breakfast right here."

"Thanks, Hon. Hey there, Princess, feel up to going to school today?"

Becky set down juice glass. "Yes, Daddy, no fever Mrs Bree was right!"

Milton eyebrows raised as Emma placed the plate of scrambled eggs and hash browns down before him.

"Her fever broke early yesterday morning and hasn't come back. In the, 'Mom's Guide to Raising Kids', it means she's ready to go back to school." Emma gently pulled Becky's hair back over her shoulder as she passed. "Besides, if she does feel bad, the nurse will call, and I'll go pick her up."

Milton nodded and reached towards the centre of the table. "Hey, Becks, hand be a piece of toast, please. I need a *pusher* for my eggs."

"Here you go, Daddy."

"Thanks. Hey, where's the Prodigal Son'?"

Emma placed another breakfast on the table and sat down. "He's dressing, I guess. He ate earlier, even before Becky." She hesitantly took a sip of her coffee and set down the cup. "Becky, clear your plate and go see if your brother is out of the bathroom. If he is, brush your teeth and finish getting ready for school…" The words barely out of her mouth before the child had removed her dishes, dropping them into the kitchen sink, and run out of the room.

Milton chuckled between bites. "Guess she's feeling better after all."

Emma laughed, but her breakfast was interrupted by the ring of the house phone. "I'll get it, you finish your breakfast, Milt."

BJ swept into the room, grabbing a piece of toast from the stack on the table. "Hi, Dad. Bye, Dad."

"Hey there, Sport, slow down."

"Milt, it's Mr Porn from the nursing home. He says, Papa Arlo's been taken to the hospital."

"Is it serious?" Milton asked concerned.

"I'm afraid so!" Emma's face told the whole story.

Tony Grant

STEPHEN HERCZEG

LHR ARRIVALS HALL, UK

Damn, I've gotta stop staring at myself in mirrors.

Tony tried to draw comfort from the fact he was finally standing in his own bathroom, but the monstrous vision staring back forced him into a world of distress. He'd travelled for the best part of a day and a half. The last leg was the shortest but the most horrid.

The flight had hit turbulence over the English Channel. The plane, having just left Amsterdam, the decadent capital of Europe, bucked around like a couple on their wedding night. The result wasn't pleasurable in Tony's mind or his innards which, well plied with Scotch for almost the entire flight from China, had let go after only a few minutes.

Luckily, he'd grabbed a sick bag to capture it all but was left with the twin joys of ensuring the results

13

didn't tip over or tear open; and nursing an acid ravaged throat until the flight attendants were able to provide service once again.

Thankfully, the flight was over in just under ninety minutes.

By the time he had disembarked, grabbed his bag and cleared immigration, he realised that he had forgotten to watch the last five minutes of his movie. Now he'd never know if the hero survived.

An hour later, the cabbie dropped him off at his Holland Park house. Tony staggered into the empty house, dropped his suitcase by the door and trudged up the two flights of stairs to his bedroom. His eyes fell on his king-sized bed.

I could sleep for a week.

He sloughed off his jacket and let it drop to the floor, then kicked off both shoes and socks. Within seconds, he was standing in just his shorts and sweat-stained vest. He pulled back the covers, ready to collapse into the bed's warm embrace, when his mobile phone vibrated on the bedside table. He peered over and saw his son's name flashing on the display.

Damn. Forgot about that.

He snatched up the phone and answered.

"Hey, Dad. How was the trip?" came James's disembodied voice.

"Terrible," Tony groaned, "Thirty-six hours to get back to London. I've hardly slept and the turbulence from Amsterdam made me throw up."

A slight chuckle came over the phone. "You got pissed again, didn't you?"

"Well I had a few, but not that many."

"Right. Well you sound horrible. Get some sleep."

"Thanks. I was just about to."

"Good. Everyone's staying home 'cause of the virus. Do the same. I'm off to Devon with Liz for the weekend. Might just stay for a week."

"Good for you. I need to report in on Monday."

"Right," came his sarcastic tone, "Too diligent you. Look after number one. Your company don't care as much about you as you think."

"Thank you, Mr Career Advisor."

"That's me. I'll give you a call later in the week. Remember, look after yourself. You're getting old, y'now."

"Okay. I'll be fine and stop reminding me of my age."

"Love you. Bye."

13

The phone went dead.

Tony stared at it for a moment before turning it off and tossing it on the nightstand. He climbed into bed, pulled the duvet up, turned the lamp off and was away with the fairies within minutes.

*****

His eyes flickered open to the radiant daylight streaming into the room. He shivered and realised he was bathed in sweat but only covered in the sheet. He grabbed for the duvet and dragged it back over himself to quell the chill.

Tony peered at the clock on the nightstand. It was after two.

Christ, I slept for fifteen hours.

He lay back and stared at the ceiling for a moment. Another shiver ran across his body.

Fuck. Did I turn off the heating?

Tony flopped his hand onto his forehead. He was burning up. He wiped his palm on the sheet to get the sweat off. A rumble from his abdomen convinced him he needed to get up. He threw back the covers and placed his feet on the thick shagpile carpet, readying himself to stand. He waited for the world to stop spinning before gaining his feet.

The bathroom was only a few metres away, but it looked like a marathon run from where he stood. Another rumble spurred him on.

He managed to sit just as his system released itself.

Good god where did that come from?

As the pressure in his bowels lessened, relief came. He relaxed and let it flow. Suddenly, he felt a chill rise on his forehead, the blood drained from his face as pain rose in his stomach. He only had enough time to point his face downward and spread his legs as wide as he could before his body ejected the entire contents of his stomach. Tony strained to remain still while fluid streamed from both ends of his body. When it finally finished, he dropped to his hands and knees, mindless of the effluent coating his skin, and lay down on the floor. Eventually, the coolness of the tiles on his face revived him, and he crawled into the shower cubicle. He started the shower, curled up, and allowed the spray to wash over him.

***

Still feeling one step above a sub-human denizen

of a dystopian underworld, Tony shuffled into the kitchen.

Coffee!!

He pressed the *primer* button on the coffee machine and listened as the internals of the device whined. He grabbed a cup and spoon and went to the fridge for milk.

"Ah, crap," he said aloud to the empty shelf.

He had emptied it before heading off. There was no milk.

Black coffee? Fuck that.

The thought of a trip to the shop plagued Tony's fevered mind almost as much as the prospect of black coffee. He stared at the empty fridge for a few moments while his brain cells stopped swimming, then closed it and shambled off to the bedroom to dress more appropriately.

***

Tony dumped his armful of items on the conveyor belt and waited his turn. He'd grabbed milk, a frozen pizza, a bottle of Scotch and the last toilet paper on the shelf.

What's with the lack of loo roll?

Ignorant of the fearful stares from those around him, his eyes were drawn to the BBC News on the wall-mounted TV. The announcer talked about the ongoing virus outbreak. Tony could barely hear what the man was saying, but a stream of subtitles screamed out words such as *COVID-20*, *mutation*, *symptoms*, *vomiting*, *diarrhoea*, *wash hands* and *facemasks*.

Tony shuffled along as the queue moved, his eyes still on the screen. One last message flashed up before Tony noticed the customer before him leave.

"Avoid personal contact of any kind."

He peered down and looked into the face of the register operator. She stared back at him from above a tightly fitted facemask that covered her nose and mouth. Her eyes never left him as she scanned his items and rang up the total. He fished out his card and brought it up to tap. It was then he saw the operator's head nod towards her right. His glanced in that direction, and he saw a stand full of green fabric facemasks. Something pinged in his mind and he turned to view the other customers in line.

Every single one wore a similar mask. Every single person's eyes bulged out of their head as they stared at him like he was some sort of abhorrent

13

monster. He realised the problem and turned back and took down one of the face masks. He smiled at the operator and said, "Sorry, just got back from an overseas trip. Didn't have any masks at home."

The woman added the mask to his shopping. Tony tapped his card, gathered his items, and bolted from the shop.

***

The suited reporter droned on as Tony stared vaguely at the TV. His intention was to find out more about the contagion. When he had left for China the country was on high alert but hadn't gone into total meltdown. On his return, it was becoming clear that Britain had gone mad.

China, after its initial panic over the outbreak, had reopened its borders and its economy to the world. Tony had encountered small pockets of the public cowering in panic, but for the most part, people went about their lives as usual. It was China after all, so finding large swathes of the population wearing facemasks was commonplace. The air was thick with exhaust fumes and the underlying tang of rot, even on a good day. His minders kept him indoors, so the need for a facemask was reduced.

England, on the other hand, was a different world. The incessant dread over Brexit had given way to heightened anxiety over the outbreak of the virus. Ordinary people's minds had gone into meltdown, leading to the hoarding of toilet paper, handwash, rice, pasta, and even sardines.

Tony considered himself lucky to have found anything.

He peered at the scattered pizza crusts on his plate, and the half empty bottle of Scotch sitting next to it.

Geez, Tony, steady on or someone might call you an alcoholic.

He smiled and aimed the remote at the TV. As he scanned the Guide, he chuckled out loud. Channel 4 was showing a rerun of *Outbreak* and ITV had *The Andromeda Strain* scheduled.

They must be taking the piss.

Tony brought up the *movies on-demand* menu. He searched for a few moments and finally smiled.

Excellent. I can finally finish that fucking movie.

He chose *purchase* under the entry for the movie he'd been watching on the plane, leaned back and closed his eyes while it downloaded.

13

***

The sun streamed into the lounge room and bathed Tony's face in light. He blinked awake and stared straight at the blank TV. Realisation dawned. He grabbed the remote and tapped a button. The menu popped up showing him that the movie he'd downloaded had finished. Trouble is, he'd fallen asleep before it even started.

"Oh, fucking hell."

He kicked the coffee table in frustration, waking up his laptop in the process. His weary eyes fell onto his inbox. Several new emails had appeared. Cursing himself, he reached for the computer and dragged it onto his lap.

He clicked on the first email. It was from Adrian, his boss at NextGen. It was a short statement that made his stomach drop into a deep pit of despair. While he'd been in China, a decision had been made at the Home Office to suspend his duties and remove him from the project.

Tony saw five years of his professional life evaporate in one line of text.

"Fuck," he swore at his computer. "That little fucking twat."

The end of the email was a request to come into the NextGen office on Monday afternoon and explain what the incoming project manager meant by the statement: "He just didn't seem to know what he was doing."

Tony stared at the email through red-rimmed eyes. He considered writing back and tendering his resignation but realised that would make Milan's victory even sweeter. Instead, he took his hands away from the keyboard and clicked on the next email.

His right hand shook as he resisted the temptation to punch the screen; it was a meeting request. From Milan Curlis. Milan, whose new job title was manager of Tony's project. Tony reread the meeting request, his body shaking. He knew it was rage building, not the effects of whatever sickness had hold of him. He read the meeting reason. The little asthmatic twat wanted a handover meeting. At ten o'clock on Monday morning.

Clever. Make me come in when everyone is there, so they can stare at the sucker who'd been ousted.

"Little shit."

Tony took a deep breath. His throat tickled, but he willed himself to resist coughing. He let the air out

13

in one long exhalation, then clicked accept before closing the email.

Things happen, mate. Don't take it personally.

He closed his eyes for a moment, but all he saw were his hands around Milan's throat, strangling the life out of the bastard. A wry smile came to his lips, but he tossed the vision aside.

He opened the next email; it was a courtesy email from Human Resources about the spread of the new mutation of the corona virus called COVID20.

The email outlined the symptoms. Tony recognised them and ticked them off in his mind.

Sore throat. *Check.* Cough. *Check.* Temperature. *Check.* Vomiting. *Oh, yeah, check.* Diarrhoea. *Definitely, check.* Shortness of breath. *No, but give it time.*

Shit. I think I've got it.

The rest of the email was a guide to avoidance. Wash hands. No physical contact, etc.

Don't need to worry about that it seems.

The last statement was interesting. It detailed a study on how long the new strain could be communicated. It could live in the air for up to ten hours, or on surfaces for three to four hours.

Jesus, hardy little sucker. Surfaces? Three to

four hours?

A plan began to form in his mind. It was the final statement that settled his train of thought.

"Don't panic. The general population is safe and will likely suffer mild symptoms. The most at risk are the elderly and those with respiratory complaints, such as emphysema or asthma."

Asthma.

He smiled.

***

Tony plodded into the office just before nine, following another rough night of sleep plagued by razor blades in his throat and a dry, wracking cough. He downed a cocktail of pain killers and cold tablets before making the journey and presented himself at the office in a clean shirt and suit and wearing his newly acquired facemask.

As expected, several sets of eyes darted away from him every time he looked up. They all knew what was coming, but they weren't the object of his concern. That person hadn't even arrived.

Tony spent the first half an hour printing off every document he'd created over the previous five

13

years and copying them to a newly acquired thumb drive. Returning from the printer, he dumped the final load of papers onto his empty desk, stared at the collected works of his tenure with the Home Office, and shook his head in defeat.

Jesus, half a decade of dedication amounts to a small pile of paper. I seriously need a career change.

With that cheery thought, he picked up his bag and laptop and carried the papers into the chosen meeting room. The clock in the room indicated he had twenty minutes before the arrival of his arch nemesis. He placed the papers and laptop on the table and pulled out the little thumb drive.

Making sure the door was shut and nobody could see through the frosted windows, he set about his plan.

First, the thumb drive was given a saliva bath. He ran his tongue over every exposed surface then placed it to the side to dry. Next, he picked up each stapled document and breathed on the front and rear pages. Some of the more important documents were given a special tongue bath at the spot where most people would grab hold.

With five minutes left before the start, he finished. His tongue and throat felt raw, and he grabbed more painkillers and took them with a deep draught of water to slake his thirst and ease the pain.

The meeting room door opened, and Milan stepped in. The normal smarmy grin was on the face that Tony had imagined punching so many times. He took a deep breath and stayed calm, standing as Milan approached him and brought his hand out of his pocket.

Assuming that Milan wanted to shake hands, he thrust his own out, colliding with the other man's. A small cylindrical object flew from Milan's grasp, clattered against the wall, and dropped to the carpet. Tony followed it, realising he'd just knocked Milan's asthma puffer out of his hand. He dropped down and picked it up, thinking quickly, grasping it in his sweat-soaked hand and fingering the mouthpiece as he stood up.

He held out the puffer towards Milan and said, "Sorry about that. Thought you wanted to shake hands."

Milan looked at him with a hint of disgust. "Why would I want to do that?" he asked, taking the puffer from Tony's hand. His Harvard ring shone in the fluorescent light as he quickly sucked a lung full of the medicine.

13

Tony took a long slow breath, keeping his anger in check, before indicating the pile before him. "As asked, I've printed everything out." He picked up the saliva coated thumb drive and handed it to Milan, noticing it was now dry. "There's an electronic copy on here."

"That's everything?"

"Yep. Everything I've done in this department over the last five years."

"Good," Milan said, looking at the stack of papers. "Maybe you did know what you were doing." He smiled, pocketed the thumb drive and picked up the documents, "That's it then. You can go." Without waiting, he turned and left the room.

Tony watched the door slowly close.

"Fucker," he mumbled.

***

Tony grumbled to himself all the way home. Several people thought he was crazy, but most just thought he was probably on the phone. Before leaving the meeting room, he sent an email out to Adrian and said he didn't feel well and would be in on Wednesday. If he was honest with himself, he didn't care if he ever went back. NextGen had thrown him under a bus and left him without support. Milan had won, for the time being anyway. Tony smiled to himself at the thought of Milan handling the virus covered thumb drive and documents.

His last act was to drop his security pass off at the front desk. If NextGen cut him loose, he knew he would never take a job at Home Affairs again. Five years had proven how dysfunctional they really were, and he'd had enough.

Back at home, he quickly sloughed off his suit and threw it on a chair in his bedroom before putting on his pyjamas and trudging downstairs to spend the rest of the day in front of the boob tube. To relieve the throbbing head and grumbling emotions, he set down a coffee, the rest of the bottle of scotch and a huge pack of crisps. Just the ticket for a day off.

As he was searching for something to watch, he remembered that he still had his movie to finish. The rental didn't end for another day, so he decided to watch the whole thing again from the start.

Bullets flew. Bodies tumbled. Blood flowed. The second time through was more fun on the big TV than the first time on the tiny aeroplane monitor. As the movie reached the climax once more, he picked

up and had another medicinal nip of Scotch. There was still a third left, he was pacing himself nicely.

The hero was once again alone and moving into the big boss's home, ready for the final confrontation. Tony readied himself.

The doorbell rang.

"Fuck," he said out loud, snatching up the remote and pausing the film. He plodded to the front door, snatched it open and almost jumped back in shock.

Standing on the doorstep were two figures covered head to toe in hazmat suits, helmets and gloves. One figure pointed what looked like a gun at his head, while the other looked at a clipboard and said, "Mr Tony Grant?"

FOSTER MARCH

SHAWN M. KLIMEK

CANARY WHARF, UK

As his headache got worse, Foster twice turned off the path towards the tube station, when alternatives briefly seemed to present themselves.

His first detour was to a fancy sushi restaurant, apparently so popular that well-dressed customers were lined up outside the door, chatting amongst themselves. As diners occasionally exited, a hostess standing behind a podium called out customer names from his waiting list. "Cunningham, party of two?"

Approaching the captive audience, Foster displayed his cracked phone and addressed himself to the group. "Excuse me. Excuse me folks," he began, raising his scratchy voice. "Would one of you good people either lend me your phone or else call me a cab?"

Most folks continued chatting, a few even raising their voices to drown out his interruption.

13

Two places short of the front of the line, however, the husband half of an elderly couple looked him in the eyes.

"You American?" he inquired.

"Yes sir," said Foster. "I'm a U.S. citizen, but I often work abroad."

"I recognised the accent!" said the man. "East coast, right? The missus here thought you were probably a mugger, or else Danish."

"My phone's broken," said Foster. "Do you have one I could borrow?"

The man smiled sympathetically and seemed about to reach inside his coat until his wife tugged at his arm.

"I'm sorry," said the man, his expression sobering. "The truth is, we're travelling too, and on a limited data plan."

Foster was just about to reply, but instead, his head drew back and then lurched forward in a sudden, noisy sneeze. The elderly couple and several others nearby recoiled in disgust.

"Cover your mouth, goddamn you," complained a woman two places further back. Foster would have never believed she'd been caught in the spray had she not wiped her face on her sleeve. She must have been downwind, he realised.

"Forgive me," said Foster before turning his head to cough.

"Goddamn it, you got me again!" cursed the same woman.

"Go away!" another customer urged.

"I did—?"

The hostess waved her hand to get his attention and raised her voice. "Sir? There are no more places left on the waiting list tonight. I'm going to have to ask you to leave."

He raised his broken phone. "I was only asking—" he began to say, but then he turned his head again, seized by a longer coughing fit.

"Please leave!" the elderly man's wife urged.

"You should go," agreed the old man. He was holding out a handkerchief. "Take this," he said. "For your nosebleed."

"Nosebleed?"

Foster's eyes widened as he noticed microdroplets of red spatter one side of the old man's face. He was guiltily relieved that it happened to be the side facing away from his wife. Putting away his phone, he accepted the handkerchief and pinched his nose. Backing quickly away, he waved his free hand

13

in surrender. "I'm going!" he said and made his escape.

Foster's second stop was a visit to the snacks and sundries kiosk just outside the tube station. Behind the counter was a dark-skinned man in a white, button-down shirt and a turban. Perhaps because they both sported beards, there was an instant simpatico. Seeing Foster approach with his head tilted back and his nose pinched closed with a bloody cloth, the prescient clerk placed a package of facial tissues on the counter.

"Thanks," said Foster, fumbling his credit card onto the counter. "Got any cough lozenges?"

"Down to your right, mate."

"Thanks."

"Been in a fight?"

"No. Been on a flight, though. That aeroplane air really dries out your sinuses."

The clerk laughed. "Ha, ha! Only dry sinuses? You got off light, mate! Did you see the news about those poor saps who just flew in from China?"

"No, I've heard nothing."

"They all got the latest killer virus. Worst one yet. Worse than bird flu, swine flu, bat flu, or whatever you can name."

"No shit." It occurred to Foster that this must be what all the Emergency Health Alerts on his phone were about. He believed he could probably guess their contents: *Don't panic. Stay out of crowds. Wash your hands.*" They'd probably sent him one message for each instruction. Silly Brits.

"There had better be no Chinese coming to my kiosk tonight. No, sir!" The clerk briefly revealed a metal baton hidden under the counter. "Need a bag, mate?"

Foster patted his pockets. "No, I'm good. Thanks."

"Well, you sound like you swallowed a frog. You had better go home and turn on a humidifier," said the clerk.

This close to the Underground, there was no point asking to borrow a phone anymore. Foster departed, waving farewell with the bloody cloth.

Once inside the tube station, Foster sought out the men's room and attempted to clean up. He washed his face and dried it with a paper towel. Crimson coins splashed into the white basin. He opened his packet of tissues and shoved little wads into each nostril, and then wiped his face with a wet paper towel. Finally, he rinsed out the bloody

13

handkerchief in the sink, squeezed out as much moisture as possible, and then held the stained cloth beneath the hot air blower beside the exit until it felt dry enough to shove into his jacket pocket.

His now throbbing headache made getting home an even greater ordeal. Friendly strangers helped direct Foster both to board the right tube and get off at the station nearest to his hotel, but as his trip progressed, the behaviour of strangers seemed to increasingly reflect growing hysteria about the rumoured newest flu out of China. When he suffered a brief coughing fit upon stepping out of the tube, there were conspicuous whispers and finger pointing. Somebody must have even been worried enough to warn a station agent, because a security guard shouted to him as got into his taxi. No one was brave enough to chase after him, however.

Arriving at his hotel, Foster went directly, via elevator, up to his room. A sign on his doorknob read, "Please Do Not Disturb." He had no recollection of having left it there but decided to leave it where it was.

A red light was blinking on the phone beside his bed. Flopping down onto the bedspread, he picked it up and listened to the message.

"Hello, Mr March. This is the hotel manager, Marvin Dawes. We have an urgent, personal message for you. When you receive this message, please notify the front desk, and then wait in your room for a response. Do not exit the room for any reason. Do not speak to any other guests or staff, except by phone. Do not use the ice or vending machines, the gym, pool, or any other facilities. All will be explained. Thank you."

With a sinking feeling, Foster began to suspect he knew what the urgent personal message might be about. Did the plane he had taken from Amsterdam originate in China? Is that what those Emergency Health Alert messages had been about? He took out his cell phone and looked at the screen again, but it was grey and blank. He dropped the useless thing onto the nightstand and picked up the TV remote. He turned on the TV and located the news. Chatter about the virus seemed to be everywhere.

Good lord. Thinking back, he recalled a passenger on the plane coughing the whole flight. And now his own symptoms were multiplying, getting worse. Every clue pointed to the same conclusion.

Muting the TV, he reached for the phone, aimed

13

a finger at the front desk button, but then hesitated. Once he called downstairs, public health authorities would probably want to interview him about everywhere he had been all day and every person with whom he'd come in contact. All those people and places needed to be warned, quarantined. That was only reasonable.

But Vicky! She needed to be warned without delay. Good Lord, he had kissed her on the mouth!

Instead of dialling the front desk, he dialled the prefix to reach an outside line, then dialled her phone number.

She picked up on the third ring.

"Hello?"

"Vicki. It's Foster."

"Foster! At last! Why haven't you been answering your phone?"

"Oh, it's broken. That's why I'm calling from the hotel."

"Oh. Well listen—"

"No, you listen first."

"Please, Foster. We can have a longer talk tomorrow, if you want to, but I can't find my purse. I know I brought it to the Bullhorn with me. Do you have it?"

"No."

"Are you sure?"

Foster thought about it for a minute. "Wait. Here it is," he lied.

"You have it? Oh, thank heavens. Can I come pick it up?"

Foster pondered this. If she came over, they might end up quarantined together. Two weeks would give them time to talk. Perhaps even work things out, rekindle old feelings.

"Come on over," he said. "I'm in Room 1342."

"Now, I don't want to talk anymore tonight," Victoria warned. "And Clyde will be coming with me."

Foster frowned. "Naturally," he said after a pause. Suddenly inspired, he added, "…but just in case I have visitors, you'd better ask him to wait for you down in the lobby."

"Alright. See you soon."

After hanging up, Foster suffered a brief coughing fit, and his still head throbbed as he lay it down on the pillow, yet in one respect, he was beginning to feel a little better.

If I time my phone call to the front desk right, he told himself, *this may all yet work out.*

13

X-DAY +7

POTUS Tweet:
We have a perfectly coordinated and fine tuned plan at the White House for our attack on CoronaVirus. We moved VERY early to close borders to certain areas, which was a Godsend. V.P. is doing a great job. The Fake News Media is doing everything possible to make us look bad. Sad!

ISOBEL AND SHEN

BLAKE JESSOP

WUHAN, CHINA

A week after Isobel left, Shen found text messages for him on the sat phone during a rare trip back to his apartment. She'd made it back to London. Shen only got home occasionally, so he'd missed a bunch of increasingly anxious texts. He sent messages back telling her what he'd been doing in as few words as he could, and promised he'd find a way to bring the camera next time.

Huge cleaning trucks swept up and down Wuhan's streets, spraying solvents and leaving a thin film of foam on the asphalt. Shen rode in the back of a pickup truck with a steel cube on the back to transport people who didn't want to go to the hospital. He worked infinite hours, and slept brief sleep, and ate tasteless food. He tried to save as many lives as he could, and the next time the military called on him, he had the camera.

13

He was working at the Guiyuan Dajue hotel, which they'd turned into a temporary hospital when the real ones ran out of beds. Even though he was technically a clinical epidemiologist, he was the chief physician, because everyone senior to him was either at one of the major hospitals or already gone.

The word *gone* was another thing that wasn't what it used to be. His fellow caregivers hadn't gone the way Isobel had—which Shen found was the last thing that caused him any emotion at all—but gone to the same place the patients went. Half the nurses Isobel had worked with were sick, and the last thing Shen had hope in was that the journalist might have gotten out before the wave had crashed over them.

"Doctor Wei, do you know the layout of the hotel?" The captain startled Shen out of his reverie, and he realised he had never learned the soldier's name. There wasn't any kind of identification on his hazmat gear other than his rank.

"Certainly. I am now the hotel's fire marshal, as well as head physician, for whatever difference that makes."

"Good. You will take some time to help my men identify the load-bearing pillars. Now."

Shen paused. "Why?"

"Doctor, when was the last time you saw a disposal truck?"

"Not for a day or two."

"Everyone here is over seventy years of age. The young are in real hospital beds. Do you seriously think many people here will recover?"

Shen tried to stare at where his eyes would be, if there really were anything behind the reflective panes of the gas mask.

"There is hope."

"Certainly, if we act decisively. We are quarantining this building. Do you understand?"

"I do," Shen said.

***

Saving lives was difficult. Shen's career, his entire being, was founded on the idea that fighting against entropy and decay took as much compassion and delicacy as it did intelligence. Preserving the living was hard, but destruction turned out to be easy.

Shen showed the soldiers around the hotel and pretended not to notice as they spray-painted marks on concrete pillars in the parking garage and in the stairwells. He knuckled under and did what he was

13

told, and the soldiers didn't notice him or his nurses passing Isobel's GoPro between them as they did their rounds. The soldiers affixed nondescript satchels to the markings, and Shen and his team watched them through Isobel's eyes.

When it was done, not much had changed. The patients still coughed and retched. The toilets still struggled to contain the desperate needs of too many sufferers. Too many sufferers couldn't stand to get to the toilets, and their smell permeated the halls, adding a sickening smell to the sound of their gasping moans. The captain found Shen doing his rounds.

"It's time to leave, doctor."

"Is it?"

"You can stay if you want," the faceless soldier said. The camera was a dead weight in Shen's pocket. He tried to imagine what Isobel would do.

"We'll go," Shen said. There was one emotion left for him to feel; shame. Humiliation at what he was about to do, or fail to do. *What would Isobel say?* Shen heard her voice as clearly as if she were standing beside him.

"We watch. We record. We bear witness. That's all we can do."

***

The soldiers hustled them into trucks. The street was deserted apart from the roar of diesel engines and the wash of yellow streetlights.

Shen tried to think of it as just a building, but couldn't. What had he told Isobel? *It's what's on the inside that counts.*

As they climbed into the truck, the charges went off with a series of flat bangs that rang in Shen's ears like the gunshots had so many days before. Not much seemed to happen, then there were puffs of smoke from the lower windows and the hotel collapsed inward on itself like a house of cards. The building, and everyone in it, were pulled inexorably, suddenly into the earth.

Fighting entropy and decay is indeed one thing, Shen thought. *Gravity is something else.*

***

Shen saw his first shadow when he returned to the University Hospital. They must have always been there, but Shen had lived his entire life under surveillance of one kind or another. It was easy not to notice. He kept working, kept trying to think of a way to get to his own apartment and his laptop and the sat phone. He felt sick, and he was starting to be sure it wasn't just a spiritual illness.

Escape seemed impossible until he did it. They were all scanned if they tried to leave the hospital, and permission from the military was required. At length, Shen stopped thinking about the problem the way Isobel would. She was cunning, and he was direct. He simply walked out.

The nurse scanning staff as they left was a young man who Shen barely knew, but he had been at the hotel, too.

"Doctor Wei," he said nervously. "Do you have a pass? Where are you going?"

"Home, there is something I need to do." Time failed to pass between them, and Shen coughed into his mask. The eyes behind the young man's mask were as frightened and wild as those of a rabbit in front of the hounds. Shen tried to remember if he had taken a turn with the GoPro.

"Go on, check me. Go on."

A shaking hand aimed the infrared scanner at Shen's forehead. It beeped.

"Well, am I positive?" he asked.

"Not today," his colleague replied, after a pause.

"Thank you," Shen said, and set off down the street.

***

The internet was down in Shen's apartment, but connecting the sat phone to his laptop quickly provided him with a connection. He opened WeChat and dialled. Waited.

"Shen?" Isobel said. Her face was pixelated on the laptop screen. Pure relief flowed through Shen for a moment. It dissipated his gloom, the stale smell of the apartment, the pain in his head. The effect lasted for a long, blissful moment, and disappeared. Isobel looked terrible.

"It's me," he said, "and you too, it looks like. When did you start showing symptoms?"

"A few days after I got back. There's no room in the hospitals, so I stayed home."

"Your colour is bad. You should go."

"I'm not sure how much difference that would make. I'm happy you're still alive."

"About that… Did our footage air?"

"In a report, not a documentary." Isobel was

pausing dully between her sentences. "No one took it too seriously until Italian hospitals started looking the same way. It didn't shake the world as much as I thought it would."

She coughed and leaned out of frame to spit. Shen felt it right through the screen. It was his future and past at the same time. Time to get down to business.

"The world was already shaking too much, I suppose, but I have something that will shake it even more."

Even through the illness, Isobel perked up. Focused. "Don't say too much. Let's think of a way to ship it out."

"No time for that. I need you to tell me how to just put it out there. I don't care what happens."

They stared at each other for a while.

"What did you see?" Isobel asked. Shen told her. It took Isobel a few moments to soak it in.

"That is so horrible I almost can't believe it. You can actually see them set the charges? On film?"

"I got the implosion, too."

Isobel let out her breath in a whoosh, and it made her cough again.

"I can tell you how to upload it straight to

Wikileaks, but you'll get caught as soon as it goes live."

"I can live with that."

"Are you willing to die here?" Isobel said in an accurate enough imitation of Shen's gruff voice that he laughed.

"I knew I chose the right doctor," Isobel said when he stopped. "Say, I've been thinking: is it possible this entire thing is some kind of conspiracy? All the way from the top?"

"The hospital certainly is—we have proof—but the virus…? You really think of China as an evil empire."

"Only because the CPC behaves like one. There's so little oversight it's scary."

"Maybe, but I can think of something scarier."

Isobel looked at him bleakly. Shen saw an old pack of cigarettes on his desk and realised he hadn't smoked in weeks. He lit one. "What if the virus just came from the wet market and we made the same mistakes we did with SARS? What if there is no conspiracy to spread it? What if the response is just incompetence and brutality and the love of power? Mother Nature is better at killing humans than we could ever be. There is no reason for this; we're all

just going to die."

Isobel's eyes stared back through the screen. They had the same look they'd had when he first met her. Hard and distant and determined.

"Not without pushing back first."

Shen smiled. "No, not without pushing back. Tell me how to get this footage somewhere everyone can see."

Isobel did. While Shen hooked the GoPro up to his laptop, Isobel wrote headlines and hash tags for it in both English and Mandarin. It took a long time to upload it all, and while the progress bar slid towards its terminal point, Shen and Isobel talked, enjoying a small feeling of connection. They spoke quietly into the night, and Isobel stayed online with him until the apartment door broke inward behind Shen with a crash. Men in grey suits filled the room. One of them slammed the laptop shut with a snap, and the connection winked out.

NIGEL

GREGG CUNNINGHAM

LONDON, UK

"Alright, treacle! Where you been, and how the fuck was Amsterdam, mate? Great result for the boys, eh!" Vinnie crowed down the phone as Nigel rolled over for the packet of Panadol on his bedside table.

"Hey, mate. Yeah, it was a blinder of a game. Got back last week and just put in a few night shifts. Was gonna call you, but hey, you know how it goes. So how you keepin?" Nigel coughed, rubbing his eyes as he sat upright, the mobile clutched to his ear with his clammy hand. His head was starting to throb.

"Shit, you sound rough as a badger's, mate? Still hungover?" Vinnie laughed as the phone crackled.

"Feels like it, mate. I think I caught something from the kid behind me on the flight back last week; feel like shit this morning and my heads rattling like

one of Barry's cowbells. How is the fucker, anyway? Did he make it back okay?"

"Yeah, the twat got a fine and was sent home before us for disrupting the peace." Barry was a country kid who worked on a farm with his family's cows; a real shit kicker. He also liked to kick off with the locals too when abroad. "He's back with Sheila and the kids, although he's in the barn with the cows now and in her bad books for spending all their rent money in Amsterdam!" Vinnie laughed.

"Yeah, well I picked up some geezer last week who flashed me a couple of bullseyes for taking him to Billingsgate, so I'm flush for a few this week if you and the boys are up for it. See if Barry wants to show off his wellies?" Nigel sniffed the snot back up his nostrils.

"A hundred nicker tip? Jesus mate, nice one. Yeah, I'm up for a few on Friday. Down the Anchor for eight? Don't take the piss out him, Nige—poor bugger misses the action!"

Nigel rubbed his sweaty bald head and squinted as his temples throbbed. "Sounds good, mate, but I can't promise you I won't rip into farmer Baz when I see him. See you there!"

"You sound well rough, Nige. You sure you're

up to a session?"

"I'm golden, Vinnie. I'll just nip down Raj's and pick up a couple of kippers to fry up and wash 'em down with a couple of whiskies. No big deal, mate. I'll be right for next weekend."

"You probably got that Corona virus shit that's going around. I heard it only affects old bastards like you!" Vinnie laughed again.

"Nah, mate, don't drink that poncy shit like you City poofs!"

Nigel hung up before Vinnie could reply to his dad joke. Truth was, he did feel lousy, and his head really was banging. He reached over to the side table and peeled a couple of pills from their foil, knocking them back with a swig of Johnny Walker, but when he tried to stand up, his whole body swayed and he had to steady himself on the bedpost. His eyes throbbed in their sockets when he opened the curtains to the midday sun, and he had to shield them like he was one of the Lost Boys. He thought a good fry up might be on the cards—just like his mother used to dish him up—and shuffled over to the front room to switch on the television while he put the kettle on.

The cupboards were bare. He hadn't been shopping since he returned from Amsterdam, and dry noodles and the last of the New Year liquor remained on the shelves. He really couldn't be bothered, but realised he had to take a wander down to the corner shop to buy some basics if he was going to shake this cold off. Beer alone would not cure this.

The news reporter on the television was talking more bullshit as the video showed ranks of soldiers patrolling Dover check points and military vehicles parked in cordoned-off areas as medics scanned lines of travellers in the terminals. He scratched his arse through his boxer briefs as he grabbed the remote control to click over to one of the morning shows. They were also talking more scare tactic bullshit about the spread of the virus in London and more footage of soldiers setting up camp at Heathrow Airport. After listening to some lard arse commander drone on about how this could be virus COVID-20 and how the government should be taking more precautionary measures to protect the people by closing airports, train stations and other open border channels, Nigel turned the TV off and picked through the pile of discarded clothes that were scattered by the end of his bed. He hadn't even unpacked his bag from the holiday, so all he had to wear was the odd socks in his drawer and his Spurs away top that was draped over the chair from before he left for Germany. Nigel sniffed out the best pair of jeans and slowly dressed, grabbing his wallet and the pile of loose change on top of the two fifties he had been tipped.

He felt all his forty-eight years aching in his bones as he toiled over his slight beer gut to get his socks on. "Fuck it." He coughed, slipped his bare feet into his work-boots instead, and made his way to the door, shuffling down the stirs, more like a man of eighty than forty-eight.

***

"What do you mean you got no bread, Shamy? Did Raj sleep in again?" Nige sighed, turning to the empty racks as he picked up another can of tomato soup from the sparse shelf.

"Sorry, Nigel. My father is very sick today, so no deliveries." Her lips pursed as she fidgeted with her bangles. "We have packets of naan bread over there though." Shamy pointed over at the Indian produce at the back of the shop, her bangles sliding up her arm and under her saree.

"Naan bread! Jesus, Shamy, I'm not catering for

one of your family get togethers, luv. Well, I hope he's up and about soon and it's nothing serious. What about milk, where're you hiding that these days?"

She frowned under her veil. "Oh, he's been terrible, Nigel…very sick…so no milk either; our driver didn't show up!" Shamy shook her head. "We have cashew milk over there though."

"I'll pass, thanks." Nigel nodded sympathetically, clutching his basket filled with Carlsberg and crisps.

"You look rather terrible yourself, Nige, are you feeling alright? Maybe too much beer last night?" Shamy smiled, lifting an imaginary can to her lips. They played this game every time they met.

"Picked up a bug on the flight last week, Shamy. Just a head cold, I think. Jesus, woman, where is all your stock? You been ram-raided by the Croydon Youth Crew or something?" Nigel swung his full basket around, inspecting the meagre fish produce in the fridge.

"Preppers. Folk are getting panicked about the bug spreading everywhere, Nigel—even the markets are closing down. I have to drive to Billingsgate for my fish now."

A radio crackled behind Shamy and she turned

to pick up the small transmitter sat by the till.

"Tell that bugger he still owes me for that whisky last week!" the voice crackled, and Nigel laughed, giving the security camera above them the finger.

"Preppers! How long do they think a loaf of bread and a carton of fucking milk is going to last them?" Nigel sighed, picking up a few pieces of not-so-fresh tuna steaks from the ice before shuffling his basket over to Shamy.

"My father asks how you are feeling after your holiday." She smiled, placing the radio back in her pocket and turning down Raj's chatter.

"Just this, luv, and a packet of Panadol. Yeh, it was an experience."

"In Amsterdam? I bet it was." She winked. "Sorry, no Panadol, Nigel!"

"What?"

"All gone. All we have is Vicks Vapour Rub and a couple of bottles of Robitussin cough syrup."

"What's the chuffing world coming too…? Alright, stick them in the bag, luv…and thrown in a bottle of Johnny as well."

"Another bottle? You're pickling your brain, Nigel! She tutted with a wink, took the whisky bottle from the display behind her and filled the bag on the counter.

"Would you like some help with the vapour rub too?" She smiled. Nigel smiled, avoiding her sultry gaze by reading the Sun newspaper headline and shaking his head.

MILITARY ASK, IS BORIS FIT TO RUN THE COUNTRY?

"Ninety-five pounds, please Nigel."

"Where's your mask, Dick Turpin?" He pulled out the two sweaty notes he was tipped and handed the rolled-up fifty's over, before lifting the plastic bag from the counter and sneezed.

"No masks, Nigel. All gone to the CDC down the road. Haven't you seen the news?" she said, straight faced. "They have taken over the Millennium Dome to use as a sick tent!"

"Really, Shamy…way to kill the holiday mood. Keep the change, use it to buy more stock, luv…and I'll hold you to that rub down!" He turned, flipped the finger to the security camera one last time. "I hope you get better soon, Raj."

"I hope you sober up before your shift, Nigel. Perhaps take a couple of days off!" The doorbell tingled as Nigel left waving, and Shamy smiled, inspecting the sweaty banknotes in her hand as her father coughed in the back room.

Nigel decided he was going to take Raj's advice and spend the next few days tucked up in bed so that he could battle the thumping head cold banging away behind his temples with another whisky bottle.

Maybe he'd kill off a few more brain cells, kill the virus the old-fashioned way?

POTUS Tweet:

So last year 37,000 Americans died from the common Flu. It averages between 27,000 and 70,000 per year. Nothing is shut down, life & the economy go on. At this moment there are 546 confirmed cases of CoronaVirus, with 22 deaths. Think about that!

Sam the Coder

JACOB BAUGHER

SECRET GOVERNMENT FACILITY, CHINA

"What's happening? What's going on?" The statesman hovers over my shoulder. His cheap cologne smells like my high school locker room.

"I-I'm not sure." I pull up a new terminal window and run a diagnostic. The results come trickling in. I scan them until I reach "Bodily Functions…thirty percent." I do some mental math. "It…it looks like he's slipped into a coma."

"A coma?"

I tense. The statesman sounds incredulous, that same tone he'd had with my supervisor before killing him. Even now, his body was spread out on the floor, a puddle of blood slowly making its way across the polished concrete. He sighs.

"Send the kill order. This is sufficient for the chairman's objectives."

I try not to let the relief show on my face as I key

13

in the code. The keys click in the silence. I run the program. On the screen, Passenger **13** twitches, reaches for his left wrist. His fingernails dig into the place where the three bars are, and draw long, bloody lines down his forearm until three small, glowing lights are exposed.

"Airborne virus exposed," I say. "Sending kill order."

And just like that, he's dead. I sit back in my chair and let out a breath I hadn't realised I'd been holding.

"Excellent," the statesman says. "You may go."

I get up, gather my coat and turn to leave—and then the tape recorder in my pocket lets out a loud, obnoxious *BEEP*. I freeze.

Wordlessly, the statesman motions to the two guards by the door. They advance, guns raised. I can't see their faces behind the gas masks that they wear. One of them lowers his rifle and reaches into my pocket, pulls out the tape recorder. He turns to the statesman.

"Give it to me," he says.

The soldier does. Then he produces a pair of black metal handcuffs and fastens them around my wrists. I don't make a sound.

"Bring him," the statesman says. "His contacts may be of use to us later."

The soldier nods and escorts me up the amphitheatre-like seating and to the door. His comrade stays behind and starts methodically putting bullets into the terminals. Their staccato *crack, crack, crack* punctuates my exit until the statesman shuts the door behind me and we make our way down the hallway that I've come to know so well over the past 13 months. Doors line the yellowing drywall. For the first time, all of them are ajar. As we pass, I sneak glances into them. They're all exact replicas of the room we'd just come from. I start to count them as we pass. One, two, three… there's certainly more than 13.

"Wait," I find myself saying. "How many other passengers were there?"

The statesman doesn't answer me. We reach the elevator at the end of the hall. He produces a key from his jacket, inserts it into the chrome keyhole in between the two flush "up" and "down" buttons, and twists it 360 degrees. An alarm starts to sound in the distance. The elevator doors *ding* and open onto…not an elevator, or even a shaft, but another long hallway, this one concrete, lined with red

emergency lighting.

"Welcome to the jungle, Mr Ashley," the statesman says.

He looks at me through his heavy lids. He reaches down to his belt and draws the pistol, presses it against my forehead. I close my eyes.

"Look at me," he says.

I do, just in time to feel the Glock twitch away from my forehead to point over my shoulder.

The statesman fires three rounds into the guard behind me—two in the chest, one to the head. I reel away, ears ringing, feeling like someone just shoved molten cotton down my ear canal. I slump against the wall and close my eyes. Something tugs around my wrists and the weight of the handcuffs drops them to the floor.

The statesman slaps me across the face, forcing my eyes open. He presses the Glock into my hand and a full magazine into the other. He draws another pistol from another concealed holster and gestures down the hallway.

"Come on," he says. "Let's get you out of here."

Together, we walk down the hallway and into darkness.

ALEX LOGAN

PAMELA JEFFS

The meeting with the psychologist didn't go to plan. But to be fair, I went in not feeling the greatest—both feverish and lethargic and with intermittent nosebleeds. Then the woman confirmed she wouldn't be re-instating me to active duty at this time. I lost it. I punched a wall. Security arrived and indelicately restrained me with a kick to the guts—a kick hard enough to make me vomit all over the Persian floor rug. Not my finest moment.

And now I've been admitted.

And I feel like fucking shit.

The Defence Hospital Unit isn't so bad. I've been given my own room, spacious and painted in calming shades of green. The window opposite my bed overlooks the car park and the hospital's emergency helipad just beyond. A helicopter landed five minutes ago. It still sits there at rest—mocking

me—the pilot's seat within representing everything I want and all I can't have.

One thing I do still have is Connor. He haunts me, sitting in the chair by my bed. But I'm glad for his company. I haven't got any family in England. I'm alone here and this sickness has got me scared.

I cough and my lungs clench around a ball of razor-blade pains. I press my fist to my chest until it eases. My arm feels heavy.

"You really do look like shit," says Connor.

I clear my throat. A ball of mucous slides up into my mouth. I spit into a tissue and frown at the blood streaking it. "I really do feel like shit."

Nurse Smith walks into my room. I can't tell if she's pretty or not due to the green facemask she always wears. She stalks over to the drip and taps the clear tube leading to the cannula in my arm.

Behind her arrives Doctor Williams, his face also masked. Tall and lithe, he moves to my bedside, graceful for a fifty-something-year-old man. "Morning Alex," he says.

"Morning."

He looks tired. "I'm afraid it's bad news," he says. "Tests have come back confirming Coronavirus."

"You'll beat it," whispers Connor.

"So how long will I be down?" I ask.

Doctor Williams frowns. "We can't say for sure. It's a mutated strain. Highly aggressive. Our priority will be to stabilise your respiratory system until it can heal."

If it heals. The words hang unspoken in the air. I bite my lip. My lungs are a constant pain in my chest, and it's growing constantly worse. The urge to cough overtakes me again. I cover my mouth, but it comes with more force than I expect. Blood splatters hot across my palm and sprays past my fingers. It paints the doctor's facemask in a sheet of gore.

Horrified, I squint up at him. "I'm so sorry…" I start to say.

The doctor's eyes are wide, but he remains calm. "It's okay. I'm okay." He gently presses me back to my pillow. My limbs, weak with fever, give way. I collapse backward.

"We will do our best to make you comfortable." He glances up at the nurse. "A dose of morphine and Temazepam to help him sleep."

The doctor turns back to me. He pats me on the arm. "Don't worry, son, we'll have you back up and about as soon as we can."

Connor stands and glares at the doctor. "You better bloody well do so," he snarls. "It's not his turn to die yet."

GEOFF'S GERMS

STEPHEN CHRISTIE

Geoff sneezed into his serviette. Moments later, with a smile, Alice, the stewardess, took it from him along with an empty sandwich packet.

"Alice," called Tina, her colleague. "Could you take over on drinks please?"

"Sure." Alice pushed the rubbish trolley back to the cabin crew station, leaving Geoff's germs on the handle. She went to the drinks trolley and picked up the coffee jug in her unclean hand.

"Would you like coffee, sir?"

"Yes, please."

She passed the man some of Geoff's germs, along with his coffee.

Behind her, Gordon now pushed the rubbish trolley back up the aisle.

POTUS Tweet:
We are doing very precise Medical Screenings at our airports. Pardon the interruptions and delays, we are moving as quickly as possible, but it is very important that we be vigilant and careful. We must get it right. Safety first!

13

STACEY

A.S. CHARLY

ON BOARD FLIGHT: LHR–FCO

Stacey swaggers up to the glass doors of Heathrow Airport's entrance hall, her little black trolley right beside her. She stops, acting as if the sunlight was her personal spotlight, and takes a quick moment to admire her own reflection.

Looking great in your new blue uniform, lovely. If just the skirt was a tad shorter... She winks at herself and enters.

Not far into the hall, the strikingly bad mood of the crowd hits her. Today, the airport is a dire contrast to the bustling life in London on this sunny spring day. There are fewer people than usual. Some suspiciously eying each other, trying to avoid any kind of contact, while others stare at the TV screens to follow the latest news on the events in China. Pictures of people collapsing in the street, queues in front of sold out shops, a hotel collapsing, and

disinfection teams sweeping through the streets.

Horrible, and it's Friday the 13th too...but luckily it's all far away. Glad I'm not doing any long-distance flights.

A bunch of guys standing together are obviously enjoying themselves.

"Hey, want another Corona?" the tall one says and hugs his blonde friend, and they all burst into laughter.

Stacey walks past them, her butt swinging temptingly to the clicking of her black heels on the stone tiles. The blondie looks at her and does a gesture as if he had burnt his hand.

Sorry, sweetheart. You're not my type...not at all.

She gives the guy a bright smile nevertheless—it's her job after all.

Then she notices another woman in blue waving at her from the "crew only" baggage drop-off counter. A brunette. It's her friend, Christine, one of the few other KLM stewardesses she actually likes. She quickens her pace to catch up with her.

"Hey, how are you doing, Chrissie?"

They are about to hug and exchange kisses when they both jerk back.

"Better not, I guess."

"Yeah, let's be careful."

They both try to laugh it off, but an odd after taste lingers on. Stacey throws her trolley on the survey belt and hands over her flight details to the attendant behind the desk. After a quick look, he nods and the little suitcase disappears behind the doors to the luggage centre. The two stewardesses wander off into the direction of the passport controls, chitchatting.

"My last flight was awful, I tell ya. A little baby was crying like hell all the way from China till here, and the mom totally wasn't up to it."

By the mention of China, Stacey tries to widen the space between them without being too obvious.

"She left the little thing with another passenger and locked herself in the toilet to have a cry! Can you believe that?" Christine continued.

Stacey shakes her head in disbelief, knowing her friend was waiting for an affirmative answer. "I don't understand why people feel the need to travel with small kids, really. It's such a bother to everyone."

"But that wasn't even the worst of it! One guy was obviously drunk, and a creepy guy kept staring at my ass, licking his palms whenever he thought no

13

one was looking!"

Disgust is written all over Stacey's face.

"The flight was awful! All the coughing and slimy wet tissues. Less than half the passengers bothered to wear a mask. You'd expect at least the Chinese to be used to it... I'm so glad I'm back now."

"I bet," Stacey replied, looking around at the waiting travellers in the airport, hoping her flight today wouldn't be stuffed with sick weirdos.

***

At the immigration control gate, they meet more of their crew members, also the handsome co-pilot. Stacey eyes him with greed.

So handsome...and only talking about his wife and kids all the time...sigh.

A security woman holds a fancy thermometer close to her forehead while a guy checks her passport. It's over so quickly she wonders if they were even looking at the result. Their whole crew is through in no time, while the lines at the passenger gates are getting longer and longer. An old grandma loudly complains as she's diagnosed with a fever.

"Out of ma way. I ain't got no time for your

stupid check-ups. I'm gonna miss ma holidays because of you lil bastard!"

She starts hitting the young man with her handbag. It's quite a scene and some people laugh, careful not to get too close to her, until security guards carry her off. After that, the silence is almost tangible.

***

At a leisurely pace, the KLM group passes the souvenir shops. The uplifting music makes it easy to ignore the few TV screens still showing news updates. The waiting area at the boarding gate is already well filled, and to Stacey's relief, they all look rather healthy.

Oh wow! Very healthy indeed!

Her eyes longingly run up and down a well-built body belonging to a dark-haired guy. She can't help but wonder how his strong arms would feel on her body—undressing her.

Soo hot!

He notices her, and she feels heat rising inside her. She puts on a seducing smile, and then turns to say a perky "Laters!" to Christine, before her cheeks get a chance to embarrass her.

Walking down the passageway to the aeroplane, she hears how someone complains to Christine and the other attendant at the gate: "Why aren't there any hand sanitisers around in times like these, and don't you have any free masks? And you dare call that well prepared, good service even?"

She rolls her eyes and hopes this guy wouldn't be seated in her section. Stacey knows exactly who she'd like to attend to, and giggles.

***

After finishing her check-up round, Stacey joins Lisa at the open aeroplane door. Not long, and the first passengers arrive. The two stewardesses welcome them with a bright smile, guiding them left and right down the aisle, according to their boarding passes. Stacey bends down to have a look at the ticket of an elderly man, and he coughs right into her face.

Gosh, you scumbag! Hope the virus gets you!

Now she totally understands the complainer from earlier. Not only should there be free masks, they should be mandatory.

"Left aisle, third row to the front," she says with

an icy smile.

Then the hottie comes in sight, accompanied by his companions. They are in a merry mood, shoving each other with their shoulders, which brings them a few disgruntled looks from the other travellers.

Stacey adjusts her working speed, hoping she'd get to talk with the cutie, and really, it works. Leaning closer than necessary, she takes a long look at his boarding pass, softly running her fingers over his hand.

Awesome! He was seated in her section!

"To the right side please, Tommy," she purrs.

"Thanks! Hope I'll see you later!"

Woah!

Enchanted by his beautiful dark voice, Stacey barely manages to keep her thoughts with the tickets being handed over to her.

Finally, all passengers are on board and she closes the door, double checking. With glee, she sees Tommy still standing in the aisle. He has a bag in his hand but is still chatting with his friend. Seizing the opportunity, Stacey walks up to him.

"May I help you, Sir?"

She takes the bag and—heart racing—presses herself against him, while she stores it in the overhead compartment. He smells heavenly. Approvingly, he rubs himself against her, and she can't help but giggle, feeling how hard he is in his pants.

Then her colleague starts the announcement, and it's time for a last walk through the aisles to check for bulky hand luggage and fastened seatbelts. Of course, she throws Tommy a dazzling smile.

A pity he has his seat belt closed already.

Stacey takes out some props and kneels down in the aisle, right next to Tommy. Trying to move as seductive as possible, she shows how to act in case of an emergency, giving him another flirty look while she demonstrates the mouthpiece of the life vest. Tommy follows her every move, fidgeting in his seat, as if he can hardly keep himself from jumping her. Pleased, she winks him goodbye while the captain continues with a message to his guests. The aeroplane starts rolling, and Stacey turns around to have a last look at "her" hottie before she disappears behind the curtain for take-off. Just as she sits down in the flight attendant seat, Tommy moves the curtains and sneaks inside. Her whole body starts to tingle.

"Well, hello there," she says in her bedroom

voice, looking at the big bulge in his trousers. This promises to be fun.

13

POTUS Tweet:

To this point, and because we have had a very strong border policy, we have had 40 deaths related to CoronaVirus. If we had weak or open borders, that number would be many times higher!

TOMMY

RICH RURSHELL

ON BOARD FLIGHT: LHR–FCO

I lower the baby-changing table as she's locking the toilet door behind us. I pull up her uniform skirt while she checks her hair or makeup in the mirror. Kissing her hard, I lift her onto the table and tear off her underwear. I find she's already wet, so I slide my finger inside her. I fumble with the button of my jeans, attempting to liberate the pulsing erection that has grown within. She'd been eyeing me up since we boarded the flight, rubbing herself against me as we lifted the bags into the overhead compartments. I was already stiff by the time she squashed Pikey's bag next to mine, her perfume setting me off like it was full of 'fuck me' pheromones.

He bet me fifty quid I couldn't get into her knickers by the time we got to Rome, and I had said I'd get her in the mile-high club before the landing gear was up.

I'd intended to get my end away this weekend, but I didn't expect it to be so soon. Scoring a stewardess should earn me some respect from the other guys on Johnny's stag party. I hope the airline don't charge extra for this, like they did for extra carry on.

My jeans drop to my ankles as I hook her legs over my shoulders. The plane hits a little patch of air turbulence and I stagger a bit. The tannoy bleeps the seatbelt warning and she giggles then reaches down and starts gliding her fist over my throbbing glans.

"Quicken up, Studley, I've got a cabin to attend to!"

I lean over to the sink and pump the hand soap into my palm a couple of times. Smearing the soap all over my cock, I bat away her hand and pull her hips towards me. I position my dick between her legs and enter her.

"Quick I can do!"

At first, I move in and out of her slowly, but it isn't long before I quicken the pace of my thrusts...and the force. In no time, she's smashing herself against me, using her legs on my shoulders for leverage. She's bucking so hard on my cock, I'm scared she's going to bend it in half, so I grab her legs and force her knees behind her ears. Then I start really pounding her.

The change in position seems to have made a difference for the better, as she starts crying out and holding onto my hips, guiding me in and out of her. Not that I need guiding now. I'm in the zone.

Someone bangs on the toilet door.

"Fuck off," I shout. I'm about to blow my load and this distraction is putting me off my stroke. I look down at my cock sliding inside her, unsure if the foam around the base of it is from her or the hand soap. Or perhaps both.

With renewed turgidity, I get back into my game and I feel the orgasm creeping into my burning thighs, hips, and dick. My balls start to fizz, and the climax hits me. Everything goes blurry and my legs begin to tremble as I go into a state of final strokes autopilot. I shout out and my voice drowns out her moaning. I collapse over her, exhausted and lie there for a moment until the baby-change table gives way, sending us both crashing onto the toilet itself.

I pull my limp cock out of her and grimace at the state of it, quickly reaching for hand towels to clean myself up. I throw a couple to her too; I'm a gentleman, after all.

13

We get to our feet and I unlock the toilet door. An old man stands outside, looking at us as he coughs into his balled fist, wishing he was thirty years younger.

"You got a problem?" I say, and he backs off.

We both walk out of the small toilet like newborn baby deer, unsteady on weak legs. I walk back into the darkness of the economy seating. Pikey's mate Ben is looking right at me.

Busted!

I walk past him to my seat, high-fiving him on the way. Can't really read his expression. Probably jealous. He'll get over it once the stag party commences and we're all up to our nuts in Italian guts.

She slips back behind the curtain down the aisle from my seat, fixing her skirt and straightening her neckerchief, and smiles. She looks like shit; like she's just done a marathon or something. I guess I'm probably not looking too great either. On the bright side, it's Friday the 13th and Tommy got lucky with a stewardess. That has got to be worth a few kudos points.

That prick who's been coughing for the whole flight is at it again, wherever he is. I hear him hacking and throat clearing like he's down the dog track at Peckham. In fact, the more I look around the flight and listen, the more coughing and spluttering I hear.

This plane is full of old folks with the death rattle. I can hear them all. As I turn around, I catch her smiling back at me, looking all needy like I'm her boyfriend or some shit. Next, she'll be coming over and wanting to swap phone numbers.

"Shall we swap numbers?" she mouths, holding up her phone.

Fucking knew it!

"Sure." I smile back through gritted teeth while getting my phone out, and she walks over with the hot tea flask for the other passengers, smiling broadly at those still awake.

"What's your number?" she asks as I type hers into my phone.

"Hang on," I say. "What's your name again, darlin'?"

POTUS press conference:
I'm not a doctor. But I'm, like, a person that has a good you-know-what.

BEN DAVIDSON

DAVID BOWMORE

ON BOARD FLIGHT: LHR-FCO

It was going to be a blinding weekend. One that Ben truly deserved. A double celebration; his divorce and a friend's stag. Well, Johnny Bond wasn't really Ben's friend; more like a friend of a friend. It had been Mike Pike—yes, that really is his name— who'd wangled a place in the party for him. Ben was determined to enjoy himself, even if half the world were going COVID-19 mad. Besides, Rome was miles away from any known cases.

So, the inventory; land at Leonardo da Vinci at 16:15, check into the hotel. Then out on the lash and a bite to eat to soak up the beer—not too much, must leave room for the drink. Then onto a notorious girlie club before crashing out at about three in the morning…if they could find the hotel. Late breakfast, and then off to the match. Watch the boys thrash the arse off the Italians and then out on the lash

again until they pass out. Breakfast. Taxi. Airport. Back to work on Monday morning with the mother of all hangovers. Piece of piss for Ben—he was used to these rugger outings.

Of course, the drinking started in one of the airport's sports bars. Other fans gathered in small groups. He, Mike, and Tommy were discussing the best match they'd ever seen. Their drinks disappeared quickly, so Ben returned to the bar for the next round. A little man came to stand next to him—well, most people were little when standing next to Ben, but this one was particularly small. And Chinese, too. Why the hell was he trying to be Ben's mate? He didn't even speak English. But Ben was in a good mood, what with finally being divorced from the bane of his life, and now on the piss with a bunch of blokes all with the same intention. So he bought the little man a drink. The stranger sipped from the pint glass, pulled a face that suggested Guinness wasn't his cup of green tea, handed it back to Ben, shook his hand, gave a little bow—perhaps he was Japanese; that's what they do, isn't it?—and then wandered off. Ben didn't even know the bloke's name. Oh well, waste not, want not. Five seconds later, the spare Guinness glubbed about in his stomach. Mike thrust another into his hands. Then the call to board came and the best man was bustling them towards gate 13.

Ben wasn't happy sitting next to the window. A big bloke needs to be able to stretch his legs. It was alright for Mike, who was about five feet tall and made Tom Cruise look like the jolly green giant, but Mike didn't want the window seat. *And why the fuck did they let people recline the seats?*

In need of space, he joined the small queue for the bogs at the back of the plane. Strangers emerged, avoiding each other's eyes as they returned to their seats. A petite blonde squeezed past. While he was admiring her retreating arse, Tommy tapped him on the shoulder and held his hand up high. Ben greeted it with his own palm. *What was that for?* He'd never been high-fived for a successful shit before. *I hope he washed his hands.* Ben rubbed his palm along the head rests. Better safe than sorry. And to top it all, the toilet was a mess, what with the baby changing unit dangling from its hinges. He expected a better build quality of KLM.

By the time they arrived at the hotel, Mike was complaining of a sore throat. The general consensus was A) planes do that sort of thing—all that recirculated air couldn't be good for you and B) lubrication was the best medicine. So they had a quick pint while the best man did the doings at the check-in desk.

During their evening meal, the groom declared that he didn't feel well. He wanted to call it a day and go back to the hotel. The thing is, no one feels tip-top when they've consumed as much alcohol as these six had. A vote was tabled and carried—no bloody way was he not seeing the stripper. The taxi dropped them outside Paradisio, supposedly the best gentleman's club in Rome. The best man had arranged for a private room. Lit with ice blue lighting, a dozen comfortable chairs surrounded a raised podium illuminated by morphing LED's. A bar occupied one wall of the room, behind which, the most beautiful woman Ben had ever seen mixed cocktails—heaven. The lights dimmed and the thumping sound of Basement Jaxx thudded against his chest. A girl emerged from behind a curtain and placed, with absolute precision, a metal folding chair in the centre of the stage.

***

Johnny, the groom, sporting a black eye and complaining of cracked ribs, needed to be carried back to the hotel by Ben and Tommy. It was a shame Johnny had vomited on the girl as she was beginning her routine. Still, you had to laugh—Mike certainly was.

Only Ben and Mike made it down to breakfast. Mike drank honey and lemon in hot water to ease his throat. But hadn't they done a lot of talking and laughing and cheering the night before? Johnny didn't even make it to the Rugby match. Not that he'd missed much—it was a poor show. Those that did paid not much heed and coughed and spluttered and blew noses. Anyone would think they'd never had a hangover before. Two more cried off the rest of the evening with headaches and blurred vision, leaving Ben, Mike and Tommy to their own devices. There is only so much drinking a rugby fanatic can do in a given set of hours, and as Ben was free and single once again, and since his chances of spending the night with one of the lovely ladies of Rome was rarer than chicken's teeth—as his grandad had used to say—he thought he might buy some company. Mike said he had never paid for it before and certainly wasn't about to start now. Tommy agreed, saying he'd already struck lucky and confusing Ben with a knowing look.

The taxi driver coughed incessantly, a proper smoker's cough deep in his chest. He was old, and a rosary hung from his rear-view mirror. He crossed himself every time he swore at a bicyclist who cut him up or when he pulled out in front of another Fiat.

It was the driver who knocked on the door of the villa in the centre of town. A tall, elegant woman answered. The taxi driver spoke in fast flowing foreign that required the use of his hands as much as it did his voice. The woman stepped back, a clear invitation for Ben to enter the dark recesses of her bordello. Puccini drifted from the interior.

"I assure you, signore, very clean girls here," the driver said, recognising Ben's hesitation. "And they talk English good. All the Americans come here for the clean girls, too."

He held out a hand and Ben passed over twenty Euros. The man smiled, coughed again using his hand as a shield, wiped it on his shirt, and then held it out for Ben to shake.

JASON WELLS

BRIAN MACGOWAN

ON BOARD FLIGHT: LHR-KEY-ORD

"For the sweet love of God," Jason Wells mumbled under his breath as he looked up from his aeroplane seat. For the whole flight from Heathrow to Reykjavik, he had been keeping a cautious eye on a passenger who was constantly coughing or going to and from the lavatory. Not just a dry throat cough, but a deep down, lung-busting cough.

Disembarking at Reykjavik, Jason kept his hands down to his sides, the thought of touching anything just made his stomach reel. He sure as Hell didn't want what that guy had.

Now on a flight from Reykjavik to Chicago, Jason clenched his jaw, he squinted his eyes in disgust. That same dumb-fuck was on his flight again, pawing every seat headrest as he stumbled up the aisle. Jason held his breath as the obviously sick man passed by. He could see the guy's sweaty

handprint on the back of the seat. *Why the Hell did they even let him board?*

Jason offered up a quick prayer of thanks to whatever deity was willing to listen that he had a window and not the aisle seat. He rolled his eyes as passengers all around him were coughing, some clearing their throats, or sniffling.

Nothing was going to make this six-hour flight on an active petri dish enjoyable. He just wanted to get back to Chicago O'Hare, then jump a commuter flight back to South Bend, Indiana. This bloody COVID-20 epidemic had everyone running scared. Even the US was finally paying attention; passengers from major international airports were being examined by health officials, sometimes whole planes were quarantined once they touched down on US soil. He didn't want to risk a direct flight from Heathrow then end up sitting on a plane with a thumb up his ass for two weeks.

Searching the Internet for flights, he'd discovered that Iceland had no reported COVID outbreaks and was not considered a serious health threat. Upon landing, passengers were still being scanned for fevers, but not with the same scrutiny as those arriving from larger hubs that would attract travellers from known COVID infected countries.

Staring out of the window as the other passengers boarded, Jason unconsciously bounced his left leg. It was a habit he had developed to help control his anger. After a bitter divorce, he thought that visiting family in London would be a therapeutic way to help him get over the ordeal. Well, at least that is what his supervisor had told him. Jason's leg started to bounce more when he recalled that he was *advised* to take some time off. That his behaviour was becoming erratic. As a bus driver for the Elkhart County School District that was wholly unacceptable. It was either take time off or get fired.

His supervisor knew damn well that Jason could not risk being fired. His ex had sole custody of their children—the only way that Jason could see them was on days when he drove them to school, along with the other sixty or so children on his daily run.

Jason's anger might have been a contributing factor to the divorce. Yes, perhaps he shouldn't have taken a sledgehammer to that guy's car. But, then again, if the guy was going to be banging his wife, why shouldn't Jason be banging the guy's car.

"Fucking bitch!" Jason said out loud.

"What did you just call me?"

Startled back into reality, Jason turned to see a beautiful Asian woman occupying the seat beside him. Hatred burned from her eyes.

"I'm so sorry. Not you." He held up his hands then held them together. "I was thinking about...it doesn't matter. I'm sorry. I didn't realize that you had sat down."

The woman eyed him for a moment then let out her breath. "Let me guess...girlfriend dumped you?"

"Don't I wish. Ex-wife."

"Ah. Lucky girl."

With an awkward smile, Jason turned back to the window. He could hear the sick passenger's wet, juicy coughing. To Jason, it sounded like the man was trying to bring up his lungs.

After a few minutes, the entry door slam shut. As the plane taxied to the runway the flight attendants reviewed the safety procedures. Like most passengers, Jason barely paid them any attention, his mind once again wandering back to his current situation. The trip was less than relaxing. He was constantly having to explain to friends and family what happened to their marriage.

"Excuse me?" His seatmate interrupted his thoughts by placing a hand on his arm.

"That's okay." Thinking she meant the accidental touching.

"Excuse me?" she repeated.

"Oh, I'm sorry, I thought you meant your hand on me."

"I would like to ask you a favour...if I may?"

Jason was intrigued by the woman's green eyes as his mind plunged down various rabbit holes wondering what type of favour a gorgeously exotic woman would ask of him. Maybe this flight won't be all that bad after all. He wondered how big the lavatory was and if two people could fit in there.

"Uhm, sure. If I can be of assistance."

"I really don't like flying. If you could hold my hand during take-off, I would gratefully appreciate it." She nodded her head and smiled. "...and landing as well."

"Oh yes, of course." Jason straightened up in his seat then held out his hand.

"I'm afraid that we got off to a bad start." She held her hand to her chest." I am Li Liu."

"Jason Wells."

"It is nice to meet you, Mr Wells."

"If we are going to hold hands, please call me Jason."

"Thank you, Jason."

Unconsciously, Jason's face registered the dampness of Li's hand in his.

"I'm sorry," she said. "My hand must feel horribly sweaty, I'm just nervous... I'm not sick, I assure you."

"Oh no, no, that's fine." Jason forced a smile.

As the plane picked up speed, Li sat back, closed her eyes and tightly squeezed Jason's hand. Once airborne, Li relaxed her grip but did not release Jason's hand.

Fighting temptation to stroke her hand, Jason took comfort in the personal contact.

"So, Li Liu, that's a pretty name. Does it mean anything?"

She opened her eyes. "Yes, Li means Plum. The plum blossom is the national flower of China."

"What about Liu?"

"It is a very common surname. It has several different meanings, such as Willow, or Destroyer."

"Destroyer?" Jason tweaked an eyebrow. "Like a destroyer of men's hearts?"

Li sat back and closed her eyes again. "Something like that."

Jason gazed at Li, mesmerised by her looks. He

admired her flawless skin, her jet-black hair accentuating her fine facial features. He smiled as his eyes skimmed down along her slim, and what appeared to be a well-toned body. Still smiling, he closed his eyes and quickly slipped into sleep.

***

With a sudden bounce of the plane, Jason woke up. Li had a death-grip on his hand. The fasten seatbelt sign flared to life. *"Ladies and gentlemen, this is the captain. We are experiencing some significant turbulence, please return to your seats and fasten your seatbelts."*

"And this is why I don't like flying."

Jason nodded his head. "Fasten your seatbelt, it is going to be a bumpy ride."

"I never unclip my belt, just because this might happen."

His face deflated that she did not acknowledge the movie reference.

"So, you are going to Chicago. Is that home for you?"

"No, I am going to Seattle for business."

"So, what—"

13

Before Jason could finish his sentence, the sick passenger raced down the aisle.

A flight attendant held out her arms in a stop gesture. "I'm sorry, sir, the seatbelt sign is on. The captain has requested all passengers return to their seats."

"I have to... I have to..." The man started heaving, his face turning red. Leaning over, he spewed the contents of his guts onto the floor and over those within his vomitus splash zone.

Jason shook his head at the spectacle. "Jesus, why am I not surprised." He leaned toward Li. "I just hope I don't get whatever he has. They should just open the door and kick him out—parachute optional."

Li put a hand to the side of his face, stroking it. "Don't worry, I know you won't get it."

"Really? How can you be so sure? Look at him. I'm surprised that he's alive."

The smile on her face made Jason once again consider how to sneak two people into an aeroplane lavatory—and not just for curiosity sake.

"I drive a school bus and I would *definitely* get fired if I got any of the kids sick."

"Trust me, Jason, in a few days you won't even

worry that he was sick."

Li reached into her purse then pulled a small perfume sample bottle. "Here, take this." She handed the bottle to Jason. "My culture believes in homeopathic remedies. Open this on your bus and it will help the children's immune system."

Jason took the bottle, but when he started to unscrew the cap, Li put her hand on his to stop him.

"Don't open it here. There is only a small amount. You don't want to waste it."

"Ah, right." Jason tucked the bottle into his pocket.

"Ladies and gentlemen, as we start our descent..."

As the pilot droned on, Li once again held Jason's hand as they prepared to land. While the plane taxied to the terminal, Jason turned to Li.

"Will you be in Chicago long? If so, perhaps we could—"

"Jason, you have been very accommodating to me, but you are *not* my type. I do wish that the rest of your life is..."—Li paused as she searched for the words—"...without too much pain and suffering."

Jason felt like he was just slapped in the face by a fully-charged electric eel. By the time he could regather his wits, she was already halfway down the aisle to the front of the plane. He sat befuddled as he waited for most of the passengers to gather their belongings and exit the plane. He collected his carry-on from the overhead locker, then slowly made his way out. The smell of Li's jasmine-scented perfume wafted heavily in the air.

At the end of the jetway, a fully masked and gloved worker pulled Jason aside. After being declared healthy, he was given a green tag to wear on his shirt. To his right, a hazmat quarantine section was set up. Jason could see red-tagged people milling about in the area. To the left was a queue of yellow-tagged passengers, most were anxious as they waited for further health status screening.

The main hallway and concourse contained those deemed healthy. Some wore masks or scarves wrapped around their faces.

A commotion down the concourse grabbed Jason's attention. A man carrying a young boy was sprinting down through the crowd. Jason could see the man had a yellow tag but the child was red tagged. Whistles were blowing as officials raced after the man. Police officers and others were yelling a cacophony of orders "Stop! Clear the way! Stop that man! Detain him! Move, move, move!"

A cadre of masked and gloved officials flooded after the police. Anyone the fleeing man came in contact with was immediately pulled aside, their green tags removed, and escorted elsewhere.

As the man approached, Jason flattened himself against the wall. Someone kicked a suitcase into the path of the man and his son, sending them both sprawling. A nearby police officer pulled his weapon then immediately tasered the man.

"Daddy! Daddy!" the son screamed. His father twitched on the floor as other officers appeared on the scene.

Not wanting to be scooped up by law enforcement, Jason high-tailed it out of the area. The crying of the boy faded in the distance as Jason made his way through the massive airport to the next terminal. From there, he boarded a puddle-jumping regional airline for the short flight to the South Bend, Indiana airport.

While in the air, Jason pulled out the perfume sample bottle. *One small sniff is surely not going to do any harm.*

Jason unscrewed the cap, he held the bottle under his nose taking a small experimental snuff. He smiled. The perfume was the same jasmine aroma as Li's. The fragrance drifted throughout the cabin of the plane.

Gate to gate the flight was over in less than an hour with more time spent taxiing than flying. It was more like a giant roller coaster ride with only one hill. Within minutes of reaching cruising altitude, the plane started its descent into South Bend.

Jason could still smell the jasmine perfume on him. Walking through the airport he felt like he was leaving a scent trail for a hungry tiger ready to pounce.

***

An hour or so later, Jason pulled into the driveway of his rented trailer park home. His school bus sat in the empty lot beside it.

The front door squeaked as he opened it. To the left was his sparse bedroom, to the right was the kitchen-living room combination. He threw his suitcase on the bed then walked straight ahead to the john. He dropped his coat and his drawers. Sitting down, he didn't bother to close the door—because what the hell, no one else was there. When he was finished he flushed, but the bowl did not fill back up. He washed his hands to find no water came from the tap.

"Aw, fuck me hard. Not fucking again!"

Jason threw his coat back on, grabbed a flashlight, and stomped outside. He peered under the trailer. A big ball of ice clung from the frozen uninsulated water pipes. His shoulders slumped. He closed his eyes in a vain attempt to contain his boiling rage. He stood up, his chest rising and falling quickly, a snarl drove his upper lip into his nose.

"Fuck. Fuck. Fuck. Fuck. Fuck!" He slammed his fist into the side of the trailer to emphasise each utterance; the last one so hard that the front door swung open.

In a blind fury, Jason pitched his flashlight at the door. "Shut the fuck up!" he commanded.

"Hey! How about *you* shut the fuck up!" a neighbour yelled out.

"Bite me, you whore sucking bastard!" Jason retorted, throwing a defiant middle finger in the air.

Jason closed his eyes again and allowed the cold night air to cool him down and dissipate his anger. Finally feeling chilled, he went back inside. Heading straight to the refrigerator, he grabbed a cold bottle

of beer. He cracked the top then took a huge swig, downing half the bottle. With the bottle still to his lips, he stopped. The beer had skunked. He closed his eyes as he forced the liquid to stay down. But it was useless; his stomach revolted, spewing the foul brew back up.

He sighed and looked up. "Jesus fucking Christ! What other shit are you going to fucking rain down on me."

While waiting for the Almighty answer, Jason cleaned up the mess, then went to bed.

***

The next morning came far too early. Even before the roosters were awake, Jason had his bus idling. Inside his trailer, Jason searched for some antacids. He assumed that the bad beer had thrown his stomach off. Giving up on the search, he went outside and clambered into the bus.

He withdrew Li's perfume sample. He opened the bottle and inhaled deeply. He felt the exotic essence enter his lungs, and as he exhaled, a calming peace settled on him.

He put the bus into gear and started his run.

Halfway through, he pulled up to the driveway of his ex-wife. She and their two children waited at the end of the drive.

"Daddy!" Alex, his son, exclaimed when the bus door opened.

"Hey kids, come on give me a hug," he said as the kids climbed aboard.

"We can't," said Jennie, the elder of the two. She put her hand on Alex's shoulder pulling him backward.

Jason gave her a quizzical look.

"Momma said that if we do, you might touch us where you aren't supposed to."

Jason looked past his children to his ex-wife. *"Bitch,"* he mouthed at her.

She just smiled.

Jason scowled at her as he closed the door.

Alex took a deep breath. "What smells nice?"

"Do you like it, Champ? A friend gave it to me. She said it will keep you strong and healthy."

Jennie took a tentative sniff. "Ew, it smells like old people."

When they reached the school, Jason noticed that the kids did seem calmer than usual. He put the cap back on the bottle. *Maybe that jasmine was a good thing.*

During the day, Jason's stomach was still bothering him, the tickle in his throat had moved on to feeling more like eighty-grit sandpaper.

On the after-school run, he opened the bottle again. The scent of jasmine hung heavy in the air, coating the kids in its bouquet.

As he dropped off his children he said, "See you tomorrow. I love you."

At the base of the stairs, Alex turned, ran back up and hugged his father. "I love you too, Daddy."

Jason could see in Jennie's eyes that she wanted in on the hug, but she held back. "Come on, Squirt, momma is waiting for us."

Back at his trailer, Jason felt like he had gone five losing rounds with a Rock'em Sock'em Robot. He had long since developed a headache. He could hardly breathe through his clogged sinuses, sucking air through his mouth made his throat burn. His stomach was revolting, but he didn't know if it was from hunger or if it just wanted to chip in on his misery. He grabbed a banana and forced a third of it past the molten glass that now occupied his throat. He could feel the mush land in his gut, then turn around and make its way back out. He clenched his mouth tight to keep everything in. Slowly, he forced the whole lot back down.

He slumped into his favourite, comfortable—well…only—chair, closing his eyes to quench the searing fire that was raging behind his eyelids. With his head lolled back, he took several deep breaths. When he opened his eyes again it was well into the night. The streetlight outside illuminated part of the kitchen. The banana sat on the counter, tempting him to gobble the rest of it down. His stomach growled in agreement. Reaching across to grab the meagre meal, his innards thought otherwise and decided to evict the mush that already occupied his digestive tract. To ensure a proper expulsion, his body voted to send it out both possible orifices.

Jason bolted to the john, fumbling with his belt along the way. He barely had his pants down before the first explosion occurred, his ass not yet on the seat. With a sigh of relief, he closed his eyes. They then flew open; he turned his head and vomited into the shower.

***

The blaring of his alarm clock jolted Jason

awake. Somehow he had made it to bed, although he was sprawled across the top of it, a pant leg still wrapped around one ankle.

He lay there attempting to determine his condition, the heat from his face radiating back at him. Sore and aching, Jason could only assume that both Rock'em Sock'em Robots came back and worked him over even more. He licked his lips and tasted a copper tang. He scraped his eyes open then ran a hand across his nose. He didn't have to look to know that it was blood. The dull glow of his clock burned in his eyes, and squinting, he made out the time. *Fuck! Too late to call off work.*

He dragged himself off the bed, then cleaned up as best he could. Going into the bathroom, he saw the result of last night. Without running water, nothing flushed. The stench forced bile up and out. He wiped his mouth with the back of his hand.

Trudging outside, he unzipped and relieved himself, writing "Fuck" in the snow. At least that's what he thought he wrote.

He pulled himself into the bus. He sat there, trying to get the strength just to fire the bus up. His gaze fell across the perfume bottle. He took a futile sniff. Blowing snot out of his nose, he tried again.

This time the scent of jasmine flooded his head, sparking him up. With renewed energy, he started the bus, closed the door, and started his morning route.

When he pulled up to his ex-wife's house, only Jennie was there.

"Where's Alex?" he asked as she boarded.

"He's sick. He was up all night, puking."

13

MILTON FINE

P.A. O'NEIL

SEATTLE, USA

"Yeah, Barb, he went downhill fast. Tell Carl, I'm not sure when I'll be back. Tradition says bury within three-days, but I must get my parents back from Israel, and…" Milton choked his words as he talked with his secretary. "Yeah, thanks, I knew I could count on you. I'll let you know the time and date. Thanks, and you take something for that cough. Bye."

Milton reclined on the couch as the sound of distant sirens wailed outside; it was the first time since receiving the call about his grandfather that he was truly alone. Emma was picking up the kids from her parents' house—when they realised Papa Arlo wasn't going to make it, she'd asked her folks to collect them from school. It was morning now, and she wanted them home.

Milton stared at his phone as if it were foreign.

13

His stomach turned as he remembered a conversation he'd had days earlier with his grandfather about his parents 'deserting' the old man. He sighed as he fingered through his contact list but was interrupted when the front door opened.

"Is it true, Daddy? Is Papa Arlo dead?" It was Becky, dressed the same as the morning before. She rushed to his side, throwing her arms around his neck.

"Yes, Princess. He died early this morning. Didn't Mommy tell you?"

Becky pulled back. "Uh-huh, but I didn't want to believe her. I know you wouldn't lie to me, Daddy."

Emma and BJ had entered in time to hear Becky's comment. Her mouth dropped open as she wordlessly hurried out of the room.

"Becky, that wasn't a nice thing to say."

"Way to go, Becks, you hurt Mom's feelings," declared BJ as he followed his mother.

"I didn't mean to hurt her feelings, Daddy. I just meant…"

"I know, I know, but Mommy and I…we're hurting too, and…" Milton turned away from his daughter, and shielding his eyes with his hand, quietly wept.

Emma later found him sitting on their bed, in his hands the *yarmulke* he kept in his nightstand. She sat next to him. "Talk to your parents yet?"

He gently rotated the soft felt and satin skullcap in his hands. "Yeah, they're catching the first flight out of Tel Aviv. I figure they'll be here sometime late tomorrow." He looked up into her eyes, puffy and red-rimmed. "Oh, Hon, I'm sure Becky didn't mean what she said. You know the way kids are."

Emma placed her head on his shoulder. "I know, she's apologised, then we did some more crying. The one who surprised me is BJ. He gave me a hug, telling me how he would miss Papa, then he cried on my shoulder as if he as a little boy again."

With his arm over her shoulders, he pulled her close and together they sat in silence.

Outside, the distant sirens continued their annoying symphony.

***

"How was your flight, Shonna?"

"Oh, Emma, I tell you…sit on an aeroplane for fifteen-hours only to have to move my watch one hour. This jet-setting is something I'll never get used to."

The two women were in the backseat, Milton and his dad in the front, on their way to the hotel. Emma nodded all the while Shonna spoke, but instead of replying, she began to cough. She turned her head, covering her mouth with her fist.

"Are you sick, my dear?"

"No, just swallowed some air. I've got a dry tickle."

Milton's mother dug in her purse. "Here, have a *Ricola*. I never go anywhere without a few." She opened her hand, offering the loosely wrapped lozenge.

"You okay, Hon?"

"You just keep your eyes on the road, Milton. I've got it all under control."

As if prompted by Emma's words, a speeding ambulance, flagged by a police escort, cut Milton off at the intersection of Wesley Street.

"Whoa there!" Milton applied the brakes quickly. "Sorry about that, are you all okay in back!"

Emma rolled the cough drop around her mouth, swallowing the sweet liquid. "Yes, I'm fine, thank you."

"Someone's in a hurry!" chirped Milton's father, winking, "and I'm sure you are Fine." The two women looked at him, then each other, and back at him.

"Barry, what are you saying to the girl?"

"I'm saying she married a Fine, so of course she is!" The older man's laughter was infectious.

The ambulance sped through the lights as the traffic waited and watched. Milton followed the procession, slowly turning down Maple Street toward the hotel.

"You know, speaking of sick, they wouldn't let us off the plane in London to stretch our legs…said something about an influenza or virus going round."

"Hmmn, I was just there last week, everything seemed okay then." Milton turned his car into the parking zone and stopped.

"Well, it's a wonder we're not all sick, with the recycled air on planes."

"Now, Ma, you arrived safe, didn't you? In fact, now we're at the hotel I arranged for you."

After collecting their luggage and registering, Shonna whispered to Emma, "You're sure you don't need us early to help set up the reception, you know how much I want to see my grandbabies."

13

"It's okay, Shonna, the ladies' group at the synagogue are hosting the reception. As for the kids, they're not exactly babies anymore." She patted the older woman's hand. "You came from the other side of the world, take some time to let your body adjust, and we'll come get you in time for breakfast. Okay?"

The older woman nodded and followed her husband to the elevator. As the doors closed, she sighed and said, "Emma's such a thoughtful girl. Hard to believe she's not Jewish."

***

"Such a lovely service, Rabbi. I'm sure my father would've appreciated your kind words in the *hesped*." Barry Fine used both hands to vigorously shake the rabbi's.

"Well, Mr Fine, I didn't do much more than repeat the obituary. Arlo was registered as a member of our congregation, but I don't recall seeing him in the synagogue."

"His world was mostly the nursing home. I'm sure if he had been ambulatory, he would've been here more often."

As the rabbi nodded, Milton approached and

placed his hand on Barry's shoulder. "Rabbi, they're ready for a blessing of the food and, Dad, Ma's waiting for you."

The three men walked towards the synagogue's great room, which was set with long tables and chairs, and other tables holding platters of food. "Look at all the people, Milton, I didn't know Papa had so many friends."

"He didn't, Dad, at least not from this congregation."

Barry raised his eyebrow. "But all the *aveilim* at the *levaya*?"

"Most of the mourners were provided by the local *Chevra Kadisha* for a modest donation. The mortuary we used specialised in Jewish ceremonies following rabbinic law which included *shmira* in their services."

"You mean you didn't sit with him or participate in purifying his body?"

Milton gently pulled his father aside and lowered his voice. "Dad, outside of a few people from the nursing home, he didn't have anyone other than us."

Looking around the room, Barry frowned and wondered who had been paid to be there. His

13

thoughts were interrupted by the sound of the rabbi's welcome and blessing of the food.

***

"You know, Mrs Fine, even though I didn't understand much of what was being said, I don't think I've ever seen a lovelier ceremony." Emma's mother blushed and quickly changed the subject. "You know, we sent flowers, but I didn't see them at the service or the graveside."

Emma turned her head and coughed into her elbow.

"It's because, Mrs Fleming, we don't have flowers at our funerals." Shonna's tone was mild, but when the other woman's face fell, she added, "But if those are them over by the guest book, they're lovely."

Mrs Fleming's face brightened. "Oh yes, there they are." Unsure what to say next, she tipped her head and smiled when a portly man approached, beads of perspiration on his forehead, with one hand extended, the other holding a hat.

"Ladies, I hope I'm not intruding?"

Emma's voice cracked. "Mr Porn, thank you for

coming. You remember my mother-in-law, and this is my mother, Mrs Fleming."

His clammy hand shook theirs in turn. "I just wanted to say how much we, myself especially, will miss Arlo. He was quite a character."

"Thank you. Yes, Papa Arlo's passing has affected all of us deeply."

"Well, if you ladies will excuse me. I need to round up staff and residents who came with me in the home van."

"Must you leave so soon?"

"Yes, Mrs Fleming, we have a few residents who aren't doing too well, they're so fragile you know. I want to return to check on them before it gets too late." He nodded, putting on his Hamburg and tipping it in their direction. "Ladies."

"He seems like a nice fellow. Arlo must've been happy there."

Emma nodded as she watched him move on towards a man in a wheelchair. "He always seemed to be, but I wonder?"

"Wonder what, dear?"

"I don't know, Mom—did they do all they could before sending him to the hospital. I mean, he went so fast."

"Well, Emma"—Shonna picked up her hand and gently patted it—"Arlo was very old, and when our time comes…"

***

"How come you're not dressed for work, Daddy?" Becky rose to clear her bowl from the breakfast table as the soft concerto interlude playing on the radio went on unnoticed.

Milton coughed and put down his coffee. "You remember, Princess, I am sitting *shiva* for a week after the burial. It's a way for me to honour my grandfather's death."

She stood close and stroked his cheek. "Will you shave then, Daddy?"

"Yes, I promise. Now, give me some sugar then brush your teeth."

She placed a sweetened kiss on his lips before skipping away.

"I'll be glad when you're through mourning; those clothes are going to smell something fierce come Saturday." Emma walked in with a full hamper, passing through to the laundry room, coughing all the way.

"Hey, at least I agreed to sponge bathe, I get credit for that?" Her laughter was interrupted by more coughing, but his attention was now on his son, as he walked into the room wearing a dress shirt and tie.

"Morning, Dad." BJ poured cereal, never taking his eyes off the bowl. "Hey, Mom, can I have a banana with my breakfast?"

"It's, 'may I have a banana,' and there's some on the counter," she called from the other room over the drone of the radio.

Milton stifled another cough as he watched BJ help himself to the fruit and a knife from the butcher block, then slice it over his cereal before adding milk. "You look nice today, son, something special happening at school?"

BJ ate with vigour, but between bites managed a conversation. "Wrestling meet today…team dresses up…shows school spirit. Say, do we have any face masks?"

Emma brought an empty cup and full coffee pot to the table. She topped off Milton's cup, filled hers, and sat down. "Don't eat so fast, you'll choke, and why would we want face masks?"

BJ downed a glass of orange juice. "You'll need

them if you want to go to the meet this afternoon. It's to stop the spread."

His parents looked at each other and sighed.

"School policy now!" B.J added and shrugged.

"I can't, son, rabbinic law won't let me."

BJ nodded. "Yeah, rabbinic law."

Emma cleared her throat and smiled. "I'll be there for sure. Flu or no flu. I'll just dope myself up with a bunch of cough syrup and see what I can find." She got up to put her arm over his shoulders. "Hey, I'll even bring Becks so she can yell for me."

"That's okay, don't put yourself out if you're sick." He shrugged off her embrace and left.

***

"Don't you have homework, Princess?" Milton found Becky, kneeling before the coffee table, carefully colouring within the lines of the printed sheet of paper.

"This is my homework, Daddy. This is what the substitute gave us to do."

Milton craned his neck to look over her shoulder as he sat. "Substitute, huh, I'd have thought your teacher would've left more work for the class to do?"

Never looking up, she replied, "She did, but we finished it yesterday."

"Yesterday, how long has she been sick?"

Satisfied, she picked up her artwork and offered it for inspection. "Do you think she'll like it, Daddy? It's a Get Well Soon card. She's been sick all week and won't be there tomorrow either. The substitute says Mrs Bree has gone to the hospital."

"Really? She must be really sick then…" He handed the sheet back just as a muffled buzzing came from his pocket. "Hmmn, I need to get this."

"I thought you couldn't use the phone until after sunset."

"Yeah, Sweetie, but I have to take this one. It's your *bubbie*." He stood and walked away. "Hey, Ma, what's up?"

"Hi, Bubbie Shonna, it's Becky!"

Milton turned and mimed a shush. "Yeah, Ma, that was Becky—Bubbie says hello, now quiet—yeah, Ma, I'm here.

"Uh-huh, does the doctor think it's serious? Do you want me to fly out? Yeah, I know I'm still sitting shiva, but if you need me? Okay, thanks for calling—remember, just call if you want me to come."

He pocketed his phone and looked at his

daughter. "Princess, it's not polite shouting when someone's on the phone."

"Is *Zayde* Barry sick, Daddy… Like Mrs Bree?"

"Yes, and it's even more impolite to listen in on phone calls."

"Was that you on the phone, Milt?" Emma walked in; her arms wrapped around her body in a deep hug, her face was pale. "I thought you weren't supposed to use the phone?"

"It was Ma, so you know, she says Dad's in the hospital. They think it's pneumonia— Hey, you don't look so good yourself."

"I'm so cold, my muscles are all cramped up."

He put his arms around her and guided her to the couch. "You're burning with fever; want me to get something?"

"Uh, yeah, some aspirin and a blanket sound nice."

"Right away. Becky move your things, let Mommy have some space." He returned with the needed items. "Anything else?"

"Yeah, since you've broken shiva, would you make the kids' dinner."

X-DAY +10

THE RAGE

ERICA SCHAEF

The cubicle walls were a pale, sickly yellow. Max had never noticed just how dull the office's interior was, until now. He was the only one left working.

Fluorescent lights buzzed above him, illuminating his sun-starved skin. He blinked up at them.

Sneeze. His heart skipped. It was probably nothing; springtime allergies; back to work. Cough. Max's bronchioles constricted. His skin prickled; hot and cold all at once. If he could only get outside for a moment, away from the stagnant office air…

Beyond, the corridors held no doors.

TESTING COMPLETE. VACCINE FAILED. RAT TWENTY, "MAX," SYMPTOMATIC FROM VIRUS EXPOSURE.

Esmir Milavić, an editor at Bosnia's N1 TV:
The vice-president is wearing a mask, while the president doesn't; some staffers wear them, some don't. Everybody acts as they please. As time passes, White House begins to look more and more like the Balkans.

JASON WELLS

BRIAN MACGOWAN

SOUTH BEND, INDIANA, USA

Blurry-eyed Jason stared at the talking-heads on the TV that blared in the medical clinic's waiting room. He knew that they were saying something, but his mental dexterity was barely working above minimum capacity. When asked his birthday upon check-in, Jason had to squint his eyes and concentrate on the answer. He got it right on the third try, or at least close enough for the almost patient receptionist to match him up in the database.

If Jason had been able to fire up a few more synapses, he would have learned that the talking-heads were mentioning a suspected coronavirus outbreak in Seattle, possibly linked to a flight from Chicago. Officially, the health department was still attempting to identify the strain, which had similar characteristics to Covid-20. They were denying rumours that this was a virus cooked up in a Chinese

13

biological lab.

Jason suspected that those bloody battling robots that had whooped him the other day had also brought along a couple of hungry, hungry hippos. He no longer felt like shit, now he felt like...warm shit that had been sat festering on the sidewalk on a hot summer day. He took a sniff. Oh God, he smelled like it too.

If he closed his eyes for too long, they would seal themselves shut. If he kept them open, it felt like molten sand was blasting them. A migraine was pulling all conscious thought from his brain. His nostrils were caked with blood. The utter rawness of his throat prevented him from eating or drinking. If he could eat, his stomach would evacuate within minutes. His chest hurt, breathing was limited to short half-breaths. Not even a feral cat would have dragged his sorry ass inside.

Jason heard his name called. He sat there as he mentally built up a head of steam. Pushing himself out of the chair, he stood there while he reoriented his balance. Looking up, he saw his cousin, Amy. At least he thought it was her; the mask and gloves made it hard to tell, but the boobs looked about right.

He shambled over to her. "Hi, Ames. I caught a

think I cold." Jason screwed his face up. "No, I..." He shook his head. "You...doctor."

Amy waved a nurse over. "Jason, this is Sherry. Go with her. I'll be right there."

Jason puppy-dogged behind Sherry as she led him down the hall to an examination room.

Smiling, Amy quickly made her way through the waiting area to the front door. There, she flipped the lock in place. At the check-in desk, she quietly spoke to the receptionist before turning to address the rest of the waiting room.

"Attention, everyone. For those who don't know me, I am Doctor Amy Fraser, I thank you for your patience. We have a suspected Covid-20 patient. I need to inform you that, in accordance with state health regulations, we have locked down the practice. No one may leave until they are cleared by the State Health Officials."

A ruckus erupted. People were shouting about their rights; how long will they be detained; that it was unconstitutional; and just general mayhem.

"I will be examining the patient in a few moments. We will need to wait for a courier to retrieve the test samples, after that it will be at least twelve hours before the results are back."

13

Lucas Hostetler stood up. "Twelve hours! I can't stick around for twelve hours. I got hogs to feed."

"I'm sorry, Lucas, but there is nothing that I can do to speed things up. Sara and the boys will just have to take care of the hogs."

"Well, I can do something about it. I'm leaving."

The thing about small towns is that everything is close by, including the police department. By the time Lucas made it to the door, one of Sheriff Johnson's deputies was standing outside.

Lucas yelled through the door. "Hey, Jimmy. I need to get home."

Deputy Jimmy just shook his head.

Amy left the din of the waiting area to the semi-quiet of the examination rooms. She tapped lightly on one of the doors then entered. Jason was lying on the examination table, his eyes closed, his breathing raspy.

She gave him a gentle shake. "Hey Jason, wake up."

Jason stirred. He tried to smile. "Hey, Ames. Are we going to play doctor?"

"Yeah, Jase." She gave him a quick visual assessment. "This may not sound overly professional. What the Hell happened to you?"

"Becca divorced me."

"Besides that."

Jason felt like his brain was plummeting into a hole. "I smelled jasmine, but I still got sick."

"When did you first notice that you were sick."

"Alex got sick too."

"I've seen Alex. We don't know what he has but it's not Covid-20. I need to know: when did *you* get sick?"

He scrunched his face up in thought. "After I got back."

"When did you get back?"

"Before I got sick," Jason said as if that was the most logical response to the question.

Amy let out an exasperated breath. "How many days ago?"

"Chicago."

"Never mind, I'll get Ed or one of his deputies to backtrack you."

She moved to a cabinet. "But first I need to test you for Covid-20. This is just like a whooping cough test. A swab up your nasal cavity, a throat culture, and spit into a cup."

Jason started to pull down his zipper.

"No! Spit, not pee. We may take a urine sample

13

later, but for now, we just need saliva."

After collecting the specimens, she sealed them in a biohazard bag. "The courier will be here soon. Sherry will be back to start you on an IV."

"Ames..." Jason mumbled. "I love you."

Amy paused at the door. "And I love you too. We'll get you feeling better. Get some rest."

Jason couldn't keep his eyes from rolling back.

Outside in the hall, Amy placed the sample into yet another biohazard bag, ensuring that she did not touch the outer bag. Then she removed her gloves and mask, placing them in a biohazard disposal bin. After washing her hands, she went to the back door to wait. When the courier arrived, they placed an open container outside the door before stepping away. Amy exited the clinic and dropped the specimen into the container. When she was back inside, the courier sealed the container and placed it into the back of his unmarked van.

***

As the hours slipped past, Amy and the nurse practitioners worked their way through the people at the clinic. Most of the patients she saw were school-aged children. Many of them exhibited the same symptoms as Jason, but not nearly as severe.

Amy and the staff gathered up a dozen or more specimens to be tested, with the courier arriving every few hours.

Jason's mind fluttered back into existence. He was mildly surprised that he could feel even worse. The elephant on his chest was keeping his breathing short and painful. His stomach had moved past revolting to a full-blown coup d'état.

As he lay there, he sensed that someone else was in the room. With an extreme amount of concentration, he brought a hand to his face and forced one eye open. He looked around expecting to see Amy or Sherry. He closed his eye again. His brain protested the amount of concentration that Jason was forcing it to do. Jason was sure that there was someone in the room.

"Whooo..." he croaked.

He opened an eye again, the other somewhat obeyed. Movement at the corner of his eye caught his attention. Jason used his hand to force his neck to turn. In the chair, swinging his feet, sat Alex.

Jason smiled. "Where's Jennie?"

"She's not here, but Grandma is."

13

Jason's mind tumbled, Alex had never met either of his grandmothers. A quiet rap on the door broke his concentration.

Amy quietly entered the room. She checked his IV and temperature then listened to his heart and lungs.

"Jace? Can you hear me?"

"Ames...where...Alex?"

"We're trying to get you a hospital bed. But everywhere is swamped. As soon as one opens up..."

"Alex..."

Utter sadness crossed Amy's face. "Jason, Alex is..."

Jason pulled in a sharp breath, his eyes rolled back, then his chest fell.

Amy quickly put her stethoscope on his chest listening to his heart.

She stood up and gazed down on his body. She wanted to wipe her eyes but couldn't. With blurred vision, she fled from the room. Outside, she stripped her gloves off. When the waste bin refused to cooperate, she threw the gloves at it. With her back to the wall, she rubbed the tears from her eyes.

Sherry came up and put a comforting hand on her shoulder. "Were you able to tell him about

Alex?"

Wiping away more tears, Amy just shook her head.

Sherry handed Amy a tissue. "Well, maybe that was for the best."

The death of one man doesn't mean that the world stops rotating. Life simply goes on.

The following day, the clinic was released from lockdown. Most of the people got to go home, a lucky few were sent to the hospital, if you could consider being so critically ill that you take priority over those who are *just* sick, lucky. Other patients in the clinic were forced to remain there until a hospital bed opened up—usually, beds only became available because someone had died.

Amy sat in the staff lounge, her eyes closed, head resting in her hand. She just wanted a few minutes of rest. She half-listened to the TV news report as it droned on about how another outbreak of an unidentified strain of the COVID-20 virus had erupted. The federal government continued their denial that this was a deliberate biological attack. But rather, that the CDC and others were working desperately to identify the strain that mutated when it reached the United States.

13

Hospitals, Urgent Care centres, medical clinics, nursing homes, and funeral parlours were being overwhelmed. Ambulance, EMTs, 911 operators were operating beyond exhaustion. The death toll was shooting upwards. Amy was convinced that it was the same damn virus that took Jason, his son Alex, another forty kids in his school, plus teachers, parents, and grandparents.

A light knocking on the door took Amy out of her thoughts.

"Doctor Fraser, there are two men here to see you."

At first, Amy didn't move, she didn't even open her eyes. She took a deep breath and sighed. "If they are reporters, tell them 'No Comment.' If they complain, send them to the mayor or the sheriff. If they are health officials, I'm working on the damn report and they'll get it when I'm done. If they are family of someone who died here...give me five minutes."

The serious tone of an unfamiliar man's voice made her eyes fly open. "Doctor Fraser, I am FBI Special Agent McLaughlin and this is Special Agent Stone. We need to talk to you about Jason Wells."

Amy sat up. Standing just inside the door was a

tall, well built, dark-haired, chiselled face man. If you had asked the good doctor what a stereotypical FBI Special Agent looked like, he would have been the perfect candidate. If you had asked, "What does a wall with feet look like?" she would have pointed to the aptly named Special Agent Stone. His massive frame filled the open doorway, his bald pate barely missed the header of the doorframe. Twinning that day, they both wore black shoes, black pants, white shirts with a dark blue tie; although McLaughlin's tie had flecks of grey. In case you got them confused with Mormon Missionaries, they both wore dark blue nylon jackets with FBI emblazoned in bright yellow.

"How may I help you, gentlemen?"

"We realise that you treated Mr Wells prior to his death. That you sent off a test that came back as negative for COVID-20."

"That is true. He exhibited all of the symptoms of the disease." Amy paused. "Did I miss something?"

McLaughlin walked forward, he indicated toward an empty chair by the table. "May I?"

Amy nodded.

McLaughlin took a seat. He produced a field notebook from his jacket and flipped it open. Stone stayed rooted in place, blocking the door.

"I am sure that you are aware of this unidentified COVID-20 strain."

"Is that what this is about? Was Jason infected with that strain."

"What we are about to discuss cannot leave this room. You are to talk to no one about this. Do you understand, Doctor Fraser?"

"Certainly."

"Not even to your husband."

"What exactly is this about?" She paused. "Was Jason in some sort of trouble? Am *I* being blamed for his death?"

The agent held up a hand. "I'm sure that you did your best to treat him." McLaughlin skipped back a few pages in his book. "It is true that Mr Wells did not have the strain of COVID-20 that is encompassing the world."

Amy's eyes widened.

McLaughlin continued. "We believe he had a weaponised version of COVID-20. This is the *unknown* strain that the news has been reporting on."

"Weaponised? I thought that was impossible."

"Yes, well, we thought so too. Until it showed up in Seattle, to some extent O'Hare, a commuter flight that landed in South Bend, and right here in Elkhart County. Your very own mini-epicentre."

"And what? You think that Jason had something to do with this?"

"That's what we are trying to determine."

"That's impossible. He was a farmer and a school bus driver."

"Mr Wells was recently out of the country. We think—"

"You think that he brought this..."—Amy waved her hand in the air—"...this weaponised version in with him? You said yourself that people in Chicago and South Bend are exhibiting the same symptoms. It is more likely that he was infected there."

"We spoke to his supervisor at the school. Mr Wells was instructed to take some time off or lose his position."

"Jason had a hard time with the divorce. His ex-wife took him for all she could."

"Yes, the divorce. His wife got sole custody of their children. He was forced to sell his farm."

Amy's eyes flared. "Our grandfather farmed that land, and so did his father and his father." She leaned toward McLaughlin, stabbing her finger on the table. "She had no right to steal that land. The cousins

13

begged her to sell it to us. To keep the farm in the family. But to spite us all, she sold it to some big Idaho corporation."

McLaughlin half-smiled. "I see where your cousin got his temper."

She brought her anger into check. "Are we done?"

"No, Doctor Fraser, we are not done." He consulted his notebook again. "Mr Wells was scheduled to fly out of Heathrow to O'Hare, but at the last minute, he changed his flight to Reykjavik and then onto O'Hare. Do you know why he would make such a change? It would seem strange that, instead of taking a direct flight, he would choose to go so far out of his way."

Amy threw up her hands. "I don't know. Maybe Iceland was on his bucket list."

"We think he did that in order to meet up with a co-conspirator."

"So, now it's a conspiracy." She rolled her eyes, then placed her hands on the table. "I have patients to tend to. Good day, gentlemen." Getting up, she strode purposively to the door, only to find it still blocked by an immovable Stone wall.

"Please sit down, Doctor. We won't be much

longer," McLaughlin called after her.

She looked Special Agent Stone in the eyes. He flicked up one eyebrow. With a huff, she turned and sat down again.

McLaughlin pulled up a photo of Li Liu on his phone. "We believe he changed his schedule to meet this woman. Witnesses on the flight reported seeing the two holding hands and possibly being intimate."

Amy shook her head. "I don't know anything about her."

"She is a former captain in the Chinese military. Her specialty...biologics."

"So you think that Jason did what? That he was a traitor? That he was actually working for the Chinese?" She was incredulous.

"In a nutshell, yes. Jason was mad, we know that from speaking to people he visited in England. That he was constantly ranting on about how he got screwed over in the divorce. How he lost the kids and the farm. How he wished that his ex-wife was dead."

Amy scoffed. "Our Brit cousins are all idiots. What the Hell do they know?"

McLaughlin brought up another photo. This time the perfume sample bottle as it sat on the dash of Jason's bus.

"Do you recognise this, Doctor?"

She shook her head. "No, what is it?"

"This is a bottle of perfume that we found on the bus that Jason drove."

"So he liked perfume. Is that a crime?"

"It is when it is the same type of perfume and bottle that we found on the body of the dead Chinese woman. When the contents were tested, guess what we found?"

Amy's eyes opened wide in disbelief.

"We found the weaponised COVID-20 strain."

"There's got to be a mistake. You're saying that Jason purposely spread the disease?" Amy frantically shook her head. "No, no, no. That is *not* possible."

McLaughlin shrugged. "Believe what you want but that's the evidence. We are still investigating how he was contacted. But we have concluded that Jason, despondent over the loss of his children and family farm, went into an 'If he can't have it, then no one can' state of mind."

"What? That he purposefully administered the infection to his children? He loved those kids."

"His ex-wife made a statement that she saw him hold the perfume bottle under their noses. He left the bottle open on the bus for maximum effectiveness. He wanted to infect as many people as possible, starting with children. The innocent children on his bus spread it throughout their school and homes.

"Neighbours reported that the night before he was drunk, they witnessed him slamming his fist into the side of his trailer, practically howling at the moon. He hated this community and he wanted to take as many with him to the grave as possible."

Amy put a hand to her forehead. "No, this is wrong, this is all wrong." She closed her eyes as she thought back on Jason. "Why are you telling me this?"

McLaughlin leaned forward. "We have already seized your medical records. We are simply tying up loose ends. I will remind you that you are not to speak of this. We cannot allow the American public to know that there is a weaponised version of the disease. If they did, there would be mass panic and chaos. For now, it remains an unknown strain. We also cannot allow China to know that we know." He looked her straight in the eyes. "It's for your own good, or else..." He let the threat hang in the air like the Sword of Damocles.

He pushed back his chair and stood. "*Now,*

Doctor, we are done."

Sam the Coder

JACOB BAUGHER

SECRET GVERNMENT FACILITY, CHINA

"Even darkness must pass." He'd whispered those words to his daughter while he boarded the plane from Perth to Wuhan, not knowing what he was walking into. Not knowing he'd be the one to help the darkness spread. Now, Samuel "The Coder" Ashley ran from the darkness of the lab, into the darkness of the tunnel, still in shock from the sudden reversal of his mission. The tape recorder hadn't been taken from him, and as far as he could tell, it was still going strong. Sure, the journalist wouldn't be getting it any time soon, but it was still recording every hitch in his step, every gasping breath of dank tunnel air.

Sam's life was measured in the bare, flickering light bulbs hanging from the tunnel ceiling. He didn't know why the statesman had saved him. He didn't even know the statesman's name, just that he was a

tubby American that reminded him of a cross between Donald "The Donald" Trump and Ted "The Zodiac Killer" Cruz.

"Even darkness must pass," he whispered to himself, in between gasping breaths and the crunch of gravel underfoot. Some small part of him knew better, knew that sometimes, the darkness *did* win and consumed vast swaths of humanity under its suffocating blanket. Katrina, the Boxing Day tsunamis, the September 11th attacks: darkness had passed for the survivors, the majority of the human race, but not for the victims, who lay in the mud swaddled by its crushing weight. But Sam knew that this particular darkness was different for him, because in this instance, Sam had *been* the darkness. He wasn't fool enough to think that God or the universe had allowed him a second chance at life. If anything, it was the devil, if you believed in that kind of thing.

"Hey!" he gasped and increased his cadence to draw even to Zodiac-Killer-Donald-Trump. "Where are we going?"

The statesman's gut flapped noisily against his gun belt. *How was he keeping up this pace?* Sam wondered.

"Hangar," came the breathless reply, accompanied by a stench of rotten onions and cheeseburger indigestion. "Up ahead."

The tunnel, which had been driving more or less into the earth at a straight line, suddenly twisted to one side and opened up on a hangar that looked, oddly, like a thawed-out version of the Rebel Base's Hoth map in the Star Wars Battlefront II PlayStation 2 game he had played as a boy. Several side tunnels opened up onto the hangar, its metallic floor and ceiling almost lost in the darkness above. Floor lights blazed to life at regular intervals and illuminated a walkway. At one end, the hangar was open to the air, and a cool breeze played across his face, blowing in from the darkness outside.

And at the end of the hangar stood a giant plane with four propellers hanging beneath its wings—an American military C-130.

And that's when the soldiers caught up with them, emerging from a tunnel opposite, across the hangar. Bullets tore into the boxes and crates around them; slammed into the far wall. Sam ducked to the ground.

"What the fuck are you doing!" the statesman yelled. "Get the fuck up and get in the goddamn

13

plane!"

He scrambled to his feet and sprinted towards it, zigzagging around crates and refuse. He reached the metallic grey exterior of the C-130 and clambered inside through the rear hatch. The statesman, somehow, had beaten him there. He slammed his hand down on a button and the rear doors started closing *much* too slowly for Sam's liking. The statesman cursed, kicked the lid off one of the many crates that littered the floor, and withdrew a rifle and a magazine. He slammed the magazine home and opened fire on the troops until the doors shut and the only sounds were the pings of bullets glancing off metal.

The statesman cleared the chamber and tossed the weapon back into the crate, then sprinted for the cockpit.

"Do you know how to fly this thing?" Sam screamed, following the statesman into the cockpit. There seemed to be an awful lot of non-bullet proof glass in here.

"In theory," the statesman yelled back. He strapped himself into the pilot's seat. Through the cockpit window, Sam could see the men getting closer, guns trained on the plane. He thought he could almost make out the flag patches on the shoulders of their uniforms in the dim light.

The plane's engines roared to life, an almost sub-audible rumble in Sam's ears, a vibration he felt in his very bones, and the C-130 started its slow, limping way down the runway, the way all taxiing planes seemed to. The sounds of the world outside had been cut off when the cargo door closed, but through the cockpit windows, Sam could see the soldiers swivel their guns to track the plane, muzzles flashing silently.

He lurched backward in his seat as the roar became thunder and the thunder became a cacophony.

Then the soldiers went from a Very Imminent Threat, to tiny pinpricks in the background, to gone all together as the earth dropped away and they flew off into the night.

The statesman let out a breath, turned to Sam, and stuck out a hand. "Special Agent Ross Cerda." Sam grasped his hand and pumped it, noticing for the first time a faint scar on the statesman's wrist in the shape of two butterflies interwoven into the biohazard symbol.

"Excuse me," the statesman said, and reached

under his shirt. There were two clicks and the potbelly flopped away from his stomach. Unbuckling another strap around his waist, he pulled it off and set it on the floor. "I hated that fucking thing."

***

They were flying above London, spiralling down, down, down, waiting for their turn to access the landing strip. Apparently, the statesman's influence had run out somewhere over Belarus. They'd had one in-air refuelling and had flown in complete silence for almost 14 hours at 28,000 feet. Sam's legs were cramped, and the world at 28,000 feet is significantly less interesting after the first three hours of flight. He spoke for the first time in about ten hours, his voice warbling over the speakers.

"So," he said in a tone that he hoped was conversational. "What the fuck is going on?"

A rush of static came that he assumed was a sigh, and then the statesman started speaking.

"In 2017, the United States Government started a coalition of scientists, philosophers, economists, and multi-billionaires to help 'Further the

Advancement of American Enterprise.'" Sam could almost hear the air quotes as he said the words. "You probably remember all the China Bogeyman talk?"

"Of course. *ChaiNya*," Sam said in his best Trump voice.

"Partially. We never had any direct contact with Donald Trump. Pelosi was my contact, but I'm sure there were others. The Coalition wanted something that would mobilise the American public against China—to cut a long story short, our scientists were able to infect a pangolin and drop it in the Wuhan Wet Market in 2018, but when COVID-18 first transmitted to humans, it was too impotent to affect any real change, so we tried again in 2019, with marginal success. Then, one insufferable jackass had an idea: nanobots and forced immunosuppression to increase the infection rate and decrease the probability of a recovery. That's where you, and COVID-20, came in."

Sam nodded, resisted the urge to dig in his pocket for the tape recorder to make sure it was on. "Yeah, I knew most of that. But,"—he gestured to the C-130—"this is an American military plane. What about the escape? The refuelling? That doesn't seem to be in the Coalition agenda." The words

13

"Deep State" floated around some corner of his mind.

"What?" A wry tone crept into the statesman's voice. "You think that everyone in the Coalition for the Furthering of the Advancement of American Enterprise just sat back and let the politicians ruin the entire world?"

The words hung in the air for a moment. "So, you're the resistance?" Sam asked.

The statesman laughed. "No. We're the cure."

"The cure?"

"This aircraft is carrying the only vaccine known to man for COVID-19 and COVID-20. We've been working on a prototype for some time, ever since El Trumpo and his cronies had the idea to blame China for the virus and create a superspreader. All we have to do is deliver it to the lab in London."

"London? Wouldn't an American lab—"

"The American healthcare system is absolute utter shit. You really wanna consign the fate of the entire world to pharma-bros?"

"Good point there. So, we're over London?"

"London."

And just like that, air traffic control came over the helmet speaker.

"You are cleared for approach on runway 3."

"Copy that," the statesman said.

They started their descent. London drew closer and closer outside the cockpit window as the statesman guided them down onto the runway. Finally, rough ground rumbled under the plane's wheels, and he let himself breathe again. He hated flying. Even the exercise with passenger-13, where he could see the entirety of the flight on the viewscreen, including the world dropping away outside the small window on the plane, had given him flight anxiety. And as the plane decelerated in that violent-ass way that all planes do, he breathed a bit easier.

That is, until he saw their welcome party.

Soldiers were lined up on the runway—a lot of soldiers, complete with an anti-aircraft gun and heavy weaponry. If the statesman saw them, he gave no indication of alarm. The plane finished its deceleration and started taxiing towards the troops. From this distance, Sam could just make out two different flags—American and the Union Jack.

"I didn't fucking sign up for this," Sam breathed out in a hiss.

"Join the club," the statesman said.

The comm crackled in the cockpit. Sam held it up to his ear as the air traffic controller's voice cut through the static.

"This plane is the property of the United States Government. Prepare to be boarded."

Sam glanced at the statesman. "What do we do?"

The man just stared straight ahead at the approaching soldiers, the aircraft gun levelled at the plane, the setting sun beyond thick cloud cover, just visible at the far end of the runway.

"Do you still have that pistol I gave you when we left?"

Sam nodded and withdrew it from the front of his jeans where he had stored it just like you weren't supposed to.

"Give it here."

He hesitated, then handed the weapon over. The statesman unbuckled himself from the pilot's chair and opened the cockpit door. He beckoned to Sam with the gun. "Sit on the floor over there. Put your hands over your head."

Sam did as he was told. The statesman produced several zip ties from his back pocket and secured Sam's hands to a metal loop in the wall so they were bent uncomfortably.

"Sorry, man, you seemed like a decent sort. Tell them nothing."

The statesman shot him in the leg and pressed an acrid-smelling cloth against his nose. The world blurred, spun, but out of the corner of his eye, he saw the statesman withdraw a small needle and drive it into Sam's arm. Then, everything went black.

***

He woke to a searing pain in his leg, a trickle of warm blood, and the sound of gunfire. Sam jerked, strained against his bindings, then went still as he took in his surroundings. An American soldier had a rifle that was Very Large And Incredibly Close pressed up against his cheek while another soldier inserted a swab into his mouth, dropped it into a vial and swirled it around. Behind them, more soldiers had piled onto the plane and were moving down the aisles. The statesman lay in a pool of blood, propped up against the cabin door, which was slightly ajar. His sightless eyes stared at Sam. *Tell them nothing.* The man's words echoed in his brain.

"It's positive for COVID-19 and COVID-20," the soldier said.

13

"Fuck," swore the other, and retreated a few steps back.

"You're already infected, Russell," said the female soldier. "No point in trying to stay away. She turned back to Sam.

"What's your name?" she asked.

Tell them nothing.

"Sam," he said, without hesitation. He wasn't going to be a hero.

"The Coder." It was a statement, not a question. He looked at her in surprise. "We have orders to process you and take you to the field hospital," she said. She glanced back to the statesman. "Did he tell you anything?"

Sam shook his head. The soldier leaned forwards and offered him her hand. "Can you walk?" On her wrist was the same scar the statesman had, two intertwined butterflies superimposed over the biohazard symbol. He tried to look like he hadn't noticed.

"I've been shot."

She snorted. "Everyone on this plane has been shot at one time or another. Come on." She handed him a mask. "Put this on. We're going to get you out of here." *Tell them nothing.*

13

ERIN

LANNAH MARSHALL

LONDON, UK

Erin's stomach had long grown accustomed to Chinese food. Not long after arriving on the mainland, she decided to stop asking what was being offered. She was more afraid of breaking etiquette and upsetting her superiors than she was about eating something questionable. The long-term food experiment had left Shepherd's Pie tasting flat in her mouth.

"How long have you lived here?" Erin asked Paula as she helped put away the dishes.

"My whole life."

"In this house?"

"Oh, heaven's no!" Paula laughed. "On this street."

"Ah." Erin stepped back to check on Jian in the lounge.

Paula coughed and rolled her shoulders. "You

327

know, I am awfully tired.”

“Are you sure you’re okay having a baby in the house?” Erin took another look at her son. He was stirring, but not awake. “He’s going to scream soon.”

“I sleep like a log,” said Paula. Another cough. “How about we leave the rest ‘til morning. Have a kip, maybe? We’ll be fine.”

No sooner had Paula headed to bed, coughing her way up the stairs, Jian let rip and tested his vocals in the new setting. Erin’s whole body rippled with tremors. There was nothing more nauseating than his cries of pain.

Moira joined her, making sure to let Erin see the hearing aid get turned off.

They took turns sharing the load of the writhing infant, and Erin’s whole body started to ache before the night had finished setting in.

Jian’s screams split the night, and Erin could picture the other inhabitants of the estate cursing each and every moment of his existence. He was a small thing, awkward and doughy to hold, but there had been nothing else in the world since he was born.

Not even sleep.

“He’s calming down now,” said Moira, eventually. “His cries are getting quieter.”

The only evidence of this was Erin being able to hear anything else at all.

"I'm going to head to bed."

"Goodnight," said Erin. "Thank you…for everything!"

Moira kissed Jian's forehead and waved as she disappeared up the stairs. Erin and Jian were alone, at last. He cried and hiccoughed and wriggled as she tried to leave him to self-soothe. He was restless.

Her skin was boiling, and her brain was water-logged. "Please sleep," she whispered. "Please."

She didn't know if he settled, as she drifted off herself, her eyes sore and jet-lagged, his screams fading…

Until another burrowed in.

Erin startled. Her body, sweat-drenched and shaking, groaned and creaked as she sat upright. Someone was screaming, and it was disturbing Jian in his make-shift cot. Erin blinked and sunlight burnt through her skull. She stumbled off the sofa and staggered towards the stairs.

"Moira?"

"Help me!" Moira was wailing; a pained, guttural cry.

Erin ran up the stairs, stumbling and fumbling

with numb and aching fingers. She burst into the nearest bedroom and staggered, dizzy with breathlessness and fatigue.

Moira was kneeling on the bed, shaking Paula who hung limp in her arms. Moira's hands cupped Paula's face, her forehead pressed against Paula's crown of silver hair. Moira shook. Erin stepped forward and her body lurched as something felt off…wrong. Paula unmoving, her bedding stained black with blood, her face awash with red smears.

When Moira looked up, Erin staggered back.

Moira's face dripped with blood, her cheeks purpled and bruised.

"What's going on?" someone cried as they burst into the room. Shoving Erin aside as they ran over to Moira, even they stopped at the sight.

***

Erin's body shook.

Paramedics came and went. They took Moira with them. Under the respirator, her face was pale and bruised. Her curls of white hair seemed flat and grey. Her breath was staggered, ever whispering, "Paula…"

"You're in shock," said the paramedic.

Erin didn't reply. Her head felt countries away, high in the mountains of Mulanshan, if a little drunk.

"We've been seeing a few cases like this these last few hours." The paramedic continued through his bag, unaware that Erin felt miles away. "If you find yourself having any respiratory problems—problems with your breathing—or persistent nosebleeds, please contact 111."

Erin's eyes fell on her son. "Was she in pain?"

"Sorry?" The paramedic leant to the side to make eye contact.

"Paula…when she died…was she in pain?"

The paramedic's eyes softened.

Erin's tongue tingled, as though allergic to the daft question that left her lips. "You don't know. She was coughing a lot last night." Erin pressed the bridge of her nose as a tension headache sprouted across the back of her eyes. "Moira is sick too. Do you think this is contagious? What about my son? He cries a lot, in the evenings. He never settles. He practically passes out from the lack of air—."

"Hush." The paramedic's voice was warm, comforting, experienced. "I will give him a look over."

13

He stood to take a closer look at Jian, but his eyes glanced to the window and stayed there. Erin saw the blue of his eyes as they widened. His brow furrowed and the front door shot open. In marched hazmat soldiers; gas masks not unlike plague doctor beaks, and white overalls filled the room.

"We need you to step outside, sir." A metallic voice demanded.

The paramedic lifted his arms and Erin followed suit.

"What's going on?"

"You need to come with us."

Erin looked to Jian, but the suits were already picking him up from his cot. "What are you doing?"

"This is urgent." A suit passed Jian over and Erin held him closer than ever before.

They pushed and prodded, not physically, but with their presence, until Erin left the house. She took a final look behind her, to the urns of Frank and George, and buried her head in Jian's thick of hair.

The street was chaos. A blaze of red and blue lights. Ambulances, NHS and St John's, and a few private ones, filled the street. Hazmat suits were loading unconscious children into the backs. Sirens wailed and every other vehicle was a police car or van. The suits shepherded the paramedics that saw to Moira into the back of a vehicle, and Erin followed.

The suits were kind, but their voices gave away an anxiety that Erin absorbed whole. As they closed the van doors behind them, Erin watched the curtains twitch around the estate, and listened to the sobs and cries of mothers and fathers chasing after the ambulances that transported their children. Suits would take them too, Erin knew. It wasn't speculation, there was something prophetic in the whole scene, as though everyone knew what character they played, and who would live to see the curtain call.

There was a pit in her gut as she clutched at Jian. He was awake, but quiet. It was the simplest and lightest relief he had to spare, and Erin took to holding him as if clinging on to life itself.

In her eyes, stained on the back of her eyelids, was Paula; blood drenched, writhing in agony as she slept. Erin imagined her gasping and coughing, begging for help, drowned out by Jian's stomach curdling screams. Maybe she'd died later, when the morning broke over the rooftops and as Erin had slept like a ragdoll on the couch.

There was nothing we could do, Erin repeated,

13

unsure of her body that seemed to be gnawing at her bones. *Better than to die alone.*

She buried her face in Jian again, desperate to pretend to smile. His face twitched. Not yet old enough to return the pretence. She whispered promises to him, in English and in Mandarin, and forced her head not to turn, not to look out into the chaos outside. She tried focusing on the brown of his eyes—so black and sparkling, like windows into the universe. She smiled at him, held him close and let him cling to her fingers. He watched her, like he always watched her. She was his sun, he was hers.

He smiled.

A gasp caught in her throat.

So innocent. So unaware.

She looked up, as though to show to paramedic beside her and boast, but they were lost, their thoughts trapped at the sight of people coughing and collapsing in the street. The sirens flooded back in, overwhelming as the static on the radio as the driver, on the other side of a thick window, rattled off information to an unknown voice over the radio.

Blood left her. Draining ice-cold as adrenalin fired shots through her body. She pulled Jian closer as she watched strangers vomiting blood-rendered bile into the street.

"What's happening?"

POTUS Fox News interview:

When asked about WHO data on the virus's death rate:
A: I think the 3.4% is really a false number... Personally, I
think the number is way under 1%.

Milton Fine

P.A. O'NEIL

SEATTLE, USA

"You should see this place, Barb, it's like a ghost town." Milton leaned back in his chair, staring out of the window at the commotion in the street, the red and blue flashing lights rippling against the opposite high-rise windows as he spoke to his absent secretary. "No, no, don't bother coming in if you need to take your mom to the doctor. There are so few people here, I'll get caught up… Far as I can tell, Carl's not here either, which buys me some time… Just don't worry, family comes first, remember? Yeah, bye." Barb hung up the other end as Milton stifled his coughing fit and wiped his sweaty brow.

He pulled his trash bin closer and began to sort the mail, some of which made a resounding thud as it landed in the garbage. Milton's deep concentration was interrupted by a heavy knock on his door. Looking up, he was surprised to see two sombre

13

looking men dressed in white protective coveralls and wearing full face protection. Behind them was an ambulance crew and several armed police guards wearing face masks.

"Gentlemen, is there something I can do for you?" He stood, the weight of the mail in his hands suddenly feeling heavy.

"Mr Milton Fine? We called at your home, but your wife said you were here." One of them slid two business cards across the desk with his finger. "I'm Special Agent Darrow of the Federal Bureau of Investigation, this is Dr Chambers of the Centres for Disease Control."

Milton inspected their identification, then looking at their melancholy faces, asked, "Would you like to come inside?"

"No, thank you, Mr Fine," Doctor Chambers said. "The fewer surfaces we touch, the safer we'll remain."

"I'm afraid I don't understand, Doctor," Milton stammered.

"Mr Fine, it took us a while to track you down, but you travelled through Heathrow Airport recently."

"Yes, I was returning from a business trip, but I

don't see why you had to 'track me down' nor bother my home." Milton's tone sharpened. "Please, come to the point or leave."

This time it was the agent who spoke. "Mr Fine, I'm sure you've heard of the COVID virus outbreak. It's killed many people in this county so far."

"I have, but I've been sitting shiva—in mourning—for the past seven days. I haven't watched television or read a paper in over a week."

"If I may ask, whom were you mourning, Mr Fine?"

"My grandfather, Dr Chambers, if it's any concern of yours."

"And he died of respiratory complications?"

"Yes, he was very old, but I believe that's what the doctor said. Why?"

The agent took a deep breath and pulled a laminated card from his breast pocket. "Mr Fine, you have the right to remain silent, anything you say…"

Milton shot up. "Miranda rights! Am I being arrested?"

"…afford an attorney, one will be provided. Do you understand these rights as I have read them to you?"

"Yes, but tell me what's going on?" he protested

13

as they began dragging him from the doorway.

With a genuine sorrow in his voice, the doctor explained, "You need to come with us, Mr Fine, for tests. We believe you're responsible for bringing a highly contagious COVID virus to this community."

It was then the phone in his pocket began to vibrate. "This is my wife, I have to take this, please."

"Don't make this harder than it has to be, Mr Fine—"

"Emma, you're not going to believe— Yeah, I was talking to Barb... They what? You bastards arrested my wife?"

"No, sir, but noticing she was sick, we conveyed her to the local hospital for treatment. Your children—"

"You keep your hands off of my children!"

"Your children will be collected from school and brought to the hospital for testing as well. Now, no more time to waste, we have a plane back to London to catch."

The onlookers were gathered, phones in their hands, to record Milton being placed in an ambulance, his objections echoing down the street as he struggled. His face contorted with anger was sure to make the news all over the globe by the evening. Another reluctant victim of the deadly virus.

POTUS Tweet:

Last year 37,000 Americans died from the common flu. Nothing is shut down, life and the economy go on... Think about that.

Are We There Yet?

GREGG CUNNINGHAM

Jim looked up at the departure board again, then over to the flight attendants by the lounge entrance, his legs bouncing impatiently as he willed Gate 57 to open before any further delays were announced. It was getting so close to boarding time, the anticipation building for the entire family for that long-awaited trip to Disney.

"Are we going now, Daddy?" Mary squealed, wiggling in her seat as the announcer walked up to the tannoy and keyed the microphone.

They were so tantalisingly close to the holiday they had save up for four years, they could already taste the fairy floss.

"We sure are honey. Any minute now!" Jim smiled.

"Sit still, Mary. Do you have ants in your pants?" Her mum smiled.

"Yes, I do, Mummy. When are we going, when are we going?" She juggled some more, waving her

13

doll in her mum's face.

The flight supervisor cleared her throat,

"Ladies and gentlemen, we regret to inform you that Flight 307 to Orlando has been cancelled. There will be no further flights to the United States of America for the foreseeable future."

BEN DAVIDSON

DAVID BOWMORE

ROME, ITALY

Sunday morning, standing in a tabac, buying cigarettes and throat lozenges—everyone else had sore throats—Ben stared at the headlines of the Italian papers. Something had happened to the super virus. Mike said they had nothing to worry about. Ben would have checked for himself if he had his mobile phone on him. For a moment, he regretted having left it at home. But then he remembered why. He didn't want the ex nagging him, demanding to know why he was wasting his money on weekends with the lads when the kids needed new shoes, or a school uniform. Which was bollocks…and she knew he knew she knew it was bollocks. All she ever wanted was another session with the Botox nurse. *It'll take more than some injections to fix everything that's wrong with that woman, Ben.* Deep down, beneath the hard-faced, entitled exterior, Jenny had

13

to know that he still loved his kids. Surely, she couldn't have forgotten their joy at becoming parents to two lovely twin boys twelve years earlier. For the time being, she could whistle for it. Let her new fella fork out for fillers for a change. Anyway, why was it Ben was always made to feel like he was the one who should be punished? After all, Jenny was the one who'd gone looking for extramarital rumpy pumpy.

No, he wasn't sick and intended to stay that way. He contemplated getting one of the masks that so many were wearing, but that would only draw attention. Several passengers were taken away prior to boarding, including the groom and best man. Armed police in black uniforms looked ready to mow down anyone who complained. Pandemonium surrounded the rapidly diminishing stag party.

Sitting on the plane, he resisted the urge to cough and popped a lozenge. The Scottish woman next to him turned away, focusing on the view outside the tiny porthole. The relief everyone felt as the plane left the ground was palpable. All anyone wanted was to arrive home safely. Across the aisle, Mike dabbed at his forehead. It was the longest four hours of Ben's life, but at least he had an aisle seat and could stretch his legs.

Several seats ahead, he could see the headline of an English paper.

COVID-19

IS IT OUT OF CONTROL?

It was a good question. In one weekend, how many people had he met? How many had his friends encountered? Pubs and bars, the restaurants, the hotel, the rugger match, the strip club and the brothel. God! If the girls were infected, he might be infected too. What if he'd infected them? His friends had all shown signs of illness as soon as they landed in Rome. Why hadn't he? He couldn't have the sickness, could he? But what if he caught it from the little Asian man at the bar? And how many people had he come into contact with? And what about the girls in the bordello? How many customers could they infect in that time? It was something a man didn't think about when he was with a woman like that—all thinking is suspended—but in an eight-hour night, how many men would a professional girl meet? Eight? Ten? As many as sixteen? Surely not! And all those men would then go about their daily routines and business meetings. Didn't the taxi driver say that a lot of Americans used the same brothel? Dear God, the numbers didn't bear thinking about. The virus must be spreading like wildfire, reaching across the globe, finding its way into every town and village. Touching everyone.

Threatening everything.

***

Now that the fun of the weekend was being subdued by the reality of COVID-19, it was time for Ben to think about family. His mum and dad still lived in Yorkshire, but his kids were with their mother near St. Albans. It was imperative that he see his children to make sure they were okay. He would insist that her new man didn't see them; not until all this COVID-19 stuff had blown over.

Better yet, he'd take them away from Jenny. He knew he was immune—surely, he must be, otherwise he'd be showing symptoms. Yes, he would take the children away. They couldn't live with her. Not until it was safe. He would take them to Yorkshire to stay with his parents.

Passing through customs, even with nothing to declare, always made Ben nervous. When they stopped him and asked him to step into a separate room he thought, *Oh shit, not another strip search.*

However, the masked woman began by taking his temperature with an electronic probe. Then the questions started.

"Are you well, Mr Davidson?"

"Apart from a bit of a hangover, fit as a flea." He smiled.

"Why do you have throat lozenges?"

"No reason. Everyone else was buying them too."

"You've come back from Italy?"

"Yes. Come on England!" She was not amused.

"We're going to take some blood and swabs, Mr Davidson," she said, unwrapping a syringe.

"Hang on a minute," Ben protested.

"Don't make any trouble, sir," a masked, gun-wielding officer said, stepping forward.

Ben opened his mouth and she ran a swab along his cheeks and gums. Then she punctured his skin with the usual warning, "Just a little scratch." As big as he was, he hated the sight of his own blood.

"Results in forty-eight hours," she said. "Two week's confinement, unless he develops symptoms." She ticked a box next to his name and indicated for him to be taken away through a different door.

"Where am I going?"

"A quarantine centre. You'll find out more when you get there."

"But what about work and my family? I haven't got my mobile with me."

"You will have the opportunity to telephone from your assigned room."

Alone on a bus loaded with worried and frightened suspect cases, Ben was eventually deposited at an anonymous-looking hotel, allocated a room, and told not to leave and that nurses would check on him every day. A pair of armed police guards made their presence felt. No one would tell him what had happened to Mike or any of the stag party. But he was told, in no uncertain terms, that to leave his room would result in arrest for breach of the peace and that anyone doing so would be moved to a more secure unit. The phone in the room was dead. The news channels were not accessible. After eight hours Ben came to the conclusion that there was no way he or anyone sane could spend two weeks in the small hotel room.

13

Tony Grant

STEPHEN HERCZEG

LONDON, UK

God, I'm bored.

Tony peered up at the TV. It was halfway through the regular daytime broadcast. The same set of bored presenters were interviewing the same set of boring celebrities that had been doing the rounds for the last three days. He looked at his laptop. No updates to his social media feed in the last thirty seconds. He refreshed just in case. His shoulders slumped. He really was bored.

He thought back to the scene out of a science fiction movie that played out on the steps of his home. The man with the gun read his temperature as thirty-nine degrees. The man with the clipboard had a list of passengers from his flight from China. They'd given him ten minutes to pack. He tried to argue that he was just a bit sick and could stay home, but the two larger men in dark hazmat suits with

351

Police stencilled on them who stepped forward at that point convinced him to obey.

Three days he'd been here. They'd taken him to an infectious diseases ward that had been set up in the Hammersmith Hospital. The ward was full of patients suffering mostly mild symptoms of COVID20. A couple of nurses came through to feed and check on them during the day, but for the most part, they were left on their own.

Tony looked around the ward. He'd tried to spark up conversations with some of the others, but after three days, they had all run out of things to talk about. Now, most were simply staring at the screen above their bed, or the one on their laps, or had simply zoned out and were staring into space.

Out of habit he took a deep breath. The scratching in his throat was diminishing, and his chest didn't feel full of cotton wool. He resisted the urge to cough and slowly let the breath out again.

He clicked his social media feed and stared as the notifications stubbornly stayed at zero.

God, I'm bored.

The doors at end of the ward crashed open as several orderlies and paramedics wheeled a gurney with yet another stricken virus sufferer on board.

Tony could only see his sandy coloured hair sticking out of the top of his full faced respirator mask. A spark of familiarity ignited in Tony's mind. It was only when he spied a thick golden ring on a limp hand hanging off the gurney, that his mind went into overdrive.

Milan!

A wry grin spread across Tony's face as he watched the gurney roll out of the ward towards the single room used for more acute sufferers.

Tony dropped to the floor and padded across to the exit. He spied Milan's destination further up the corridor and stood waiting for the commotion to die down.

After several minutes, he stepped back to allow the paramedics with their gurney back through the ward. Each one nodded, a small smile hidden behind their masks, as they passed him.

"Boring as hell in here, ay?" one of them said.

Tony nodded and replied, "Only excitement all day."

When they had gone, and he noticed no further movement in Milan's room, he walked slowly up the corridor, stopped at the doorway and peered in.

His foe lay on his bed, deflated. All of the

13

swagger had left him. He was in an alien environment. No longer in control of himself or those around him. A clear plastic mask covered his mouth and nose, with a plastic line running to the wall supply of oxygen. A heart monitor beeped intermittently in the corner. Milan's heart rate was steady in the low sixties.

Tony stepped into the room and quietly closed the door behind him. Milan's eyes opened as he heard the click, then widened when he recognised Tony.

"You," he rasped, with the sound of a throat raked by razor blades. "You did this to me, didn't you?"

Tony moved up beside the bed and stared down at his blonde-haired enemy.

"Looks like it worked," he said.

"Why would you do this?" Milan wheezed. "I'm dying. I never hurt you."

Rather than feel pity, Tony's heart turned to stone. "Really? You didn't think that maybe stripping me of all the work I dedicated myself to for the last five years would affect me?"

Milan stared at Tony with red-rimmed eyes.

"It was only business," he gasped. "I never

meant—"

Tony leaned in and cut him off, "No. You never meant anything, did you? You didn't think, did you? Don't give me any bullshit excuses, you knew what you were doing, every step of the way." He jabbed Milan in the chest, eliciting a slight cough. "You're a virus. You infect an organisation, latch on to someone else's healthy work, then kill the host with your rumours and innuendos. I've seen the likes of you before and I've been sickened, but I've always survived. I'll survive you as well."

Milan started to cough. Lightly at first, but it suddenly became hoarser and more serious. His body was wracked by convulsions as the cough ran deeper into his infected lungs. Suddenly, a great gob of red-tinged mucus appeared on the inside of his mask.

Tony stepped back in revulsion.

The blonde man sat up as the coughing fit worsened. To Tony, it sounded like his lungs were ripping apart. Milan let out a gurgling sound and a great gush of blood spewed out into his mask. He tore at the straps but couldn't gain any purchase and the masked stayed stubbornly in place. More blood spurted from his mouth and sprayed out of the tiny holes giving him the look of a red novelty fountain.

The heart monitor beat out a frenetic accompaniment.

Suddenly, he breathed in, dragging the liquid back into his lungs. The coughing doubled, throwing his body into spasms and slamming his head back into his nest of pillows.

Tony's resolve began to fray as he watched the pitiful scene before him, but he remembered who this man was and what he represented. He stepped backwards to the door and opened it quietly as the tumultuous performance on the bed began to play out to its denouement.

Milan thrashed about, blood spraying out in all directions and showering the walls and bedding in a speckled pattern of gore. His only sounds were the coughing and gurgling as he choked on the same fluid erupting from his lungs.

Then, without warning, it stopped. Milan fell back on the bed and lay still. His breathing faded to a shallow gasp for air.

Tony stared at the blood-soaked supine form before him. He searched his feelings, but failing to find any vestige of sympathy, turned and left the room. As the door slowly shut, a single beep filtered out, triggering alarms further down the corridor and the sudden rush of feet.

It seems I did know what I was doing.

13

X-DAY +12

 13

POTUS (while numbers are plateauing or increasing):
Coronavirus numbers are looking MUCH better, going down almost everywhere.

BEN DAVIDSON

DAVID BOWMORE

QUARANTINE FACILITY, LONDON, UK

Apparently, they needed fresh air. For this reason, the windows were unlocked.

Quietly, Ben climbed out of his ground floor room. Even the lights of the courtyard were extinguished at that hour of the night. Thank God for Greta, her annoying crusade and those extinction rebellion tossers. Keeping to the shadows and trying to spot CCTV cameras, he inched his way around the horseshoe-shaped enclosure, which made up the interior yard of the hotel. As he rounded one end of the complex, he found himself opposite the main entrance. Inside a police Land Rover, he could see someone's face, illuminated by a phone, stifling a yawn.

Wondering where the other policeman might be, Ben headed in the opposite direction from the vehicle. He only had about seven hours before

breakfast was brought to his room and they noticed that he was missing.

He found a scooter in a state of partial disrepair next to an old ice-cream van, in the front garden of a house on the road out of town. The seat was attached, as were the handlebars and wheels, but the head lamp had been removed. The fool who owned it hadn't expected a bloke with a childhood interest in these things to come along. Not everyone knows that with the starter motor disconnected, one doesn't need a key to get the machine going, and as best as he could tell from the glow of the moon, the required parts were indeed missing. He picked the rear end up and guided the moped to the end of the street on its front wheel.

He had settled himself onto the seat and was about to press the 'on' switch when someone called his name. He turned to see Tommy from the stag do, halfway down the street, jogging in his direction up the centre of the road.

"Watch ya, Ben," he called, raising his arm and waving. "I didn't know you were in clink too. Wait for me, would ya? I could do with a lift."

Ben raised his finger to his lips indicating that silence would be essential for a successful escape.

Tommy slid to a halt as a policeman on foot emerged from a side road, clearly drawn by Tommy's ill-timed imitation of a town crier. Standing between Tommy and Ben, the policeman looked from one to the other as if unsure of the situation.

The Mexican standoff was broken when Tommy turned and fled at full pelt in the opposite direction, forcing the officer of the law to take chase. Part of Ben knew the right thing to do would be to help Tommy. Instead, he hit the switch and stepped on the kick starter pedal. The sound of the machine coming to life brought a smile to his face and his heart raced as he *phut-phutted* his way south.

The roads were quiet, but it was still only two in the morning. Even at a top speed of fifty miles an hour, he would be able to make good headway, providing he didn't crash from tiredness—he hadn't slept in nearly twenty-four hours—or get pulled by the rozzers.

***

He hammered on the front door of the detached house that had once been his home. The boys would be sitting in the kitchen looking at iPhones and eating toast. A TV in the living room would be showing the BBC News channel. No one would be watching it.

"I want the boys, Jenny. They're coming with me," he said as she opened the door. She tried to slam it, but he thrust it wide open, sending her crashing to the ground with a scream.

"Sam, Adam. Get your things. You're coming with me," he said stepping over his ex-wife.

Dressed in Ben's old towelling robe, the man who had stolen his family stepped out from the kitchen. "What do you think you're doing, Ben?" he asked. The very picture of reasonableness. Already tired and well beyond the point of thinking straight, Ben grabbed his boss—soon to be ex-boss, but fuck it—by the lapels and landed the perfect head butt on his nose. Blood gushed over the white robe as he fell to the floor.

He could hear Jenny, behind him, damning him to hell like a harpy on acid. But right now, he needed to protect his kids.

"Get your things, boys," Ben shouted.

Tears mingled with blood as the bastard curled into a ball at his feet. Ben kicked him for good measure.

"You've got a hashtag, Dad," Adam said.

"What?" He looked up to see his children standing in the doorway of the kitchen.

"Hashtag: bendavidson. Hashtag: fugitive," Adam said, holding his phone out so Ben could see his own face looking back at him.

"What?" Ben said again.

"You've gone viral, Dad," Sam said.

And then everything went black.

TOMMY

RICH RURSHELL

QUARANTINE FACILITY, LONDON, UK

Getting out of the quarantine accommodation had been easy. Pretty much just walked out. I even saw Pikey's mate Ben. We were spotted by a copper though. I had to do a runner. He shot off on a moped. He looked a right knob. Bloody great bloke racing along on one of them. Glad he got out too though. He's a proper lad. Not like Pikey and all those other pussies. Ben kept with the plan and hit the stag party like a champ. It doesn't surprise me he got out. I bet all the others are playing along and waiting for bed baths.

After half an hour or so of hedge-hopping, I manage to lose the pig.

My phone vibrates in my pocket. I take a look. Jesus. Stacey again. Since fucking her on the plane to Italy, she had been messaging me five or six times a day. Man, this is one needy cow.

13

Jesus, we had sex in a toilet. Once. She's hot for sure, but not the sharpest tool in the box.

Though this time, her message was different.

Jesus. How many more questions? I keep my reply simple.

Pikey had been banging on about corona virus all weekend. A quick Google search took me to an article about a Brit in Wuhan who beat corona with Hot Toddies. So I'd been hitting the whisky, milk, and honey for the rest of the weekend, and feel pretty good right now.

It seems all that Corona virus stuff has got way out of hand, and the streets are empty, except for the patrols. I need to find some supplies. Food, water, whisky, milk, and honey.

Again, my phone vibrates.

with them. The news is saying all sorts
of things. I don't know what to do.

I send back a quick reply.

Probably best you stay. Had to escape
quarantine. UK paranoid. Watch too much
news.

I see the convenience store sign down the street and keep to the shadows as I approach. I'm probably beyond the view of the quarantine patrols now, but best to be safe.

I walk through the doors to find two guys filling bags with pasta, tinned food, toilet rolls, booze and cigarettes.

"Back off, mate. We got here first."

"Whatever, boys," I reply. "I'm not here for your swag. I've just come to pick up a few bits."

The shorter of the two pulls out a blade.

"Fuck off, mate."

"Gonna make me?"

He lunges at me with the blade, though the attack is not committed, he's just trying to spook me. I push away his arm and land a solid cross on his chin. He drops his bags, and tins and bog rolls spill out onto the floor. He collapses back against the cigarette cabinet and then hits the deck, unconscious. The other guy leaps forward and cracks me in the eye with a jab. I cover up as he throws a flurry of punches at me, then throw all my weight into his midsection, taking him down to the floor. My eyebrow is pissing blood into my eye as we wrestle behind the counter. He's probably a cage fighter or something, as he quickly takes a dominant position and starts battering my face with punches. Again, I cover up, but he winds his hands between my arms and tries to strangle me. I flail around, trying to find purchase. Some leverage of some kind.

I find the knife instead and plunge it into the guy's neck.

He lets go of my windpipe and clutches his own, blood spilling through his fingers, covering my face and chest. He makes a rasping noise and gets to his feet. I take this opportunity and get up from the floor. I pick up one of their bags, and sprint out of the shop, taking the knife with me.

Helicopters buzz overhead, heading towards the Thames, and I dart into the shadows of a shop. The place smells of curry powder and death. The shelves have been cleaned out, only the dry naan breads remain and the cashew milk cartons lying discarded on the floor.

I have to leave this place and get home.

***

No fucking tin opener. As I walk along the train tracks back towards my district, I swig from a bottle of Whyte and Mackay. At least I got one of the things on my shopping list. The toilet rolls will come in handy at some point too. I'm keeping a low profile since the fight in the store, but it seems no one is around anyway.

I hop the railway fence close to my house and make my way up the street towards my door. My phone vibrates. I take it out of my pocket. My brother has messaged me.

```
Tommy, you dick. Your face is all over
the news. The pigs have been here and
round to mum's house. They say you
bunked the quarantine at the airport,
and then killed some guy in a shop right
in front of the CCTV, you mug. Don't
come here. Or to Mum's. Or home if you
don't want to get caught. I'd probably
dump this phone too. They'll be
tracking it.
```

13

Two guys get out of a car across the street from my place.

Fuck. I need to run.

Find somewhere safe, somewhere quiet where I can get my head down without the worry of any dick finding me and trying to screw me over.

#MariaExquisito

DAVID BOWMORE

TWITTER

Maria Garcia @TheRealMariaExquisito

Maria has tested positive for Coronavirus and has put herself into isolation. Thank you in advance for your messages of concern.

Sue Smith @SSue1973

OMG !!!!! Prayers for a quick recovery. #coronavirus #mariaforever

Tobias Wahl @TobyW55

Prayers For You And Yours. You're The Best. Heart You Maria.

Richard Hopkirk @idontcare

i thought she was dead already. #coronavirus #waisteofspace #idontcare

Pammy Price @SmartyPrice

What a fuckin dick! I hope your die in pain @idontcare. #wanker #diebastard

JoLee Lee @Joleelee

luv u lots maría. praying for u. #prayers

***

BBC NEWS

"New cases of Coronavirus have doubled today to 5,000. True figures may be much higher. The government has urged anyone with even a mild cough or temperature to isolate immediately.

"Maria Exquisito, whose real name is Maria Garcia, has self-isolated after testing positive for Coronavirus, her agent and manager has confirmed on social media today.

"Miss Garcia first shot to super stardom in 1981 with her song 'Evil Man, Easy Woman'. Her wild routines and videos often drew comment from the Vatican. Mary Whitehouse famously wrote to the BBC demanding that her videos be destroyed for the moral health of all young people everywhere.

"In recent years, she has garnered a new reputation as an opera singer.

"And now the weather..."

***

TWITTER

Maria Garcia @TheRealMariaExquisito

It with regret and tremendous sadness that we must inform the world of the passing of Maria Garcia. She died peacefully at home. A memorial fundraiser concert will be arranged shortly.

Sue Smith @SSue1973

OMG - this is the worste news ever. my eyes are never gonna stop crying.

Tobias Wahl @TobyW55

#Heartbroken This Has To Stop Before More People Die. Why Arent They Doin Anythink?

Pammy Price @SmartyPrice

Are you happy now @idontcare you peece of shit scum bastard

JoLee Lee @Joleelee

this is the worste news ever. god help us all. must get tickets. #mariaforever.

Richard Hopkirk @idontcare

i bet it wasnt peacefull. that covid-20 shit is painfull.

***

BBC NEWS

"Cases of the new stain of Coronavirus, Covid-20, in the United Kingdom have more than doubled in the last twenty-four hours bringing official figures to 12,936. Further deaths have been reported including the singer, Maria Garcia, more popularly known as Maria Exquisito. She was years fifty-nine years old.

"Meanwhile, The Prime Minister, Mr Johnson, is to hold a special COBRA tomorrow morning via

video link from 10 Downing Street."

***

TWITTER

Richard Hopkirk @idontcare

@BorisJohnson is holding a cobra meeting for Maria Exquisito. Why?

JoLee Lee @Joleelee

perhaps he can bring her back. praying for a miricle. #mariaforever #resurection

Tobias Wahl @TobyW55

She was a beautiful person. The world is a worste place without her. #makemariaasaint.

GOD @TheCreator

IT IS TIME FOR A NEW START.

#REVELATIONS

#APOCALYPSE

#CORONAVIRUS

#COVID-20

STACEY

A.S. CHARLY

TYROL, ITALY

Stacey hugs her blanket, moaning during her dream. Restlessly, she moves around in her bed. Sweat is running down her temples.

Tommy...

A phone call wakes her.

Could it be?

Butterflies rise in her stomach, and still a bit disoriented, she answers her phone.

"This is KLM headquarters calling."

Disappointed, she listens and nods a few times.

"Yes, sure. I understand. Goodbye."

For a while, she sits silently on the bed, her face white as snow. Then she gets up, kicks her already packed trolley out of the way and marches into the kitchen. Pouring milk over her cereal, she grumbles to herself.

"Today's flight cancelled...use up your

remaining holidays. Damn it!"

Shivering, she reaches for her yoga pants and a pullover before she leaves to sit in her favourite place; the Winter Garden. She had been thrilled when the old building had been renovated last year, and all the balconies got a closed glass front, but today she does not care much for the beautiful view over the old Italian city.

At least I'm still on short-time work. It could be worse, I guess.

Stacey sighs and wonders what she should do with her unexpected free time. With all big events cancelled, and the advice to avoid large gatherings, it is difficult to think of much. It is difficult to think of anything but Tommy, really—his sexy voice and awesome body. Glancing at her phone, she cannot help but send another message.

```
How are you, sweetheart?
Will you call me today?
I miss you!
```

Before she can add another one, Nonna calls. Chatting with her grandmother helps Stacey relax. Unfortunately, Nonna is rather worried about the whole situation, especially now that Mom got stuck.

"Don't be worried, Nonna. You gotta be

positive. It's a hotel room with everything she needs, great view of the ocean, free internet, TV...tons of eBooks. She's not going to get bored anytime soon."

"And what about poor me? Who's going to entertain me?"

"You know what? I can visit you and grandad for a few days. Would you like that?"

Her grandmother is thrilled, and Stacey feels refreshed. She adds a few things to her trolley before she jumps into her car. Of course, she finds enough time to send some more kisses and hearts to Tommy before she starts her four-hour drive to South Tyrol.

***

The highway is almost empty, just a few cars and several trucks are on their way. It is unexplainably hot inside the old Peugeot, and it gets increasingly difficult for Stacey to concentrate. Her stomach spins, and she is feeling dizzy.

I better take a break, get some fresh air. Oh! It's way past lunchtime too. Maybe I should eat something.

Stacey pulls in at the next highway station, only to find it closed. At least the neighbouring fuel station is still open, and she has a chocolate bar while reading Tommy's answer.

```
I'm alright.
I don't know.
```

She sighs, wondering if all guys are so laconic. Taking another bite of her chocolate, her fingers fly over the keyboard.

```
How do you feel about us?
I   think   we   have   something   really
special.
Do you love me?
```

After starring at the screen for a while, she gives up and returns to her car.

***

The sun is sinking behind the mountains, as Stacey drives uphill to the little village where her grandparents live. Her throat is burning again, but her water is empty, so she decides to have a quick stop at the supermarket just outside the village. While getting out of the car, a young woman passes her with a fully loaded shopping cart—just toilet paper and nothing else. Stacey shakes her head in disbelief. Inside the store, there are tons of signs to remind people to keep their distance and not shake hands. Many shelves are empty, despite products being limited to one or two per person.

What the heck...are people going crazy, or what?

Stacey knows her grandparents cannot afford to bulk buy, so she decides to get more than just another drink. The guy at the cash register looks pretty cute in his mask and rubber gloves. Stacey gives him one of her charming smiles, and he blushes.

"Have a wonderful day, gorgeous. I hope I'll see you again," he whispers to her while handing her back her change.

Stacey giggles.

That would indeed be lovely...

***

With a fully loaded trunk, she slowly drives up to her grandparent's house. All those cobblestones were probably not very good for the groceries. They definitely did not do her any good. Exhausted, she gets out of the car and sees her grandmother waiting with open arms.

That's not the very best idea right now, Nonna.

13

Her grandmother does not give her a chance to complain, and hugs and kisses her despite her hesitation.

"Just in time for dinner, my little butterfly!"

***

Dishevelled and tired from the long trip, Stacey sits with her grandparents at the dining table. The lasagne smells as delicious as it tastes, but she only pokes it around her plate half-heartedly.

"You've barely touched your food, child? Are you alright?" her grandfather inquires between coughing and blowing his nose. He has been rather quiet today, apart from his sneezing.

Stacey gives him a weary smile.

"Please don't be worried, Grandpa. I'm perfectly fine. It's just all that driving—annoyed my stomach and made me feel a bit giddy."

Understanding, he nods and continues with his meal, nervously glancing at the news on the TV behind them. Her grandmother, though, gives Stacey a long questioning look.

"You're not pregnant, are you?"

For a moment, Stacey thinks her last bite of

lasagne might get stuck in her throat.

Oh my god...nooooo! That can't be... Or could it?

"Damn no, Grandma! Where do you get those silly ideas from?" she manages to answer indignantly. "Why the heck is this the first question anyone asks a girl if she's not feeling well?"

"Alright, alright. I was just wondering, my dear."

Her grandmother starts clearing away the dishes, and Stacey's thoughts drift off to Tommy again. A bit worried, she decides to Google a few things, when her grandfather turns up the volume.

"As the death toll rises, Italian government has ordered a complete lockdown starting tomorrow. Tourists are urged to return to their homes. Our citizens are to stay home if not needed at work. Please avoid any unnecessary human contact. Medical facilities, pharmacies, and grocery shops will remain open. Police will be patrolling to assure these measurements are put into action."

Catatonically, the three of them watch the rest of the news, then Stacey's grandfather turns the TV off.

"You better stay here, my dear. It makes little sense to drive back all the way to the city to be locked away alone. Supplies might be easier to get here in the countryside anyway."

He looks as if he has aged a decade in the last minute. Grandmother leaves for the pantry, mumbling to herself.

"Of course..."

Stacey nods, her face even whiter than in the morning. She takes her phone to see if Tommy is around.

```
Tommy, how are you? Please reply.
I'm scared. Are you ill too?
Where are you?
```

Her phone vibrates on her lap. What a pleasure—he is online!

```
OK. No, not really. London.
```

His answer is as short as always. She sighs.

```
You're in London? They let you back in?
My grandparents suggested I should stay
here. They are saying all kinds of
things in the news. I don't know what
to do.
Probably best you stay. Had to escape
quarantine. UK paranoid. Watch too much
news.
```

Oh my god! He had been in quarantine! He must

have been ill... or still was! What if he died?

Without noticing, Stacey bites her nails. It feels as if an iron clamp tightens around her chest, and she can hardly breathe.

***

Loud noises from outside rouse Stacey from her slumber. She has a look at her phone, but there are no new messages. Tired after another restless night, she opens the curtains. The bright light hurts her eyes, and intensifies her headache, but when she sees what is going on, she smiles. The people of the village are singing on their balconies, a young girl is playing a guitar, and further down the road she can hear an accordion. Cheered up, she goes downstairs to have breakfast.

In the kitchen, she finds her grandmother desperately flicking through the newspaper.

"What's up, Nonna? Is something wrong?"

"It's your grandpa. He hasn't been well for days, and now he's gotten a fever, but I can't find which doctor is on duty."

You know, you could have mentioned that he's ill when you called, Nonna...thanks a lot.

"No worries, Grandma. I can have a look and take him there."

388

X-DAY +14

13

POTUS talking on Capitol Hill:
Well, this was unexpected. This was something that came out of China, and it hit us and many other countries. You look at the numbers; I see the numbers with just by watching you folks. I see it — it's over 100 different countries. And it hit the world. And we're prepared, and we're doing a great job with it. And it will go away. Just stay calm. It will go away.

RETREAT

DAVID GREEN

Beth had spent four weeks of blissful silent retreat in the mountains. Just herself and nature. No phones or electricity.

Damn allergies, she thought, rubbing at her eyes on her drive back to the city. The roads seemed oddly deserted.

Turning a corner, a checkpoint across the road made her stop. Someone in a hazmat suit approached. Beth opened her window timidly.

"What's happened?" she spluttered, phlegm catching in her throat.

"Cougher, we've got a cougher. Get her to quarantine!"

Similar clad people ran towards Beth, dragging her from the car as her screams about

allergies fell on ignorant ears.

POTUS meeting with the Irish Prime Minister:
I mean, think of it: The United States, because of what I did and what the administration did with China, we have 32 deaths at this point. Other countries that are smaller countries have many, many deaths. Thirty-two is a lot. Thirty-two is too many. But when you look at the kind of numbers that you're seeing coming out of other countries, it's pretty amazing when you think of it. So, that's it.

Nigel

GREGG CUNNINGHAM

LONDON, UK

The Hope and Anchor had been quiet for a Friday night so Nigel took the Circle Line into town to meet up with the other boys in Soho. It seemed most punters had decided to comply with the wishes of the government to stay at home and not take the bars up on the opportunity of the cheap lagers on offer. Vinnie and Nigel caught up over a few large ones, discussing the shit that was going down around the world, before the rest of the crew showed face. Mostly they talked the usual bullshit—the sweeping virus that was knocking the old folks off their feet, or the upturn in hospital trips he was making. Barry got ribbed about his farm duties and they wondered if he even had permission to be out that late from his missus, much to the groans from the others. There was even talk between them all about a curfew needing to be set up around London to stop all

13

foreigners getting in to spread their filthy germs. All this while tucking into their special fried rice dishes in Chinatown.

"What we really need, Vinnie, is to stop all those twats coming over and infecting us, mate. Send them packing. We don't want them here!" Nigel was displaying all the symptoms of your typical ill-informed uneducated thug, his views on life being as stubborn to remove as the gang affiliation tattoo inked on his neck.

The group drank on into the night as the rain came down, and then stumbled their separate ways through the puddles out of Soho early on Saturday morning to the sound of the usual distant sirens, having put the world to rights. Nigel, three sheets to the wind, was giving out his own personal rendition of "Singing in the Rain" as Vinnie struggled with his jacket zip, the pair of them doing their best to kick a discarded lager can along the empty street, the waft of the Saturday morning fish market hanging in the air.

Nigel was trying his best to remember his pin number at the ATM, squinting at the screen requests, while Vinnie relieved himself up against wall as nightclub bins somewhere nearby rattled with the sound of empty bottles being poured inside their metal bellies.

"What the hell's going on over *there*?" Vinnie pointed over the city to the helicopter searchlights lighting the sky above Canary Wharf like they were searching for the Luftwaffe bombers during the Blitz.

"Uh?" Nigel swayed trying to get the notes from the machine.

"Choppers over by the Dome…look."

Nigel however was too busy staggering back against a lamppost with his wallet open and wiping his running nose with the cuff of his jacket while squinting into the night sky like he was spotting for icebergs from a crow's nest.

Vinnie zipped himself up and grabbed Nigel's collar, turning his head skyward.

"Over there, you muppet, by the bridge. There's loads of them up there."

"Jesus, there must be twenty of them buzzing around!" he said as he wiped snot across his face. Blood smeared across his cheeks as he stared at the flickering lights.

"Looks like the streets are filled with coppers too, Nige. Check out the flashing red and blues—"

13

He stopped mid-sentence, staring at the blood on Nigel's face as it ran from his nose.

"Christ, Nige! What the fuck have you done?"

"Uh?"

"Your nose, mate. Who smacked you?" Vinnie had Nigel's head in his hands and was inspecting the bridge of his nose for damage as Nigel clung to the lamppost like Gene Kelly about to give another off-key rendition.

"Uh?" Nigel could barely stand upright.

"Did you fall, you dopey fucker?" He was laughing now as he wiped the snotty blood from his mate's face. "Come on, let's grab the Tube and get you home."

They wandered along the street like they were on the deck of a fishing boat, swaying left to right until they made it to the main road where the roar of an ambulance engine suddenly sped past them, emergency lights flashing and siren screaming, followed by another, then another. Vinnie had to pull Nigel back onto the path before a speeding police car nearly took him out. As they watched, another line of vehicles turned the corner—this time it was three large four-toner army trucks trundling their way along. Masked-up soldiers sat at the back with rifles between their knees, staring out menacingly.

"Are the Hammers playing tonight, Vinnie?" Nigel laughed, saluting the trucks as they passed.

"Nah… Must be the Scousers in town mate!" Vinnie laughed, slapping Nigel's back. "Come on, mate, let's get you home before the bastards nick your shoes."

Together they made the sobering long walk down to Tower Hill Tube Station as the screech of truck tyres echoed in the alleyway ahead.

"Tubes closed to the public guys, take a hike!" one of the armed soldiers rasped through his respirator mask, the trio standing by the station entrance like a troop of Terracotta statues. The other two closed ranks as Nigel tried to squirm his way through.

"What do you mean *closed*, mate?" Vinnie replied, squaring up to the sergeant.

"I mean as in not open. So fuck off!" he replied, pushing Vinnie back with his SA80 rifle against his chest. The other soldiers shuffled into formation, blocking Nigel.

"How the hell are we going to get home if you twats close the Circle Line, its three in the fucking morning mate, what's your problem?"

13

"You're my problem…twat. Call a cab!" The sergeant leaned forward. "Now piss off before I have you thrown in the back of the truck with the rest of the nonces!" Vinnie glanced around and saw the hazmat suits in the back of the four-ton military truck and sobered up. Three nurses with full body protective suits and masks were restraining somebody inside the cabin, who was not looking too happy about it. The truck further down the road also had numerous soldiers with riot shields and respirator masks slowly clambering from the tail gate and wearily lining up along the roadside, looking as excited to be there as he did.

"Nige…" He shuffled backwards as the soldiers closed ranks on Nigel.

"Sarg, looks like we got another one here. This one has the bleeds!" The raspy voice from the respirator caused Vinnie to break his gaze from the nurses in their protective suits and turn to see Nigel shoving the soldiers in an attempt to pass the blockade.

"Shit. Well you know the procedure: restrain him, Private." He was wiping his respirator lenses as they fogged up from the inside, his breath becoming faster in the mask.

"Nigel, time to fold 'em cards, mate!" Vinnie said as the sirens wailed around the city and the helicopters swooped over the Thames. He heard the faint sound of bullhorns over the other embankment but couldn't make out the orders being given out; something about a curfew being enforced. The young soldier also heard the echoing commands and hesitated as Nigel pushed him.

"Come with me, sir!" the inexperienced soldier stammered, his mask also fogging up as the tension mounted.

"Nah, mate, you gestapo grunts can't push us around; this is our turf not yours!" Nigel turned to the soldier closest. "You boys wanna watch where you point those things; might do yourselves an injury." Nigel puffed out his chest and pushed the soldier's rifle aside. The soldier looked uncertain; he glanced at his superior for guidance on his next move, not fully understanding the situation he found himself in. The kid just wanted to drink piss with his mates and get laid, just like Nigel and Vinnie.

"Restrain him, Private. You have your orders!" The sergeant turned back to Vinnie who was now shuffling away from the guards.

"Nige, fucking leave it!" Vinnie was scared.

This wasn't Saturday afternoon cop patrols with truncheons, herding the footy away fans from the locals…his was a proper lockdown he was seeing, with guns and tanks and shit. This was the real deal, and the deal was just about done.

Vinnie stood as the rain fell, watching the soldiers as both sides realised this was how it was going to be, this was a real situation. Guns *were* being pointed at them both, safety catches *were* being slid from safe.

"NIGE!" Vinnie lunged forward as the soldier pushed Nigel back, but he grabbed at the rifle barrel and twisted the weapon in the private's hand, pushing back. The other soldier raised his rifle butt and smacked it down hard against Nigel's skull, sending him to the gutter with a splash.

"Army! Stand back!" He warned, wide eyed in disbelief.

Vinnie was stumbling backwards too, blood pouring from a deep gash in his forehead—delivered by the sergeant's rifle—as Nigel scrambled from the melee on his hands and knees. Two other soldiers grabbed him and flipped him onto his back as he lashed out, grabbing the air cannister of one soldiers and ripping the mask from his face. His helmet went tumbling as Nigel spat a bloody wad in the kids panicked face, fists flapping in the air like it was some new yoga session, striking the soldier's chin with a lucky swipe.

"FUCKING MILLWALL SCUM!" Nigel cried out, having flashbacks to happier days with his crew as the other soldier backed off and took aim.

The sergeant cursing before shouting, "Queen's Guard… Stop or I'll fire!"

Vinnie shoulder-charged the sergeant, sending him rolling on his boot heels, then grabbed Nigel by the coat collar and dragged him to his feet. The rain was falling heavy, and the guards were caught out by the aggression of the two drunk men up for a Friday night rumble.

"Let's get the fuck out of here, Nige!" Nigel was up, blood streaming into his eyes, as Vinnie turned shouting for him to run, ignoring the orders to stop. But Nigel was grinning—it was just like old times, only with the guns.

How the hell did this turn so fast? Vinnie wondered.

They both heard the *click clack* of the rifle behind them, the sudden reality hitting Nigel as the single gunshot rang out in his ears. He watched in

13

disbelief as Vinnie spun around violently, slumping to the cobbled road as if Bruce Lee had just done a front leg sweep and floored him, his head missing the right-side of his face as it hit the smooth stones in a thick matted bloody splat of teeth and gristle.

"Vinnie!"

Nigel saw the sergeant take aim again and instinctively made a run for the alley without looking back.

"Army! Stop or I *will* fire!"

SAM THE CODER

JACOB BAUGHER

LONDON, UK

The River Thames flowed dark and swift beneath London's overcast sky. A light rain sprinkled down from the disparaging clouds, shredding like burning cloth before the setting sun. The red horizon seemed somehow ominous yet peaceful, almost as if the very sky was in mourning for the millions of souls needlessly lost.

Millions of souls that you had a hand in exterminating, a small voice whispered in Sam's head. He tried to ignore it, tried to repeat that saying that now seemed ages old to him: that he was doing it for his family, that, once the journalist approached him, he was doing it for the greater good. Strange, how quickly he started to sound like the Nazi's after World War II when it was his ass on the line. Eugenics, he knew now, is never the answer.

He exited the London ExCel building—the

emergency hospital the soldiers had taken him to—with a crowd of others who had also been discharged today. One man who looked like a gym rat and had the gleam of a freshly shaved and waxed head nudged him. Sam recognised him. He'd been in the bed across from the man until they'd taken him to the ICU.

"We're going to get a drink, mate." He gestured to a few others behind him. "Try and drown this whole fucking experience. You in?"

Sam shook his head. "No." He turned slowly around in a circle, trying to take in the city. The river; the wet-rock-and-rain smell of it that mixed with asphalt and car exhaust and industry is hanging on a humid spring breeze. "I have a plane to catch." He grasped the recorder in his jacket pocket. Somehow, he'd held on to it through all this.

"Suit yourself, mate." And the man turned to leave.

Sam dug in his pocket for his phone, powered it on, and texted his wife: `Coming home. Where should I meet you?` Then he put the phone back in his pocket.

"Hey!" he shouted to the man. "My phone just crapped out on me. Can I borrow yours?"

"Sure thing," he said.

"Thanks. I'll only be a minute." He dialled the reporter's number.

"This is Dean," a voice said after exactly three rings.

"It's Sam."

"Sam…?" The voice trailed off.

"From Wu— From the lab."

Silence, then rustling, and what sounded like the soft *beep* of a digital tape recorder. "Sam! I was hoping you'd contact me. I've been gathering stories of the pandemic ever since we talked. I thought you were dead."

"Not for lack of trying," he said. "I have information for you."

"I'm at Caffe Nero next to the Golden Hinde. Give me 15 minutes—"

"I'm in Australia," Sam lied. "Where can I send it?"

"But—"

"This is a one-time offer," Sam talked over him

"I...sure." The reporter rattled off a London address. Sam ended the call without bothering to confirm the information.

He hailed a cab and headed to the airport, but not

before he dropped the tape recorder in the mail in a high-priority box with a note that read "Samuel Ashley THE CODER — chronicling Passenger-13 project, escape, COVID-20 recovery. The world deserves the truth."

***

The flight passed without incident. Sam slept from wheels-up to wheels-down at Broome airport. He rented a car at Thrifty, paid extra for the 2020 model of the Dodge Challenger and headed down the coast. He'd stopped in town for two West Coast Eagles caps—one for him and one junior size for Lucy—a football, and a metric shitload of sand toys and sandcastle moulds.

The beach house—the one he'd bought his wife with the advance from the Passenger-13 project—was modest as far as beach houses go. A tall, brick structure with an ocean-view and several bedrooms that they had planned to fill with children. His wife had texted him on the road—she and Lucy were out on the beach. He'd promised he'd meet them out there. Just the thought of seeing them both again...he shook the thought away as the road began to blur.

When he finally did pull up to the house, his allergies were acting up and he'd wiped his sunglasses on his shirt multiple times from his watering eyes. He rolled down the window and just listened to the distant ocean as he got his "allergies" under control. He took several deep breaths, grabbed his bags of goodies, walked up the paved brick sidewalk to the red oak front door, and let himself in.

The CIA agent was waiting for him in the kitchen. Sam was pouring himself a beer from the fridge into a chilled glass that he found in the freezer, when he heard someone clear their throat. He turned, bare feet whispering on the ceramic tiles.

"Sam Ashley?" An American accent. The man was sitting at his wooden kitchen table, identification badge in front of him. "Please take a seat."

Tell them nothing, the statesman's voice whispered in his ear.

"What are you doing in my house?"

The agent cleared his throat again. "Sorry, I'm just getting over something. I'm here to talk to you about the Passenger-13 project. There's been a reporter in the UK that goes by the name of Dean Hawkshaw who we think has uncovered some sensitive information about the mission. Through our

UK agents, we've come into information that he may be trying to contact you. If he does…"—the agent slid a business card across the table to him and stood—"give us a call."

"I've never heard of him," Sam said, "but thank you."

The agent left. When the front door closed behind him, he crumpled up the business card and dropped it in the trash. He grabbed his beer from the counter and walked out into the sun.

The darkness would come again, this time for him. He knew that. Even now, clouds were brewing out at sea on the horizon, but he didn't much care. When the reporter analysed the tape, he'd be able to see the extent of the conspiracy. Then they'd come for him. He walked onto the hot sand, located his wife and daughter, and made for them.

The darkness could wait. Right now, it was time to build sandcastles.

TOMMY

RICH RURSHELL

LONDON, UK

I'm staring down at Stacey, spread-eagled in front of me, on my mum's dining room table, but my dick hangs limp and lifeless between my legs.

"Tommy, I thought we had something special," she says, frowning at me.

"Don't worry, dear! I'm his fluffer for today." A voice drifts over our shoulders and I turn to see my grandma standing behind us in her birthday suit.

I scream out and wake up on the back seat of Pikey's car. Since he's getting his bed baths in the quarantine area, he won't be needing his wheels, so breaking into it last night was the only option I had.

Shivering, I wipe my nose, and my hand comes away covered in blood. I can't believe my nose is still bleeding. My head aches like hell. I cough, and a pain in my chest is accompanied by a mouthful of coppery phlegm. I open the car door and spit it out. The dead

leaves on the ground are reddened with my blood.

I'm not well, the cramps in my belly feel like I've had one of Pikey's dodgy curries and it takes me all my effort to reach into my pocket for my phone.

"Stacey, it's me…Tommy. I think I'm fucking dying. Can you come and get me?"

No answer. I try again.

`Please Stacey, I need you.`

This time the blood is like a fountain gushing from my nose.

Shit.

STACEY

A.S. CHARLY

TYROL, ITALY

Half an hour later, Stacey and her grandfather arrive at the doctor's. There are notices hanging all over the door. The biggest one says: DO NOT ENTER if you have had contact with a confirmed CORONAVIRUS case or FLU-LIKE SYMPTOMS.

Her grandfather looks pale. He coughs wetly, and Stacey suggests he should wait in the car. After reading through all the signs, she joins him. Still shivering from the icy wind, she dials the emergency hotline number she has found. She smiles encouragingly at her grandfather, but the line is busy.

After waiting for a couple of minutes, she hangs up and tries again, with the same result.

"Ah, come on...screw it. They're too busy, they ain't got no time for an old lad like me. Let's go home. It's cold," her grandfather says.

Irritated, she waits another couple of minutes,

13

but then does as suggested.

On her way back, the phone rings, and shortly afterwards she can hear the familiar sound of an incoming message. Hoping it would be from Tommy, she fidgets around in her driver's seat, but she does not dare to look while driving.

Back home, she opens the door for her grandfather and offers him a hand.

"Shall I help you get back in?"

"Thank you, my dear. Go and entertain Grandma a bit. I'll have a sunbath here."

He sits down on the bench in the front yard and closes his eyes. Stacey takes a last worried look at him, but knows it is hopeless arguing, so she hurries upstairs to check her phone.

A voicemail...*from Tommy!*

"Stacey, it's me... Tommy. I think I'm fucking dying. Can you come and get me?"

Stacey's heart skips a beat. Breathing heavily, she opens his message.

`Please, Stacey. I need you...`

Tears well up in her eyes, slowly running down her cheeks, wetting the sheets of her bed. With a heart-breaking scream, she jumps up and storms back to the car. With squealing wheels, she drives off, not noticing her grandfather lying on the backseat, sound asleep.

***

Stacey is driving through a valley heading north. Tiny snowflakes are swirling around, lightly sticking to the front window. Her thoughts are already in London, while physically she is still in Italy. The Austrian border is getting close when she sees a police car in the distance.

"You know they are going to send us back, right?"

The car swerves for a moment before Stacey can get it back under control.

"Grandpa! You almost gave me a heart attack! What you're you doing here?"

"I could ask you the very same thing, my dear. It's not the best time to go shopping at the Brenner."

"I was more thinking of going to London, really. My friend..."

Her voice breaks away.

One of the policemen is waving, gesturing her to stop, and she slows down.

"Poor kid. Things seem so important when

you're still young," her grandfather mumbles. "That little side street there leads up to a pass to Austria, you know."

He leans forward and points at the steep, narrow road starting a few meters behind the police car. It is closed, but only with traffic cones. She gives him a questioning look.

"Are you serious?"

Her grandfather looks out the window with a mischievous grin. "That's gonna make a fine tale once we're back." Her grandfather giggles, but then starts coughing again.

"What are you doing here, anyway? Shouldn't you be in bed?"

"Well, I had to escape somewhere. Your grandmother is driving me crazy with all her worrying."

They look at each other through the back mirror and start laughing.

Well, here we go...

Stacey steps hard on the gas pedal, and the car jumps forward with squealing tires. The car shoots past the surprised policeman, who is starring after them with a dull expression. His colleague is more daring, and he jumps into the middle of the road, hands crossed over his head. He is screaming something, but Stacey only hears her blood rushing through her ears. She feels dizzy. Her vision darkens, and *BANG*! They crash full speed against the parked police car. The driver's airbag pops up. Then the impact sends their car spinning across the street, right into a hedge. Snowflakes keep falling, turning red as they hit the ground.

***

"Good Morning. Stacey, right?"

Someone takes her hand.

Hmmm...feels nice.

A friendly male voice keeps talking to her, luring her out of dreamland. Stacey opens her eyes and finds the owner as charming as the voice itself.

"Hi. I'm Dr Marten."

"Hi."

She feels herself blushing, as she realises that she is naked under the sheets, and smiles shyly.

"I'm sure you'll be happy to hear that you're quite alright. You were very lucky."

Stacey vaguely remembers driving in her car...her grandfather.

The crash!

"How's Granddad? Can I see him?"

Dr Marten flips through the pages on his clipboard. "Your grandfather seems to be in ICU. I'll see if I can find out more, but you'll have to stay here with me in the isolation centre for another two weeks. You've been tested positive for COVID-19."

With him... How lovely!

"You don't have any severe symptoms, so I'll leave you to the nurse for now, but I'll be back to check on you later."

He winks at her and walks off.

Yeah...come and check me out later...I'd like that, blonde angel.

ERIN

LANNAH MARSHALL

LONDON, UK

"Negative," said one of the hazmat nurses. She looked tired, her face bruised with fatigue and raw from the straps of her face mask. Up close, Erin saw the shadows of her eyes and the reflection of the bright white lights of a makeshift hospital.

"Negative," another suit beside her said as he wrote it down. "And you came from Wuhan?"

"That's what I said." Erin's patience was slipping. Beneath her skin felt oily with sweat and itchy, like her bones were turning into nettles. Days upon days, with tests that felt every few minutes. Her skin was an open wound now. "And my son?"

"Also, negative."

The hazmat nurse turned away, rustling through equipment before taking away the blood pressure cuff.

"Test him again," said Erin, her teeth chattering

as she swallowed rising bile before it hit her eyes. "He screams every night, for hours. He's in pain."

The nurse turned to her, tilting her head and drawing Erin away from the man that was beginning to grate through her head.

"It's colic," said the nurse.

"What?"

"Colic." The nurse sounded relieved, but Erin's head swam with the word.

"Sorry, what?"

Something simple. Something common. Something temporary. Relief was a current inside her as she leant down and picked him up from his cot. His smiling was all she had now, in the tiniest of rooms.

"This is your third negative test," said the nurse. "What we're going to do now is discharge you. You'll need to follow me to, uh, be cleaned, and then we'll take you to an isolation house. Once there, you will need to stay in quarantine for fourteen days. Once this happens…"

The nurse may have continued talking, but Erin stopped taking it in.

"I'm free."

***

The shower was chemical in every sense of the word. Fortunately, Jian was spared this and wiped down by cooing nurses. By the red of their glassy eyes and the hoarse in their throat, Erin could tell this wasn't a particularly common ritual. They could probably count the number of patients allowed to leave with the fingers on their hands.

The fever was rising, but all the tests were negative. Ibuprofen and tea, that's what the doctor told her. They'd offered her accommodation with security, should she need assistance, but promised she wasn't sick with what had gripped the world.

The world.

Wuhan.

Hongqi. She'd escaped him, but something toxic still followed her across the continents, and something was still tormenting her son. Colic. It was too easy.

In her new room with her new clothes and her infant son, Erin couldn't stop staring at the blank walls. She tried to rest. She tried sitting down and reading books, but the words spun inky webs across the pages. Whatever had gripped her felt alive.

Growing. It didn't like her, but it was stuck inside her skin and gnawing its way through every part of her being. It leaked from her skull as torrential sweat and evacuated in clumps of bile as she wretched. It was trying to leave her. Flashes of hot and cold, a microscopic war for her body, and she scoffed at the thought of having any conscious choice in winning.

Sick, drenched in fever sweat and delirious on memories playing across her eyes, Erin sat against the window and watched the world fall apart. Jian in hand, consuming all the formula, Erin saw silence on the streets, then faceless looters descend in mobs. Part of her told her she was dreaming, the rest told her to run.

Her phone rang, the first time since landing.

"Lien?" Erin answered, her throat flesh and nettles.

"Erin! You're okay!" An old friend a million miles away. "Oh, my god! I've been trying to reach you."

Erin's mind pulsed in and out, between walking the students to the classroom and dancing with Lien on nights out in the city. Her first friend in China.

"Erin?"

"Yes, sorry, I'm quite tired."

"You heard about the pandemic?" It didn't sound like a question, but it was, with an upturn to somewhere dark. Or maybe that was Erin's mind playing tricks on her.

"What's wrong, Lien?"

Silence. It was broken on both sides by the sound of sirens. Some looters across the street finally made their way into a shop. When one keeled over, they scattered like flies.

"People are dead."

"I know."

"No, I mean… some of our students. Some teachers."

"Hongqi?" Erin asked. She didn't mean to sound hopeful, but her voice betrayed her.

"Yes," said Lien. A cough. "I don't know what happened between you two, but—"

"No." Erin pushed herself up from the door and looked down as the rioters came back, Molotov cocktails in hand. "You don't." She hung up and stepped back from the window as the inert body below erupted with liquid fire.

* * *

13

Erin slipped out not long after the security guard collapsed.

He'd been coughing, and Erin recognised the grate in his wheeze. He sounded like her, but worse. An older gentleman. Now a dead one.

The number she had been told to call no longer rang, and advice and answers stopped trickling through the apartments. Food was low. Tension was high. Jian was screaming into the night, and now the rioters weren't scared of the building anymore.

Taking the guard's rifle and car keys, she checked her aim. She wasn't a sure shot, she knew this—Britain wasn't exactly known for its gun ranges—but she knew she would aim true if it meant saving her son from what lurked below.

At some point, the army had been rolled in, and they left like a tide, leaving bits of carcasses in their wake. From what she could tell on the news, their attention was being pulled elsewhere, by other riots, by their own dead. Whatever else was said in the reports, it didn't stick.

That thing inside her body was cruel and spineless. It gouged her lungs, with every cough rising like a nest of nettles in her throat, but all that came out was sticky air. It clung to her bones, pulling ever downwards as she walked through the halls and out into the carpark—a monster in her veins, burning hot and oozing out into her skin as sweat and blood.

"Hey, you okay?" someone asked across the lot. A man not much older than Erin. A knife in hand. His pace not slowing. "You got food?"

Erin, bent double from the pain, raised the gun, and the man stopped.

"Hey, woah, I don't want any trouble."

"And what does your knife want?" Erin asked. "Back off."

The man cocked his head. His eyes on the weapon. He didn't look as scared now he'd had time to think. A few spaces away. At some point he'd clocked Jian.

She's not going to fire, Erin imagined him thinking.

His foot swept out, slow, as he tested the distance between them.

Erin narrowed her eyes.

"You know what I want?" Erin asked, sweat smearing with the blood on her palms.

"Listen." The man stepped slower, like a game of Mr Wolf, except her back wasn't turned and her teeth were bullets. "How about we make a deal. You scratch my back and I scratch yours."

"Or," said Erin as she swayed to stand, "you fuck off."

His eyes betrayed him. She watched them flick between them, counting steps—no, lunges—and she straightened her resolve. Chin up, she aimed.

"You're not gonna shoot," he said with a wry, acid smile. "Look at you! You're dying!"

"I'm not dying here!"

"You think you can hit me?" He scoffed and opened his arms. "What you gonna do when you shoot, miss me and land on your arse?" He pointed his knife at her. "What do you think I'm gonna do? To you? To your ki—"

She fired.

The gun jerked back into a bone that cracked clean. She span and hit the ground with a hot, airless thud.

The man was dead.

The bullet struck him in the throat.

Erin lay there, cold and breathless, unable to will herself to move. Jian was screaming, but Erin's fingers twitched instead of lifted. Her feet spasmed instead of walked. She was too hot.

Too hot.

Too cold.

Too hot.

***

Black came the night, and Erin rose from the near-death she slept in. Jian was quiet. Sleeping. No coughing. Only sleeping.

He's strong, Erin promised herself, stronger than his father.

Dizzy and sweating, delirious on a delayed adrenalin-high, Erin placed Jian in the guard's car and drove. She didn't expect to go far, just somewhere new. She was sick, and all she ever did when she was sick was listen to her mother.

"I'm dying," she whispered into the steering wheel. "And Jian's alone." Tears drenched pink stains down her shirt, sweaty and coppery when they passed her lips.

Mum, I don't want to die. I'm so sorry. She sent the text, with dull, numb fingers.

The roads were empty. Roadblocks breached. Cars and the dead littered the motorways, but Erin could still picture the way home. She could see herself, maybe six years old, gasping in awe at the passenger window.

"Fairyland!" she'd squealed to her mother, pointing to the distant streetlights that lit the horizon. She fell asleep to the stories her mother told of magic and fairy courts. She'd wake somewhere new, with her mother by her side.

"This is so dangerous," Erin said. Her mind momentarily clear, like the monster's fog was lifting, and the claws it dug into her throat was easing, widening. "I'm going to crash." Floods of hot and cold washed over, and the fog descended. The car pulled to a stop and Erin dragged herself out. Dawn on the horizon, she walked.

One step, she promised herself. *One more step.*

With every staggered step, Jian's weight doubled, and shortly before the sun broke, he screamed. Erin collapsed and echoed his cries. It burned her. A virus spreading. Consuming. Fog descending across her eyes. Jian's screams pulled her in. Her sun, dimming, her son, disappearing into the darkness across her eyes.

X-DAY +15

NIGEL

GREGG CUNNINGHAM

LONDON, UK

Nigel woke to the sound of a distant dog barking, slumped awkwardly in a dim alleyway, with no idea where he had run too. All he knew was his mate was dead and the army were now running things. His head was spinning, vomit and blood smeared his stumbled chin.

Had there been a coup?

His heart was beating fast as he peered from the pile of stinking rubbish bags, realising he was outside the fish market once more, his trousers soaking up the rotten fish juice and cold rain as it ran from the guttering above him. Down the road he heard the rumble of military wheels. It seemed they were everywhere, like swarming ants over a carcass.

Was it even possible for the military to take control so fast? Nigel knew Boris was a twat, but what would they gain by allowing the military to take

13

control like this. And shooting civilians in the street. Jesus fucking Christ! Were they taking a page out of China's policies?

He pulled out his phone to call the others, but found it had no connection, no internet.

In London!

Jesus Christ, it is a coup.

Vinnie was dead and the fucking army was running the country! Was the virus spreading that fast over here now?

Inside the market, Nigel could hear the engines and the bustle of the early morning traders, and quickly realised he could hide inside, away from the rifles and the soldiers. He got to his feet and stumbled into the market area, his head throbbing and his chest aching. He had to get somewhere where it was busy, get lost in the rush of people before the soldiers found him and stood him up against the wall. Because that's what they do. That's what his head was telling him would happen if they caught him.

They'd parade him in front of everybody and make him read from a laminated sheet of paper, telling anyone else that wanted to fight the supreme leader that there would be serious consequences.

Nigel grabbed his face and screamed. What the

fuck was going on in his head?

"Shut the hell up!" He bounced off the wall, banging his fists against his temples as his nose began to bleed again. It was like whispering phantoms were licking his earlobes and tonguing his ears, sirens talking bullshit, just like the talking heads on the television. Propaganda sirens infiltrating his thoughts and showing him images of dead babies in the streets. Marching armies invaded his thoughts as he struggled with his sanity.

"Nigel, is that you?"

He felt the soft touch grab his arm and recoiled into the shadows.

"Oh my god, Nigel! What is the matter with you?" Shamy had a hold of his arm, leaning over him as he rocked on his heels.

"Oh, Nigel…what are you doing here? Tell me, what is the matter…are you sick?" Shamy hugged his huge frame, feeling his entire body shake.

"Please, come take a seat over here, you look ill… Is that blood?"

Shamy looked shocked at the sight of him. Sure, she'd seen him drunk before, but this was nothing short of hysterics—the man was a wreck.

"We need to get you to a hospital, Nigel…you

13

look terrible, you are ill!"

Becoming aware of Shamy's presence, Nigel dropped his hands as the voices in his head eased.

"No, no hospital, Shamy. I need to get home. Have you got a ride?" he asked, his eyes darting from exit to exit, stall to stall. Around them, traders were bartering for fish, or stared at phones, or shouted as money exchanged hands.

"Yes, I have my delivery wagon, but they are blocking the roads."

"Who are?" Nigel said, trying to compose himself as she pulled a hanky from the sleeve of her flowing Saree, her bangles jingling up her slender arm.

"The army men. They are closing everywhere north of the bridges. It is so worrying, I need to get back to my father, he is so sick." She looked as worried as he did. A crowd was gathering by a stall where a tall man with a radio held in the air was hushing people as more gathered around him, some sniffing, others holding hankies to their noses.

"Shhhhh people, listen to the newsman." He stood on the table, pushing away the fish to the side as Shamy took Nigel's arm and guided him closer. The man in the turban turned the volume to maximum and the crowd stood silent.

"...This is a public announcement. All unnecessary travel is now prohibited within the M25. A curfew is now enforced from the Dartford tunnel to Heathrow airport and surrounding areas. Anyone moving within these aeras as from 1300 hours will be apprehended and detained for questioning by the Armed Forces. Please return to your homes and await further instructions. If you are infected or know of anybody infected, call this number... Attention, this is a public announcement..."

Someone began yelling from the doorway as soldiers entered with rifles raised.

Shamy looked up at Nigel, whose mouth was now just opening and closing like the fish on the slab in front of him. *Did the announcer just say the whole of fucking London was now in shut down?*

"We have to go. Gimme your keys, Shamy!" He held out his hand.

"But I have stock to pick up, Nigel. I can't just…"

"They just killed Vinnie!" Nigel interrupted, "Blew his fucking brains out while we tried to catch the Tube, Shamy. These guys are serious!"

She stared back at him, her eyes widening in

horror. "Who did, Nigel?"

"Them! The fucking army! We need to go!" He tried to snatch her keys as he pulled her along through the group of rowdy retailers who were now shouting incoherently.

"No, I'll drive. I need to get to Raj. He's ill!" Her voice was firm, but disbelieving.

"Okay, but we need to go now. We'll get Raj, then try and find a way out of the city. Is your phone working?"

Shamy checked her mobile as they made their way to the car park. Several other traders were leaving through the door as two army trucks screeched to a halt, blocking the exit.

"No, I have no signal!" she gasped, shaking her phone in an attempt to find a connection.

"Where are you parked, Shamy?" Nigel panted, his head pounding. She pointed to the rusty red Nissan Patrol by the trees. "Okay get in and keep your head down!"

They bundled inside and Shamy started the engine. Several soldiers in full masks were rounding up stragglers and herding them back inside the market hanger, rifle butts to the head of those refusing to move and shooting the wheels of any parked cars.

"Over there, through the gap. Quickly!"

Shamy hesitated, giving him a second look, before glancing in her rear-view mirror and gasping in horror. Her colleagues were being manhandled and physically restrained by the soldiers; bags being placed over their heads like they were criminals.

"Oh my god, what are they doing?"

"Now!" Nigel prompted, and she hit the accelerator pedal. The rusty Nissan mounted the kerb before crashing through a row of gorse bushes and back out into the road, the wheels spinning on the grass verge as the soldiers turned and pointed their rifles.

"Take a left!" Nigel shouted over the gunfire as the rear window shattered and they bounced out into the street.

"But it's one way!" Shamy panicked.

"Just do it, it's a short cut out of here…then take a right!" Nigel said, hanging onto the roof handle and pointing to the small turning.

The Nissan crunched against the parked cars as more gunfire erupted behind them, the masked soldiers in the alley pulling more civilians from their slumber and marking the doors with large red crosses.

"What is this madness?" Shamy screamed as they barrelled down the one-way street the wrong way.

"Trust me… Take the next right…down that alley!" He was a cab driver after all.

They saw bodies piled in the alley as teams of people in hazmat suits jumped out of the way. Trucks loaded with people in masks bound for who knows where struggled to free themselves from the zip ties around their wrists.

"DOWN THERE!" Nigel pointed again as more soldiers opened fire on Shamy's car. Side windows exploded as the rounds made dull thuds against the door panels, and side mirrors crunched against parked vehicles. The car went spinning out onto the pavement as they turned down another side street, away from the soldiers.

"WHY ARE THEY DOING THIS!" Shamy screamed, the wheel spinning in her grip, her eyes widening at the scene ahead.

Two police vehicles had blocked the end of the road. Masked officers held a row of people in their pyjamas up against the wall as a doctor tested temperatures and a tannoy system blared out instructions: "Please obey all commands. Those who do not adhere by the law will face the maximum penalty… This area is infected! You are infected!"

Nigel wondered just what the maximum penalty was as he grabbed the wheel and mounted the curb.

"Hit the horn and step on it!" he shouted, as the police turned to see the Nissan hurtle towards them. Shamy yelled out from between her palms, like she was watching some late-night horror film from behind a pillow, as the engine revved and Nigel steered straight towards the officers.

They all scattered, the civilians screaming with Shamy, as Nigel smashed his way through the cordon and out onto the open road, the cars bumper spinning high into the air and the windscreen shattering. Above them, helicopters swooped as more gunfire popped—this time, accompanied by an explosion that sound like it came from the adjacent block. Sirens seemed to wail from every direction and screaming people fled the streets like ship-wrecked rats. Cars were being filled with possessions as panicked citizens fled for sanctuary outside the ring that was being sealed around London. Every road they sped down, they saw the same thing; scared people fleeing for their lives; bodies piled in the

13

streets; soldiers raiding indiscriminately.

Disinfectant trucks slowly idled, spraying huge plumes of detergent into the air from hoses, forcing choking people back into their residences as the skies above were blocked in a shroud of grey dust.

It was as if Big Ben had just struck half past Madness and the curtain had lifted to show the world exactly what chaos lay under the thin veil of normality.

"Jesus Christ! They're clearing London." Nigel choked on detergent spray as he steered the Nissan from the passenger seat, out onto the empty street, struggling to make out which side of the road he should be on.

"Move over, Shamy. I'll take it from here, luv!" They wriggled across the broken glass together, swapping seats as the Nissan rolled into the clearing. The small two-way radio in Shamy's saree squelched as they neared the corner shop

"Shamy! Can you hear me?" Raj was calling her, his coughing heavy.

"Yes, Father. We are coming for you!" Shamy replied into the walkie talkie just as Nigel swung a tight left into a tunnel filled with a chanting mob.

"NO, no! You must stay away...*cough*... They

are searching the building…*cough*…they have a flight manifest with Nigel from upstairs on. He's infected!" Raj's voice faded as a volley of coughs erupted through the speaker. "Please! You must stay away from here. The whole area is infected. Darling, I love you very much. Please stay away!"

Shamy stared at Nigel who was weaving the Nissan through the crowd of angry demonstrators.

"Nigel is here with me. He saved me from the soldiers. They came to the market and—"

Nigel saw the police blockade ahead and brought the Nissan to a violent stop. Soldiers watched, their rifles raised, as the mob approached the car, Molotov cocktails burning in their hands.

"What did you say, Shamy? Shamy?" Raj's voice called out from under the passenger seat.

"Jesus fucking Christ… Get down!" Nigel grabbed Shamy and pulled her down to the seat as the soldiers opened fire. Bottles rained down on the police cars, the mob scattering in all directions.

"Keep your head down!"

Fireballs engulfed soldiers and policemen alike. Nigel turned around, grabbing the headrest, and floored the Nissan again, this time in reverse. Rounds shattered the windscreen, and several soldiers broke ranks, running toward the car as it gathered speed. Nigel frantically fought with the wheel, applying the handbrake and spinning the leather, jerking the Nissan in a cartwheel manoeuvre until they faced the other way.

One of the soldiers grabbed the door handle and yanked it open, but Shamy, sobbing, smacked him on the side of his face, grabbed his respirator, and pulled it from his face as her radio bounced to the bitumen outside. She knocked the soldier to the ground, making Nigel smile. Sticking the car into first gear again, he sped out of the burning tunnel towards Islington, praying he still knew all the short cuts.

***

They crawled down the terraces until they pulled up a few hundred yards from Shamy's father's convenience store. The whole area ahead was in lockdown, with tape and hazmat suits walking around with detergent sprays. Several body bags lay by a truck; similar scenes to those they'd already seen.

"Oh no!" Shamy gasped, her hands to her face, and Nigel turned and saw what she was looking at.

Two hazmat-suited doctors, chaperoned by armed soldiers, were carrying a body bag from Raj's store. They placed it with others already lined up on the footpath. Nigel counted at least twenty. He comforted Shamy as she became hysterical.

"Shamy, stop. Stop! We need to go. We need to get as far away from here as we can. It's not safe here anymore!" He had her head tight against his chest as she sobbed, her black hair pressed against his chin.

"They killed…they….my father…!"

"I know. The government killed a lot of people today, but we need to go. Look, my cab is just over there!" He nodded over to the verge, thankful for once that parking was terrible the night before and he had to park all the way down the road.

"We can't go very far in this, we have to move. Now."

"Where can we go? They are everywhere?" She wiped her face.

Nigel thought for a moment. *God, I need a drink.*

"We can go to my mate, Barry… He has a farm out on the M4. We'll be safe there for now."

Nigel turned off the idling Nissan. He took Shamy's hand, and crouching down, they ducked behind parked cars, hidden from the view of the circus further up the street. When they reached the black cab, Nigel unlocked the rear door and helped Shamy inside.

"Where to luv?" he said, sliding into the driver's seat and smiling in the rear-view mirror. But Shamy was distant, her thoughts with her father, as she moved Nigel's bags from the seat to the floor, noticing the bottle of Johnny Walker poking from it.

"Yeah, pass me that Shamy, will you? I think I need a touch of the hair of the dog for this next trip!"

Shamy sighed. "This stuff will kill your brain, Nigel!"

Gunfire suddenly erupted without warning, shattering the rear cab window and spraying the street with lead. The soldiers outside the convenience store turned towards the armed protestors and returned fire.

Protestors spilling into the side streets were stopped in their tracks in a hail of machine gun fire that tore through parked cars and bone alike, showering the street in a bloody mess. Fires erupted from the Molotov cocktail bombs thrown at the hazmat suited collectors, and they dropped everything to run after the trucks that were already retreating.

Shamy clutched at her neck, blood soaking into her saree. She slid down the seat, her eyes pleading for Nigel. In a flash, he was outside, yanking her door open and pulling her to the safety of the nature strip and the tree line of the square.

"We need to get you help!"

The crowd passed by, throwing anything they could find at the retreating trucks. Nigel pulled Shamy deeper into the undergrowth as the foot battle moved on.

"The shop, Nigel," Shamy gasped. "In the back room…medical bag."

Nigel hoisted Shamy onto his shoulder and ran for the safety of the shop.

"Don't look, Shamy!" he said as he passed the row of body bags abandoned outside. "Just don't look."

But she did.

13

X-DAY +16

POTUS White House briefing:
Today I am instructing my administration to halt funding of the World Health Organization while a review is conducted to assess the World Health Organization's role in severely mismanaging and covering up the spread of the coronavirus.

ERIN

LANNAH MARSHALL

LONDON, UK

Erin woke to fire.

Long tendrils across her vision, copper-coloured, that bled into hues of oranges and pinks in the dawn behind it.

Not fire.

Hair.

"You're awake!" Mother's rolling tongue hitched, and Erin's whole body almost convulsed with relief.

"You're a dream," whispered Erin, eyes rolling.

"No, no, I got your text. I'm so happy you remembered this road," whispered Mother, pressing her forehead into Erin's. She was cool, wrapped in plastic, and breathless. She spoke through a mask, but it was her. Behind those goggles were her eyes. "We're going to move you now."

"What?"

13

Erin was lifted and pulled into the back of a van. It stank of mud and oil, like it was moonlighting as a plumber's vehicle. No gurney. Old school P.E mats on the floor. Erin gasped as a cold cloth was pressed against her skin and Jian's car seat placed next to her.

"I-Is he okay?" Erin whispered, her fingers reaching out for him.

"He is," someone said.

"What's his name?" Mother asked.

"Jian." Erin's mouth twitched into a soft, smitten smile.

"What does that mean?"

"Strong," Erin coughed and grinned. "Healthy."

"He is healthy, if a little cold." They were fussing over him, checking his temperature.

"He's not got it?"

"Must be immune."

"That's my grandson." Mother's voice was warm. Proud. "He's beautiful."

"He screams."

"He does," said Mother. "That's how we found you. Sounds like he has colic. Thank fuck."

Erin rolled her head back and sighed. A soothing cold was gripping at her bones. An ointment to the fire that burned there, that hid there as embers beneath her skin.

"Why didn't you tell me?" Mother asked. "Why didn't you come straight home?"

Tears spilled from Erin's eyes as she reached up to her mother's waiting hand. The van was moving now, but Erin couldn't feel it. Only see it.

"I thought you'd be mad," said Erin. "I thought…I thought you'd be disappointed…in me."

"Oh, my baby," Mother gasped and embraced her, pulling her up and cradling Erin's head like she was a baby again. Like she was small, sick with flu.

Erin held her back, clinging with the little strength she had, until all at once it left her, and traded it for sleep.

"You silly girl."

MAGGIE

GREGG CUNNINGHAM

The old man sobbed, watching his wife jump overboard, following without thought.

Only the waves replied as the infected *Goddess of the Sea* lolled on the ocean.

"MAGGIE!" he gurgled as sea water stung his lungs. Blood trailed behind his dangling severed leg as he crawled from the frothing ocean.

He tried to stop the blood flow from his wife's neck, his own twisted leg almost pulled from the tendons barely holding the limb to his thigh muscle.

Nobody came to help.

"SOMEBODY HELP ME!" he pleaded. His own wounds barked for attention as he frantically tried to stem the hot, flowing stream pumping from his dying partners neck.

Nobody came. Nobody wanted to catch this new mutated infection. Instead, the people watched the tugboats from the harbour wall, pulling the

Cruiseliner away from the dock under the order of the authorities—the fuel stop request denied yet again—as the two elderly passengers jumped from the ship.

Videos would show their plight, though.

They'd swim through shark infested waters for each other.

Alex Logan

PAMELA JEFFS

A MILITARY HOSPITAL, LONDON, UK

I wake, woozy. My mouth tastes like old blood and my lungs are two pools of fire in my chest. It's dark, both in my room and outside the window. I search for Connor. He's there, pacing by the exit door. His eyes are glued to the small viewing panel that looks out into the corridor. He must sense me. He turns. His ruined face is revealed; half cast in shadow and half in the blue-white flickering lights slipping in through the glass in the door. His lips press thin.

"What's happening?" I ask.

"Go back to sleep, Alex," he says.

"Why?"

"It's not good out there."

"Is that gunfire I hear?"

Connor stalks to my bed. "Don't worry about anything, Alex," he says. "I'm here. I'll watch over you."

I'm so tired. I close my eyes and do as he says. Darkness welcomes me with open arms.

Every Day at 3:15pm

PETER J. FOOTE

"Every day at 3:15pm, and for one hundred and eighty-seven stinking days, that kid practices the same song. When self-isolation was mandated, I assumed I could handle it, but this is cruel and unusual punishment."

Eyes flicking between wristwatch and open bathroom window, the man waits as the seconds tick away, his breathing the only sound reaching his ears.

Across the alley, in the next apartment building, a bedroom door opens. A sandy-haired teen steps in carrying a trombone.

"Never again," the man mutters. He chambers a round and sights along his rifle. The shot rings out, echoing between the buildings.

The deed done. Sirens perform a different tune, one that grows closer and closer.

"I wonder what the bribe is for murder nowadays…four or five rolls of toilet paper?"

Jacinda Ardern, New Zealand Prime Minister:
Go hard and go early

X-DAY +3 WEEKS

POTUS Tweet:
A great early result from a drug that will start tomorrow in New York and other places!

Beata

SHAWN M. KLIMEK

It all began last winter, when Beata caught the flu.

Then Beata sneezed on Ava, so that Ava caught it,
too.

When tender-hearted Lexi gave her sisters both a
hug,

The squeeze made Ava cough, which is how Lexi
caught the bug.

Now Kylie, being eldest of her sisters, and thus
wiser,

Knew that 99 percent of germs are killed by
sanitizer.

But what she didn't know, and present misery
confirms,

Is that flus are caused by viruses, which aren't the
same as germs.

When folks ask how it all began, tell them this
much is true:

It all began last winter, when Beata caught the flu.

13

POTUS Tweet:
HYDROXYCHLOROQUINE & AZITHROMYCIN, taken together, have a real chance to be one of the biggest game changers in the history of medicine. The FDA has moved mountains - Thank You!

LILY

D.M. BURDETT

SURREY, UK

Lily quietly placed the glass of water on the bedside table next to Joseph. "Make sure you drink some, Joey," she said, softly.

Joseph lifted his head from his mother's shoulder and eyed the glass. Tears had left clean rivulets on his dirty cheeks. "I'm so hungry, Lily."

Lily looked over at the window. Although the curtains were drawn, a sliver of morning light was peeking through the gap. "If Mum doesn't get up today, I'll go out and find something."

Joseph's eyes widened, and he sat up with a jerk. Reaching up, he grabbed Lily's hand in his small, pudgy fingers. "No, Lily," he said, fear in his voice. "You can't leave me here."

Lily smiled, but no light touched her lips. "Don't worry about it now," she said, putting a hand on his cheek. "I'm sure Mum will be ok by tonight."

They both turned to look at their mother.

Andie Sullivan lay on her back, head propped on a pillow, dead to the world but for the shallow rise and fall of her chest and the rasping breaths. Dark veins marbled her grey face, and cold sweat dampened her skin. Joseph had placed her hands, fingers entwined, below her breasts and they accentuated the slow movements.

Joseph laid his head back on his mother's shoulder, his arm draped gently over her stomach.

Lily watched them for a moment before retreating downstairs. She sat in front of the television, the only thing playing, on a loop, being the emergency procedure: "…isolate…mark your door…someone will be with you soon…stay indoors…keep your distance…make your way to a processing point…isolate…" On and on it went while Lily's stomach grumbled.

She remembered back to the day they'd come for her dad.

The sign had been on the door for four days before the truck came, slowly rumbling into their street. Lily, Joseph, and Andie had watched its slow progress from the window, Joseph's head buried in

Andie's stomach, tears flowing freely.

The three men, head to toe in biohazard suits, entered the house without knocking. They stood in the hallway for a moment, like aliens visiting from another world, before the leader asked, "Upstairs?"

Mum had nodded then, and the three men wearily trudged the stairs to the first floor. After not much time, they returned, carrying the black body bag between them. Dad had died days before, a horrible gurgling death, blood and foam bubbling from his lungs, and red tears streaming down his face.

They watched as he was loaded unceremoniously into the back of the van, stacking him on top of a growing pile. The suits got back in the van and carried on the slow roll again, stopping nine or ten houses down.

All that time, Joseph cried into Mum's cardigan.

Lily knew time was running out for her mum— she could hear it in the wheezy rattles that Andie sighed out in tortured breaths. She was so tired; tired of keeping up the pretence in front of Joseph. She broke down and cried into her sleeve until the sun set behind the neighbouring houses, filling the lounge with darkness once more.

***

Something…imperceptible…changed. Hardly noticeable. But Lily woke with a start.

Disorientated for a moment, she blinked into the weak light squeezing through the blinds before she realised what had woken her.

It was the silence.

She lifted her head to look at her mother, and pain etched its way across her face. She lifted a hand to touch Mum's greying face, and Lily closed her mother's unblinking eyes with gentle fingertips.

At least it's over, Lily thought; her only comfort. The inevitable had happened.

Lily stood and made her way to the other side of the bed. "Joe-joe?" she whispered softly, shaking Joseph's shoulders gently. He stirred a little. "Joe?"

He opened his eyes at last. The look on Lily's face must have spoken a thousand words because he started to cry, not even needing to turn his head to look at his mother. He climbed from the bed and wrapped his arms around Lily. She squeezed him back, and he sneezed into her shoulder through his wailing.

She gave him a moment, but then she took his hand and they left the room together, never looking back.

***

Two men in hazmat suits carried out the body bag while a third held open the door. He eyed the children, his eyes wrinkled with worry. "You kids gonna be ok?" he asked, his voice muffled through the mask.

"Yes." Lily nodded, hesitantly.

"Where's your dad?"

Lily's eyes went to the window where she could see the black bag being placed in the back of the van.

"Fuck," the man muttered under his breath. "You got food?"

Lily nodded again, hugging Joseph close as he peered at the man from beneath her arm. "We got some crackers. And a few tins of tuna."

The man stared at her for a moment, then glanced towards the kitchen. He seemed to be thinking of more to say, but then he shook his head and left the house.

13

After a few moments, he returned, his oversized gloves clutching a cellophane-wrapped sandwich. He held it out to Lily, and she took it slowly, tears welling up in her eyes.

"I'll call it in to the office, tell 'em we got home alone kids out here. Someone'll come out to you, but it might take a few days…maybe a week," he said. "You gotta stay in the house, though. You hear me?"

Lily nodded.

"I mean it, kid. It's not safe out there. You wait here till the bus comes. OK?"

They both stared with wide eyes. The man shook his head, and without looking back, left the house, closing the door behind him.

Lily looked at the sandwich, her stomach aching, as Joseph sniffled. "Looks like ham," she said. As the van's engine grumbled into life and it recommenced its slow journey down the street, she led Joe into the kitchen.

They sat at the table, the plastic-wrapped sandwich sitting between them, and she poured water into mugs. Once the cellophane was pulled back from the little package, they looked at one another before they swooped in, taking a half each. Lily wolfed hers down in seconds, savouring the butter…ham…bread… Joe sat in silence; the only sign he was still crying were the fat tears that leaked from his eyes now and then.

Later, Lily took inventory. "We need to go out," she said as she checked out the last of the food in the cupboard; a tin of tuna and three dry crackers.

"The man… He said he would talk to his office," Joseph said.

"He said it could take a week, we can't last on a tin of tuna and some crackers for a week, Joe-joe."

"But we had a big lunch today."

Lily looked at the empty packaging, and remorse hit her hard. "We shouldn't haven't eaten it all. Should have saved some for tomorrow."

Joseph eyed the balled-up cellophane.

"We'll go to Auntie Margaret's. Like Mum said we should do."

"But there're no buses, Lil."

"I know. We'll have to walk."

Joseph looked towards the window. "The man said it's not safe."

Lily's brow furrowed, and she sighed. "Joseph," she said, more harshly than she'd meant. "We can get picked up by the child catcher," she said, using the words Mum had used to refer to the child protection services van that collected lone children in the streets. "We can sit here and starve, get picked up by the meat wagon. Or we can walk. OK?"

Joseph stared at her, eyes beginning to brim again. "OK," he mumbled. "I can walk."

Relenting, Lily leaned down and gave her brother a hug. "Sorry."

"How long will it take?" he asked.

"I don't know. A few days, maybe? Hang on…" She left the room, returning a few minutes later with some street maps from her dad's study, and a pen. She opened one out on the table, and finding the street, circled it in red. "This is where we are." She checked the index, located the right square on the paper, and marked another street in red. "This is Auntie Margaret's."

They both sat staring at the spaghetti mess of streets in between.

"A few days?" Joseph repeated, blinking at the map.

Lily shrugged. "I don't really know, but hopefully. It doesn't look so far, does it, Joe-Joe?"

"It looks a long way to me."

"We'll need to rest at night, find somewhere warm."

"Break into houses?" Joseph said, his eyes alight with adventure.

"We might have to. But there are some hospitals on the way. We might be able to stay there." She dotted a few places on the map that were marked with Hs.

"When will we leave?"

Lily checked her watch and then looked at Joseph for a moment. "I guess there's no reason to stay. It's late now, and getting dark, we could set out first thing in the morning."

"OK," Joseph said, a hint of excitement in his voice.

"Go and pack a bag. Not too much, because you need to be able to carry it, Joe," she said, envisioning the myriad of toys he would want to take. "You need underwear, your wash kit. We'll split the food between us in case…" Her voice trailed off, not wanting to think about them getting split up.

Joe slid from his seat and left the room. As Lily heard his socked feet on the stairs, and then a small cough from the landing above, she dropped her head onto her arms on the table and cried quietly.

POTUS Press Conference:
So, if we have thousands or hundreds of thousands of people that get better just by, you know, sitting around and even going to work — some of them go to work, but they get better...

BEN DAVIDSON

DAVID BOWMORE

A HOSPITAL, LONDON, UK

He woke with a startled cry. Sweat prickled his forehead. He tried to raise his left hand to wipe the tears from his eyes but was halted by a rigid pair of handcuffs keeping his arm attached to the metal frame of the bed. In anger, he yanked at the bound wrist, once, twice and finally once more. The cuffs rattled on the metal bar, but held firm.

"What's going on? Is anyone there? Someone answer me." His dry throat produced a weak croak.

No one came. He shuffled back into the pillows so he was in a semi-recumbent position, and took stock of his situation.

The room was small. From the window he could see, through vertical blinds, the sun blazing in the middle of a clear blue sky. The room was stocked with medical machines, the likes of which he might have seen had he been one of those sad tossers who watched medical programmes. *How do you know you're not one of those sad tossers, Ben?*

"Ben," he said. "My name is Ben."

Then he ran his uncuffed hand over his head, finding it thoroughly bandaged. The back of his head was tender to the touch, even under thick wadding.

"Shit."

Twisting around on the bed, he saw a thick wire with a plastic button hanging from a hook on the bedside cabinet. Snatching it from its resting place, he pressed the button repeatedly while calling out for help.

Still no one came.

Sticky pads attached to his temples had fine wires running to the dead machines next to his bed. He pulled these from his skin, still calling for help and trying to control the panic that he knew might lead to one of his episodes. A tube from his nostril was hooked over his right ear and taped to his stubbly cheek. It was slippery with bodily goo and made him gag as he felt the end pass up his throat. It fell from his nostril, a trail of sticky blood smeared across his chin. Another tube ran from the back of the handcuffed hand. He yanked it free, leaving a small trickle of blood and a bruise in its wake.

He rubbed at his eyes and then blew his nose on

the bedsheets.

"Think, Ben. What happened?" he said out aloud, but nothing came to his panicking mind…except a crowded plane. Had he been on holiday? Where?

He awkwardly poured himself a glass of water. It was warm. How long had it been sitting there?

"Time to move, Ben."

He climbed over the edge of the bed, only to realise another tube was inserted into his penis. The other end was attached to a bag of yellow liquid hanging below the bed.

"Oh shit!" He slammed a fist into the bed. "Where the fuck is everybody? Help me. This is a hospital, isn't it?"

He tried to tug the tube free, only to find an intense pain somewhere deep inside. And now he had the urge to take a leak, but that wouldn't be possible until he found someone to drain the bag.

"Double shit."

He opened three of the brakes on the wheels of the bed, but the fourth was beyond his reach. He dragged the bed away from the wall, wincing as the machines clattered and shattered to the floor. He would have to be careful; his feet were bare, as were his back and arse in the exposed hospital gown he wore.

Standing at the head end and grabbing the steel safety bars that prevent patients falling out, he dragged the bed backwards towards the door.

The corridor he emerged into was empty; empty of life, empty of sound. His past experience of hospitals was of constant noise; groaning and moaning, air conditioning units, elevators, squeaking footsteps on polished floors and chattering nurses. But not today, today everything was silent.

"Hello. Anybody?"

Panting, he and the bed arrived at the lifts only to find them inoperable, with no sound, light or movement. He knew it would be the case, but it still made him angry.

"Shit-fucking-shit-bollocks. Sixth floor! How the fuck am I going to get out of here with this dead fucking weight?"

The stairs were opposite the elevators. He pushed the bed through double doors. Facing him were floor to ceiling windows, confirming his elevated position in the world. Each floor had a set of dog-leg stairs descending to the next. Each section of steps had twelve risers. The bed would have to go first, that way he could bear the weight. If he went first, the bed would be more difficult to control, and might come crashing down on top of him.

Soon the bed was at a forty-five-degree angle, and although heavy, not far from the little landing and the half-way point to the fifth floor.

His confidence grew as he turned onto the second flight of stairs. The rattle, thump, rattle, thump was some sort of rhythmic comfort in the unnaturally quiet building.

Soon, his cuffed wrist had taken enough wrenches to justify a rest. And he badly needed to take a leak. He found a nurses' station not far from the double doors of the fifth floor. Sitting by the blank computer monitor was a half-full plastic bottle of water. Sweet Jesus, he was thirsty…part of him had imagined he would have to go all Bear Grylls and drink from his piss bag.

Where was everybody? Where were all the staff? His bare feet were sore from the slapping on the hard floor, and his exposed behind should really be covered up. He decided shoes and trousers were a priority, after he had found someone to remove the catheter and the bed. Then, as he pushed the trolley-bed into a ward, all thoughts of help were swept from

13

his mind.

Every bed housed a dead woman, their faces pale and hair encrusted with vomit. The smell of puke and bodily waste brought the water he had drank back up and he fell to his knees. He looked up again. One woman had a newborn clasped to her bosom. It didn't move. Then he saw the little cots beside each bed and, afraid of what he would see if he were to look too closely, he fled the room, dragging the bed back to the stairs.

He bashed the trolley through the double doors to the stairs with an almighty clatter and began a hasty descent to the fourth floor. He was not prepared to take the weight. The bed began to pull him forward until all control was lost. He landed in a heap, his wrist and arm twisting so much he thought it might have broken. Miraculously, the trolley was still upright, even though he was on his knees and his cuffed wrist awkwardly in place above his head.

"Fuck! What the fuck happened? Heeelp."

Then he realised the bag of foul-smelling urine had split and his own bladder was adding to the puddle he was kneeling in. A chuckle made itself present as he thought of his situation. He was still laughing as he tried to dry himself with the bed sheet.

Once recovered, Ben decided to try for the next floor, and taking it steady, realised the wheel that had previously been locked had opened during the tumble. Perhaps things were going his way after all?

"Take it easy, Ben. Slow and steady wins the race." Grandad always said that. "I should have listened to you more, Grandad. What did I do to get into this mess?"

The sun was setting. Jesus, how long had it been since he'd woken up? An hour, perhaps two? It felt like a whole day. He climbed back onto the bed to inspect the piss pipe dangling from his manhood. About eight inches along the length, the pipe split in two. One tube went to the now useless bag. The other tube ended in a green piece of hard plastic the size of a lime. Upon careful inspection, he saw a valve recessed about a centimetre into the lime. His conclusion was that this, somehow, locked the entire tube in place inside his bladder. *Probably a vacuum.*

He leaned forward, and with images of teenage experimentation, put his lips tight around the plastic valve. After counting to three he gave a suck and was rewarded with a small amount of liquid; salty liquid and not piss as he had feared. Then he started the slow process of sucking some liquid from the tube and spitting, sucking and spitting, until the liquid was gone. Tentatively, he pulled on the tube and felt it begin to slide roughly from his penis. He tried to imagine the sadistic bastard who had devised such a contraption burning in the pits of Hell, as it scraped its way free, tugging and hooking on the delicate inner workings of his organ. With a sigh of relief and a whispered, "Thank fuck," his prick flopped free and dribbled a small amount of watery blood.

Leaning back against the wall, sleep overtook him.

LILY

D.M. BURDETT

SURREY, UK

It's early when Lily closes the front door behind them, and they step out the gate and onto the front pavement for the first time in a month.

As they make their way down to the main road, the streets are silent and eerie. A cat stares at them from the bonnet of a car, pausing in its rhythmic licking of a paw to watch them cross the street.

At the corner with the main road, Mrs Richardson from number one peers down at them from an upstairs window. Lily raises her hand to wave, but Mrs Richardson shakes her head grimly, and then drops the net curtain back into place.

"Well, that's rude," Joseph said, looking up at the empty window.

Lily shrugged. "Come on."

They walked for an hour, leaving the village of Bagshot behind, without seeing another soul. But

then a crashing of glass brought them to a stop. Joseph reached up and grasped Lily's hand. "What was that?"

Lily stared around the residential street, unable to locate where the sound was coming from, but then across the street, a few houses down, a blonde head popped out of a window, followed by a red t-shirt and blue jeans. The boy—who Lily thought seemed only slightly older than herself—balanced on the windowsill on one knee as he looked around, his head cocked to one side. He scanned the neighbourhood, his eyes eventually finding them and widening in surprise.

At the same moment, two men ran from one side of the street to the other, one of them spilling cans from a bag as he went. He stopped, scampering around to collect up the food, until a voice hollered, "You bastards," and a gunshot rang out, making Joseph and Lily clutch at each other. The blonde head at the window down the street disappeared back into the house.

A woman, dressed in a giraffe onesie and wellington boots, stomped out from behind a wall, raised her gun, and pulled the trigger again, but the two men had already scattered down the street, racing off between abandoned cars. "Fucking bastards," the woman muttered.

She stooped down to pick up the cans that had been left behind, and her eyes found the children as she stood back up. She stared at them for a moment before yelling up the street, waving the weapon. "You want some of this, too, you little fuckers?"

Lily, eyes wide, shook her head haltingly.

Seemingly satisfied, the woman went back in the direction she'd come, her eyes still scanning the ground, and Lily hurried Joseph across the road and down a side street.

***

After a few more streets, they turned a corner into a dual carriageway where no cars travelled anymore. The road, the businesses, the houses on either side…they all looked deserted.

"This is the A30," Lily said, her finger tracing a line on the street map and then pointing across the empty junction at Stationers. "If we go down here to Feltham, it will be starting to get late and we'll need to find somewhere to keep warm for the night. Do you think you can manage another mile…that's about an hour or so at the speed you're wa—"

Movement out of the corner of her eye caught her attention—the blur of a red t-shirt disappearing behind a building further up the road—and she narrowed her eyes suspiciously.

"Come on," she said, and holding hands, she pulled him across the road to the central reservation, walking between the metal barriers, and looking to the distant high-rise blocks ahead.

After a short while, Joseph let out a faint, low mewl. "What's up, Joe-Joe?" His steps shortened, and he curled his arm into Lily's and pressed his face into her coat sleeve. "What is it?" He pointed to the side of the road where a bloodied bootee lay next to a small unmoving bundle. "Don't look," Lily said, and she tightened her grip on his hand, walking faster, putting distance between them and the tiny shoe.

As they got closer to the city high-rises, Lily realised they were being followed. Every so often, the red blur would dash from one place to the next.

"For goodness' sake," Lily muttered under her breath.

"What is it, Lily?"

"That boy. He's still with us."

Joseph began to turn.

"No! Don't look!"

"What are we going to do?"

Lily thought as they walked. "We're going to find out what he wants." And then she turned and shouted. "Come out. We know you're there."

Nothing moved for a moment or two, and then the boy stepped out slowly from behind a bin up the street. He stopped, one hand on the bin lid, and stared at them.

"What are you doing?" Lily called, but the boy continued to stare.

"For the love of cheesy Wotsits," Lily breathed. "What's he doing?"

"He's being a boy. You're all idiots." She scowled, and then shouted again, "Stay there."

Dragging Joseph with her, she stomped towards the boy. He looked flighty, as if he might disappear at any moment, but then he stood his ground.

"What are you doing?" Lily said when they reached him.

He had the good sense to look sheepish. "Nothing."

"Then why are you following us."

The boy looked at his feet, stabbing the

pavement with his toe, and shrugged.

"Where's your family?"

"Gone," the boy said quietly, still inspecting his shoes.

Lily glanced at Joseph.

"You're on your own?"

The boy nodded.

Lily looked him up and down and sighed. "Do you want to come with us?"

Joseph pulled on her arm. "No Lily," he said urgently. "We don't know him."

"Shush, Joe," she said, frowning at him. "Do you?" she said, turning back to the boy.

He shrugged and then nodded.

She sighed again. "OK, come on. Let's go," she turned and started to walk, and after two houses, the boy caught up with them and got into step beside them.

"What's your name?" Lily asked.

"Jayden."

"I'm Lily, and this is Joseph." Jayden nodded at Joseph who squinted back at him.

"Where are you from, Jayden? Where's your house?"

"Brighton."

Lily's eyes widened. "That's a long way to

come. You walked all the way?"

"I've been…on my own…for almost a week. I was running out of food, so I had to come out and find some. I got a lift to the Victoria Barracks at Windsor with another family—we were told there was a processing point, but there was nothing when we got there, it was abandoned. So, I walked for a few days and ended up here."

"The van didn't come for you?"

"The van?"

Joseph and Lily looked at each other. "We were told after, after Mum…left us…that they would call it in, and someone would come for us. We were told to stay in the house until they came."

Jayden shook his head. "No one came."

"What did they say when they…collected…your parents?"

Jayden shook his head. "No one came."

Lily gasped. "Did you put the sign on your door? Like they tell you to?"

"Yes. I painted the sign on a sheet and hung it over the front door when Mum died. No one came. I waited by the window the whole time."

"That's terrible," Lily said as Joseph tightened his grip on her hand. "So, your parents were…"

13

"Mum died 13 days ago. Dad died two days later. They were in their bed upstairs. I put the sign up after Mum..." A single tear slid down Jayden's cheek. "No one came. I ran out of food last week, so I left them there."

Although he made no sound, Jayden's shoulders shook with the tears he tried to conceal. Lily patted him on the shoulder, and they walked on in silence until they reached the inner-city streets. Day was turning to dusk, and their shadows were getting long and hard.

"We need to stop somewhere for the night," Lily said. "What about that alley?"

They headed over the road into a well-lit alley and cautiously walked its length. Finding it empty, they hunkered down at one end, behind empty bins, and opened their bags. Between them they shared some of their food, and as dusk turned to dark, Joseph and Lily huddled up, Joseph's head on Lily's knee.

Much later, her breath frosting on the air, Lily was woken by Joseph coughing into her leg, his little body heaved with the effort. She patted his back softly. "It's OK, Joe-joe," she whispered. As he settled back down, she looked over at Jayden, who gave her a look she couldn't decipher.

BEN DAVIDSON

DAVID BOWMORE

A HOSPITAL, LONDON, UK

The rising sun warmed Ben to consciousness as it glared through the tall glass. His dreams had been filled with loneliness, death, and a pretty girl with bobbed hair and tattoos on her back.

His stomach grumbled, but food was far from the front of his mind. He was determined to get out of the hospital from Hell, and the only way to do that was by descending the stairs. A smell ascended the stairwell, bringing images he hoped were pure imagination.

He turned his mind to more practical matters; mainly the detachment of the bed from his wrist. Somewhere in the hospital there must be a storeroom, a place where the caretakers kept tools for day to day repairs.

He lowered the bed one stair at a time until he was on the little landing window, and took a long

13

hard look at the familiar vista. How in all the seven Hells had he ended up slap bang in the middle of London, in a hospital on the other side of the Thames from the Houses of Parliament?

But where had everyone gone? An open-top double decker bus lay on its side, halfway across the bridge. All was still except for several plumes of smoke spiralling into the clear sky in the distance.

He rattled his foggy brain to figure out a way to free himself. If he remembered London correctly, he wasn't too far from Waterloo Station, and surely such a place would have cutters or some other heavy-duty tools he could use to cut the bastard bed free. He guessed that no more than a mile separated him from the means to his freedom. Easy. Especially with no traffic on the roads to hinder his journey. The clock at the top of the famous building read eight forty-five. The streets should have been busy with commuters on their way to work.

The stench worsened with every footstep he took. By the time he reached the ground floor, flies not only buzzed but swarmed. The double doors only partially opened as he pushed on them. He shoved harder and they began to give. When there was room, he had to nudge the corpse of an elderly man with his foot. He tripped and fell to his knees, but the fall was broken by the body of yet another corpse.

All along the ground floor, bodies were piled two or three to a trolley. The dead lined the floors, young and old alike, stinking of death and secretions. Bloated stomachs and bulging eyes looked up at him as he dragged his bed along the corridor. He made silent apologies every time the heavy trolley rolled over the outstretched limbs and he heard the snap of bone. He tried not to think of what he was stepping in as his sore feet slapped through sludgy puddles of muck.

The reception area was full, many people having died in the chairs waiting for help. A young couple holding hands, a young toddler in her arms, looked like they were sleeping. Many more corpses had toppled to the floor. Gases escaped the bodies with farts and groans as he pulled the bed over them. Soon the lower half of his legs were covered in the gore of the dead. The thought of infection and disease hammered away at his brain. As a chef, he was more than aware of the need for proper and correct hygiene, but what he was walking through was beyond comprehension.

He wondered how long he had been unconscious

13

for all this to have happened, and why he had survived such a catastrophe.

Eventually, he dragged the bed through the large sliding doors to breathe beautiful, fresh, glorious air. It filled his lungs and chilled the tears on his cheeks.

"Thank you, God. Thank you."

It had rained during the night. He crouched in a puddle and tried to wash the blood and grime from his lower legs.

"Less than a mile, Ben. You can do this."

Dragging the bed out onto the roads of London, he looked once again at the Houses of Parliament. "Where were all you bastards when we needed you?" he said.

He could see boats in a marina bobbing; their rigging calling to him with gentle tinkling. Birdsong came from every direction. Somewhere in the distance, a dog howled. No traffic or trains or radios or any number of daily noises that are always taken for granted. Only the sounds of nature.

He lurched away from the bridge, following the signs for Waterloo Station. Many cars had been abandoned; several had crashed. Bodies lay haphazardly about, often in a pool of vomit and muck. Rats feasted and did little to avoid Ben and his trundling bed.

One of the wheels fell from the trolley and his estimate of an hour to reach the train station was thrown out the window. He swore at the world in the loudest, vulgarest way possible.

The vibrations of the trolley in combination with the tight cuff rubbed the flesh of his wrist to the point where it oozed blood. And he daren't look at his feet, fearing they would be raw from walking on the hard tarmac. It would be just his luck to survive some kind of deadly plague only to die of a simple infection. *Not plague, Ben. COVID-19.* Fragments of memory returned. A stag party in Rome. A newspaper headline. A moped.

He wanted to lie down and sleep. He wanted someone to take the cuff off, and he wanted someone to help with his wounds. But stopping now, when he was so close to freedom, was not an option. What if he were not the only survivor? What if others came across him, almost naked and attached to the bed? His fears were confirmed as he passed the body of an elderly woman. The bullet hole in her head unmistakably the work of another human being. Had she been put out of her misery, or had she been attacked?

13

He stopped as another memory surfaced; he was groggy, his vision blurred, and he was lying on the floor looking at the ceiling…and then Jenny had stepped into view, the cricket bat held ready to strike again.

"I think he's unconscious," she'd said into the phone.

But what had he done to receive such treatment?

As he once again began his journey, the locking hinges that normally kept the bed at one of several heights rattled loose, and with a painful twist to his bloodied wrist, dragged him to his knees.

"You fucking cunt wanker!" He gasped for breath and tried to lift the bed so as to drag it, but it being heavy and he being tired and weary, he was forced to bend double and continue the journey bent over.

He nearly missed it, so intent was he on his task, but he passed by the front of a small DIY store. A smile cracked his face as he paused to stretch his back and he saw the sign: Home & Trade.

"You fucking beauty, you."

Someone has already taken a brick to the glass door and he had no trouble entering, as long as he didn't mind walking on broken glass. But his feet were too sore, and his need too great, to feel the cuts.

He found industrial cutters in the third aisle, and within minutes, had cut through the steel bar of the bed either side of the handcuff. Then he set to on the cuff itself. Eventually, his bruised and bloodied wrist was free of the bastard.

After an age, he wiped his eyes and began to inspect the soles of his feet. Blisters had been raised and broken. He removed several pieces of glass and was satisfied that none remained. Although sore, in time they should heal.

Ben pulled on a pair of tradesmen's trousers with far too many pockets, and a pair of size nine steel toe capped trainers. He needed food, so helped himself to chocolate bars at the counter. A coffee pot had a thin layer of green mould floating on top of it, so he grabbed a warm tin of pop from the fridge. He was about to leave when he remembered the lady with the bullet hole and returned to find a hammer. It was better than nothing,

By the time he reached Waterloo Station, the sun had set. Some streetlights illuminated the dead roads, but inside, the complex was almost entirely dark. Emergency lighting cast everything in a green hue. Ben didn't care. All he wanted was to lie down and

sleep. And he did so on a bench inside a plastic pub. It was the sort of place that could be found in every train station in every city and town of England, but the Scotch was still sound and served as a perfectly acceptable nightcap.

LILY

D.M. BURDETT

SURREY, UK

Waking up in Feltham

They woke early, the morning sun taking the chill out of the air, and ate frugally—a cracker and water—to save their supplies, but Lily thought she heard the heavy clank of tins when Jayden lifted his bag and she wondered if the boy had more than he was saying. Perhaps the last week on his own had been hard on him and he was scared of being hungry. She couldn't blame him, but her stomach grumbled at her reasonableness.

After a full minute of coughing, his hands on his knees for balance, Lily helped Joseph wipe bloody sputum from his lips, all the time aware of Jayden's heavy stare on her back.

"Are we ready?" she said jovially as she stood, hiding the tissue in her pocket.

Jayden nodded slowly and headed out of the

alley, walking ahead. After an hour, he disappeared into the distance, and Lily and Joseph were once again alone.

***

Richmond

"Auntie Margaret!"

"I don't think she's at home, Joey."

"Where's she going to be? Everyone is supposed to be stuck inside."

Lily looked up at the bedroom windows where the curtains were open. "Let's try round the back."

At the back of the house, the patio doors were locked up, but Lily found the key under the leg of the barbeque where it always was. She unlocked the door and slid it open, stepping into the cool room.

"Auntie Margaret?" Joseph called again.

"Go and see if the car is in the garage," she said, and Joseph raced off to the kitchen. She went up the stairs to the upper floors and poked her head into each of the bedrooms. In Auntie Margaret's room, the wardrobes stood open and most of the clothes were missing or strewn on the bed. Lily stepped across the threshold and opened the top drawers in her aunt's dresser. Finding it empty of the huge cotton knickers that she knew were stored there, she closed the drawer and went back downstairs, just as Joseph returned to the lounger.

"Car's gone," he said sadly.

"Looks like she packed up her clothes and left."

"What now?"

Lily shrugged with a sigh. "I guess to the Dome then."

They left the house by the same route and retuned the spare key to the bottom of the barbeque leg.

***

Later in the day, as the sun began to sink below the apartment buildings in the distance, Lily heard footsteps behind.

"Hi," said Jayden sheepishly.

Lily scowled at him. "Where have you been? Didn't you think we'd be worried?"

"I wasn't worried," Joseph said with a mucusy sniff as he gave Jayden a side-long look.

Lily tutted.

"I saw you at that house."

497

"You followed us there?" Lily asked, incredulously.

Jayden shrugged. "I've nowhere else to go."

"She's already left. We're going to the Dome now. That's what the TV says to do. We need to find somewhere to stay the night. The weather's too cool in the alleyways for Joseph, with his…cold."

Jayden eyed Joseph for a moment before saying, "I found some food in a house a few streets away. It's empty, but there're still some cans in the cupboards." He opened his bag to show Lily, and she saw baked beans and cans of cola on the top. Jayden dug into his pockets. "I got these too," he said, holding out some paracetamol and ibuprofen packets. "For his *cold…*"

Lily glanced at Joseph and back again before taking the pills and stuffing them in the side pocket of her backpack. "Thank you, Jayden. That was very thoughtful."

"I thought we could stay there tonight, as it's getting dark. There's clean, made-up beds and hot water."

"Hot water?" Lily said, her eyebrows raising. Jayden shrugged. "What are we waiting for?"

***

East Sheen

Jayden turned, and they followed him through the streets for an hour until they reached the house, set back on a leafy street with hyacinths in neat borders against a white picket fence.

"The back door is unlocked," Jayden said, heading for the side gate. They slipped through into an immaculate backyard full of roses.

In the small kitchen, everything was tidy and clean, and Lily rushed to the cupboards and flung open the doors. Neat lines of cans filled every shelf, and she beamed over her shoulder at Jayden and Joseph.

"I told you," Jayden said as he leaned on the kitchen counter.

"We need to fill our bags before we leave in the morning," Lily said. "But just what we need to last us to the checkpoint, leave the rest for someone who might need it more."

"The gas works too," Jayden said, nodding at the hob.

Joseph's eyes lit up. "Can we have hot baked beans?" he asked excitedly, and Lily laughed.

"I think I can manage that," she said with a laugh

and started opening cupboards to look for a pan.

Later, Joseph took a cool shower to help with his temperature. He dressed in clean clothes and climbed into the double bed in one of the bedrooms. Lily rifled through a drawer of T-shirts and pulled one out with a large open mouth on the front, tongue stuck out, and *Rolling Stones* printed across the top—it reminded her of one her father had owned and she stifled a sob for Joseph's sake. She took it with her to the bathroom and washed away the days of dirt in hot soapy water, feeling more relaxed than she had in a while.

After the shower, she dressed in the clean t-shirt and her dirty jeans and climbed into bed next to her brother. The warm water having helped make her sleepy, she was just starting to drift off when she heard voices. Her eyes snapped open, and she held her breath, listening to the sounds coming from below. Flicking back the duvet, she slid out of bed and quietly opened the door an inch.

"Always a bonus when they're pretty," said a man's voice.

"Yeah, about twelve or 13, I think." Jayden's voice was quiet.

"What are we gonna do with the boy, though."

A second man.

"He'll be dead soon." Jayden again. "He's got the snots and was puking up bubbles this morning."

The first man spoke again, "We can just leave him here, then. Just take the girl."

"When do I get paid?" asked Jayden. "You said I'd get the food if I brought them here."

"Oh, yeah…definitely food," Man Two said with a chortle, and Man One joined him.

Lily had heard enough and silently pushed the door closed again.

"Joseph, wake up!" she whispered into his ear, shaking him urgently. She pressed a finger to his lips as he opened his eyes. "Shhh… We need to go."

Thankful that they'd got dressed after their showers, she pushed the last few of their belongings into the backpacks and pointed Joseph to the window. Opening it slowly, minimising any noise, she looked out to find the flat asphalt roof of an extension not far below, and relief washed over her.

Joseph lifted a leg up to the window still and, when he stopped to cough up bloody phlegm, she could hear the conversation stop downstairs. "Hurry," she whispered again, and he slipped over the edge and onto the roof below. She quickly wriggled down next to him and they tiptoed to the edge and peered over.

"Bin," Lily said, indicating the wheelie bin stored up against the garage door below, and Joseph sprawled flat on the roof, flipped his legs over the edge, and pushed himself off, landing with a soft *whump* on the bin below. Lily followed him down with as much ease, and then they ran away into the dark.

After a few blocks, Joseph's coughs became more insistent and he stopped, bent over, his small hands on his knees, as foamy bile exploded onto the pavement. Lily looked around, and seeing an alleyway a few steps away, dragged Joseph down there. They drop behind a dumpster.

Joseph's breath came in pants as he tried to steady his breath, and Lily pulled out the last of their water. "Drink some. We'll rest here for a while," she said.

He nodded as he gulped down mouthfuls of water.

"Lie down, get some sleep," she said, pulling his hood over his head. He put his head in her lap and looked up at her, a smile on his face despite his red watering eyes.

"It'll be ok, Lily," he said before closing his eyes.

He was asleep within minutes, and before long, Lily's world also faded to black.

13

The Trading Post

ROWANNE S. CARBERRY

The streets are empty.

A ghost town without ghosts.

A swirling black fog of despair engulfs her, two months in; it's only getting worse.

The sound of an engine has her diving for cover.

She's gotten used to doing the run for supplies and risking her life, she's learnt how best to hide.

When it's finally safe, she moves again, careful not to make a sound.

The pharmacy in site, the mask goes on, she covers her hair and takes out what she's got to trade: pasta and toilet roll.

A few steps to go and she freezes at the only other noise that everyone dreads more than the police.

Coughing.

 **13**

Dany Shoham, a former Israeli military intelligence officer who has studied Chinese biological warfare:
Certain laboratories in the institute have probably been engaged, in terms of research and development, in Chinese [biological weapons], at least collaterally, yet not as a principal facility of the Chinese BW alignment. Work on biological weapons is conducted as part of dual civilian-military research and is definitely covert.

NB: Theory debunked as testing shows virus was not manufactured or manipulated

BEN DAVIDSON

DAVID BOWMORE

A HOSPITAL, LONDON, UK

When he woke the next morning, he found a chemist and filled a bag with ointments and painkillers, then breakfasted on chocolate, crisps and a tin of Guinness from a Tesco Express. The same headline ran on all the papers

COVID-20

Government Gagged Media

Like the day before, the silence struck him more than anything else.

Deciding he would have to travel north, perhaps to his parent's place in Yorkshire, he began the return journey to Westminster Bridge. Thankfully, without the bed, he made better time. A blockade had been set up south of the river preventing traffic from crossing. It would be a long journey by foot.

He wandered down to the marina. Stripped out

13

of his clothes and leapt into the clear, cold water. It was as good as any other way to wash the filth of the previous forty-eight hours away. It might take longer to cleanse his memory.

Ben climbed up the dive ladder of a random yacht and stretched out, letting the sun dry him off. Then he planned. Clothes, he needed clothes and good ones too. He'd get a suit. None of your made in China or Vietnam, sold on the high street shite. One of the yachts might have something suitable. And a watch, he needed a watch – a Rolex would do the job nicely. *And a car, don't forget to get a car, Ben. Something sporty and powerful. And Italian. A Ferrari.*

He didn't mind being alone and he supposed others may have survived, but could he trust anyone? What would people be capable of with no law to worry about? He raised a hand and started to unwind the wet bandage, trying to remember why Jenny had cracked him over the head with a cricket bat.

As the bloodied wadding fell to the deck and he tentatively probed the lump and stitches at the back of his shaved head, an image gathered at the front of his mind. His boss lying on the ground, cradling his nose and trying to wriggle backwards. A look of terror on his face. His mind's eye shifted, and he saw his children in the kitchen doorway. He would have to find them again and heaven help anyone who tried to stop him.

"Dad's coming, kids," he said, getting to his feet.

WHO Organisation:
5G mobile networks DO NOT spread COVID-19
Viruses cannot travel on radio waves/mobile networks. COVID-19 is spreading in many countries that do not have 5G mobile networks.
COVID-19 is spread through respiratory droplets when an infected person coughs, sneezes or speaks. People can also be infected by touching a contaminated surface and then their eyes, mouth or nose.

LILY

D.M. BURDETT

SURREY, UK

Somewhere in Battersea Park

Gurgling woke Lily with a jolt, and she sat up quickly.

Joseph, red-streaked yellow bile foaming from his mouth, eyes rolling into his head, jittered next to her, his whole tiny body tensing and relaxing rhythmically.

"Joey!" Lily cried, and she sat him up and held him against her. He coughed up a putrid stream of foam before his body ceased its vibrating and Lily was able to wipe away the blood and puss from his face.

"Joe?" she said as he leaned against her, breath wheezing in his chest. "Come on, Joe-joe. It's not too far to the Dome from here, we can make it. They'll have medicine." She dragged him up onto his feet.

Holding him close, she waited a moment for him

to be steady on his feet, but when she let go, he collapsed to his knees again, puking bloody sputum on the ground.

"I can't go, Lily. Let me sleep," Joey said, his body shivering. "Tomorrow," he said as his eyes began to close.

Lily slid down the wall, tears stinging her cheeks, and pulled Joe's head into her lap, wiping sweaty hair from his face. "I'm so sorry, Joey. I was supposed to look after you," she whispered through her tears.

Hours went by as Lily watched Joseph's chest rise and fall in raspy tortured breaths until, sometime in the dark of the night, Joey croaked, "Momma?"

"Joey?" Lily said, her hand on his cold, grey face. "It's Lily, Joe-Joe." She watched his eyelids flicker, but he didn't open them, and then his dry, blue lips moved for the last time as he breathed out, "Momma," before lying completely still.

"No, Joe-joe," she cried into Joseph's coat.

UNTITLED

DAVID BOWMORE

I washed my hands and counted to twenty while singing the theme tune to *The Dukes of Hazard*.

We all took extra vitamins and ate fresh fruit and veg. We had enough pasta, bog roll and frozen meat to see us through a nuclear winter.

But we still contracted the unstoppable, incurable virus.

My wife is lifeless beside me. My son is dead on the sofa downstairs. I'm prepared to join them in the afterlife.

The dog has water and the front door is open. For the time being, he sleeps across my stomach, whining.

The cats have already fled.

Anonymous Tweet:
Please DO NOT POP bubble wrap packing. It has Chinese air inside and the Corona Virus can spread FYI

ALEX LOGAN

PAMELA JEFFS

A MILITARY HOSPITAL, LONDON, UK

The beeping of an alarm pulls me from sleep. The drip must be empty. My eyes, crusted with sleep and sickness, sting as I blink, struggling to make out the details of my darkened room. It's stuffy in here. I can barely breathe. Who turned the air-con off? And I really need to take a piss. I ease myself up from my pillow. The door to the en suite is close, but it may as well be a thousand kilometres away. For while my limbs feel slightly stronger and my lungs don't hurt quite as much, I'm still weak.

I press the nurse-call buzzer. It echoes outside. I wait a full three minutes, but no one comes. Where are they? I decide I am just going to have to make my own way to the toilet.

I peel back my blankets and swing my feet over the side of the bed. My vision swims. I suppress the urge to vomit and grip the mobile frame of the drip and use it to lever myself up. The vinyl floor leeches

13

cold into the pads of my feet. I stand swaying for a moment and then shuffle towards the bathroom.

Connor appears by my side. "That's right, just one step at a time. Focus on your feet."

"Where is everybody?" I ask, eyes fixed on the bathroom.

Connor glances at the exit door, then back. "Just get to the toilet," he says. "We don't want you to make a mess out here."

It's a relief to reach the bowl. Connor gives me my privacy as I work to adjust my hospital gown, his back to me as he hovers by the door.

"We need to find a way to get you out of here," he says.

"I'm still sick." I finish. The toilet flushes with a harsh gurgle. I grip the drip frame like it's my only lifeline.

"The situation's changed." He glances at me. "Think you are up to flying? Can you make it to the helipad? It's about 100 meters away, across the car park."

My vision swims. "I crashed the last helicopter I flew," I say thinking back to my Uncle's cattle property in Australia, near Darwin.

"That's 'cause you're a shit pilot." The ghost of

a smile touches his ruined lips. "Seriously though. You got the strength to do it?"

My lungs still hurt. My throat and nose are clogged with snot and clotted blood. But the fever is down. I nod. "I could if I needed too."

"You need to," says Connor.

Death has leant Connor a certain, unsettling gravity. He's different to the jovial man he was in life. A chill crawls down my spine. Hallucination or not, I decide to trust him.

The door to my room opens out into chaos. My brain refuses to process the scene—a scene cut straight from a horror movie. Fluorescent lights flicker in the grid ceilings. On and off, punctuating flash point images of the corridor and nurse station. Trolleys lay toppled, their cargos of multi-coloured medications and paper cups spilled out like confetti. Blood and vomit stains walls and floors, a miasma of stench rising from it all. I gag and press my sleeve to my nose. *Fuck. What the hell happened here?*

A trail of blood smears the pale green vinyl floor. The streaked blade of scarlet leads into the nurse station.

It's there I find the first body.

Nurse Smith.

13

She lays face up, eyes open, on the floor in the centre of the room. Her mask has slipped askew, revealing lips blackened in death. The front of her uniform is ruined—stained with vomit and blood. A sheet of paper lies next to her lax hand. I lean in. It's a fax. A government logo glares at me from the top left corner. Black letters dance before my eyes.

COVID-20 VIRUS

Attn: Doctor John Williams

We hereby advise that John Radcliffe Hospital is quarantined due to fatal virus outbreak. All patients and staff are to be secured within the building.

Any persons breaching quarantine borders will be shot on sight.

I've never been one for being caged. A sudden urge to escape the hospital's confines consumes me. The nurse is beyond my help, so I shuffle further down the hall, still gripping the frame but moving faster now. Connor stalks ahead of me, his boots making no sound as they pound the floor. He checks the rooms, left to right. Always the soldier.

More bodies line the corridor, sprawled in various states of decomposition. I pass one man, a patient by the look of his gown, huddled in a corner, fists clutched to his chest and face bloodied to his chin. Three more nurses are crumpled on the floor by the coffee machine in the small dining area, corpses—black and bloated—starting to stink.

My training keeps me calm on the surface, but somewhere deep in my chest, my heart is battering uneasy against my ribs. If I leave the hospital will I be shot? I cough. I cough again. But then I realise, it's not a cough at all. It's a sob.

I don't want to die. I didn't want to die in Syria. I definitely don't want it to end here.

"Steady mate," whispers Connor, his voice sounding far away. "We'll get you out of here."

"Why are you helping me? I failed you. You died because of me!"

"No. Alex. I died because it was my time. Keep going. Follow my voice."

But it's hard. Each step is like walking through concrete. The urge to stop tempts me—to just stop and slump down and let it all go.

The pain. The delusions.

The need to live.

"Get up Alex!"

I don't remember hitting the floor. But here I am

with the drip frame fallen across my legs. I taste vomit at the back of my throat.

"Get up NOW!"

"I hate you, Connor." I snarl. Pushing myself up, I shuffle forward. The exit is so close. The grey light of dawn filters in through the glazed main entrance doors.

One step.

Two steps.

The helipad is a beacon across the car park. A helicopter sits, waiting.

Freedom.

Connor stands by the door. His eyes lock onto mine. "We get to the helicopter. You get inside, start it and then head hell-for-leather out of town."

"Why is a helicopter even here?" I ask. It all seems too convenient.

Conner frowns. "Pilot got trapped here in the lockdown. He tried to leave but didn't make it."

I glance back at the helipad. This time I notice the helicopter's cockpit door hanging half open; the bullet-riddled windshield and a corpse slumped in the pilot's seat.

The world spins. Grey into white into black. I cough and a stream of blood dribbles down my lip. I can't do this. I'm not going to make it.

"Fucking man up," says Connor, "and get your arse to that chopper. Get there or die here. You're the last one alive in this place. There's no one left to help you."

And I know he's right. This building is a tomb. I grit my teeth. The auto entry door slides open on my approach. A blast of cold, English air brushes over my face. I sigh, relishing the sensation. Just got to get to the helicopter. I take a deep breath.

"I'm right by your side," whispers Connor.

I run.

My bare feet slap the concrete of the helipad just as the sound of gunfire erupts.

I fall.

Connor screams at me. "GET UP!"

I want to. I really do. But I'm done.

Connor snarls. His ice-cold hands grip me around my shoulders and I cry out in pain. It's like he is tearing my soul from my bones. But in moments he has me upright and again running for the helicopter. I'm not sure how I do, but I make it. I pull the corpse free of the seat and let it slither to the ground. I scramble into the cockpit. My breaths are fire in my lungs; my heart threatens to explode. I activate the ignition and rotors amidst another hail of gunfire.

The helicopter lifts uncertainly into the air. I grin at Connor, now sitting in the co-pilot seat. But he doesn't grin back.

"Head for the coast," he says.

I nod and take one last glance down at the hospital with its military quarantine barricades and armed forces in Hazmat suits that service it.

I'm out of here.

My whole body hurts, but the *whoop, whoop* of the helicopter's blades is comforting. I push the stick and turn, heading for London and the coast.

Everything is better now I'm in cockpit and in control.

***

London city emerges on the horizon, cloaked in a miasma of shifting smoke. As we draw closer, details refine. Charred buildings border ruined streets that are either barricaded or on fire. Ant-like figures dart desperately from one set of cover to the next. By Westminster Palace, the Thames runs thick with rubbish—cars, cruise boats with their backs broken and bodies.

I swallow, sickened by more than just the virus. In the nursery rhyme it's London Bridge that's said to fall, but here and now, in reality London herself has fallen—the once-queen of cities, stripped of her jewels and her dignity.

Conner leans forward in his seat.

"Holy hell," he says. "What's the world come to?"

"I don't know. But we've gotta get out of here." I glance at the fuel gauge, trying to ignore the pain in my lungs and the taste of blood at the back of my throat. "Tanks are full. We should be able to make it to Calais. Maybe things are different there."

"Or maybe not," mutters Conner, his eyes fixed to the laid-bare corpse of London.

The helicopter rises. The Clock Tower emerges from the smoke, the tower's turret a black spire against the grey backdrop. Its hands point to 10 and 6—mid-morning.

Plenty of daylight to make the trip.

I push the stick. The helicopter dips left on cue, but a hissing sound catches my attention, swallowing the drone of the rotor blades. My stomach drops. It's a sound I know all too well.

A sound I heard over Syria.

A sound Conner recognises as well.

"Brace for impact!" he screams.

A ground-to-air missile, fired from within the palace barricade, collides with the midsection of the helicopter. The stick is torn from my hand. Metal tears with a whine and the aircraft's nose dips sickeningly. We spin.

The cabin is filled with smoke and heat prickles the back of my neck. Alarms blare. "Fuck!" I scream, fighting to right and hold the craft on even keel.

But it's no good. This isn't Syria.

There's no landing for me this time.

The Clock Tower looms close, the clock's face a single white eye, growing larger and larger. The helicopter, as if taking offence, ploughs into it— through it.

Fire, heat, the shear of metal and the roar of crumbling masonry.

***

The street is solid beneath my feet. Around me lie the scattered parts of a helicopter. There is a body too, bloodied and broken, sprawled face down on the bitumen. The muscled form, with its blonde hair and hospital gown, seem familiar.

"Don't look," says Connor. "You can't change it. We just move forward from here."

"Is that me? Am I dead?"

Connor presses his hand to my torn chest. His touch is warm this time.

"You are here with me."

"That's not an answer."

"You don't need me to answer."

"But I don't want to move forward," I say.

Conner sighs. "It's a hell of a lot better than moving back."

I glance again at my own corpse. He's right.

Whatever this is—death, life, half-life—it's better than the wreck of what is left behind.

"C'mon," says Conner, squeezing my shoulder. "Let's find another plane and get out of here."

Yes. That's all I really want.

To be back in the pilot's seat again.

Back in the cockpit and in control.

13

POTUS Tweet:
The Coronavirus is very much under control in the USA. We are in contact with everyone and all relevant countries. CDC & World Health have been working hard and very smart. Stock Market starting to look very good to me!

NIGEL

GREGG CUNNINGHAM

LONDON, UK

Nigel had heard nothing but the broken orders over Shamy's radio for a week as he tended to her neck wound in her father's shop. After burying her father in the commons square under the cover of darkness, he had hidden his cab in the lock-up at the back of the shop and then barricaded the front door, stock-piling what was left on the shelves. It gave them enough food for three nights locked away from the madness outside.

"He was a good man, Shamy," he said, holding her hand in the darkness of the storeroom.

"Thank you, Nigel," she replied faintly. "You're a good man, too."

He left her to grieve after that, monitoring the riots through the barricade, ready to protect what little they had.

The helicopters had moved on and the gunfire

was now just an echo from over the water. The radio reported running street battles around Parliament, and protestors trying to flee over bridges that were now in the control of the army. But slowly, the radio messages dropped from the air, leaving only the evacuation advertisement about everyone being 'in it together.'

"Damn straight…together up to our necks in the shit!" Nigel cursed.

The two-way radio faintly picked up the odd instruction calling for the army to pull back across the Thames. By the sound of it, they had lost control of everything north of London. Nigel knew they should move on; it was too dangerous to sit around any longer.

If they were to make it out of the city alive, it had to be now, before the looting and the roaming kangaroo courts got into session. This was no place to try and survive without the law to protect them.

"Can you move, Shamy?" He dabbed her forehead and she nodded.

"I think so."

"Good, because the cab's waiting outside and the meter's running."

***

Nigel slowly rolled his cab out of the street as Shamy's radio crackled in her hand.

The black cab made its way through every burned out back-street labyrinth and short cut through Enfield that Nigel could remember from "the knowledge."

Whitechapel burned, sand-bagged check points lay abandoned across Prescot Street, and Nigel had to swerve down several alleyways to avoid body bags being used as makeshift barricades all the way down to Tower Bridge. Smoke drifted from the bridge, and he realised there was no way in hell he was passing through the barbed wire fencing across the escape route to the south. A static garbled message came from Shamy's radio and she held it up to the glass barrier between them. "Nigel, listen!"

"*...We've got incoming on Westminster, Sergeant...*"

"Christ they've shut every bloody route out of here. Hold on, Shamy."

"*...Take them out, keep that bloody bridge open at all costs Corporal...*"

Westminster Bridge, in the heart of London!

Christ! Nigel shook his head. "Okay, only one thing for it!" Nigel hit the gas and slid his cab down towards Parliament. Trafalgar was a mess, both soldiers and civilians lay on the roadside outside the looted shop windows. Vehicles had been bulldozed, pushed to the side of the roundabout to clear a pathway through to the concrete bollards around the perimeter of the Parliament building. Bullet-riddled vehicles lay missing their windscreens like poached elephants robbed of their ivory.

Nigel floored the pedal when he heard the familiar sound of helicopter blades cutting the air above. He stuck his head out the window and peered up at the medical red cross insignia of the helicopter as his cab bounced onto the pedestrian walkway. Smoke was belching from its engine as it veered and lurched in the grey sky towards the clock face of Big Ben's tower.

This was it, surely! They were lining the cab up in their sights to blow them up…so close to reaching the bridge and safety.

"Oh Christ, Shamy. When I say jump, I need you to get away from here as fast as—"

The explosion above the cab rattled his teeth and burning pieces of helicopter panelling and Victorian architecture dropped from the sky onto the road around them.

Nigel fought with the wheel as he bounced from kerb to kerb, struggling to avoid the falling clock face masonry bouncing like one of Barnes Wallis's engineered bombs behind them. His whisky bottle fell into the footwell, jamming under the brake pedal as the wheels squealed on the cobbled street.

"Look!" Shamy screamed as a soldier with an RPG missile launcher reloaded his weapon and aimed it straight at the cab.

"I see it, Shamy!" Nigel cursed as he kicked out at the bottle, trying to stop the cab from fishtailing, and frantically fought to steady his aim for the sandbags positioned across the bridge.

The soldier stared on wide-eyed as the cab lurched at him, taking out the sandbags like it was splitting bowling pins and crunching soldiers beneath its speeding wheels.

The vehicle barrelled through the lone sentry post, but Nigel didn't stop. Westminster Bridge was soon cleared, and they were over into Lambeth without any more blockades.

Once they were on the other side of the river, the carnage seemed to ease slightly, and Nigel was able to breathe. He pulled the cab up to take stock of the damage and check on Shamy. "You okay, luv?" He turned and saw her sobbing in the back seat.

"Did you hit them?" she sobbed, still clutching the crackling radio. Nigel grabbed the whisky bottle that had been rolling on the floor and unscrewed the cap.

"It's okay, Shamy, they're gone. I promise you, I'll get us out of here. You just keep your head down till we get to Barry's farm. It will be safe there."

He glanced out through the shattered window, back at the smoke rising from the city embankment, not fully convinced of his own words. He took a large swig of the whisky then, smiling, passed Shamy the whisky bottle in shaking hands.

"Here you go, luv. Have one for the road, Shamy. It will calm our nerves."

Behind them, London burned, but they never looked back.

BEN DAVIDSON

DAVID BOWMORE

LONDON, UK

If Ben were to find his two sons, then he would have to figure out a way through London and judging by the roadblocks at this end of Westminster Bridge, most of the roads would be impassable. It would be a long walk. He would probably find another motorbike or perhaps a bicycle, but even so, it would be an unpleasant journey and more than likely dangerous. Who knew what mood the surviving natives might be in? The one thing that would get him killed now was stupidity. He never did consider himself a fool, despite what his ex-wife always said.

The anchor rested in the corner of the deck. It made sense not to use it if the boat was moored up, so with a grunt he hefted it up and used it to break into the cabin. In his search for clothing, the only thing he found was a blue and white striped jumper. It was a perfect fit, if he ignored his exposed navel.

13

A cooler in the galley had half a dozen bottles of Dom Perignon rested on their sides and a jar of Beluga Caviar. He had never been a fan of Sturgeon roe, but what the Hell, he could always wash it down with Champagne. While searching the drawers for a spoon to eat the fish eggs with, he found a keyring with two keys attached and a fob with the words 'Gloriana's Sunset' printed on it.

It might be a longer, more circuitous journey, but it would probably be quicker in the long run. He only had to get outside London and then make his way over to St. Albans. Of course, he had never driven a boat before, but how hard could it be?

The cabin was luxuriously appointed with several beds to relax on if needed. Oh yes, there definitely were worse ways to travel.

He returned to the deck and hopped over to the jetty to loosen the tie ropes in preparation to cast off. A movement out of the corner of his eye forced him to spin around only to see a young girl standing halfway along the jetty. She swayed on her feet.

"Hello there," he said, taking a step towards her.

She started to turn away.

"No, don't go. I won't hurt you."

She paused, looking over her shoulder.

"You like the Rolling Stones, do you?" he said referring to the T-Shirt that swamped her. She shrugged her shoulders.

"I was just going to take this boat down the river. You know, try and get out of town," he said, before adding, "Do you want to come with me?" Well, he had to offer, didn't he? She was obviously alone and scared. And he hoped that someone would be good enough to look after his kids too, if they were alive.

"They said it was dangerous, but I didn't really know how bad it would be," she said.

"Who did?"

"The men in special suits who took Mum away."

"Ah well, I think they're probably right. But I'm looking for my sons, you see. They're about your age. How old are you? Twelve or 13?" Ben looked around, he thought he could hear a helicopter.

"Twelve."

"Have you eaten? There's caviar if you can stomach it."

The drone of the helicopter grew louder.

"Come on board. We can help each other drive this thing if you like."

And then the chopper came into view and both Ben and the girl looked up holding their hands to shield their eyes from the sunlight. A sudden streak of something fiery left a smoking trail that led back to the Houses of Parliament. Smoke billowed from the midsection of the chopper.

The pilot was clearly struggling to control the machine, and with a sudden lurch, the helicopter took a sideways nosedive straight into Big Ben's clock face. Ben covered his head with his hands and arms. After a few seconds, he looked over at the girl, but she was running in the opposite direction. Oh well, no one could say he hadn't tried.

He jumped back into the boat, positioning himself in front of the steering wheel. Debris fell all around. The helicopter had continued its downward journey destroying the entire east wing of Westminster Palace. Ben found the keyslot and the first key slid home. With a smile, he twisted it to the right, but the engine remained static.

"Oh, you fucking fucker. Don't you dare be out of fucking petrol."

He searched the cockpit for anything that might get the boat going. He was thinking that maybe the girl had made the right decision and was about to follow in her footsteps when he found the answer— a Start/Stop button. As he pressed it, the engine came to life at the same time as an explosion ripped through what was left of the great building. He was sure that the heat coming off the inferno would melt his skin.

He was tempted to fully open the throttle and get away as quickly as possible, but with poor, dusty visibility that was sure to be the most stupid thing to do. So, he carefully eased the boat into the Thames. *Slow and steady*, he heard his grandfather say.

Pieces of burning wood, plaster and brickwork continued to fall, but at least he was moving away from the disaster zone. Ben wasn't sure which direction he was heading, but he could always rethink things later, once he was safely away from the capital.

Ten minutes into his slow dash for freedom, the dust began to clear. He turned to see the havoc caused by the helicopter and stared, opened mouthed, as he realised London was finished. The fire had spread to several other buildings and it looked like there was no one left to fight it. Alarms sounded but no one responded. Windows shattered in nearby buildings and another explosion sent great plumes of smoke billowing into the air. Great sucking gusts of wind rocked the pleasure cruiser as the flames ate into the structures north of the river.

Ben turned his back on London's burning and pushed *Gloriana's Sunset* to the max while, behind him, one thousand years of democracy and power continued to destroy itself.

EPILOGUE

540

X-DAY +28 DAYS

D.M. BURDETT

THE O2, CHECKPOINT 17, UK

"Fuck." Baker's lip curled as he looked down and inspected the sandwich, its crusts dried at the edges.

"What's up, mate?" Smith asked through his own dried-out lunch. He closed his eyes and leaned his head back against the wall.

"Fucking cheese. Again," Baker complained before stuffing half the offending meal into his mouth. Spitting crumbs down his uniform, he continued, "Bet the fucking big wigs"—he flicked his head in the general direction of the buildings beyond the armed checkpoint— "didn't eat fucking cheese sandwiches every meal this week."

Smith opened his eyes and took another bite of his lunch, finishing it off before wiping the packaging from the bench. He stood up and picked up his gun, holding it above his head in both hands,

stretching his stiff muscles. "This is fucking boring, mate. Haven't seen a Bubbler in days," he muttered, his eyes sweeping the deserted road ahead of them.

"Ugh, I'm eating, you fucker. That's all I need— a vision of that red foamy puss-filled puke to go with this cheese and ketchup monstrosity!"

A movement in the distance caught Smith's eye, and he squinted into the evening haze. "What's that?"

Baker looked up from his sandwich. "What's what?" he said around stale cheddar.

"There," Smith said, pointing into the distance. "You see it?"

Baker raised his hand to his brow, shielding his eyes from the last of the day's sun rays. "Is that a kid?" he asked, surprise in his voice. He stood, picking up his gun and laying it across his arm, and took a step to stand by his partner's side.

They watched for a few minutes as the girl stumbled and limped towards them, before Baker raised his gun. "Halt. This is a military checkpoint," he shouted.

The girl carried on walking, her head hanging loose, bobbing with each wobbly step.

Smith glanced over at Baker and then raised his

own gun. "Stand still, kid. Or this will get ugly."

For a moment, the child stopped. "Please help me," she breathed, but then continued her unsteady gait.

"Fuck," Baker breathed, almost imperceptibly, before shouting again. "Halt or I'll shoot!"

Smith glanced over at him again. "It's just a kid," he said.

As the girl lifted her head, Baker said, "Look. She's a Bubbler."

Smith's eyes flicked back to the child, taking in the pussy red foam that caked her face and the front of her oversized Rolling Stones t-shirt.

"Shit," Smith muttered. "I'm gonna need fucking therapy after this assignment," he said as he focused through his weapon's sights. He squeezed the trigger, and the Bubbler dropped to the ground.

"Clean up needed in aisle six," Baker barked into his radio.

AUTHOR BIOGRAPHIES

PASSENGER-01

A.S. CHARLY loves to lose herself in fantastical worlds far away between the stars, filled with magic and wonder. A good way to lure her back, or out of lockdown, is chocolate. Her writing has been published in various anthologies and online publications. Some of the most recent ones include *Love* and *Hate* by Black Hare Press, *Mythica* by Iron Faerie Publishing, and the upcoming science fiction anthology *Raygun Retro* by Zombie Pirate Publishing.

She would also like to take this opportunity to thank all every-day-heroes who continually provide help and support for people in need. Thank you!

Facebook: A.S.Charlydreams
Amazon: amazon.com/author/a.s.charly

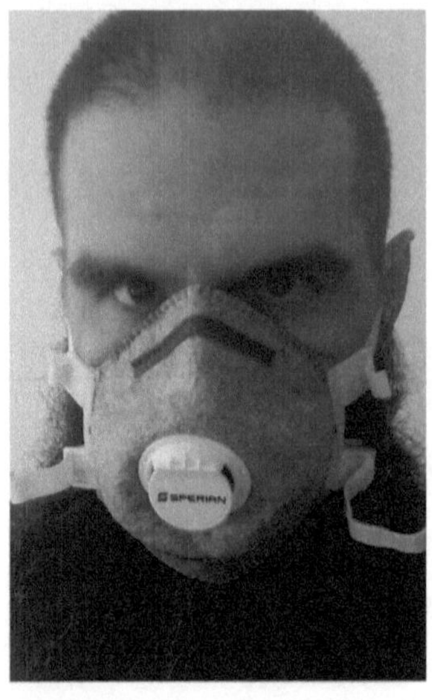

PASSENGER-02

BLAKE JESSOP is a Canadian author of sci-fi, fantasy and horror stories with a master's degree from the University of Adelaide.

You can read more of his speculative fiction in *Triangulation: Dark Skies* from Parsec Ink, or follow him on Twitter @everydayjisei.

PASSENGER-03

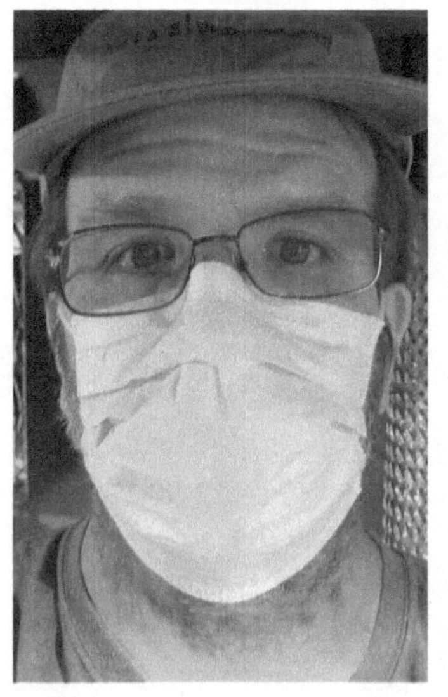

BRIAN MACGOWAN hails from the east coast of Canada. He currently resides in Indiana, USA with his wife and their two daughters. Brian enjoys confusing his coworkers with the Canadian spelling and pronunciation of many words. He receives particular enjoyment when he gets to spell any word that contains a zed. Contrary to the photos on Brian's passport and driver's license he is not the crazed homicidal maniac that his IDs suggest; although his writings do seem to substantiate the photo evidence.

PASSENGER-04

D.M. BURDETT initially roamed as an army brat, but now lives in Australia where she spends her days avoiding drop bears and killer spiders. She has published a Sci-Fi series, has short stories in various anthologies, and has published two children's series. She is currently working on the first book in a dystopian series.

She has worked in software development for three decades and has published a children's series—with the help of a canny kangaroo–on the subject. A life of roaming the shores of Australia in her teardrop caravan calls to her but, until then, there always seems to be just one more software project to complete.

Website: www.dmburdett.com
Facebook: DMBurdett

PASSENGER-05A

DAVID BOWMORE has lived here, there and everywhere, but now lives in Yorkshire with his wonderful wife and a small white poodle. He has worn many hats in his time; head chef, teacher and landscape gardener.

His first collection of short stories *The Magic of Deben Market* is available from Clarendon House.

Website: davidbowmore.co.uk
Facebook: davidbowmoreauthor

PASSENGER-05B

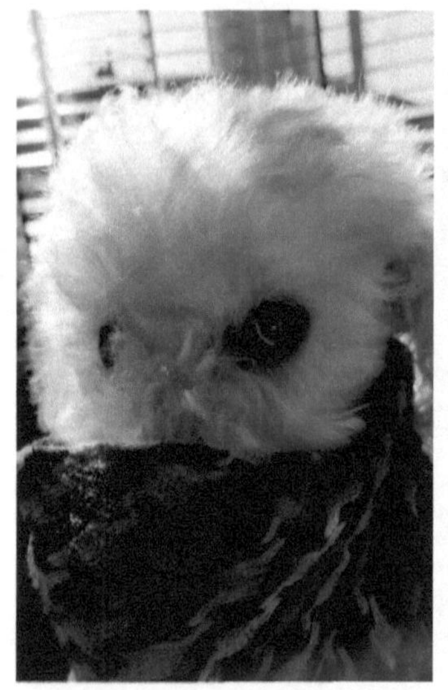

FLOYD BOWMORE is a nine-year-old poodle of style and taste. When not putting his head in holes he can be found asleep in one of his numerous baskets.

Trained from an early age to fetch balls and close doors, he soon learned the art looking cute.

Well known for whispering story ideas into one of his human's ears, he has recently self-published his first book: *Look Cute, Get Away With Everything*. Chapters include How to Look Hungry, and How To Look Innocent When You've Been Sick In The Middle Of Their Bed.

You can follow Floyd on Twitter: @FloydThePoodle

PASSENGER-06

GREGG CUNNINGHAM, 49, is a short story writer from Western Australia who has contributed to various genre anthology books since 2014.

In 2019 he was accepted into several anthology books published, Black Hare Press, including *Deep Space, Storming Area51, Bad Romance* and *Jibbernocky*.

His latest short story, *Wardenclyffe*, was published earlier this year by Black Hare Press; a tale about an eccentric English officer fighting off invaders set to destroy his beloved England in an alternate timeline.

Twitter: @GGGcunningham
Website: cortlandsdogs.wordpress.com

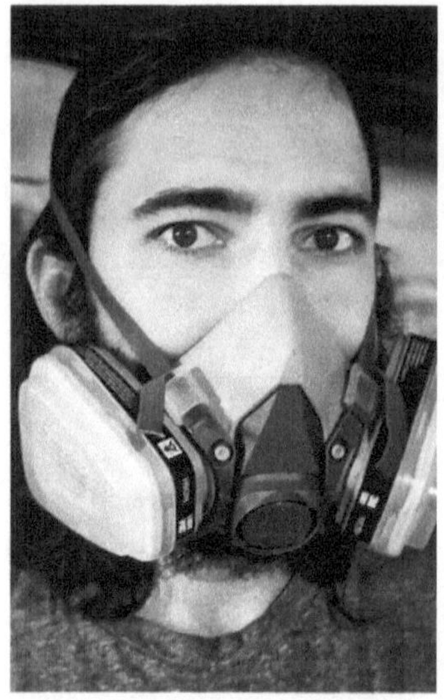

PASSENGER-07

JACOB BAUGHER teaches Creative Writing at a small college in Ohio. When he's not teaching or coaching the track team, he can be found in the Cuyahoga Valley hiking with his wife and son or brewing beer on his front porch.

He's received honourable mentions for his work in the Writers of the Future contest and he co-edits a series of Fantasy and Science Fiction anthologies titled *Continuum*.

Website: www.authorjbaugher.com.

PASSENGER-08

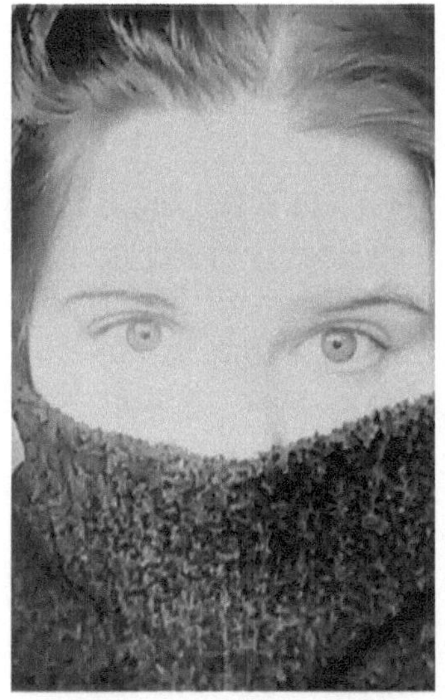

LANNAH MARSHALL is a speculative fiction author from the UK. Her flash fiction piece, "Waterways and Dreamscapes" was shortlisted for the Nature of Cities 2099 competition, while her short stories have been published in such anthologies as *Shoal*, *Dark Lane Anthology Vol 7*, and *Witches Vs Wizards*, with a smattering of others available to read online at Thanetwriters.com.

Lannah is also an illustrator, with graphic novels such as 'Colourless' being created as a means to articulate living with autism. She also has a Facebook page, but regularly forgets to post there.

PASSENGER-09

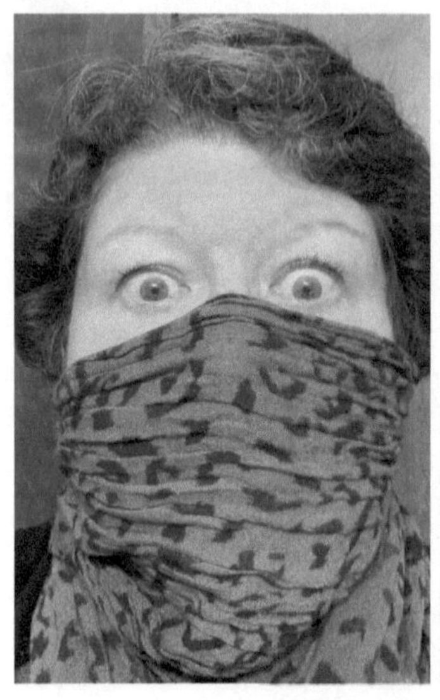

P.A. O'NEIL has been writing professionally for just over three years. In that time, her stories have been featured in multiple anthologies (many of them international best-sellers), as well as on-line journals and magazines from several continents. She and her husband reside in Olympia, Washington, with her adult children living nearby.

She has just released her first collection, *Witness Testimony and Other Tales*, available from Amazon

For links to books which feature her stories, look under the Photo sections of her Facebook author.

Facebook: P.A. O'Neil, Storyteller
Amazon: amazon.com/P-A-ONeil/e/B07BF2D8SP

PASSENGER-10

PAMELA JEFFS is an Aurealis Award nominated speculative fiction author from Queensland, Australia. She has numerous short fiction pieces published in national and international anthologies and magazines. She has released several short fiction collections including *Red Hour and Other Strange Tales, Saloons & Stardust: A Collection* and *Five Dragons*.

Website: www.pamelajeffs.com
Facebook: @pamelajeffsauthor

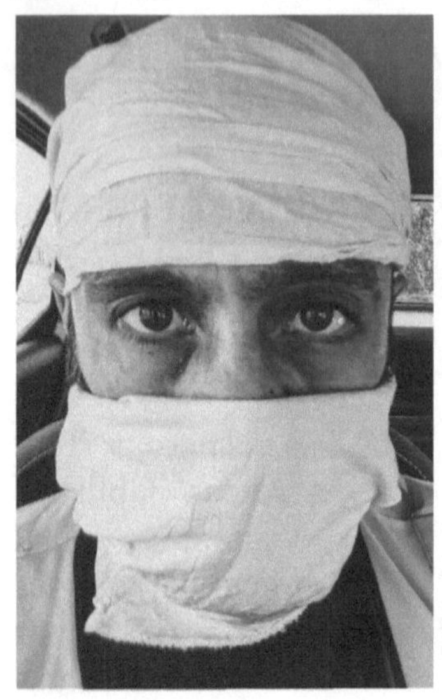

PASSENGER-11

RICH RURSHELL is a writer of Horror, Fantasy, and Science Fiction. From his home in Suffolk, England, Rich likes to ponder the existence of the sinister, the fantastic, and the downright terrifying. He likes to explore the darker side of life and what lies within us, and celebrate the beauty in the world and what lies beyond.

PASSENGER-12A

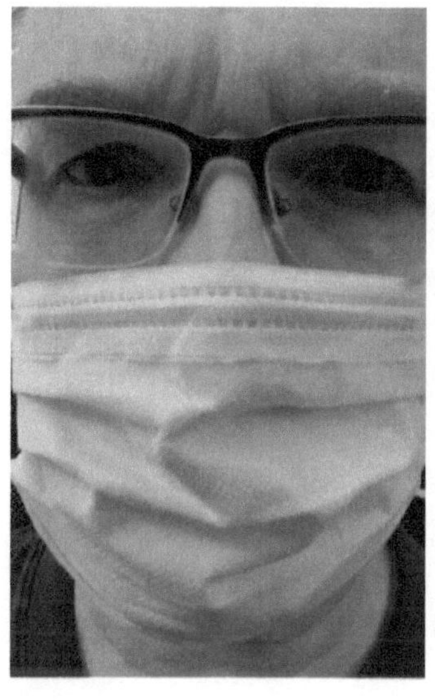

SHAWN M. KLIMEK is the author of the illustrated poetic-fantasy book, *Hungry Thing*, and more than 150 published poems and short stories, including BHP's *Deep Space, Eerie Christmas, Jibbernocky* and every book so far in the Dark Drabbles series.

He lives in Illinois with his military-nurse wife and their Maltese

Website: jotinthedark.blogspot.com
Facebook: shawnmklimekauthor
Twitter: @shawnmklimek

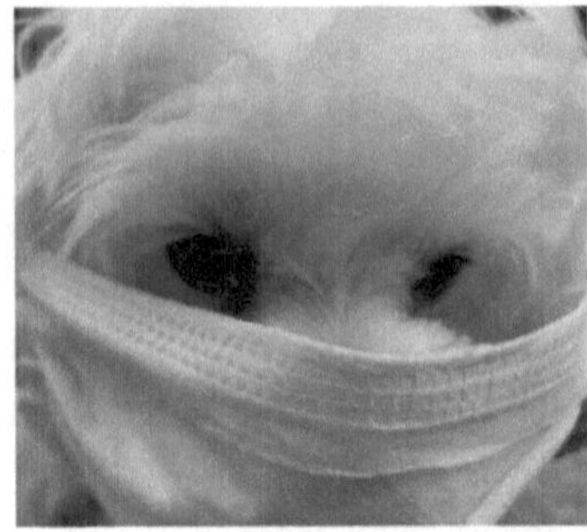

PASSENGER-12B

NONEKO "NANI" KLIMEK (whose first name means "not a cat") is a Japanese-born Maltese living in Illinois.

She is a full-time muse and aspiring writer, whose WIPs include a gourmet recipe book, *Forbidden Foods Worth Vomiting* and two mysteries, *Why Can't I Come with You?* and *What's That Noise?*

PASSENGER-13

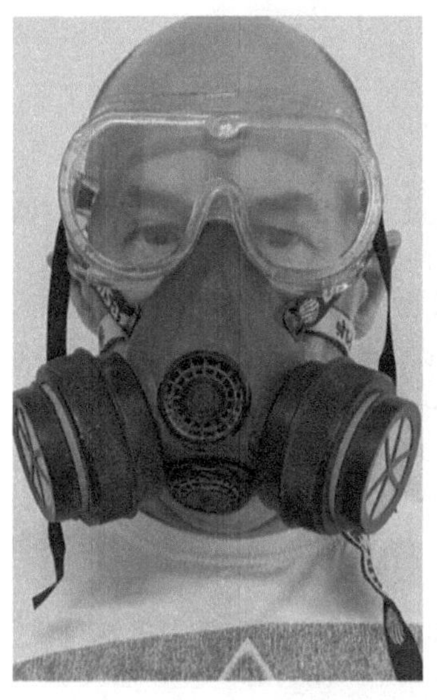

STEPHEN HERCZEG is an IT Geek based in Canberra Australia. He has been writing for over twenty years and has completed a couple of dodgy novels, sixteen feature length screenplays and numerous short stories and scripts. His horror work has featured in *Sproutlings, Hells Bells, Below the Stairs, Trickster's Treats #1 and #2, Shades of Santa, Behind the Mask, Beyond the Infinite; The Body Horror Book, Anemone Enemy, Petrified Punks* and *Beginnings*. He has also had numerous Sherlock Holmes stories published through Belanger Books' *Sherlock Holmes* anthologies.

Amazon: amazon.com/-/e/B07916SQQS
Facebook: stephenherczegauthor

RED SHIRTS

DAVID GREEN grew up between Manchester, UK and Galway, Ireland. A reader from an early age, David had long harboured dreams of writing himself. Throwing himself into any genre, David enjoys creating breathing characters to challenge—and finds horror a wonderfully terrifying space to work in. Twitter: @davidpgreen83

ERICA SCHAEF is a speculative fiction writer whose work has been featured in a variety of literary journals, magazines and anthologies. She lives in rural Tennessee with her husband and two children. Facebook: ericaschaef

ROWANNE S. CARBERRY was born in England in 1990. She has always loved writing, with her first piece published at age 15. Although Rowanne writes in varied genres, each piece has a darkness to it, which helped coin her brand, Poisoned Quill Writing—Wicked words from a poisoned quill. Facebook: PoisonedQuillWriting

STEPHEN CHRISTIE, a lifelong bookworm, cinephile, and wine connoisseur, has decided to lay off the drink, and try his a little creative writing of his own. A fan of Horror, Science Fiction, Military Fiction, and Historical Fiction, he hopes his years of enjoying great books will aid him in this endeavour.

PETER J. FOOTE is a bestselling speculative fiction writer from Nova Scotia, Canada. Many of Peter's stories are a reflection of his personal life, as he is a firm believer in the adage that a writer should write what they know. He believes the writing community is stronger when it works together.
Facebook: peterjfooteauthor

ABOUT THE PUBLISHER

BLACK HARE PRESS is a small, independent publisher based in Melbourne, Australia.

Founded in 2018, our aim has always been to champion emerging authors from all around the globe and offer opportunities for them to participate in speculative fiction and horror short story anthologies.

www.blackharepress.com